PENGUIN BOOKS

The Harp in the South

Ruth Park began writing early in life and by the time she left her homeland New Zealand in 1942 had considerable literary and editorial experience. She intended to join the staff of a Sydney daily newspaper, but instead married her longtime correspondent, the young writer D'Arcy Niland. She accompanied him on his wanderings in the outback, working at any job that came to hand. Eventually they settled temporarily in the neglected and archaic Surry Hills area of Sydney. The rich and often shocking street life of this enclave opened her literary eyes. The result was her first novel, *The Harp in the South* (1948), which won the prize for best novel in the inaugural literary competition of the *Sydney Morning Herald*. This book established her reputation as a writer, along with its sequel, *Poor Man's Orange* (1949). After the death of Niland in 1967, Ruth Park moved to Europe, then lived on Norfolk Island between 1973 and 1985.

Ruth Park has written over fifty books, including ten novels and nearly thirty children's books, as well as much successful non-fiction. Her many prizes include the prestigious Miles Franklin Award for her novel *Swords and Crowns and Rings* (1977), and the 1981 Australian Children's Book of the Year Award and the *Boston Globe* Award for *Playing Beatie Bow* (1980). She has published two volumes of autobiography: *A Fence Around the Cuckoo* (1992), which was the Melbourne *Age* Book of the Year, and *Fishing in the Styx* (1993), winner of the FAW Herb Thomas Literary Award. She is a member of the Order of Australia.

Jill Greaves completed her doctoral thesis, a study of Ruth Park's major works, at James Cook University of North Queensland, Australia. Her main interest lies in Australian literature and she has published on this subject. She has taught literature and academic writing at James Cook University and is currently working as an editor and manuscript consultant with both the university and with commercial publishers.

RUTH PARK

The Harp in the South

With an Introduction by Jill Greaves

PENGUIN BOOKS

PENGUIN BOOKS

Published by the Penguin Group
Penguin Books Ltd, 80 Strand, London WC2R ORL, England
Penguin Putnam Inc., 375 Hudson Street, New York, New York 10014, USA
Penguin Books Australia Ltd, Ringwood, Victoria, Australia
Penguin Books Canada Ltd, 10 Alcorn Avenue, Toronto, Ontario, Canada M4V 3B2
Penguin Books India (P) Ltd, 11, Community Centre, Panchsheel Park, New Delhi – 110 017, India
Penguin Books (NZ) Ltd, Private Bag 102902, NSMC, Auckland, New Zealand
Penguin Books (South Africa) (Pty) Ltd, 24 Sturdee Avenue, Rosebank 2196, South Africa

Penguin Books Ltd, Registered Offices: 80 Strand, London WC2R ORL, England

First published by Angus & Robertson Ltd, 1948
Published by Penguin Books Australia Ltd, 1951
Reissued 1975
Reprinted in Penguin Classics, 2001
1

Copyright © Ruth Park, 1948
Introduction copyright © Jill Greaves, 2001

Set in 11/12.5 Monotype Fournier
Typeset by Rowland Phototypesetting Ltd, Bury St Edmunds, Suffolk
Printed in England by Clays Ltd, St Ives plc

Introduction

In 1946, in Australia, with the war finally over and a new era of peace and prosperity seemingly assured, optimism was high; and, in this spirit, the *Sydney Morning Herald* announced its inaugural literary competition. First prize in the novel section was the enormous sum of £2,000, together with a guarantee of publication by the prestigious firm of Angus and Robertson. Ruth Park heard about the competition during a visit to her family in New Zealand; a few years earlier she had left her homeland, travelling to Sydney in the midst of war, in order to marry fellow author D'Arcy Niland. Together they had embarked on careers as freelance writers, raising a family on the income from their output at a time when it was generally considered impossible to make a living from writing in Australia. Although their total dependence on the typewriter made it imperative that their literary wares should be eclectic, neither of them had ever written a novel, because the exigencies of their financial position demanded prompt payment and a book would simply take too long to write. Spurred on, however, by that almost unimaginable first prize, Park completed her first novel in six weeks (working at night after the children had gone to bed), and submitted the manuscript, together with entries in the poetry and short story sections. Since competition rules stipulated that entries should be submitted under a *nom de plume*, Park chose Hesperus, because she 'felt like a wreck'.[1] Later, upon obeying a summons to the imposing offices of the *Herald* and being informed that she was a prizewinner, she was obliged to enquire, nervously, 'In which section?'

It was the novel section, and her winning entry was, of course, *The Harp in the South*. Limited finance, coupled with Sydney's acute wartime housing shortage[2], had forced Park and Niland to live, for a time, in the Sydney suburb of Surry Hills and the *Harp*'s fiction is drawn from the facts of their experience of slum conditions and slum dwellers. The competition prizewinners were announced, with considerable fanfare, on the front page of the *Sydney Morning Herald* on Saturday 28 December 1946, and not only was the competition the subject of the editorial, but two further pages were devoted to the judges' reports, synopses of the first-, second- and third-placed novel entries and the 'Personal Stories' of their authors. An immediate outcry followed! During January 1947, while the *Herald* published the *Harp* in serialized form, telephone calls, telegrams and letters poured into the office, most praising the novel but many condemning it. The controversy was obviously good for business,[3] and the *Herald* exploited the situation, not only by publishing many of the most vehement opinions, but also by announcing, each day, the mounting total of letters for and against, rather like a progressive cricket score. That a book which, over the years, has become something of an Australian institution, a fixture in many homes and a text frequently set on school reading lists, should have created such an uproar in 1947, being denounced by some as 'an outrage against decency' and 'no better than an open sewer, spreading disease and death all around',[4] is a fascinating comment on the cultural and societal mores of Australia, both then and now.

Reflecting on the incident fifty years later, Ruth Park came to the conclusion that the novel was denounced for two reasons: first because she was not an Australian (as her 'Personal Story' had made clear) and second because she was a woman. The novel which had secured second place, *You Can't See Round Corners*, had also been set in the slums of Sydney, but was written by a male Australian, Jon Cleary, and had attracted no criticism. Certainly, in the 1940s, ladylike behaviour was dictated by social mores and shibboleths which no longer prevail, and some letters contained denunciations such as: 'I have five nieces and I am sure I should not like to give them this story to read' and 'If the story was really written by a woman, then I am very sorry, for it destroys all the nice things I have believed about women's minds.'[5] There is, however, another strand in the negative letters, which may be even more pertinent. In his review and synopsis of the novel, published in the *Herald*, Shawn O'Leary had commented, significantly, that it 'will be accepted overseas as one of the finest things out of Australia'.[6] Although the Second World War, which had devastated so many older nations, had not reached the island continent, many young Australians had gone overseas, experiencing other cultures for the first time, and now the great waves of postwar immigration were about to begin. Australia's legendary isolation was suddenly diminished. While staunchly maintaining the superiority of the Australian Way of Life, many inhabitants of the new land simultaneously suspected that their nascent culture might appear raw and gauche in comparison with that of older societies.[7] Some of the more vociferous protests seem to have been triggered by O'Leary's remark, betraying an almost adolescent hypersensitivity on this point:

Miss Park's novel . . . is . . . a misleading one and not a book that one would send out of the country (Surry Hills)

To think that in a young clean country (clean as compared with the older countries) such unadulterated filth should be given first prize and put out to the world as representing Australian life, makes my blood boil (Anderson)

I shall be sorry if the outside world has to hear all this dirt about Australia (Wilson)

It must inevitably bring Sydney and many of its citizens into contempt (Steel).[8]

The reaction in literary circles was as mixed as that of the general populace. Some critics praised the novel for its realism, the photographic quality of its street scenes, the authenticity of its characters, while others denounced its lack of plot and of a central hero and heroine. Again, however, the national image was a consideration. Australian intellectuals had long awaited the Great Australian Novel, the novel that was to mark the maturation of Australian writing, its equality with and independence from older literatures, and the *Herald* competition seemed the perfect occasion for such a debut. A novel about slums, one which not only featured violence, prostitutes and bedbugs but which also portrayed its major characters as feckless and apathetic, did not fit the bill. This was partly because the tradition of the bush, enshrined in poetry and painting, was still firmly ingrained in the Australian consciousness at all levels; the distinctive flora and fauna and the rugged landscape seemed to symbolize the independence and fortitude of the unique Australian temperament. More significantly, the general, if tacit, opinion seems to have been that Australian literature was under an obligation to foster enthusiasm, both at home and abroad, for the newborn nation, with its limitless opportunities, its less constricted, more confident way of life. A story of life in the slums did not illustrate this.

Even the publishers, Angus and Robertson, informed Park that 'It's not the kind of book A & R cares to publish but we have a gentlemen's agreement with the *Herald*.'[9] (Ironically, *The Harp in the South* has never been out of print since Angus and Robertson honoured their commitment in 1948.) Nevertheless the publishers' attitude, in regarding Australian novels as part of national publicity, was typical of the period. For instance, in her autobiography, *The Missing Heir*, Kylie Tennant, who also wrote about the poor in Australia, reports: 'I was forced to send all my earlier books to England to be published because, as Ken Prior [editor of the influential journal, the *Bulletin*] told me, they were "such a bad advertisement for Australia"'.[10] Similarly, in his biography *Patrick White: A Life*, David Marr notes that the Nobel prizewinner 'was dogged all his career by the demand that he put aside his private vision and write optimistically about decent Australians'.[11]

The majority of readers, however, blithely ignored all this negativity and took the novel to their hearts. Sales of *The Harp*, both in Australia and overseas, were and continue to be enormous, yet it is also a book of which well-thumbed copies are handed down through family generations. Indeed, when it was adapted for television in 1987, the producer felt constrained to keep modification to a minimum, commenting that it was 'necessary to stick as close as possible to the original [because] many Australians feel very possessive about the novel. We have letters begging us not to spoil it'.[12] The reasons for this positive attitude are as complex as those for the negativity and, again, are bound up with the Australian psyche.

For one thing, the Darcys are Irish–Australian, like a very large percentage of the real population.[13] For another, they are poor and, perhaps most significantly of all, they are city-dwellers. For all its vaunted bush legends, Australia has one of the most urbanized populations on earth, yet the bush tradition had encouraged these 'city people' with their 'pallid faces . . . their stunted forms and weedy'[14] to regard themselves unfavourably by comparison with the tall, lean, sun-browned bushman. (A notable feature of *The Harp*, especially for the period in which it was written, is that women, excluded from the bush tradition, are the strong characters and their concerns are central.) Everybody knows somebody like the Darcys, and nobody is likely to be daunted by them; indeed, with their poverty and fecklessness, they foster a comfortable sense of superiority not unmixed with empathy. For the Darcys are recognizably ordinary: their struggles, their griefs and joys, successes and failures are not epic but life-sized. Their problems are endemic and are not solved neatly at the conclusion of the novel, yet in defeat they remain undefeated. The indomitability of the human spirit is a recurring theme in Park's work, one that she finds exemplified in the Australian character by a 'wiry endurance . . . and the larrikin touch',[15] and which often finds expression in a subversive, Bakhtinian humour.

The Darcys, like many people both then and now, are entrapped by poverty. Their condition is obviously not as stark as that of millions in underdeveloped countries, but their problems are real and endemic amongst the underprivileged and undereducated every-where. They have enough to feed and clothe themselves, they have a roof over their heads, but there is little to spare. Although Hughie squanders money on alcohol, the sums involved are very small. His irresponsibility may not be justifiable, but it is understandable when one realizes that even the most rigid economizing would not provide his family with a way out of Surry Hills: his wages are too low. (The apathy of slum dwellers, the state of learned helplessness, is a phenomenon well known to sociologists.) Yet, in spite of their resignation, their apparent lethargy, the Darcys and the various residents of Surry Hills share that saving, subversive sense of humour from which even the narrator appears not to be immune. In the opening paragraphs, as the squalor of Twelve-and-a-Half Plymouth Street is revealed, the effect is relieved, and the larrikin fecklessness of its occupants intimated, by the 'drunken garbage can [which] stood with its lid over one ear'.[16] The resilience of the slum-dwellers is epitomized by eighty-three-year-old Grandma, 'who [has] borne so many children, who [has] worked and laughed and despaired and grieved' and who now has reached 'the evening of her life with nothing whatsoever in her hands'.[17] Yet this in no way impedes her from trouncing Hughie in the battle of the pudding, from deceiving the good nuns with amoral ingenuity or from joining with gusto in the potato barrage of the New Year bonfire.

If Grandma epitomizes the larrikin resilience which Park sees as integral to the Australian character, the bonfire is pure carnival. Mikhail Bakhtin has traced the origins of carnival to medieval culture; he describes it as a time when normal law and order are suspended, and when the prevailing mood is mocking and subversive. 'Deeply ambivalent,' he notes also, '. . . is the image of *fire* in carnival. It is a fire that simultaneously destroys and renews the world'.[18] The inhabitants of Surry Hills traditionally celebrate the passing of the old year and the birth of the new with a bonfire, an event which is routinely prohibited, and then ignored, by the authorities, whose uncharacteristic intervention on this occasion is met with a fusillade of potatoes. Further ambivalences characteristic of carnival, as identified by Bakhtin, are present in the bonfire episode: the combinations of life and death, death and rebirth, laughter and sorrow, wisdom and stupidity, youth and age. On this New Year in Surry Hills, in the midst of the laughter and festivity, both Miss Sheily and Mumma remember their sons who will never again celebrate such an occasion; while Grandma, reminded joyously, in the thick of the action, of her rebellious Irish youth, receives a thorough drenching that will result, eventually, in her death. Then, simultaneously with the death of the Old Year and the birth of the New, Mrs Siciliano gives 'a shrill scream and [bends] over, clasping her hands to her abdomen'; a new little Siciliano is about to be born.[19]

Bakhtin also emphasizes that carnival is a celebration of community: 'The main arena for carnival acts was the square and the streets adjoining it . . . for by its very idea carnival *belongs to the whole people*, it is *universal, everyone* must participate in its familiar contact'.[20] In Surry Hills, the traditional bonfire is built 'where Coronation Street met Plymouth Street [and where] there was a rough rectangle striped silver with tramlines',[21] and everyone contributes and participates, even the normally reclusive Miss Sheily and Lick Jimmy. Such tacit acknowledgement of communality, once taken for granted, not only in Surry Hills but in towns and cities everywhere, is no longer a facet of urban life. Social commentators note the passing from modern culture of the village atmosphere, those times when residents knew not only their neighbours but also their neighbours' business; times when people looked after each other, when all the children played together, when doors could be left unlocked and families and individuals were not isolated units.[22] Today, sociologists, historians and human geographers all cite *The Harp in the South* for its accurate depictions of life in a poor suburb of an Australian city of the 1940s.[23] Perhaps this was one reason for the book's initial popularity: people both in Australia and overseas responded to the unmistakable authenticity of the text. And if that is the case, nostalgia may be one reason for its continuing success, nostalgia not only for a community spirit but also for the once unquestioned security of family life. (It is perhaps significant that even the affectionate title Mumma, once so common in Australia, has fallen into disuse.) In spite of their factiousness, the Darcys face the world from within the bastion of the family circle; even Hughie, for all his irresponsibility, is a loving father and recognizes his obligations towards his mother-in-law.

For any and all of these reasons, *The Harp in the South* is a fixture on the Australian literary scene. Perhaps, through the acute observations of a friendly newcomer, Australians have been able to see themselves more clearly. If so, the effect of this novel, in both reflecting and thereby shaping Australian culture, has been, and continues to be, considerable.

Jill Greaves

Notes

1. Ruth Park, *Fishing in the Styx* (Ringwood: Penguin Viking, 1993), p. 141.
2. Carolyn Allport reports that: 'On the eve of the war there was an estimated shortage of 120,000 dwellings in Australia. By 1945, with the pressure and restrictions of war, this shortage had reached 300,000 together with a normal annual requirement of 40,000 homes. In Sydney alone the shortage was estimated to be near 69,000.' 'The Unrealised Promise: Plans for Sydney Housing in the Forties', *Twentieth Century Sydney: Studies in Urban and Social History*, ed. Jill Roe (Sydney: Hale & Iremonger, 1980), p. 48.
3. The drama critic, Leslie Rees, remembers 'walking through Wynyard station one morning and noting a long queue outside a bookstall waiting for their *Herald* containing the latest *Harp* instalment, a phenomenon I'd never seen before and have never, as applied to a novelist's work, seen since'. *Hold Fast to Dreams* (Sydney: APCOL, 1982), p. 194.
4. 'Letters to the Editor' (*Sydney Morning Herald*, 11 January 1947), p. 2.
5. Ibid., p. 2.
6. Shawn O'Leary, 'Reviews of the Prize-Winning Novels: 1st Prize Is a Social Document' (*Sydney Morning Herald*, 28 December 1946), p. 8.
7. In 1950, A. A. Phillips was to coin the phrase 'The Cultural Cringe', which has since become embedded in Australians' social consciousness. *The Australian Tradition: Studies in a Colonial Culture* (Melbourne: Cheshire, 1958).
8. 'Letters to the Editor', p. 2.
9. Ruth Park, *Fishing in the Styx*, p. 151
10. Kylie Tennant, *The Missing Heir* (South Melbourne: Macmillan, 1986), p. 91.
11. David Marr, *Patrick White: A Life* (New York: Knopf, 1992), p. 178.
12. Jane Sullivan, 'A Rich Tale of Poverty' (*The Age*, 7 May 1987), p. 1.
13. In *The Irish in Australia* (Rev. ed., Sydney: NSWUP, 1993), Patrick O'Farrell records that circa 1906 'Irish Catholics were 20–25 per cent of Australia's population' (p. 120), and that, even in 1988, 'Australians of Irish origin [made up] 17.24 per cent of the then population of 16.3 million' (p. 318).
14. 'Clancy of the Overflow' a bush ballad very well known in Australia, by A. B. Paterson.
15. Janet Hawley, 'Real Life is Sometimes ... Too Fictional' (*Sydney Morning Herald*, 31 August 1985), p. 10

16. Ruth Park, *The Harp in the South*, p. 2.

17. Ibid. p. 61.

18. Mikhail Bakhtin, *Problems of Dostoevsky's Poetics* (ed. and trans. Caryl Emerson, *Theory and History of Literature 8*, (Minneapolis: University of Minnesota Press, 1984), p. 122.

19. Ruth Park, *The Harp in the South*, p. 92.

20. Mikhail Bakhtin, op. cit., p. 128.

21. Ruth Park, *The Harp in the South*, p. 84.

22. See, for instance, Kate Legge, 'Our Street: An Australian Chronicle 1900–1994' (*The Australian Magazine*, 12–13 March 1994), pp. 8–15.

23. See, for instance, Carolyn Allport, 'The Unrealised Promise: Plans for Sydney Housing in the Forties' (*Twentieth Century Sydney: Studies in Urban and Social History* (Sydney: Hale and Iremonger, 1980)); Elizabeth Kenworthy Teacher, 'Early Postwar Sydney: A Comparison of Its Portrayal in Fiction and in Official Documents' (*Australian Geographical Studies: Journal of the Institute of Australian Geographers 28*, 1990), pp. 204–23.

One

The hills are full of Irish people. When their grandfathers and great-grandfathers arrived in Sydney they went naturally to Shanty Town, not because they were dirty or lazy, though many of them were that, but because they were poor. And wherever there are poor you will find landlords who build tenements: cramming two on a piece of land no bigger than a pocket handkerchief, and letting them for the rent of four. In the squalid, mazy streets of sandstone double-decker houses, each with its little balcony edged with rusty iron lace, and its door opening on to the street, or four square feet of 'front', every second name is an Irish one. There are Brodies, and Caseys and Murphys and O'Briens, and down by the corner are Casement and Grogan and Kell, and, although here and there you find a Simich, or a Siciliano, or a Jewish shopkeeper, or a Chinese laundryman, most are Irish.

Even the names of the streets tell the story of those old emigrants who came looking for roads cobbled with gold, and found them made of stone harder than an overseer's heart. There is Fahy Street running off Riley Street, and both of them branching from Coronation Street, which had the name of Kelleher before they changed it to honour Queen Victoria. And there is Ryan Street running down into Redfern, and Brophy Street, mean and horrible, flowing into Elizabeth Street, which leads to the city.

This was the place where the Darcys lived – Plymouth Street, Surry Hills, Sydney, in an unlucky house which the landlord had renumbered from Thirteen to Twelve-and-a-Half.

It was the oldest in Plymouth Street, a cranky brown house, with a blistered green door, and a step worn into dimples and hollows that collected the rain in little pools in which Roie and Dolour, when little, had always expected to find frogs.

There were many houses like Number Twelve-and-a-Half, smelling of leaking gas, and rats, and mouldering wallpaper which has soaked up the odours of a thousand meals. The stairs were very dark and steep, and built on a slant as though the architect were drunk, so that from the top landing you couldn't see the bottom. On the top landing hung a little globe, very high up, so that the tenants could not steal it. It was as small as a star and as yellow as a lemon.

Downstairs there was a dark bedroom without windows or skylight, a kitchen with a broken floor, and a scullery with one window overlooking the flagged yard, where a drunken garbage can stood with its lid over one ear. Upstairs were three cramped attic bedrooms. Hughie and Mumma had slept in one of these for a long time, but it had a sloping roof, so that anybody bouncing hastily out of the left-hand side of the bed hit himself a terrific blow on top of the head, and fell prostrate again. Hughie had done this a thousand times, both drunk and sober, and it was the main cause of his frequent absence from work; as he pointed out to Mumma, by the time he'd shaken his brains back into their proper place it was past the hour and no use going to work at all, seeing that a man was fined for every minute he was late. He had promised himself time and time again that he'd move the bed, but somehow it never got done, for it meant rearranging all the furniture, and that would take a full afternoon of time. He could not afford that, for Saturday afternoon he always spent at the pub, and Sunday afternoon he spent sleeping off Saturday afternoon.

So the simplest thing was to move the children into the attic, while he and Mumma took the dark bedroom downstairs.

Once Roie and Dolour had had a little brother, Thady. When he was six, and Roie nine, and Dolour two, he had been sent out on to the footpath to play, for the backyard was too small and dirty and sunless. And he had just disappeared. Nothing was ever heard of him again. No one had seen a man or woman leading him off, or a car carry him away. There was just a little box cart left lying on the roadway, and that was all. Hughie had rampaged round the streets and through the alleyways like a madman; he had accompanied the police as they patrolled the sewers. Grim-lipped and devil-faced, he had sworn that God and he would never be friends while the agony and mystery of Thady's disappearance hung over them.

But Mumma had never given up hope. She often stood at the gates of boys' schools, looking and looking, adding the slow years to Thady's stature, and maturity to his little round face. It was ten years since he had disappeared. Dolour did not remember him at all, and Roie only a little, but he was a living presence in that house. He was like a ghost who is not dead.

In the other attic rooms, which Mumma let, furnished, for seven and sixpence a week each, lived Mr Patrick Diamond and Miss Sheily. Mr Diamond was a real Irishman, born in Ireland, an Orangeman who was friendly with Hughie and liked all the Darcys except on St Patrick's Day, when his Orange blood boiled up, and he called them all pope-worshippers and mummers, and stamped upstairs and slammed the door, and banged on the wall if Roie or Dolour gave as much as a squeak. He had been christened Patrick in error by a gin-bemused neighbour, and all his life it had been a cross to him and a confusion to his friends. But his pride and his stubbornness forbade his changing it to William or James, much as he would have liked to.

Miss Sheily was a tiny thin woman, as bitter as a draught of alum water, with a parchment face and subtle black eyes. She had been well educated, and consequently Mumma always felt a little shy of her. Hughie tended to become rumbustious, just to prove that he was as good as she was, and a damn sight better. But he liked her more than the others did. Roie and Dolour were a little bit frightened of her. It seemed to them that Miss Sheily, with her piercing eyes, and birdlike sophisticated voice, knew a world wider than theirs. It would not have surprised them if she had one day thrown open her attic window and darted out on a broom, over the narrow canyon of Plymouth Street, and into the maze of alleyways which makes up the Hills.

The funny thing about Miss Sheily was that nobody knew her Christian name, or had even seen her initial. When she left a note pinned to the door for the iceman or the butcher's boy, she always signed it 'Miss Sheily'. Roie and Dolour and Mumma often had guessing competitions about Miss Sheily's name, but nobody had ever proved her guess correct. Dolour thought that Agnes or Amy was most likely, and Roie said scornfully that Belle or Grace was right up Miss Sheily's alley, seeing that neither fitted. But Mumma, with the stubborn and unpredictable romanticism that she sometimes displayed, voted for Stella.

'Oh, Mumma! Fancy Stella!' cried Roie. 'Why the dickens should she have a name like that?'

'Because she's a lady,' said Mumma obstinately. And, although both Roie and Dolour, as well as the rest of Plymouth Street, knew that this could not possibly be so, they did not dare say anything, for Mumma hated the mere mention of illegitimacy. So they could not quote Johnny as an argument against Miss Sheily's ladyhood.

For Johnny Sheily, the poor unfortunate with his crooked back and great square box of a head, was Miss Sheily's son, and she did not make the slightest attempt to hide it.

'Johnny!' she would scream down the stairs. 'Johnny, where are you?' and to Mr Diamond, who might emerge across the landing just then, 'Have you seen that great lump of a son of mine, Mr Diamond?'

Johnny, sitting beneath the mangy-leaved phoenix palm in the backyard and gently moving some incomprehensible cipher of pebbles back and forth in the dirt, would raise his buttermilk blue eyes and call back: 'Ike ummin, Umma', for his tongue, like the rest of him, was twisted.

Roie was one of those who cannot bear to see the deformed. The dark little currant eyes of an idiot, his chinless face, and thick neck and bowed legs, was enough to fill her day with horror, though she saw him but passingly from a tram. And every day she walked a quarter of a mile out of her path so that she would not have to pass a certain doorway where an old legless man with blind milky eyes sat in the sun.

She tried to conquer this, for it was against the principles which had been instilled in her soul from the time she began to speak. Mumma had always said: 'God has struck them as the wild lightning

4

strikes a tree, and no one knows why.' And she had said: 'It might be you with the harelip, or the nose like a strawberry, and if ever I catch you calling names or hurting the feelings of the misfortunate, I'll beat the bottom off you.'

So when Roie shrank from Johnny Sheily, or turned away her face when he mumbled some mysterious greeting, she committed a double sin, that of uncharity and that of pride. For almost unconsciously her hand would go up to her own small slender face, and trace the contours of slanting eyes and soft chin, and the little delicate mouth that had its outline slightly raised as though it were in relief. It was almost as though, with that very gesture, her hand said: 'Thank God that I am not as you.' Realizing this, she was always trying to atone, offering Masses for poor Johnny Sheily, and forcing herself to look in his bleary eye and smile as she passed.

But Mumma loved him in her own acidulous, contrary way, and never once did she hear Miss Sheily beating him that she did not shed a tear of mingled grief and rage.

Johnny was often naughty, for all that he was twenty or more, for his poor bewildered brain, that saw a sparrow as big as a goose, and peopled the air around him with butterflies and other things that needed to be snatched at, and caught, did not take in every word he heard, and consequently he was always doing the wrong thing, and being walloped for it.

'The woman hates him, it's my solemn belief,' said Mumma one day, staring at the ceiling, her cup of tea growing cold and curdly on the table.

Hughie laughed: 'Hate her own child? What are you talking about?'

Mumma shook her head. 'It's possible, Hughie. He's the cause of her shame, and she blames him for it.'

'Better blame herself for getting all hot and bothered when she didn't ought to,' chuckled Hughie coarsely. Mumma flushed.

'Shut yer big trap,' she snapped, and Hughie laughed uproariously and put his arms round her wide waist and mumbled in her ear. She brought the side of her hand in a sharp chop across the back of his neck.

'You're a dirty old man, Hughie, and that's a fact.'

'I'm not, now. I'm neither dirty nor old. I'm just a man,' protested Hughie. Mumma opened her mouth to retort, but almost instantly the whimpering wails of Johnny upstairs broke into shrill shrieks.

'She's murdering him, the old hag, that's what she's doing,' cried Hughie. His eyes blazed, and he burst through the doorway and pounded up the stairs. There in the darkness he stood, hammering on Miss Sheily's door and yelling to her to open up. Mumma pounded after him, protesting, for in the live and let live law of the slums there is a clause that nobody shall interfere in anybody else's fight.

'Open the door or I'll kick it in,' yelled Hughie, the brilliant white light of the crusader filling his heart. There was a split second's wait, and then Mumma quietly tried the door. It was not locked. Hughie burst in, and Mumma caught a glimpse of Miss Sheily's room, its streaky blue kalsomined walls, the sloping ceiling stuck with pictures, and the gas ring flaring yellow and smoky in one dim corner. The air was thick with the fumes of burnt fat, stale food, and old unwashed clothing. On the floor was a litter of scraps of paper and crumbs of food that had been trodden flat into the grease and dirt.

And there against a wall was Johnny, his hands tied around a disused gas jet. As soon as Mumma saw his grotesque figure she gave a shriek and her anger surpassed Hughie's.

'Why, you old Borgia,' she cried. 'Tying the poor kid up to slam the daylights out of him.'

Beside Johnny Miss Sheily stood trembling, thin as a piece of wire, her drooping black skirt hardly hiding the bones which stood fragilely beneath it. In her hand was a piece of knotted electric flex. Her white face was a smudge under the dim light which filtered from the skylight, but Mumma could easily see the hatred and passion which glared from it. It was almost as though Miss Sheily were as transparent as a light globe, and the very force of her bitter spirit illuminated her.

'Get out of here,' she spat. 'What do you mean by it? By God, if it's the last thing I do I'll see you in gaol for this. It's forced entry, that's what it is.'

'What have you done to the poor little devil?' groaned Mumma, her fingers running over Johnny's bare back, wet with oozing serum from a dozen wounds. He sluggishly turned his head, and his bristly hair brushed her face. His pale blue eyes had an opaque opal sheen in the dimness.

'The Red Cross'll hear about this,' promised Hughie. 'Yeah, and the RSPCA, too. You can talk about putting other people in boob, you old vulture.'

And, indeed, Miss Sheily did look like a vulture standing there quaking with temper, her long white nose curved downwards and her blue lips as thin and bitter as a snake's. Out of those lips came no words, only shrill birdlike sounds that spoke as no words could of the maelstrom of loathing in her soul. Mumma gave a yank with her strong hands and broke the bootlaces which linked Johnny's hands over the gas jet. He stood there giggling under his breath, his great oblong head cocked over one shoulder and his long arms dangling like an ape's.

'You should be black ashamed, Miss Sheily,' said Mumma.

Miss Sheily's fury lapped over as a river in flood brims its banks. She began to speak in a high, hoarse voice upon which her refined accent sat grotesquely. 'I'm sick of him! I'm sick of the look of him!'

Mumma put her arm around Johnny. His shoulders were so broad that her fingers barely grasped his other arm.

'It's not his fault he's a cripple. And you shouldn't be reminding him of it,' she reproached.

Hughie had a mindful of scintillating sentences which he could not wait to utter, but every time he opened his mouth one of the women took advantage of the moment and spoke in his place.

Miss Sheily's eyes blazed so much they were like the eyes of a mad woman. 'I hate the way he looks. Every time I realize he's my child I could cut my throat.'

'Easy to do,' cried Hughie hurriedly, before anyone could snatch the moment from him. 'Easier to do than lashing the hide off him.'

'Hating your own child,' said Mumma, shocked to her heart and yet exultant, because she had suspected it all along. 'You shouldn't ever have had a child.'

'I didn't want him,' screamed Miss Sheily. 'I tried every way I knew to get rid of him before he was born. And then when he came he was like this, a monster. I hate him. I hate him!'

'Why don't you put him in an orphanage, then?' said Hughie.

Miss Sheily answered sulkily, 'I don't want to.'

'No,' said Hughie astutely; 'and you can get a pretty big pension for him, can't you, so that you needn't go to work. Oh, no, you're quite the lady. You may as well say that Johnny's hump is working for you, Miss Sheily.'

He laughed uproariously. Already he was tasting the applause of the boys at the pub as they listened open-mouthed to his recountal of the story. To Miss Sheily his wide mouth and little screwed-up eyes looked like the mask of a devil. She lashed out with the flex, but before the blow fell Hughie grabbed her thin arm, as dry and mummified as that of a skeleton, and warded it off.

'Oan urt umma,' croaked Johnny, throwing himself upon Hughie. His great weight thrust the man off his balance, and Hughie rolled in the dirt with Johnny on top of him. But the boy had no strength, and squatted there with tears bubbling out of his eyes in a stream, his blubbery mouth pursed in a ludicrous parody of a child's.

'Ah, God in heaven,' said Hughie in disgust, scrambling up and thrusting his face close to Miss Sheily's paper-white one, 'if I hear one more yell from this room I'll report to the cops as sure as God's up there.'

He pointed a dramatic finger at the ceiling and stumped out of the room. Mumma hovered a moment, then followed him.

That night, in the silence Roie and Dolour, lying cold and uncomfortable in their bed next door, heard Miss Sheily crying – faraway, hiccuping sobs which told them she had her head buried in a pillow. And then there was a muffled bellow from Johnny, and sharp sentences from his mother in a voice which was nasal with tears. Dolour whispered:

'Crumbs, she's a funny old tart. I say, Ro, do you reckon Miss Sheily is really his mother?'

Roie was on the verge of sleep, caught between consciousness and unconsciousness; she replied in a voice which seemed to come from down a long corridor: 'I guess that's why she hates him so much.'

Dolour scoffed: 'But she couldn't have hated him when he was a little weeny baby, even if he was all bumpy and queer.'

'Imagine if Miss Sheily loved someone,' said Roie, her voice laden with sleep, but her mind clear and remote. 'Imagine if he threw her up when he found she was going to have a baby . . . and then she tried to get rid of it . . .'

'How can you get rid of a baby?' asked Dolour. The little clear voice coming out of the darkness made Roie feel ashamed. She remembered the shock and horror she had felt when she first learned about abortion. She said quickly: 'Oh, ways.'

'Oh,' said Dolour. They were quiet for a while. Beyond the violet-blue oblong of the window, rimmed with the blowing shadows of the ragged curtain, a flight of white stars slanted across the sky. Dolour said dreamily: 'Have you ever been in love, Roie?'

Immediately she was sorry, and the blood beat in her ears for she knew she should not have asked, and she was frightened in case Roie rebuffed her stingingly, and hurt her feelings. But all Roie said was: 'No, never at all.'

'I wonder if girls feel about boys like they do about film stars?' asked Dolour shyly.

'I won't,' said Roie. 'It'll be all different.'

'How do you know?' asked Dolour curiously. She felt Roie's slim body move beside her, and felt the faint scent of her talcum power. All of a sudden Roie wasn't her sister any more; she was in some queer way mysterious, like a strange woman. Dolour realized sinkingly that Roie was grown up and she was still a child. She wanted to ask some more questions, but it was no use, for Roie was asleep. Dolour sighed and turned over.

Next door Miss Sheily, her head feeling as though it were swollen and yet filled with a most malignant emptiness, buried her face in the lumpy, ill-smelling mattress and tried to shut out the sounds of the night: Johnny snuffling in his blankets near the window, Mrs Darcy rattling about washing supper dishes downstairs, Mr Diamond clumping on large bare feet down the stairs to the yard. She could also hear a tied-up dog howling, the vagrant song of a drunken man, and the distant rattle and clang of a homegoing tram.

9

As the darkness grew deeper the bugs came out of their cracks in the walls, from under the paper, and out of the cavities in the old iron bedsteads, where they hung by day in grape-like clusters. They were thin and flat and starved, but before the dawn they would return to their foul hiding-places round and glistening and bloated with blood, so fat they could hardly waddle.

Captain Phillip brought them in the rotten timbers of his First Fleet, and ever since they have remained in the old tenement houses of Sydney, ferocious, ineradicable, the haunters of the tormented sleep of the poor.

Two

Next door to Number Twelve-and-a-Half was an empty shop. It had been empty for so long that Mumma often groaned and grunted her way through a hole in the paling fence and hung her washing in the back yard. When Roie and Dolour were little they had often peered through the black glass, clotted with spider web, that lighted the little kitchen, cavernous and forlorn; and they had scampered, naked and joyous, under the rain that spouted from the gutterless roof.

When the rent man told Mumma that the shop at last was to be occupied, it was a great blow to the Darcys. What sort of people would come to live there? Someone with lots of children, forever yelling, and lobbing stones on the roof? Someone with a curious profession like fishmongering, which meant that they would get all the smells?

But it wasn't. It was a Chinese, a small, neat, compact, elderly lemon-yellow creature with polished shoes and eyes as glossy as jet. He appeared one day in the yard, bowed to Mumma across the fence, and proceeded to clean the tumble-down dwelling with energy and intensity equalled only by a cyclone's.

'There!' wailed Mumma, peering out of the upper window at the clouds of dust which billowed from his. 'Chow gramophones miawing all night. Prawns lying around the yard. Heaven knows what going on.'

The next day the Chinese, having spent a mysterious night of bumpings and thumpings, and sharp staccato hammerings, cleaned out his window. To Dolour and the other children, standing spellbound before his door, he was at first only a ghost amidst the yellow dust. Then, before his polishing cloth, crystal lanes and highways appeared on the coated glass, and they saw him, calm and ivory and smiling, chasing the last cobwebs and dirt clots from the window.

'Wonder what his name is?' whispered Dolour, and one of the Drummy kids, cheekier than the others, yelled out: 'Hey, you! Your name John or Charlie?'

The Chinese did not reply. He picked up a small brush and pot of black paint, and trotted outside with a step-ladder. In precise and level letters he inscribed across his window the words, 'Lick Jimmy, Fruiterer.'

Dolour and the others were delighted. They had never before seen so exotic a name. An old woman, doddering past with a billy in her hand, stopped and blinked her little dead eyes.

'What's he givin' us? An invite?'

Ever afterwards, Lick Jimmy was the delight of every wit in Plymouth Street. Even the tiniest child, going to his shop for a penny soup-bunch and thrippence-worth of mandarins, inquired: 'Where do you want to be licked today, Jimmy?' And never once did Jimmy fail to smile, for he was not destined to learn the intricacies of Surry Hills English.

How Dolour loved little old Jimmy! A lonely hermit of a man, he did not appear to have either wife or friend. His heavily curtained windows might have concealed almost anything, and occasionally Mumma, who was legitimately curious about her neighbour, reported that she had seen lights bobbing about in more than one room at a time.

Also, occasionally, there were wild bursts of fire-crackers from the upper room, for which nobody could account, but when Hughie irascibly asked Jimmy the next day what all the bang-o had been about, all he got was a silken smile, the offer of a splendid brown pear, and the beguiling words, 'My blirtday, misser.'

Jimmy had a great idea of colour, but none at all of form. He liked to pile everything higgledy-piggledy into his window, the carrot-tops feathering out of the apples, and the celery, like pale-green ivory, mathematically grooved, lying side by side with a heap of crimson cherries. Jimmy counted the change on a worn black abacus, sliding the beads very swiftly with his smooth creamy fingers. Dolour could not work it out. Did the big beads represent the shillings and the little ones the pence? Then she realized that Jimmy thought in Chinese, and heaven alone knew what queer hieroglyphics the beads stood for.

The St Patrick's Day when she was thirteen, her mother gave her a shilling and said: 'There now, God bless you, and for his dear sake get out from under me feet until I get the stew going.'

It was a fine March day, with amber in the sun, and the leaves on the plane trees blotched with clear bright yellow. Reluctantly the summer was departing and after it whirled the leaves on the rising wind. Joyfully, her shilling so hard and substantial in her hand, Dolour ran down the hall to the door. She heard someone shouting upstairs, in a thick, coarse, wine-soaked voice, and as the top door swung open she caught a glimpse of Patrick Diamond standing in front of the mirror and toasting himself with a tumbler of something. He saw her white triangle of face, and lurching to the stair-rail, he yelled: 'Gert, yer little pope-worshipper!'

Promptly Dolour yelled back: 'Garn, yer old proddy-hopper!' She ran blithely down the street, not bothering to wonder why it was that Mr Patrick Diamond hated them all so bitterly on St Patrick's Day. He had been that way as long as she could remember. Dolour bought thrippence-worth of acid drops, lime-green and sour, currant-red and sweet; a twisted liquorice strap, four large leathery-brown buns with coarse sugar grains glued to the top. Then she returned to Lick Jimmy's to spend her remaining threepence. There was much to choose from there, for it had been a good fruit season, and oranges as red as a setting sun were two for a penny. And there were rich autumnal pears, too, and Queensland sugar bananas like little fat fingers. Dolour pondered for a long time, for there was always the problem of getting for your money something that would last in spite of many suckings or nibblings. At last she decided on the bananas, for Hughie loved bananas, and that would mean he mightn't eat his bun, and then she could have that as well as the rest of her share.

Lick Jimmy, patient and tranquil, sat and watched her, stuffing long silky shreds of pale golden tobacco into his little pipe at intervals, and caressing the back of his maternal cat, which lay at ease in a box half full of rhubarb. He had no curiosity whatsoever about Dolour Darcy; he knew all about her, for Lick Jimmy, too, liked to stand behind a dark curtain and watch the life of his neighbours.

'It's me birthday, Jimmy,' said Dolour apologetically, to atone for the delay in her purchase.

'Oh, yeah?' chirped Jimmy. He rose and flip-flopped into the inner room. When he came back he bore a kite, a lovely rose-red thing of finest paper pasted on bones of white wood. It was all there, the thick bank of string, and the fairylike tail like a procession of butterflies, for Jimmy had used the torn-up pages of an old Chinese calendar. Dolour was so overcome that she didn't know what to do. She stammered:

'Not for me? Oh, gee whiz!'

The lovely thing vibrated in her hand. It was like a pair of wings, disembodied, with lift and eagerness in them, ready for the tumult of the wind, and the placid lakes of the upper air.

'You like?' inquired Lick Jimmy, his face a web of smiling lines.

'Oh, Jimmy,' stammered Dolour. 'I *do* like!'

She dropped a kiss on the hand that rested on the counter, and ran from the shop. Lick Jimmy, a strange inscrutable expression on his face, slowly rubbed the kiss away, then went back and sat in his corner behind the window, puffing quietly at his pipe, and rubbing the back of the happy cat. And nobody knew what he thought.

Dolour tore pellmell into the kitchen. 'Mumma! Oh, look!'

She pulled up short, for there was Patrick Diamond, and in a perfect devil of a St Patrick's temper. His attitude was that of an early politician immortalized in stone, one hand thrust inside his waistcoat, and the other pointing waveringly to the smoke-stained ceiling.

'Bowing and scraping to heathen idols, that's all you're doing, Mrs Darcy, and taking wilful pleasure in scarlet mummery not fit to be performed, that's what.'

It was a strange thing that every time St Pat's Day came around, and the Orange blood rose rich and rare to Mr Diamond's head, he wanted to convert Mumma. Dolour had long ago got used to it, but Mumma never did. She gave Mr Diamond a look that would brand a pig.

There she stood in front of Puffing Billy, the coal range, who, unheeded, hiccuped and belched against the back of her skirt. Her face bore two brick-red banners of anger, but unfortunately Mr Diamond spoke so fast she did not have the chance to get a word in sideways.

Dolour, however, did. 'Look what Lick Jimmy gave me, Mumma!' she yelled, waving the kite like a monstrous poppy-red moth before Mr Diamond's loathing eyes.

'It's no better than a heathen show you've got here, with your holy pictures on the wall, and your holy water in the bottle. Does it cure Hughie of the DT's when he's got them, or does it take the rheumaticks from your own bones, Mrs Darcy, tell me now?'

Puffing Billy suddenly gave a croaking sound deep down in his throat, and panted rhythmically. Great puffs of soot-laden smoke curled out of every crack in his God-forsaken front and filled the kitchen with stinging fog. Mr Diamond reeled away, and Mumma burst into tears of anger, for she had all the preparations for dinner laid out on the table, and now everything was freckled thickly with smuts. She seized the potato-masher and beat Mr Diamond over the head with it.

'Go on, get out of here, you old bastard, or I'll smarther yer! Coming into me own kitchen abusing me about me holy pictures! Get out of here or I'll brand you!'

She crashed the potato masher down on Mr Diamond's bald head once more, and he with a growling oath caught her wrist and twisted it.

'Smarther me, it is, and you not far from the brink of hell yerself with yer curses and whatnot to call a decent working man.'

Puffing Billy suddenly gave a great sobbing inhalation, and all the smoke vanished as though by magic from the room, disappearing in thin wreaths and rings through the rifts in the iron. Dolour saw her mother and Mr Diamond with sudden clarity. She gave a shriek and flung herself upon the drunken man, yelling at the top of her voice and beating his stomach with her clenched fists.

At this moment Hughie came in, considerably the worse for St Patrick's Day, for he had been shouted by more than one of his friends. He seized Mr Diamond by the back of the collar, and it seemed as though all the fury of the Battle of the Boyne were in his grip. Mr Diamond glugged and gripped his throat, the words coming in spurts from his lips:

'She called me a bastard, she did, Hughie.'

Hughie gave a snort of admiration: 'Do you tell me so! Yer dirty swaddler, and what are yer but an illegitimate, to put it in a gentlemanly way. Coming in here to make up to me missus, no doubt, yer Calvinist.'

He hurled Mr Diamond into a corner, where he lay in a huddle of arms and legs. Dolour flew into her father's arms, breathing in the fumes of liquor with an almost reverent air: 'Oh, Dadda! Dadda! You fixed him.'

'It just goes to show what an Orangeman will do when he's left alone with two defenceless women,' said Hughie, very loudly, so that Mr Diamond would hear no matter how battered he might be. Mumma wiped some of the soot off her face with the corner of her apron. She was trying to hide the tears of anger and fright that were in her eyes.

'Mumma called him a "bastard",' whispered Dolour with a shocked giggle, for she had never before heard such a word from her Mumma's lips. Hughie frowned.

'Don't you let me hear you repeating such things!' he roared, and Dolour wriggled down from his arms in terror. Mumma whimpered:

'I'm sorry, Hughie love. I am, so. But I was so angry with the soot and everything, all over me apple charlotte. And now you've killed him!' She burst into hysterical sobs.

Hughie turned to the prostrate body of his friend and snorted. 'You can't kill an Orangeman with an axe!' he said derisively. Then Dolour saw his eyes widen.

'By God, me girl, maybe yer right!' He turned Mr Diamond over on to his back, and peered down into his face. It was plum-red; more than that, it was claret, and a great purple swollen vein ran down the side of his temple from scalp to eyebrow. Mr Diamond was snoring so hard that his upper lip fluttered with every breath; his mouth hung open and showed his tobacco-stained teeth. It was a sight not only hideous, it was in some way terrible. Dolour, breathless, held on to her mother's skirt.

'God be between us and harm, the man's had a stroke!' whispered Mumma, blessing herself. 'He'll die on us, Hughie. Get a doctor, quick!'

Hughie turned a face from which all the flush and the bravado had died. 'And have to say that I hit him, and maybe killed him dead?'

Dolour was still clutching her kite. The rustle of it broke through the frozen layer of terror which filmed her consciousness. Suddenly she broke from her mother and plunged out the door.

'Dolour! Come back here!' she heard her Mumma cry after her, but she did not stop. She flew into Lick Jimmy's shop.

'Jimmy! Come quick! Mr Diamond . . . he's dying!'

Without a word Lick Jimmy rose and followed her. He padded as quietly as a tiger down the passage and into the room where Mumma and Hughie still stood in a tableau of indecision.

'Ha!' said Jimmy. He brushed past Hughie and knelt by Mr Diamond. 'Ha! Him plenty sick.'

He looked up at Hughie, and in a moment his whole face was different. The tranquil pale yellow mask was gone; there was vitality and energy in that face, and the black glossy eyes were full of intelligence. Hughie felt a passing wave of chagrin that he had been so cheated into believing that Lick Jimmy was just the same as any other Chink. He stammered: 'What do you think we better do, Lick?'

Lick Jimmy rolled up his sleeves. He said curtly to Mumma: 'Fetch basin. Plenty hot water. Stleng.'

Without a word Mumma vanished into the kitchen, and Hughie asked fearfully: 'What you gonna do, Lick?'

'Take blood,' said Lick Jimmy. 'Him have stloke soon. You watch. Him have stloke and go sssst!' He snapped his fingers.

'Oh, God, it was me that hit him,' babbled Hughie. 'And he had plenty of wine in. Oh, God, I've murdered me mate. Patrick, man, I've killed yer.'

Mumma ran back with an enamel basin and a kettle of hot water. She said no word. Somehow the demeanour of the Chinese had filled her with trust.

Jimmy and she rolled back the sleeve of the unconscious man. There was a soft click, and Dolour, with dilated eyes, saw an open penknife in Jimmy's hand.

'My God, what you up to?' croaked Hughie. Jimmy did not answer. He thrust the tip of the knife firmly into the big vein which throbbed in the crook of Mr Diamond's elbow. Dolour, frozen to the spot, saw the blood come trickling, then throbbing, then spurting, hitting the side of the basin as the milk from a cow's udder hits the side of a bucket. She couldn't turn her eyes away. All she could do was to stare at that rising ruby flood. Mumma turned her face away, and her shoulders heaved. Jimmy did not look at anybody. He saw the colour of Mr Diamond's face turn from burgundy to claret, and then to pink. As it became a sickly mushroom colour, Jimmy put his thumb upon the vein, and the blood, diverted, splashed in a great dark star upon the floor. As he applied pressure, it became a driblet, and then merely a series of reluctant beads.

Hughie ran outside and was sick in the drain. 'Oh, glory-lory-ory!' he kept moaning, wiping the sickly sweat from his brow, and trying to be ill again. When he returned Lick Jimmy had already applied a tourniquet to Mr Diamond's arm, and a square of sticking plaster was on the puncture in the skin.

'Fline, fline!' chirped Lick Jimmy cheerily. 'Come, puttee Misser Dlimon on sofa.'

They lifted the man and put him gently on the old horse-hair couch. He looked very ill; his head sagging heavily, and his eyelids shivering rapidly from side to side. He looked old and pathetic, and Hughie suddenly remembered that Mr Diamond did not have a soul in the world to care whether he lived, died, or berated Catholics about pope-worshipping.

'You give cuppee tea,' suggested Jimmy. He gave the suggestion of a bow, and the Darcys had the definite impression that the whole incident was at an end and Lick Jimmy was required in his shop. They did not say a word as he padded quietly away. Hughie, pale-faced, and no longer even slightly drunk, burst out:

'He mighta killed poor Patrick!'

Mumma's face flushed. 'Don't go covering up yer embarrassment that way, Hugh Darcy. It's gratitude you ought to be feeling to Jimmy. Ah, it's a sad thing to think that poor little yeller heathen won't ever see the face of God in heaven,' she ruminated.

Mr Diamond opened his eyes and said feebly: 'What am I doing lying down in yer house, Hugh Darcy?'

Hugh replied soothingly: 'Yer fainted, Pat, and cut yer arm on the chair. But I fixed it up for you. Be quiet now, and the missus'll have a cup of tea for yer in a minute.'

Mumma threw a tea-towel over the basin of blood and whisked it out of the room. Dolour followed.

'Gee whiz, can I look? All that blood!' She peered under the tea-towel. The blood was as dark as wine, already starting to become jellified where the air touched it. The rich colour, the smoothness of it, fascinated Dolour. It seemed to her to be the most wonderful stuff she had ever seen. It was hard to believe that only half an hour before it was pulsing through Mr Diamond's heart. It was almost like looking at life itself.

'Ain't it beautiful, Mumma?' She dipped a finger in it, and the next moment received a stinging slap across the ear.

'Don't be filthy, yer dirty strap!' said Mumma hysterically, as she poured the blood down the drain, holding her face away in nausea. 'Now, get a cloth and help me flick the smuts off me charlotte.'

Dolour, with trembling lips and smarting eyes, groped around for the cloth. Then her mother's warm breast was against her shoulder, and arms went around her and held her close.

'Ah, Dolour, me darling, I'm sorry. I shouldn't have slapped you and you only a little inquisitive child. But I'm upset.'

Dolour's hot heart flamed with love for her mother. 'I should think you would be, with that old coot knocking you around.'

Her mother dumbly shook her head. 'No, it's not that. It's because I allowed a bad word to cross my tongue.'

Dolour's wide eyes were astonished, 'You mean "bastard"?' Mumma blushed.

'Will yer please forget, Dolour! I won't be content till I get it off me soul in confession. It's no word for a woman, and no word for a mother. Now, forget it, or I'll clip yer ears good and wholesome.'

So Dolour obediently did, but she never after saw Mr Patrick Diamond without muttering under her breath: 'Dirty old proddy-hopper. Old bastard.'

Three

One Friday it happened that Roie had a half day, for the machinery at the box factory had broken down, and the two hundred girls who were its slaves were liberated into the mellow afternoon. Roie had almost forgotten what a weekday afternoon was like, so much more magical than Saturday afternoon, which was noisy and drunken, or Sunday afternoon, which was dull. She walked along, saying to herself: 'I'm married, and I've been doing the shopping, and I'm going home to cook the tea for my husband, and then we're going to the pictures, and he'll buy me an ice-cream, and put his arm around me.' For Roie's heart was full of sweet timid yearnings for the security and contentment of love. Then she laughed, and forgot all about it for it was an exultant, promising afternoon. The road curved upwards and down in a long, graceful bow. The sky was purest blue, not convolvulus, or harebell, or cobalt, nor the happy vapour-laden blue of the sky over the sea; it was as though the air had at last become colour, burnished by the dauntless dying sun, and scoured to brilliance by the vast sandy winds from the desert inland. Roie felt as though anything might happen, and to ensure that it would be good, she ran up the hollowed sandstone steps of the church and into its chilly duskiness. Even there the excitement of the unexpected afternoon off did not leave her. She took no notice of the lame old woman limping around the Stations of the Cross, or of the queer man with his hat still on, who sat counting something that clinked. It was as though Roie spoke to a young and understanding person, not at all as if she were praying to God who had been hoary when the world was still a thought.

'Dear Lord, don't let Mumma get sick. Don't let Dad be drunk this weekend. Let Dolour get her arithmetic right in the exam. And Lord, don't let me get too old before anyone wants to marry me.'

Mumma was pleased to see her come in. She said:

'Dolour will be out of school in a moment. Why don't you and her go down to the Paddy's Market and get me enough vegetables to last for the week?'

Roie groaned: 'Oh, gosh, lugging pumpkin and things all that way?'

Mumma winked, and reached into her little flat black purse that was always being lost under cushions and mattresses, and at the back of the knife-box.

'Here's five bob I've been scrimping from the house money. If you see anything pretty down there, you buy it for yerself, seeing that it's yer birthday next week, Roie love.'

Roie took the two florins and the shilling. She felt their slipperiness and their clean milled edges, and a gush of love filled her heart. She hugged her mother and said roughly: 'You're an old rat stealing from the house like that, but thanks, Mumma. I guess I'll buy a lace dress from the old clothes stall and go out and get myself a millionaire.'

Dolour was so excited at the thought of a visit to the Paddy's Market that she ran round and round the kitchen like a wet puppy. She had lived in Surry Hills all her life, but she had never been to the zoo, the museum, the circus or the market.

Roie and she took a sugar-bag, rolled up in newspaper, and walked down into the city, past the smelly stable where the brewery horses, big white whiskery old fellows, spent their ammonia-scented nights, and through the narrow, drab lanes where the old ochre-coloured tenements shouldered and frowned. Washing hung out over the upper iron railings of the balconies, and dirty-nosed children darted like rabbits in and out of the warren-like alleys.

Soon they had crossed George Street, and were headed toward Darling Harbour. Everywhere there were barrowmen, with lean bowed horses plodding along in front of barbarically painted little waggons laden two and three feet high with fruit or vegetables. Here went a man with a cargo of radiant hothouse tomatoes, blushing beneath a gauzy counterpane of fern which shielded them from the sun. There a gipsy-like fat woman with a black moustache backed a frightened white pony and a barrow of lettuces between two gigantic drays laden to the gunwales with leaden, staring-eyed fish. The noise of people calling their wares became louder and louder, as an increasing tide becomes louder. The girls passed little shops of which the floors were golden with spilt wheat, or silver with spilt barley; there were others where young russet-faced Chinese peasants who could not speak English, but never made an error in the change, sold dried octopus and seaweed for the delectation of budgerigars.

'Cripes!' gasped Dolour. She had never heard so much noise, or seen so much simultaneous movement.

And there was the market, with wide gaping dark doors through which a surf of sound was flowing. Roie tried to look blasé and unconcerned, but even she felt excited, for she hadn't been to the Paddy's Market since she was a little girl. Thady had been with her and dadda that time, and they had stroked the little yellow chicks at the livestock stall, and laughed at their thin cheepings.

'What do they sell?' gasped Dolour.

'Everything,' answered Roie. They hurried forward, and were submerged in the endlessly flowing crowd. The stalls were arranged on long counters which stretched, seemingly interminably, from one end of the vast building to the other. Above each pitch, on a wooden notice-board which swung like an inn-sign in the gust of cold air from the street, was the dealer's name. 'Miss Emily Heplinstall, Licensed Old Clothes Dealer,' and 'Jose Halmera, Old Silver and Chinaware,' or just plain 'Jack Hoop, Fruit Man.'

The passages between were crammed with a seething mass of people, hot, loud-voiced, but always good-tempered. Some of them bore perforated cardboard boxes of yellow fluff . . . baby Orpingtons going home to a suburban foster-mother. Others clutched immense sheaves of dark russet chrysanthemums or held above the heads of everyone else little green enamel pots of velvety-leaved begonia. But the majority of the customers had fruit or fish.

Roie felt as though she were only twelve instead of nineteen, and she let the giggling, sparkling-eyed Dolour lead her, darting from one stall to another. Their greedy, grubby hands pawed over the collection of red and yellow and purple and green macaroni necklaces, all enamelled and strung for an hour's flaunting. They looked idly at the vast array of old books, limp and battered and inconceivably dirty, which had reached the last stop on their *via crucis* to the incinerator. Astute book dealers were here in dozens, pawing over the wrecks, calculating how presentable they would be when cleaned and mended and fumigated – and buying them six for a shilling. Dolour picked up one book with a faded brown inscription on the flyleaf: 'From Ernestine to dear Papa, 1873.' In her dirty, bitten-nailed little hands the old book seemed to protest its lost gentility and gave forth a tiny odour of violets and mothballs. Roie sniffed.

'Funny. Wonder what happened to Ernestine?'

'Got old and conked out, I guess,' said Dolour. She threw the book down and picked up an odd volume of Shakespeare; she fluttered the torn pages and said: 'I like that bit about the billows curling their monstrous heads and hanging them with deafening clamour in the slippery shrouds.'

'What's it mean?' asked Roie. Dolour felt suddenly embarrassed, as though she had been showing off, and said: 'I just learned it off by heart, silly tripe. Look, ain't he got a dome!' The book thumped down on to the pile, and the portrait of Shakespeare went on staring out into the crowd which was so much like his own loud-voiced, unruly Elizabethan one.

Best of all, Dolour and Roie liked the old-clothes stalls. There were dozens of these; some of them sold shoes, all neatly arranged like lines of cargo vessels drawn up at a wharf, and every one plainly bearing the imprint of the corns and bunions of someone's feet. Here was a broad-bowed merchantman that had plainly gone hundreds of miles on shopping tours; here was a dainty triangular-toed pair of wrinkled black patents with a heel worn down the way a fat woman wears it, into a fray of broken wood. And there were tiny shoes, too; little white ones with scuffed toes and needle marks on the straps where the button had been moved back and back until at last there was no more room for expansion. And there was one pair of Russian boots with a haughty furry top and a long aristocratic toe. Dolour stared in hypnotic fascination; it seemed to her that at any moment the boots would leap forward and begin kicking in some wild Cossack dance.

'Gee, look,' breathed Roie suddenly. She pushed aside an Indian lascar in a red velveteen fez. He looked at her with glazy burning eyes and remarked: 'Chi-chi.'

There on the counter was a lovely red silk shawl with a trailing fringe knotted in a strange and exotic pattern. Seagreen flowers bloomed on the silk, and the softness of their padded needlework was like a jewel amongst all the dross of black Italian cloth bloomers and darned lisle stockings and faded print working dresses.

'How much?' asked Dolour timidly of the woman behind the counter, a delicate, genteel little woman with a peculiar cloche hat made of rusty black rooster feathers. She gave Dolour a sharp look, and said in a high, noisy voice: 'Whatcher want it for? To cut up and dress up with?'

Roie stammered: 'Oh, no, I just thought that . . .'

The woman's eyes were sharper than needles. 'Whatcher think?'

Roie said boldly: 'I just wanted it to look at.'

The woman patted the shawl. The sharpness went from her face. 'It's pretty, ain't it? Me sister made it. Ten years on her back, she was. 'Ip disease. I didn't want to get it destroyed, that's why I asked.' She added with sudden briskness, 'Ten shillings.'

The light died out of Roie's eyes. 'I only got five,' she said.

Dolour nudged her elbow. 'There's the other five Mumma gave us for the vegetables,' she reminded. The woman's acute ears caught her hoarse whisper, so she said obstinately, 'Ten bob. Take it or leave it.'

Roie felt a pang in her heart. She knew she could not leave the lovely shawl. Wordlessly she handed over the two five shillingses, and with them went all Mumma's potatoes, the soup tomatoes, the good piece of ironbark pumpkin, the sixpenn'orth of yellow belly, and the strip of barracouta, nice and thick, which she had down on the list.

With the money safe in her possession, the woman pushed her hat up on her forehead so that the tips of the coq feathers mingled with her eyebrows, and said in a friendly, relieved tone: 'I'm real pleased you're taking it dearie. It's been knocking around on the counter ever since me poor sister died, and getting dirtier every week. Two pounds I was asking for it to start with, and I wouldn't let it go to any old trollop who'd wipe the floor with it quicker than kiss yer foot. Here, dearie, try it on, and see how it looks on yer.'

She pushed a brass-rimmed mirror over towards Roie. Dolour giggled:

'How would you wear a shawl, Ro? Like an old granny?'

Roie did not say a word. A thousand Irish girls who had bequeathed to her their blood and manner of thinking guided her fingers. She draped it gently about her head, and looped the fringe over her shoulders. Oblivious of the crowd that looked at her, and then looked somewhere else, at odd boots, or patched buckets, or other things that better merited attention, she gazed into the mirror at the pale creamy face, with the strangely clear glossy skin of the underfed, the dark blue eyes, and the little scarlet rosette of a mouth, so much darker than the silk.

'I'm awfully glad you bought it, Roie!' cried Dolour, her eyes shining. Roie looked shyly across the counter for the woman's approval, but she was gone, and was showing some underpants to an old man further along. In her place was a young man. He was not much more than a boy, with black tousled hair and a thin, sallow Jewish face. One felt that some exotic accent should touch his voice, but it was broad Surry Hills, with every vowel lengthened into two.

'Oh, rose of all the world,' he said. Roie stared, taken aback. He might have said: 'Cripes, you look grouse in that,' or 'Trust a sheila to try a thing on as soon as she buys it,' or even 'Get a move on, willya. Yer blockin' the customers' way.'

Any of these things Roie would have accepted as natural, but the other made her blush painfully. She snatched the shawl from her head, rolled it up haphazardly, and said furiously: 'Shut yer big mouth will you?'

The young man did not seem to mind. He said: 'I've seen you before.'

'Oh, yeah?' flashed Roie. 'I've never been here before.'

'I didn't say it was here, did I? I seen you in Coronation Street.'

Roie was confused. She muttered something and began to move away. The young man called: 'What's yer hurry? Scared I'll bite?'

Dolour meantime had been staring very hard at him. Then she glanced at the board above his head. 'Joseph Mendel,' it read, 'Licensed Vendor of Old Wares.'

'Mendel!' squeaked Dolour. 'You ain't old Joseph Mendel?'

The young man seemed to find the question distasteful. 'Hell, what do you think? I'm his nephew, Tommy.'

It was almost as though they had been introduced by some close friend and relative. Both Roie and Dolour had been in and out of the Mendel establishment in Coronation Street a score of times, for the Darcy family was always popping something, and then popping something else to redeem the first pledge.

'Gee,' stammered Roie. 'I'm sorry if I was rude. You just got my goat laughing at me.'

'I wasn't laughing at you,' he protested. 'You just looked like a picture my Uncle Joseph has in his shop.'

'Oh.' Roie did not know what to say. She looked away foolishly, and pretended to be watching a lascar pawing over the garments at the next pitch. Dolour chirped: 'She's Rowena Darcy and I'm Dolour Darcy.'

The two girls stared at him, and he stared back. Dolour noticed that his hair was loose and curly, and he had a little yellow scar under one eye, and the marks of three boils on his neck. He had a gay green-printed tie, and a tweed suit which seemed too cumbrous and important for his slender boyish body. Roie noticed only that his eyes were dark and melancholy. She had the strangest feeling that her blood was running backwards; down arteries and veins it cascaded where it should have climbed, and through the valves of her heart it pulsed in reverse. She felt quite giddy and lightheaded, but it was a wonderful, intoxicating feeling. All the beauty and promise of the day seemed to come to fruition in this moment.

Tommy said: 'Can I come round and take you to the flicks some time?'

Roie said ungraciously: 'Oh, I suppose so. I live at Twelve-and-a-Half Plymouth Street.'

'Can I come tonight?'

'I'm not doing anything,' said Roie.

She wanted, and he wanted, to say words that were not crude and banal, but their imagination fell flat, unsupported by education or intuition. The boy, shy and sidelong with adolescence's indecisive shames and inferiorities, wanted to say something that would show this girl that he was a man. She, simpler, wanted nothing more than that he liked her. But inarticulate as most of their class, they could do no more than utter bald phrases forgotten as soon as they were spoken. He said harshly: 'First I gotta show you something. Take a squiz over here.'

Puzzled, Dolour and Roie craned over the counter, and they saw that he wore a heavy boot on one foot. For a moment Roie unconsciously felt the same sickness of repugnance and fear that she felt when she looked at poor Johnny Sheily. But it was only for a moment. It was different with Tommy Mendel. She felt a vast surge of pity which so filled her throat she could not speak. She stammered, and the boy's eyes closed to a pinpoint of bitter blackness.

'Now's yer cue to say you ain't going to be seen with no hop-and-go-fetch-it,' he said. Roie blushed. She did not know what to say. She looked away and laughed, saying: 'Gosh, you do say silly things, don't you?'

Dolour cried eagerly: 'There's a whacko cowboy pitcher on at the Palace tonight. Why don't you go to that, Ro?'

'I'd like that,' said Roie shyly. The boy laughed out loud with relief. 'Me, too,' he said.

Roie said awkwardly, 'Well, I better be going.' She backed out into the flowing crowd and walked rapidly. Dolour trotted beside her, skipping to catch up.

'You forgot to say what time he was to pick you up,' she cried anxiously.

'He knows the pitcher starts at eight. He isn't a boob,' answered Roie with tranquil assurance. 'He'll be around about a quarter past seven. You see.'

Dolour was so excited one would have thought that Tommy was going to be her boy. 'He's handsome, ain't he?'

'You reckon?' asked Roie proudly.

'What give him the boils on his neck?' wondered Dolour. Roie gave her a look of angry scorn.

'What are you talking about? He ain't got no boils. You're crazy.'

'But he has, Ro,' persisted Dolour. 'I saw them. Little marks . . .'

'Ah, shut up!' snapped Roie. She, too, had seen the scars, but she steadfastly shut her mind to them. Boils did not fit in with her dreamlike and exhilarated mood. She thought: 'I'll wear my pink dress, and do my hair up in front. I'll clean my white shoes . . .'

In silence they walked through the long lanes of little primitive bazaar-shops, each with its flapping sign above. All the way home Roie spoke little save cross and grumpy monosyllables. She had the feeling that worshippers have had at the portals of great temples, that to make a sound is to commit a sacrilege. Inarticulate, dumb at her heart, Roie could only feel that the chapter of her girlhood was nearly closed.

'You're going to get it,' promised Dolour, half-fearful, expectant, as they entered the long dark hall of Number Twelve-and-a-Half. 'Wait till Mumma sees what sort of vegetables you've bought!'

'Well, it's your fault too,' answered Roie unfairly. 'You give me the idea.'

'Well, by gosh!' exploded Dolour. 'You're a squib, if ever there was one, Roie.'

'For the love of heaven will yer stop squabbling like magpies under me very nose?' bawled Mr Patrick Diamond from the landing. He was at that time on very good terms with Mumma and Hughie, as St Patrick's Day was safely behind, so Dolour and Roie, glancing at each other, and muttering 'Old stinker!' and 'Dirty old proddy-hopper!' under their breaths, went silently into their own apartment and slammed the door.

Mumma had been waiting their return impatiently, for Hughie was due home, and she feared that he would be drunk, and anxious to start a fight.

'You've been a time, you have!' she cried. 'Give me the fish so I can get it started before he comes in. And Dolour you start skinning the pumpkin.'

Dolour giggled. 'Go on, show Mumma the pumpkin, Roie!'

Roie silently unrolled the newspaper in which she had wrapped the shawl. The silk, lustrous, poppy-red, spilled upon the table, and under its glossy fringe the old heat-marked timber looked as cheap as deal. Mumma, amazed, picked up a corner of it.

'It's pretty,' she said. 'It'd knock the two eyes out of yer head.'

'I didn't get any pumpkin,' confessed Roie.

'Or fish, either,' added Dolour, greedy for sensation.

Mumma wanted to be angry, but she couldn't, for she remembered the time when her Ma had given her a shilling for some sausages, and instead she had bought a little cup of glossy blue china she had coveted for a long time. She gently stroked the silk with her raspy fingers.

'Ah, well,' she said, trying to sound as though there were some justification for Roie's action, 'I suppose this will last.'

She dug in the little black purse and gave two shillings to Dolour.

'Here, now, go to the fried fish shop and get a couple of thick battered pieces for your Dadda's tea. Potatoes will do us.'

Dolour could hardly wait until she had finished speaking, for she wanted to break the news before Roie did.

'Roie made a hit with a boy, too,' she boasted, her eyes dancing. 'Didn't you, Ro?'

'Aw, shut up,' answered her sister angrily as she turned away and began folding the shawl. Mumma shut her lips tight and nodded with a pleased, knowing look, as though this were the beginning and it was no surprise to her. Dolour pranced to the door. 'He's got brown eyes and a funny foot.'

'Quit that, or I'll clout you!' shouted Roie, her temper flaming with the swiftness common to those who know little about the simulation of feelings they do not possess.

With a jeering giggle Dolour vanished up the hall. On the way she passed Johnny Sheily, who was squatting in the shadow of the stairs. She peered down at him and he smiled shyly, ducking his head away. Lately he had taken to making strange grimaces, pulling down the corner of his lip until it was two inches long, and showing the whites of his big aimless eyes until he looked like a bloodhound. He did this now, and Dolour protested: 'Oh, crumbs, Johnny, you give me the creeps.' She patted him on the top of his huge bristly head and skipped onwards, hearing from the top of the stairs the suspicious voice of Miss Sheily:

'What're you doing down there, Johnny?'

'Nothing, umma,' crooned Johnny from the darkness.

A few minutes later Dolour ran out of the fish shop, a grease-stained, pleasantly warm parcel in her hand. She had ideas of tearing a hole in one corner and extracting some of the salt-encrusted bluish potato chips that nestled about the little knobbly yellow lumps of fish.

It was five o'clock and the street was full of traffic. The tramp of a thousand factory workers sounded like a hundred drums – beat, beat, beat – the tributaries of the lanes and alleyways resounding sharper and hollower, all running into the central channel of Plymouth Street. Great red trucks laden with empty milk cans, oil drums, jolting planks, or scattered with the dropped cabbage leaves and the odd carrots of a load sold at the markets, rattled and boomed down the streets, and amongst them darted the fleet-footed starveling urchins, bearing billies of milk and unwrapped loaves of bread.

Dolour was fifty yards from her gate when all of a sudden out came Johnny Sheily. It was the very first time she had seen him outside the house or the backyard. At first she thought that Miss Sheily was going to take him for a walk, and then she saw that he was alone. He stood there, confused at the tumult of traffic, his big oblong head cocked sideways and his lip pulled long and straight.

Dolour yelled, half anxious: 'You'd better go back before your mother catches you.'

He turned slowly on his big flat feet and stared up the road at her, waving his fat sausage fingers. Several little boys barging past stopped and jeered: 'Lookut the loony! Lookut the loony!'

Johnny did not like their voices. His lips trembled. Perhaps they seemed as big as elephants to him, or small as rats, with dirty leering faces and little red mouths open to bite. He backed off the street into the gutter, and a car moving out from the kerb caught him with its fender and threw him into the path of a heavy brewery truck that was jolting homewards. He fell sprawling before the wheels.

Dolour heard the skip and crash of the barrels in the truck as its wheel rose and fell. She stood as still as though she had been frozen, her mouth open, her hand raised, even a smile still upon her face. She stood still and stared at the red squashed melon on the road, with the little teeth scattered about like grains of bloodstained corn. It was truly like a dream, seeing his poor tattered body lying there, and no head at all. She was not aware of the screams of passers-by, or of police whistles, or of the truck-driver tumbling out of his cab and being violently ill quite near her, moaning all the time, 'Oh, God forgive me, I didn't mean it. Oh, God forgive me, I didn't mean it.'

Dolour turned and walked stiffly inside. Miss Sheily brushed past her in the hall, saying shrilly, 'Have you seen Johnny? Have you seen Johnny?'

Dolour still with a smile fixed immovably on her face, did not answer. She walked sedately into the kitchen and stood in the doorway. She saw Hughie's red face and Mumma's worried one, and then she began to scream and scream, on a thin high-pitched note, like a rabbit in a trap.

'What's the matter with yer?' bawled Hughie in alarm.

Mumma ran up to her and shook her. 'For God's sake, darling, what's got into yer?'

Dolour's mouth was wide open, her eyes staring blindly. She went on screaming. Hughie brought the flat of his hand in a sharp slap across her cheek, and she stopped screaming instantly. Slowly she rubbed her cheek, and then toppled forward in a dead faint.

It was not really a faint; it was a nightmare, an ebony thing blotched with scarlet, that flapped about her with roaring and fading sounds that nearly deafened her, and then shrank away to a tiny niggling noise like a mouse at the end of a long passage. Dolour fought to remain unconscious, but it was no use. She became aware of something cold and prickling on her forehead, and the bitter stifling smell of ammonia in her nostrils. Then her mother said, very loud and close: 'She's over it now. She's coming out of it now.'

Then Dolour heard the sound of someone sobbing loudly; and with astonishment she realized it was Roie.

'What's the matter with Roie?' she asked with a sort of feeble irritability. The sound of her voice was at first shrill, then hoarse, and then, as though shaking itself into focus, was normal. The room seemed to be full of people. Mr Diamond, pale and aimless, was wandering about falling over chairs and begging people's pardon, and then rushing out to the kitchen to get a cup of smoky hot water from the kettle, for the shock of the accident had brought his indigestion on.

Mumma's face was streaked with tear-marks, and Dadda's nose was red, and not only with wine. And Roie was crying in the corner, all huddled up like a wet sparrow in winter.

'What's the matter with Roie?' asked Dolour. 'She didn't see the accident. I did.'

'She ran out and saw it afterwards,' said Mumma stroking her head. 'But you mustn't worry about Johnny any more, darling. It's all over for him now, God rest his poor soul, and maybe it's a good thing he's out of it, him being as he was.'

Dolour said to herself: 'I saw Johnny killed. I was right there.' She tried it over two or three times, but already the shock and horror of it was fading from her resilient mind. She found that she could even feel a certain pride that she had been there. Of all the people who had been walking up and down Plymouth Street she had been the last one to speak to Johnny.

Roie went on crying. She did not know what for. She only knew that the ache in her throat and the constriction in her chest needed tears. The picture of Johnny was before the eyes of her mind. She closed her lids, and it was there; she opened them, and it was bright as paint upon the wall.

'Ah, darling, it's all for the best,' soothed Hughie, putting a distraught clumsy hand upon her hair. 'Who'd want to go on living like Johnny, him all minced up at birth and never got over it?'

'He was happy,' sobbed Roie. 'He didn't know there was anything the matter with him.'

'I'll bet Miss Sheily's glad. I'll bet she's up at the hospital laughing like anything,' cried Dolour, sitting bolt upright and saying the words with a sour intensity that mated oddly with her childish voice.

'Shut up that talk,' said Hughie fiercely.

Dolour yelled: 'She always hated him! She did! She did!' She burst into savage tears. 'She was always beating him.'

'She was a good mother,' said Mumma contrarily. 'She always fed him well, and he was never allowed out when there was danger. Nobody can go slinging dirt at Miss Sheily and saying she neglected him.'

'Now, Mrs Darcy, missus,' protested Patrick Diamond. 'And you only a few weeks ago going up there and finding him tied up and lashed like a dog.'

But Mumma in the strength of her sorrow for Miss Sheily refused to remember it, and they argued inconsequentially, punctuated by Roie's weeping.

Roie wanted to go out and find a quiet, dark place amongst the trees somewhere, and lie down and think it all out and ease the hurt in her chest. But there was nowhere to go. Like all the poor, she had nowhere to be private except in the lavatory, and even that had no lock on the door, so she could not be sure of being uninterrupted. The sorrow of this, so intimate a need for solitariness, that had never in all her life been satisfied, became all mixed up with her grief for Johnny and she cried: 'I can't stand it! I can't stand it!' Just as she had done when she was a little girl with the toothache.

There was a knock on the door. Mr Diamond answered it, with an air of subdued importance mingled with trepidation, for he feared that it might be Miss Sheily back from the hospital. But instead, it was a strange young man with dark sombre eyes and hair sleeked down with oil.

'Excuse me,' he said, 'but does Miss Darcy live here?'

'Two Miss Darcys live here,' answered Mr Diamond. 'Which one do you want to see?'

'I want to see the big one,' said the young man, losing his careful composure and looking for an instant as though he were inwardly trembling with nervousness.

Dolour's eyes glistened through her tears. 'Gee,' she croaked, 'I forgot. It's him, Ro.'

'Send him away,' sobbed Roie. 'I can't see him tonight. I don't want to see him.'

'Of course you do,' said Mumma practically, for she had made up her mind to see this young man who wanted to be her daughter's escort to the pictures. She marched to the door, opened it wide, and said: 'Come in, son. You'll have to excuse the mess, because there's just been a terrible accident and we're all upset.'

'Not in the family,' said Hughie, gruffly, seeing the reluctance upon the boy's face. 'Just in the house.'

'I saw it happen,' said Dolour proudly. Roie hid her swollen and tear-blotched face in her hands. She felt a hand on her shoulder, less assured than her father's, yet warmer, and more comforting. The tears welled unbidden out of her eyes.

'I'm sorry I can't go out,' she choked. 'Please, please go away now.'

She rose and ran into the bedroom, throwing herself on her face on the bed. The young man looked at Mumma.

'Please can I go in and see if I can do anything for her?' he asked. Mumma was pleased and proud at his delicacy in asking first. She said: 'I wish to heaven you would.' She explained about Johnny. The young man's face grew sickly. He shook his head silently.

'Crook business. Kids are always getting run over in these streets.' An idea sprang into his mind. He shyly extended his foot with the big boot. 'A motor bike did that to me when I was a nipper. One leg grew shorter than the other.'

Ready tears welled into Mumma's eyes. 'You poor boy. Go on in to Roie, and I'll get a cup of tea for yez both.'

The boy felt warm and exultant. It was not everyone who would have thought so well on the spur of the moment. He felt proud of himself, and for the first time since his foot had been paralysed a few years before, he almost looked upon his disfiguring boot as an asset. It had gained him attention and sympathy. He went through the glass doors into the bedroom.

It was dim and cold in there, for there was no window, and the sun had not touched its walls for nearly seventy years. There was a smell of old clothes, and mustiness, and down one wall was the great map-like stain of last winter's rain. The dressing-table was a litter of rubbish, old powder-puffs and broken boxes; a grubby, balding hair-brush, and some cheap photographs. From one wall the melancholy face of the Madonna looked down into the half dusk.

Tommy sat down upon the bed. He was trembling with excitement. The way the edge of it swayed and dipped under his weight, the dim intimacy of the room, and the long slim body of the girl, lying there face downwards beside him, made him feel as though he were taking part in something curiously dramatic. He was twenty, and had never had a girl. Shy, sullen, and tormented with the frustrations and brooding ambitions of adolescence, he had longed futilely for a girl of his own, about whom he could boast to his pals, and thus prove himself, in spite of his foot, a man amongst men.

He put a hand on her back. It was damp with sweat, though the room was chill. He tried to think of something to say. He formed two or three sentences in his mind but none seemed memorable enough. Finally, he said: 'Forget it, kid.'

Roie wiped the back of her hand across her wet face. 'I'll never forget it as long as I live,' she choked.

Tommy said: 'I did.' She stared at him, sitting up beside him, knowing that in the gloom he could not see her disfigured face. He told her the same lie he had told her Mumma, elaborating on it until it seemed to him so real and vivid that a momentary shock of horror filled his soul. It was almost as though it had really happened . . . the little dark Jewish boy running across the street, and the motor bike crashing into him . . . the crush of bone, and the screams and the blood trickling. Tommy's voice shuddered into hoarseness. Ah, God, it might have well happened that way!

In an instant Roie forgot all her own pain, and flung her arms around him. Clumsily he returned the embrace. They put their soft cheeks together.

'Ah, Tommy, Tommy . . . you must have got a terrible fright.' Her voice broke again.

'Yeah. I still dream about it.'

She held him tighter. In a moment their position had changed. She was comforting and protecting him, who had so wanted to comfort.

Four

The day Miss Sheily came home from her sister's place, where she had gone for a little rest after Johnny's death, was a great one for Number Twelve-and-a-Half. She did not look much different. Her black suit was as neatly pressed, the big round gold brooch at her collar just as precisely fastened. Only her face, as white as dough, gave the impression that Miss Sheily had died some time before. She came in the front door without a word and stumped upstairs on her sharp-heeled shoes. Mumma ran to the door and stood there panting for a word. But there was none. Mumma was very disappointed. She had secretly expected something dramatic and surprising to happen, such as Miss Sheily drinking phenyl and dying in convulsions, or perhaps hanging herself from the very same gas-jet where she had tied Johnny.

But Miss Sheily did none of those things. She made toast, for they could hear her scraping the burnt pieces with a knife; she went out and did her shopping down the mean street, as she had always done; and on Saturdays she disappeared for the whole afternoon and came home late, as had been her custom for years. And if she met anyone she spoke ordinarily and that was all. Yes, Mumma was disappointed.

'She's got no heart, that one,' she said to Hughie. 'No doubt she's pleased the poor misfortunate is gone. The puzzle to me is why she don't go and live at her sister's.'

'Because probably her sister won't have a drunk on her hands,' said Hughie bluntly. Mumma scoffed. Miss Sheily was a lady, even though she had had an illegal child. Miss Sheily didn't drink.

'You ain't heard her at night-time, clinking bottles,' said Roie.

'And you ain't met her in the hallway, either, and smelt her breath,' added Hughie.

'You're the one who'd recognize it, then,' flared Mumma. 'Drinking her breath in like perfume, there's no doubt, you old tosspot.'

'Tosspot or not,' bellowed Hughie, aggrieved, 'Miss Sheily knows how to throw up her little finger, you take it from me. And I'll thank you to keep me own weaknesses out of the conversation.'

But Mumma did not give up hope, and the next day when Miss Sheily came down to do her bit of washing in the copper, Mumma went out and fussed about there with the broom, looking yearningly meanwhile at Miss Sheily. Ah, she had a queer face, that one, with a beaky high-class nose, and eyes deep back in like jet pieces. Mumma's mind, which was innocent and fiercely chaste, in spite of the life she had led, tiptoed down avenues of inquiring thought about Miss Sheily. Somehow she could not imagine her being kissed or beloved by any man, no matter how remote. And yet she had had Johnny, and on the wrong side of the counterpane, too. Mumma blushed, and dragged her errant mind back from its wanderings, scolding it ferociously. Suddenly Miss Sheily turned around and said:

'You're not going to get any change out of me, Mrs Darcy, so you needn't be snooping around for any information about my feelings.'

'Well, indeed . . .' stammered Mumma, so taken aback her mouth fell open. Miss Sheily's eyes sparked cold glitters.

'I'm not sorry he's gone, if that's any use to you,' she said, watching Mumma's consternation with an icy interest. Mumma's mother-heart burned for poor Johnny.

'Ah, the dirty drop's in yer, there's no mistake!' she exploded, and waddled out of the laundry. All the morning she repeated to herself the things she might have said to Miss Sheily, brilliant, cutting things, but in the afternoon when she saw her again, the rancour had all gone, and they spoke civilly to each other, with a sort of wary politeness.

But if Mumma were curious, the rest of the establishment cared little about Miss Sheily's strange and secretive character.

Dolour was happy, for the end of the year was approaching, and though examinations were yet to be faced the brightly-gilded picture of Christmas filled her mind like a lovely ghost.

In the schoolroom they were already making preparations. All the year's drawings and mottoes and scrolls had been rubbed off the blackboard into a cloud of mingled red and yellow and green dust which vanished for ever as Dolour shook the duster out the window. It was just as though she could see the year vanishing, first brilliant, and then vague and dispersed, whirling and scattering, day after day, and hour after hour.

'Dolour, what are you dreaming about?' inquired Sister Theophilus from her desk. Dolour withdrew her head and blushed. Sister, a tall slender figure in a classically designed brown habit, her wide sleeves rolled up a little so that her slim sallow arms showed, went to the board, six beautiful, untouched, velvety-pointed sticks of coloured chalk before her.

'It is two months to Christmas,' observed Sister Theophilus. 'But I think we will decorate the blackboard so that we may have Christmas in our thoughts.'

Spellbound, the children watched her draw in one top corner a large five-pointed shape. Upon this she stuck a star she had already cut out from silver foil. It fitted perfectly, and to her pupils this seemed to be a good omen. Some of them shivered with joy, for already they could scent in the air the peculiar smell of orange peel and boiled pudding and incense which was Christmas's.

Sister Theophilus took the blue powdery chalk delicately in two fingers, and a thumb, and shaded in a long strip of sky. As she did so, chalk dust fell in a soft rain to the floor.

'What you going to draw in the other corner, Sister?' called Harry Drummy, who was busy pricking his name on the top of his desk, and knew that silence would draw suspicion upon him.

'You'll see.'

Dolour sat up and stared intently. She saw a strange snake-like thing grow under the mole-coloured chalk in Sister's hand.

'It's . . . it's a dragon.'

'No.'

'It's a lizard.'

'No.'

'What is it, then, Sister?'

'You'll see.'

The serpentine head grew; it had big heavy-lidded eyes and a sardonic shaped mouth. It had a long neck which swooped upwards into a hump and downwards into a tasselled tail.

'It's a camel! It's a camel!' shrilled Harry Drummy, who had seen one in a circus.

'It's the Three Wise Men,' said Dolour softly. The picture grew rapidly under Sister's fingers. It was beautiful to see how the blunt chalk made delicate little lines, and how blue smudged into green to make a twilight sky, and how the Wise Kings had each a different turban. And soon there they all were, travelling over the lonely brown desert to find the little Child whose house wore a star above its chimney.

There was a sharp rap at the door. Sister put down her chalk and dusted her fingers.

'Now,' she said. 'You all know the story of the Three Kings. Write down all you know about them. Harry Drummy, what are you doing with that compass?'

'Nothing, Sister,' answered Harry promptly.

'Then you can write an essay on that, too,' said Sister, sweeping to the door. She closed it firmly behind her, but Dolour caught one glimpse of the visitor.

'Crumbs!' she breathed. 'It's old Delie Stock!'

'What's she seeing Sister for?'

'Someone's been bunging goolies through her window.'

'She's going to tell on someone.'

'She might get tough with Sister. She might call her somepin.'

They were all dumb at the thought, for although terms that in better districts would have caused disgust and shock were used in nearly all their homes, and certainly on every street corner, the idea of them applied to Sister Theophilus was alien, and somehow frightening.

But Delie Stock hadn't come because of stones bunged through her windows, though there were plenty of them. She had come with a purse full of money.

Sister knew her, of course. Hurrying home through a winter afternoon, long ago, she had seen a young Delie Stock squatting on the church steps and being sick between her shoes; and another time she had seen her violently hammering a policeman on the head as he half-carried, half-dragged her to a small dark green van that was waiting. And, even in the seclusion of the Convent, Sister had heard the rumours, the legends and the fabulous scandal that had sprung up about this woman.

Her heart beat a little faster, for though she was secure in the poise and tranquillity of her profession, yet she felt a little frightened. She looked at the other woman, and in the second before she spoke a welcome she had taken in the expensive coat and hat, food-stained and dribbled all over with cigarette ash; the grey hair frousled and yellow at the ends; the old humpy black shoes; and the face. Above all she saw the face of Delie Stock.

Delie Stock's was an interesting face, not yet fifty years old, but with a sort of ancient, timeless air about it. It was not really dirty, and yet one felt that Delie Stock had not washed it for a long, long time. It had a grey-ivory look, and wrinkles like tiny vertical lines sketched with a fine pen covered it in a net. Out of this, rimmed with short spiky eyelashes, looked Delie Stock's eyes, furtive, small with middle-age, brazen with amorality, and yet with a queer habit of scuttling away from the stare of the beholder. They might have been the eyes of a number of people . . . of a woman with no sense of morality at all, whose conscience never kept her awake at night . . . of a devil who chose their opaque brown to hide his greedy ferocity . . . or just of a dirty old prostitute with no mind, no soul, and not much body.

Sister's own eyes, fascinated, kept returning to them, as to a window through which could be seen some mysterious and appalling scene. It was only by the utmost effort of politeness that she looked away.

'How do you do? Do you wish to see me?'

'I'm Delie Stock, Mrs Stock,' said the woman, her voice deepened and rasped by gallons of rough native wine. Sister bowed slightly and extended her hand. Delie Stock looked surprised, and giggled awkwardly, looking away to cover her momentary embarrassment.

'I'm Sister Theophilus.'

'Well, it's this way, Sister. I was thinking of the kids the other day . . . all the kids here, the Drummys and the Stevenses, and the Brodies and all the rest, poor dirty-nosed little arabs. And I said to meself, Delie, it's time you did something about them little bastards. Give 'em a bit of fun. You see what I mean, Sister?' The hot eyes looked into the nun's for a moment, and then hurried away.

Sister said, yes, she did, but what . . . ?

Delie Stock gave another chuckle, a pleased, proud guffaw. It was plain that some mystic psychological change was taking place in her mind. She was growing in stature as her charity unfolded itself. 'So I'm going to give 'em a picnic, see? The whole shebang. Hire a bus. Two buses. Ice-cream, plenty of tucker. Beach and everythink. And maybe we can get a magician bloke to give 'em the works. How many kids in this school, Sister Theoctopus?'

'Why . . . there's . . . there's . . . two hundred odd,' stammered Sister Theophilus.

'Here, then,' said Delie Stock. She opened her stuffed shabby purse, and it was crammed to the lip with notes.

'Holy Mary, Mother of God,' said Sister Theophilus, but it was a prayer and not an exclamation. She had never seen so much money before. Delie Stock shook it all out on the bench amongst the children's hats and caps and lunch-packets. There were dirty, crumpled green notes, and smooth blue linen ones, and lavender ones which had faded to tobacco-stained lilac. They fell in a rustling heap which the wind riffled and teased. Delie Stock wished that she had taken another nip before she left. The tall, brown-faced nun, old and yet young-eyed, with her clean face that had never known powder or even scented soap, somehow made her feel all feet, and too loud-voiced. She gave a hitch to her coat collar and reminded herself that she owned six houses and more than forty girls, and she had the right to hold her head up with anyone. So she gave the notes a slap and cried loudly:

'There they are, take 'em or leave 'em.'

Sister Theophilus had a temptation to say: 'Oh crumbs!' like Harry Drummy or Dolour Darcy, for her whole mind was a circus of delight. In the space of twenty seconds she saw the whole picnic, Deewhy perhaps, or Collaroy, and the great double-decker buses, pied red and yellow, drawing up, and all her two hundred children pouring, shrill and hysterical with excitement, towards the biscuit-brown beach and the great majestic foam-topped breakers. She smelt the sea, and she saw the sunshine of gum-leaves, glossy and curved like a rooster's tail-feathers; she shook sand out of sandwiches, and smeared liniment on stone bruises; she taught the little ones how to make forts, and she gathered tiny yellow grooved shells like grains of wheat. Then she said: 'Oh, Mrs Stock! Oh, Mrs Stock! But how much is there?'

'A hundred and thirty,' said Delie Stock. Then she boasted a little, for she was feeling proud and happy. 'I would have made it more, but . . . well, perhaps I can put another tenner to it.'

'Oh, no,' cried Sister Theophilus, aghast. 'It's more than enough. Oh, Mrs Stock . . . the children will . . . I just can't say thank you sufficiently.'

There was a firm step on the porch, the brush of boots on the mat, for Father Cooley had never lost the Irish habit of scraping the bog off his feet. Then in he walked. He was a stout, compact man with a pleasant red face and silky white hair. His feet were large, and his strong practical boots showed strangely prosaic under the skirt of his soutane.

'Oh, pardon me, Sister, I didn't know you had a visitor.' His eyes flickered with quiet civility over Delie Stock, for though he knew all about her, he had no dealings with her, and she was no business of his. Then he saw the notes on the table.

'The Lord look down on us!'

Sister Theophilus clasped her hands. 'Isn't it wonderful, Father? Mrs Stock has donated all this money for the children . . . for a picnic for Christmas!'

'Ice-cream for the poor little . . . beggars,' said Delie Stock.

The priest put his hand on the faintly crackling notes; they were like dried leaves, impregnated with the powder and dirt and tobacco crumbs of a thousand pockets. He did not have the rapid imagination of Sister Theophilus; his, tranquil, silent, slow, saw only the entry in his ledger: 'One hundred and thirty pounds donated to school by Delie Stock.'

'Hope there's enough,' blared Delie Stock, with something of defiance and preparatory argumentativeness creeping into her voice, for she did not like the priest's silence.

Sister Theophilus, with clasped hands, rushed in: 'I thought perhaps Collaroy . . . I went there once for a holiday . . . it's a lovely beach . . . and a nice ride in a bus . . .' her voice trailed away. For the priest shook his head. He chased his imagination back into its cubbyhole in his brain and shut the door sharply.

'I'm sorry, Mrs Stock. Sister and I do appreciate your offer, but we cannot accept it.'

'Oh, Father,' said Sister Theophilus. Then a faint red crept into her smooth sallow cheeks and she dropped her glance. Delie Stock's dark eyes became snapping pinpoints. She knew what was coming. Hadn't she had it a dozen times, whenever she'd tried to give some money away to one of these boneheads in an upside-down collar?

'Why not?' she demanded roughly. Unconsciously her arms, in a habitual way of the slum women, tired-backed from too many babies and too much carrying of heavy loads, folded themselves over her bosom and in this belligerent attitude she waited.

'Mrs Stock, your generosity will long be remembered by us, but I'm afraid that what you suggest would be quite impossible.'

Delie Stock did not blush; she could no longer feel shame, but she could feel anger and bitter resentment against those who thought that she should. Her tight wrinkled mouth fell open and showed the narrow, yellow-stained bottoms of her lower teeth.

'So, you ain't taking me money, is that it? You don't want old Delie's tainted dough. There's a hundred and thirty good quids there, and no mangy old bible-banger is going to keep those kids in there from getting it. See?'

Father Cooley gathered the notes into a bundle, tidied it up, and offered it politely and calmly.

'Mrs Stock, you are frank, so I will be as well. I am afraid it would be against my principles to take this money. It is tantamount to stolen property.'

'Stolen from who?' flamed the woman.

'Stolen from the wives and children of the men who spend it in your foul places of pleasure,' thundered the priest. Then abruptly he turned to Sister Theophilus and said: 'Please leave us, Sister.'

Sister Theophilus, with trembling lips, flew back into the school-room. There was a subdued sort of bedlam there, but not so much that the children did not notice her expression. She said sharply: 'Harry, have you finished your essay?'

Harry muttered: 'Can't think of nothing.'

'Sit down and do it, or I'll give you the cane,' commanded Sister Theophilus. Abashed, he sat down. Ashamed of herself, she seated herself and forced her hands to move slowly over the desk in their little accustomed tasks. Calm, calculated movements, like rhythmic words, soothed her mind, and it was soon tranquil again. Her mind was like a deep pool, which the wildest wind might ruffle only for a minute.

Father Cooley's, however, was not so easily subdued. All his life he had deplored, and battled, and scourged his temper, but it was still like an electric wire, forever ready to be charged with extra voltage. Now he felt it rising in him, and ignored it, keeping his voice low and his manners gentle. But it was no good. His face grew crimson and his white hair bristled almost perceptibly. He felt sick with passion and remorse at the same time.

Delie Stock, on the other hand, loved and petted her temper. It was like a horse that she caressed and fed and teased when necessary. When it suddenly rose and took control of her, it gave her an exhilaration comparable with that of drink. Now it was well away, in a tossing gallop, upsetting one more restraint each split second. She longed to see shock and disgust come over the red face of this respectable man, and to hate and despise him because it was there.

'Ha!' she yelled. 'So you're going to diddle those poor little bastards in there out of a bit of fun, are yer? Just because you're too damned pure and holy to touch my money, that was earned honest.

Yeah, yer call yourself a Christian. Do you think God would have done that? Yeah, when Mary Magdalene came along to him, did he tell her to take her precious hair-oil somewhere else? Go on, answer that, you old buffalo.'

Father Cooley choked. He stared at the woman with her sly beetle eyes, and her face that knew everything and respected none of it. How could he preach about hell when this woman had been there? All the knowledge and disillusion of the devil was hers; her bawdy houses were filled with poor Surry Hills and Redfern kids that grew up starved and ignorant, knowing nothing, trained for nothing, and cast out to earn their livings by their own instincts. She peddled dope; she sold liquor that was manufactured in her own backyard, laced with foul fuel spirits and given a tang with tobacco . . . liquor that filled the brain with madness and murder, and had been the cause of dozens of terrible bloody brawls in those dark back alleys. Did she really know what she was doing? On her deathbed, would she feel horror and fear, or would she feel she had been a successful business woman? Father Cooley, wondering, did not answer. Delie Stock leaped into the silence.

'You call me a bad woman. Yeah, I'm the worst woman in the district, the coppers say, and I'm not ashamed to repeat it. But who comes across with fifty quid when there's a funeral? When Johnny Sheily got hit with a truck, who gives his ma enough dough to go away for a good holiday to get over it? You? No, old Delie Stock, that's who.'

Father Cooley said swiftly: 'Just to square your conscience? Is that it?' And as soon as he said it his soul shuddered and he inwardly prayed: 'Oh, Lord, when would you have said a thing like that?' And simultaneously his Irish blood remarked gleefully: 'Now, there's one in the eye for the old pig.'

Delie Stock half-closed her eyes. A dozen rich and luscious phrases, thick with imagery and laden with obscenity, rushed into her mind, but she discarded them all. She felt like playing with this man, like bringing him down so hard that he would kiss her feet. She caressed the head of her temper softly, and it stamped its feet and shook its mane, but did not bolt.

She said in a hoarse, sad voice: 'It's a nice thing when a minister says things like that. I thought you was different, Father, from all the others.'

'What others?' asked the priest, doubtfully.

'The reverend over at the Methodist Church, and all the others, I've been around to them all at some time, and they all think they are too good to be in the same room with me.'

'Mrs Stock, if you think I can help you to make a new start in life you know I am at your service. But still that has nothing to do with the moral question of whether I should accept your donation.'

Delie Stock suddenly felt grieved and utterly alone. The alcohol in her bloodstream affected some part of her brain where melancholy lurked like a raven. Here she was, the worst woman in the district, trying to give away some money for a cause that ought to get into the papers. And this evil-minded old codfish wouldn't look at it. She was a character; she had a whole book of police court clippings about herself; drunks got out of her way, and kids thought they were gutsy to chuck a few stones through her windows. She sniffled, and a lone sticky tear rolled down her withered cheek. It wasn't fair. It wasn't fair.

'I was just a little bit of a sheila when I started,' she said, her voice breaking into a croak. She leaned against the table and played with the shabby purse, clicking the broken clasp in and out. 'Just a boy here and there . . . never got a bean for it. And then I got into a good house. Up on the corner of Murphy Street it was. You wouldn't believe it, but no customers were allowed after twelve at night. Well, when the old girl died, she left the house to me, and that's how I got me start. It's been hard work and good business brains that done it. You've got no call to be looking down at me, Father Cooley.'

'Start!' exploded Father Cooley. 'Start on the road to hell!'

'You wouldn't say that if you were a girl,' said Delie Stock, still quietly and sombrely. 'You don't know what it's like being a woman. Everyone's got it in for you, even God. Even God,' she repeated sadly. 'What chance does any woman get around here? Starved and dirty and walked on to the end of your days, that's all, unless you kick over the traces and make the most of what yer got. I'm as good a woman as anyone else, and what's more,' bawled Delie Stock, sticking the spurs into her temper and giving it a slap on the rump for good measure, 'that money wasn't earned the way you think. I won it in a lottery, and if you want to know which one, just stick yer beak in the newspaper and read me name amongst the prizewinners.'

Father Cooley realized once more that he was a lamb amongst goats, and hardly knew more than his prayers. He resolved that he would go without a smoke all the next month in order to atone for his sin of uncharity against one who should be pitied. Perhaps even admired. Had he been so great a sinner, would he have bothered to throw such drops of water into the flames of hell as fifty pounds to a widow at a funeral, or a hundred and thirty for a children's picnic?

He thought humbly: 'No, I wouldn't. I'd go the whole hog and be damned to me, there's not a doubt.'

Aloud he said: 'Please pardon me, Mrs Stock. Indeed, and the children will be most grateful to you.'

'Well, now,' said Delie Stock, 'that's better talk.' She shook her shoulder like a ruffled parrot, and marched out.

Father Cooley took up the money and stuck it in his wallet. There was more than would go in comfortably. For the very first time he could not get his wallet shut. Usually the flap wrapped over three times. He rapped on the door, stuck his head in, and beckoned Sister Theophilus. She said a word to the children and came out with her gliding step.

'Do you think they heard, Sister?' whispered Father Cooley with an anxious face. Sister understood instantly what he meant.

'I got them reciting, Father. But she did shout a bit now and then,' she answered. Eager expectancy was in her face.

'Well, I found out that the money was earned honestly enough, even though in a lottery. For if the Government condones it . . .' Father Cooley drifted for a moment into puzzlement about the ethics of lotteries, and then he shrugged his thick shoulders and continued: 'We'll be having the picnic.'

Sister Theophilus clasped her hands like an excited child. 'Oh, Father, thank you, thank you. I've been saying ejaculations under my breath all the time.'

The priest said rather sadly: 'You never can tell with people, can you Sister?' She said, flushing: 'We can pray for her. Nobody is beyond help.'

'No,' said Father Cooley. Then, more heartily: 'Well, I hope you good Sisters will get together tonight at recreation and jot down a selection of ideas for the picnic.'

'Oh, we'll do that gladly, Father,' she cried, and a dimple split her cheek for a moment, so that she did not look at all like the head-mistress of a poor and difficult school.

'Um,' said Father Cooley. He gruffly added; 'It's strange, the queer sort of people who win the lotteries, isn't it, Sister?'

There was an almost wistful tone in his voice.

Five

And so it was arranged. The children of St Brandan's were to go for a picnic. The whole of Surry Hills knew about it in no time. In every narrow back alley littered with rusty garbage tins and sleeping bony cats, somebody leaned over a bent corrugated iron fence and called: 'Didja hear about it, dearie? Ole Delie Stock's put down a hundred quid flat and give the kids a treat for Christmas. Young Kathie's going, and Mrs Wilson's Bernie is wetting his pants with temper cause he's a Protestant and can't go.'

The feeling was one of pleasant excitement, and geniality towards Delie Stock, so now when her big black car drew up in front of the grog shop in Little Ryan Street, people gave her a jovial jerk of the head instead of an intimidated one. They had always been proud of Delie Stock; she was tough and hard, and she had got on in the world, though there were those who remembered her as a little snivelling fancy-girl being hauled off to the station by the Vice Squad. The people thought, you didn't catch any of them flash nightclub-hoppers from Rose Bay and Potts Point donating hard cash to give a lot of poor kids a picnic.

Dolour had never been to a picnic in her life. She was not even sure of what it was, except that it involved swimming, and races on the sand, and sunburn, and a great deal to eat. Roie was superior, for she dimly remembered outings with her mother and father and Thady in the country long ago. She remembered a hedge, dark green and speckled with some sweet-smelling bewhiskered white flower, and some mushrooms which she found in a furrow, pale brown and peaked, with delicate stalks. And although she was happy for Dolour's sake, Roie was a little jealous that nobody had sent St Brandan's kids for picnics while she was there. She tried to make up for this jealousy by lending Dolour her new pink slip, which was much too large for the child and had to be held up by four safety pins. But Dolour loved wearing it.

At last the wonderful day came. It was the first of December, an enchanted date, for then the year turned on its axis and a shower of heat and light, and burning, burning blue fell upon Australia. Already the smell of the scorching hinterlands was stealing upon the city; the odour of river-beds appearing through brackish dwindling water, and of soil dried into dust and whipped into whirlwinds that vanished like smoke. Dolour climbed out of bed at five in the morning, for she had slept lightly and excitedly, and through the skylight the sun was already pouring in a flood of yellow. She rose on tiptoe and looked out through the window, and through the ragged fronds of the phoenix palm in the backyard she saw the stainless sky and the haze on the distant buildings. Like onion-shaped domes and slender spires they rose, an eastern city dreaming in the early morning.

All the children attended early Mass, for as Sister Theophilus told them, God loves to receive the offering of our pleasure as well as our pain. Never before had the old church seemed so lovely to them. They loved Sister Theophilus, kneeling so straight and silent, only the faintly hollowed black wooden beads slipping through her fingers. They loved Father Cooley, strange in his vestments, moving ceremoniously about the altar. They loved each other; Harry Drummy and the seven Stevenses, Dolour Darcy with her petticoat hanging down, all the Rileys and the Archibald boys with their ears rimmed with dirt, the Mulligans, the Brogans, the host of gipsy-eyed Sicilianos, the Brophys and the O'Donohues. They glanced about with the bright unselfconscious eyes of birds, their tousled, home-cut hair bobbing, their clothes washed, and pressed with flatirons that left tell-tale freckles of soot behind, and their bare calloused feet restless with delight and anticipation under the seats. They prayed for everyone they could think of, mainly Sister Theophilus, and one even remembered to pray for Sister Beatrix, who was old and cross and rheumaticky, and laid it in with a cane very frequently. After they had had their breakfasts, they all met on the corner of Plymouth

Street. It was now half-past eight, and lots of mothers came down to see the children off, feeling vicarious excitement, and many wishing that they, too, were going off to Collaroy in one of the two big double-decker red and yellow buses which waited like docile monsters at the corner.

'Now, don't you be going too far out,' explained Mumma anxiously to Dolour. 'Them sharks,' she added. Sister Theophilus, who was standing nearby with her big black umbrella shading her face from the sun, said: 'They'll only be allowed in the baths, where it's perfectly safe, Mrs Darcy, so don't you worry.'

Sister Theophilus was as excited as the children. She had every intention of finding a secluded spot and making sand castles, and even paddling in the shallow clear lips of the breakers as they spent their force after the long roll in from the Pacific.

Mumma watched the buses roll away. There was quite a crowd gathered on the footpath, even a reporter with a square leather case in which he carried a camera. He took a lot of shots, of Harry Drummy biting into a big apple, of Rosie Siciliano climbing upon the back platform of the bus, and then of all the children waving farewell out of the upper windows. The crowd knew quite well what would be over or under those pictures when they appeared in the paper . . . 'Underprivileged Children at Christmas Treat,' or 'Santa Claus comes to Surry Hills,' which would be self-explanatory. Some of the women felt a little resentful, and glared at the newspaperman, for they were fiercely aware of the fact that they were just as good as anyone else in Sydney, and if the rest of Sydney persisted in looking down on them, then the rest of Sydney could just lump it. But others thought it lovely that their children should be in the papers, for it meant that you could clip the picture out, and that was as good as having a real photograph.

Mumma walked slowly home, for the corn on the ball of her foot was bothering her, in spite of its being a fine day, and she felt hot and uncomfortable. Her winter dress was mended and tight under the arms, for she had not yet saved up enough money to go poking around the second-hand shops after a cotton one for summer. She called in and bought some bread and six-penn'orth of garlic sausage, for Hughie was still in bed, not feeling very well after last night's bottle of muscat, which had not been all it had promised. Mumma thought sadly of the lost money, which they could so ill afford, but she was used to going without her full complement of housekeeping money.

She had barely reached the gate before the postman came along. There was a letter for Miss Sheily, and one for herself. Mumma shrieked up the stairs for Miss Sheily, meanwhile shaking the envelope busily to see if it contained anything more solid than paper. She left the envelope on the stair-post and hurried into her own flat. A letter was so rare that she was half-frightened to open it, for it was plain to see that it was from sister Josie, who lived at Albany, and had five children, and looked after Grandma.

Mumma muttered: 'Now, Lord, don't be too hard on me,' as she tore open the envelope. She sat down and read it, and as soon as she had finished she commented: 'Lord, sometimes I can't understand you.'

Then a little excitement filled her mind, and she hurried heavily into the bedroom, crying: 'Wake up, Hughie, I've had a letter from Josie, and she's got important news.'

Hughie was lying sulkily awake, rhythmically rubbing his bristly chin in an effort to smooth down the pain which tickled him in every portion of his face. He did not like Josie, she was fat and putty-featured, with a coarse habit of saying exactly as she thought. The very remembrance of her made his head feel much worse.

'Yeah, what does she say, the old ratbag?'

'She says she can't possibly go on looking after Grandma. She's got fallen arches.'

'Who, Grandma?'

'No, Josie. She says she can hardly crawl from her bed.'

'Well, what about it? Does she expect us to brace 'em up for her?' inquired Hughie, with almost a grin. Then suddenly the significance of Josie's arches struck him, and the top of his head palpitated almost visibly. He sank back with a groan. 'I think I'm getting brain fever.'

'Is that what's the matter with yer?' asked Mumma satirically. She sat on the edge of the bed, feeling bolder.

Hughie whispered: 'Grandma wants to come and live with us again. I can see it writ all over yer ugly face.'

'Well, where else can the poor dear live?' cried Mumma, her temper rising. 'Josie's had her for eighteen months, and if she's sick then she's done her duty and no one can ask more. Grandma'll just have to come back here, that's all.'

'That means to say I've got to go out on the couch again,' protested Hughie, 'while Grandma sleeps in here with you. It's not right. Not by no manner of means. A man shouldn't be separated from his wife.' He added, rather wistfully, 'not that it's so bad now, with me growing older every minute.' He brooded for a while on this, then exploded: 'I won't be having that old dragon breathing fire at me every time I come home with more than one drink in me!'

'She's my own mother, and while I live she won't be turned into the street,' proclaimed Mumma ferociously. Hughie closed his eyes.

'Now, who's talking about turning the old battleaxe into the street?' he protested. 'All right, I'll shift out on to the couch, and when I want to kiss you, I'll have to take you out into the scullery.'

Mumma sniffed. 'And when do you ever want to kiss me, Hugh Darcy? No more'n Lick Jimmy does.'

A brief twinkle was born in Hughie's eyes. 'Ah, so you've been encouraging that pagan cabbage-seller, have yer? Wiggling yer bottom at him, no doubt.'

Mumma refused to be a party to the pleasantry. She glared. 'And what's more, Ma's coming next Tuesday. So we'd better be getting the place cleaned up, and it's a blessing you're home today to give me a hand.'

Hughie groaned. 'I might 'ave known this was me unlucky day. Metho in me booze last night, and Grandma in me bed this morning.'

'Ah, yer poor old mug,' sympathized Mumma. 'Well, I'll bring you in some tea and a nice slicer toast.' She smiled down at Hughie, for now that she had won her battle, such as it was, she felt strongly the affection which always lay in her heart for him.

'Now, would you do that?' asked Hughie, gratified. She was delighted. 'Don't you come smoodging around me. Look at the grey in yer whiskers.'

She bustled off and happily made a pot of tea.

At half-past seven that night Dolour, almost purple with sunburn, and with sand in everything except her mouth, came bursting into the room. Behind her was the brilliant memory of a day at the beach, of bus rides, of yelling 'Waltzing Matilda' and 'Little Nellie Kelly' and 'Hail Queen of Heaven'; of swooping white roads and sudden revelations of cobalt seas iced with foam; of Harry Drummy being sick all over three Sicilianos, and Father Cooley being forced to take Bertie Stevens aside and explain to him about the gigantic hole in the seat of his trunks; of Sister Theophilus sitting calmly hour by hour making high turreted sand-castles which were wiped into spinning dust and pigmy willy-willies by the afternoon wind. There were so many things to talk about. Dolour had experienced them all in one day, but it took her weeks to tell about them.

Roie came in late, having spent the evening with Tommy. She listened with a sort of dreamy content. Having at last found someone who seemed to fit into her ideal of love, she found that there had mysteriously developed in her a sort of divine aloofness. She was isolated in her own happiness, watching from a distance the squabbles and scraps and little excitements of others. A new tolerance grew in her heart. Consequently, when Mumma timorously broached the subject of Grandma's coming home, she was surprised when Roie readily agreed.

'Poor old thing. After all, Auntie Josie's got all them kids to look after. It must be pretty solid for her with Grandma as well.'

'I like Grandma,' said Dolour decisively. 'She's got a nice nose.'

'Hooked like a vulture's,' chuckled Hughie. Mumma's eyes flashed, particularly as Hughie was correct.

'I can remember the time when my mother's nose was as straight as a die. And the skin she had. Like milk. And she never washed it with anything but common old yellow soap.'

'Now she doesn't wash it at all,' observed Hughie.

'You mark my words, Hugh Darcy, when you're eighty-three you won't be bothered with washing your face, neither. You'll be a dirty old man, or I miss my guess.'

'You bet I will,' affirmed Hughie, his voice growing loud and hearty. 'I'll never wash me hoofs once I pass me sixtieth birthday.'

'Where are you going to put Grandma?' asked Roie. Mumma shook her head vexedly.

'She'll just have to come in with me, and Dadda'll have to come out here on the couch again,' she said.

Hughie looked at the shiny, lumpy couch, too short for anyone over the age of twelve, and too narrow for anyone over eight stone weight. He well remembered his sojourn there during Grandma's last visit, with his feet stacked up on a chair at the end of the couch, and the blankets slipping off him all night long, first one side and then the other. At last he sat up against the curved end of the ancient bit of furniture, and reclined there with his chin boring into his second shirt button, so that by the time morning came he had a savage crick in the neck.

'Gawd,' he said dolefully. Roie laughed, and Mumma thought lovingly how beguiling her little teeth looked with those tiny spaces between them, and how the wide white space between her eyebrows emphasized her slanting eyes.

'Couldn't we put the couch up in our room, Dolour, and then you could sleep on it, and Grandma could sleep with me? I don't think it's right for husbands and wives to be separated.'

She lapsed into silence as Dolour burst into loud lamentations and protest, and Mumma saw with astonishment that she was thinking of how she would feel if she were married to Tommy Mendel and was forced to sleep away from him. As mysteriously as though she were right inside Roie's head, Mumma felt forlornness and loneliness because she did not have a tousled dark head to press into the hollow of her shoulder, or a slender, warm, young man's body to relax in drowsiness beside her own.

She thought, protesting: 'It's not like that, Roie love. It all goes after a while, and he's just a man who snores, and smells of tobacco, and hauls all the bedclothes off you every time he turns over.'

'Not that I wouldn't rather sleep on the couch than with Grandma,' Dolour's voice became audible to her. 'I slept with Grandma once, and she stuck her great big bony knees into my back all night. All crooked up like a safety-pin she was, and cold as a frog. And in the morning when I woke up she was smoking a pipe and setting the blankets on fire.'

'Hush,' said Mumma hurriedly, for she liked to preserve the legend that nobody but herself knew about Grandma's fondness for her little clay cutty.

'No,' said Hughie obstinately. 'I'll tell you what we'll do. We'll hang a sheet up in the bedroom and divide the room, and Grandma can sleep in there, all nice and private.'

'On the couch?' asked Mumma, scandalized.

Hughie shook his head. He had a surprise. 'On the stretcher Johnny Sheily had. We'll borrow it from Miss Sheily, and glad she'll be to be rid of it, with the bugs in it and all.'

'Oh, no, you don't,' stated Mumma with determination. 'My mother's not going to sleep in any bed where Johnny Sheily died, poor creature.'

'He didn't die in it. He died right out there in the road,' said Dolour, and her face went sickly under the sunburn. Mumma hurriedly back-tracked, and agreed that it would be a fine thing, and so it was arranged.

On Tuesday Grandma arrived, as fresh as paint after her long journey. Once she had been a tall and slender woman, with lovely white skin and a bun of dark red hair, and blue eyes with the devil in them, and innocence, too. But now her bones had descended one upon the other, and she was a little old creature, not very bent, but giving you the impression that at any moment she would shrink still further. She walked along with a brisk pigeon-toed step, chewing rapidly at nothing at all, and occasionally having a short, sharp conversation with herself, which nobody else could get the gist of. Grandma had lived on and off with the Darcys for years. In Hughie's turbulent youth she had often thrown things at him, and he had thrown them right back, for they were much of a kind, and secretly admired each other. Immediately they heard her step, Roie and Dolour flew out into the hall to greet her, for they loved her very much.

'Ah, you've grown up something splendid, Dolour,' observed Grandma, reaching up to pat her tall granddaughter on the head.

Then she ostentatiously rubbed the cheek where Roie had kissed her, and said: 'You'll never get past St Peter with all that paint on your face, Rowena, me jewel.'

'Oh, you're an old hussy yourself,' answered Roie pertly. 'Don't try to kid me you didn't put on a bit of colour to attract the boys when you were young.'

'Oh, maybe a bit of chewed-up geranium leaf,' said Grandma calmly, 'and I'd have them all twirling their moustaches like to drop off.'

The moment Grandma put her nose inside the door Mumma began clucking like a hen. She flew at her and helped her out of the mouldy old rabbit-skin coat which had been referred to from time immemorial as 'me tippet', and unclutched her hand from the canvas kit that held all her belongings.

'Ah, Ma, it's thin you are. What's that Josie been doing to yer?' she asked, smoothing back her mother's coarse shiny white hair.

'Starving me, the baggage, on three good meals a day,' chuckled Grandma. 'Ah, poor Josie, her with fallen arches that bad, and going to have an addition to the family, too. It's a pity she don't go out of business.'

Dolour blushed crossly, for she was getting to the stage where much that had hitherto passed over the head of even her slum precocity was penetrating her mind. It seemed to her that Grandma's tongue was getting what Sister Theophilus referred to as 'piggy', and she resolved on the spot to offer her next Mass for her Grandma, for she had no wish to stop on the road to heaven and see that long nose poking through the bars of the gates of hell.

Mumma suddenly stopped and twitched up Grandma's skirts.

'Oh, Ma!' she remonstrated, 'where's yer warm bloomers?'

'Up there, somewhere,' returned Grandma absently.

Roie giggled. She said: 'It's nice to have you home for Christmas, Grandma, so that you can make the puddin'.'

'Oh, no, she don't,' said Hughie, who wandered in at this moment, vexed and sharp-tongued with dirt and weariness. 'This year yours truly is going to make the pud. How are yer, yer old hellcat?'

'Fit to break your brain-box in,' shrilled Grandma, a devilish glint appearing in her eye. 'And nobody's going to make any pudding in this house barring me.'

Now Hughie had, long ago, been a shearers' cook, and could make a curry hot, sweet and luscious, with surprising bits of chopped-up date, green peaches, and sliced banana floating mysteriously in it. And he could make soup, and brownie, and the curiously named sea pie, which is nothing more than a stew with an oversize dumpling roofing it. But, best of all, he could make a boiled pudding, dark as midnight and rich as Persia, and containing so many dates, prunes, cherries, sultanas, and currants, that, as Hughie himself modestly said: 'You couldn't spit between them.'

This year he had been determined to make the Christmas pudding well in advance, and tie it to the scullery rafters to 'season' before the great day arrived. By that time, Hughie calculated, it would not only be rich – it would be intoxicating. But, as Grandma pointed out, she, too, had a hand with puddings, and had made one every year since she was eleven and living with her dad in Faroe Street, Cookstown, Ireland. And be damned to anyone, said Grandma, if she was going to stop now.

The pudding argument went on for days after Grandma had settled in at Number Twelve-and-a-Half.

It was a strange thing how her advent changed the personalities and outlook of those already in the house. Old as she was, Grandma had some exciting element in her; the courage and restlessness which had driven her forth at eighteen to emigrate to the new colony had not left her; soon Mumma found herself unconsciously giving her speech an Irish twist, and even the girls, brought up as they had been to the quick Irish idiom and wit, discovered that their voices had a new softness and purl. It was as though the real Celticism, not only of blood, but of memory and association, were catching, and the Australian blood, if there was such a thing, were vanishing before the red blood of the Irish.

Grandma unpacked her canvas bag, and Dolour, watching, thought nothing of the fact that Grandma possessed in all the world only two winceyette nightdresses, yellowed and ragged around the armholes; an extra pair of moth-eaten black bloomers; a curious maroon garment of the fashions of twenty years before, and known as 'me house dress'; seven or eight strings of rosary beads, all broken, and an ancient prayer-book which had been used so many times that the bottom corners of the pages were yellow and illegible from the grip of Grandma's thumb.

Dolour had never thought about age, but she had an instinctive feeling that as you grew older you needed fewer possessions, and she seemed to see behind Grandma a long road which extended into her childhood, dotted with the discarded treasures and necessities of Grandma's discarded years.

But Roie, with the curious, subjective sensitivity which love had brought her, found her heart filling with sadness. It stung her eyes and tightened her throat. It seemed so strange that Grandma, who had borne so many children, who had worked and laughed and despaired and grieved, should reach the evening of her life with nothing whatsoever in her hands. She was like a little bird in the sunset hour, safe beneath the eave, chirping and cheeping, possessed of complete poverty.

'Maybe I'll finish up like that, too,' she thought. 'Maybe Tommy will.' She remembered the countless dirty old lonely men around the city, living in some cheap and squalid room, or even half a room; with no one to talk to save park-bench acquaintances; spending their meagre pensions on buttered rolls and scanty cups of tea and mean grey Devon sausage, because eighteen bob a week went nowhere at all once you took your rent out of it.

Roie did not understand her thoughts; she hated them, and because she did and was confused she took it out on Grandma.

'Why don't you get some more clothes?' she said. 'Anyone would think you were as poor as a mouse. Look at that filthy old nightdress – I wouldn't be found dead in it. You just don't care any more – no respect for yourself. You just ought to make your pension go further.'

'What am I, a magic-an? I'm dubersome if you'd make me pension go half as far, Roie me girl,' cried Grandma. 'You've taken leave of yer seven small senses, and what manners yer have, too.'

'Ah, God!' cried Roie, and she ran out of the room. Grandma jerked a black-nailed thumb after her.

'Now what's come up her back?'

Dolour jigged her shoulders in a shrug. She was dying to explain all about the Haymarket and Tommy Mendel. Grandma loved to hear about anyone falling in love. Her interest was a combination of vindictiveness and nostalgia. She sat on the sagging bed and nodded her head like a Chinese mandarin. At the conclusion she shook it.

'It's a good thing, it is, for Roie to have a boy. It makes the mind broader to know how the men think, and if you live too long without finding out you grow into a peculiar one-eyed sort of body. But I'm not so keen on the Jewish,' she added thoughtfully.

At that moment a curious odour, half flavour and half perfume, stole through the door, and Grandma's nose quivered like an anteater's.

'Vanilla, God help us – and that fladdy-faced Hughie of a father of yours is stealing a march on me and making the Christmas pudding.'

She trotted rapidly out to the kitchen, holding an agitated conversation with herself as she went. And Grandma's nose had not lied. There was Hughie, his black brows bent downwards into a solid line, concentrating on a series of sticky brown-paper bags before him, the contents of which he was measuring out into the washing-up basin.

'Ah, yer tom todger,' commenced Grandma mildly, in a tone which brought to mind the precise and gentle pacings of a bull before he starts tearing up the earth.

'Go on, skedaddle out of here,' threatened Hughie jovially. He was in a good mood. Ostentatiously and luxuriously he sniffed at a cupful of raisins soaking in brandy. Grandma dipped her nose downwards too.

'Where'd yer get the brandy, Hughie?' she asked.

Hughie smiled mysteriously. 'Guv to me by a friend,' he explained. Grandma looked longingly at it, and her slaty eyes flicked a glance along the mantelshelf and into the dark cubbyhole beyond the sink. But there was no bottle to be seen. Hughie was mean enough to buy it in a cup, she reflected bitterly, for brandy was one of the few pleasures left in her life. It put the marrow back into her bones and the red into her blood, and for a narrow space she was young and tall and the world had a prickle in it again.

'Can I have the cup after you've finished with it, Hughie?' asked Grandma humbly.

'Will yer keep outa me kitchen if I give yer maybe a sip or two?' inquired Hughie cunningly. Grandma dipped her flag without compunction.

'You won't tell herself, Hughie?'

'Never a word outa me mouth, Grandma!'

'Ah, dotie, it's a fine boyo you are, sometimes, and perhaps I've been hard,' she confessed, thinking of the many times that he'd come in rolling drunk and made Mumma cry, when she'd gone for him with anything handy.

Hughie pondered the times Grandma had been hard on him.

'You have that,' he agreed, savouring Grandma's comedown, and pouring a cupful of yellow, wrinkled sultanas into the bowl. He added chopped dates, clumpy with flour.

'But I always liked you, Hughie,' cajoled Grandma, sniffing lingeringly at the brandy cup. 'I remember when you used to come around when you were courting and Pa used to say: "Here comes the lad with the ellafump ears."'

'Ellafump!' jeered Hughie. 'Poor old Pa. Remember the arms of him like blocks of carved wood.'

'That's right,' marvelled Grandma, of the husband she had not thought of for years.

'And the head of him,' said Hughie ferociously. 'Like a block of carved wood, too.'

'He was the finest man that ever brought a block of ice into a house,' declared Grandma loyally. 'And at the icemen's picnic he won the hammer throw and got an elegant brass clock I'd have yet if you hadn't pawned it, bad cess to you, Hugh Darcy.'

'Stop yer nagging, or you'll ruin me nerve and I'll be putting the wrong amount of suet into me pudding,' protested Hughie. He wiped his floury hand down the side of his pants and groped about under the sink. From out of the ill-smelling recesses around the loops and coils of plumbing he produced a medicine bottle half full of brandy.

Grandma's eyes glistened. With pursed lips, Hughie poured a table-spoonful into the bottom of the cup she held out to him. Then he decisively corked the bottle and put it on the mantelpiece, high up out of her reach.

'There now, that'll keep your old bones together,' he remarked with repulsive magnanimity. Grandma peered forlornly into the white bowl of the cup to the minute pool of pungent amber at the bottom.

'Ah, Hughie, you're a mullet-headed sheeny if ever there was one,' she cried. There was a short sharp conversation between herself and some person unknown, conducted in a voice inaudible to anyone but Grandma, and she had decided that she would sacrifice the brandy to the cause of war. She put down the cup, well out of Hughie's reach, and then attacked him with tooth and tongue.

'Look at it, look at it, Hugh Darcy. No more than a spoonful, and you call yourself an Irishman. There's not enough there to warm a kitten. Ah, it'll be a glorious day for me when you're old and aching and knobbly in every joint, and some tight-fisted jeremiah of a son-in-law deprives you of yer wee sup of brandy.'

'Leave it then,' said Hughie unconcernedly, 'and I'll season me pudding with it.'

'Your pudding!' shrilled Grandma, 'and me going to sell me soul and me rights for the sake of that wee driblet of brandy. Get away from that bowl, Hugh Darcy, for I'm going to make the pudding meself, and you can make up yer mind to it.'

The lines in Hughie's face went sour and perpendicular; his eyebrows formed themselves into a line as forbidding as any seen on the battlefield. He plunged his arms nearly to the elbow into the pudding basin, and jammed both hands full of suet, sultanas, and flour.

'Now get out of it, Grandma, before I lose me temper.'

'Temper!' jeered Grandma. 'As though the Darcys ever had any temper worth speaking of, barring the dirty bit of liverishness that passes for it in some families.'

She rolled up her sleeves and put her long knobby fingers into the flour. Hughie's face was dark crimson. He shouted: 'I'm warning you, Mrs Kilker. I'm warning yer that I'll bust the basin over yer scone rather than let you make the pudding this year. I've got me mind set on it.'

Grandma went on kneading the flour, pressing the whole lumps of fat in as though her fingers had done it for centuries.

'Mrs Kilker is it now? You've become mighty polite, Hugh Darcy. More so than yer dadda was, I must admit.'

Hughie cracked her fingers hard with the wooden spoon. 'Leave me suet alone, or you'll get worse, you meddlesome old murphy. And leave me father alone, he was a fine man.'

'He was,' agreed Grandma sweetly, 'save for the teeth of him.'

'What was the matter with me father's teeth?'

'Like clothes pegs,' said Grandma sadly, rubbing her fingers under cover of the flour, for they still hurt. 'And the scandalous manners of a pig under a bed. But the Darcys were always like that. Will you ever forget yer Aunt Kathy, her that had eight children and a pillar of the Church for a husband, and then went mad and danced Salome's dance in her skin and an umbrella.'

'I'm not interested in me Aunt Kathy,' said Hughie loftily, stirring rapidly with the wooden spoon, and involving Grandma's fingers with every stir.

'Ah, it's all in the blood,' ruminated Grandma. 'What about Molly Brody, her what was cousin to yer mother, and married a Lanigan from Limerick way?'

'What's the matter with that, to be properly married to a Lanigan?'

'But he was a hangman,' explained Grandma, 'and kept his rope and noose under the bed. That's a fine bed to be laying on. And it was Molly Brody, own cousin to yer mother who lay on it. You can't say there was any good in a woman like that.'

'Listen to who's talking,' retorted Hughie. 'Who was it got bailed up by the skipper coming out from Ireland and was found with six shirts on, and all other people's?'

Grandma's eyes sparkled, for if there was anything she really loved, it was a fight, and one was steaming up in the best possible way. 'Keep your brazen tongue off me father, Hugh, or as sure as I'm standing on me own two feet it'll be worse for you.'

'Brazen, is it?'

'It is. Me father suffered from the cold, that's all, and if any of them passengers said otherwise he was a liar, and I'd tell him so to his ugly face.'

'Fat chance,' jeered Hughie. 'And them all dead sixty year ago, like your dadda.'

'God rest his soul.'

'God rest it,' assented Hughie piously. Grandma had no intention of letting the quarrel get away from her. She grabbed it by its disappearing tail and brought it back.

'It was sad for me when me poor dear husband consented to your marriage with our girl.'

'Oh, is that so? And she was well on the way to being an old maid when I took pity on her.'

He added sorrowfully, for Grandma's breath appeared to be short. 'No, it was me was the mug, and look what I've come down to.' He gestured flourily at the dirt, the drabness, the overpowering poverty of the dark and greasy scullery, scarred with seventy years. Grandma felt tears of futile fury rising in her throat. In spite of herself her voice quavered: 'Hughie, you're not saying me girl dragged you down to this? Her that's worked so hard, and reared your children and always gone to her duty?'

Hughie was abashed. He had not meant any such thing. It had just sounded good. 'Who said such a thing?' he jeered. 'But it might be true, for all that. It's disencouragement that drives a man to the drink, and if she was a different sort, and not always whining and complaining and crying about me, I wouldn't do it.'

Hughie had a brief vision of a heroic woman, a mixture of Norse goddess and film star and plain everyday mother, who would have listened to his maudlin self-pityings without bothering him with suggestions for a cure. Wistfully he marvelled at the number of women exactly like that there must be in this world, and how bad had been his luck that he hadn't chosen one.

'No,' he repeated, 'taking it right back to the beginning, it's her that drove me to the drink.'

Grandma promptly snatched the spoon out of his hand and

hit him so smartly across what she described as 'his long snout,' that tears came into his eyes. She stood there, tiny, blazing, and indomitable.

'Go on now, hit an old woman, Hughie Darcy. Show what sort of a man you are, blaming your evil doings on your poor wife that's worked her fingers to the bone for you and your children, and then hitting her poor old mother.'

'I haven't hit you yet,' protested Hughie, but Grandma behaved as though he had, crying out and weeping, and calling to Miss Sheily and Patrick Diamond for assistance against the big lout of a son-in-law who'd hit her and take her pension off her, and drink it to the last penny.

Grandma was not conscious of maligning Hughie; by the time she had finished her tirade she was righteously angry and as lamentary as if Hughie had actually beaten her up.

Hughie could hardly speak. His rage choked him. He wiped his floury hands down the sides of his trousers, and crammed his hat on his head, hissing:

'I'd like to see your throat cut by a buck nigger, you old morepork,' and strode out of the room. Grandma, satisfied, plunged with eager enthusiasm into the pudding, and by the time Mumma returned from her shopping it was tied up, a jetty cannon-ball, in its tea-towel, and bubbling and knocking in the black enamel saucepan.

'Where's Hughie?' asked Mumma. Grandma tucked in her lips and tried to look grieved and wise at one and the same time.

'I suppose he's drowning his woes,' she shrugged. 'Flung outa here like a tomcat with a tin on his tail.'

Mumma looked distressed. 'Now, Ma, I hope you haven't been annoying him, when he was so good and all, making the pudding and not a peep out of him.'

Grandma was indignant. 'Him make that pudding! It was meself and no other, though he might have helped a bit with the mixing. And you'll be able to tell from the taste, too.' Grandma was feeling good, not only because she had vanquished Hughie, and at eighty-three, too, but because she had licked out the luscious fragrant brandy cup and got more than a drop. Mumma looked at her doubtfully, and went on with the tea-making. Already a cold and melancholy foreboding was settling over her soul, as though a fog of the spirit were coming down. She felt sure that Hughie was going to go on a Christmas spree.

And so he was. He was already getting drunk. It is easy to get drunk in Australia. Things have been so arranged that a man can buy a bottle of muscat for four and six and get madder on it than a cow on a patch of poison-weed. For it did not come from any vineyard. No deep and autumnal southern sun ripened its grapes; no pungent vat housed it before it was bottled. It was born of an oilwell in Texas, seasoned with wine dregs, coloured with raspberry syrup or beetroot juice, and even, occasionally, pepped up with tan boot polish. It was easy to become a god on it, or a maniac.

There are intelligent drinkers and stupid drinkers. Hughie was one of the first. His intelligence told him that he was weak and without any importance in the world he both feared and loved, and so he drank to drown it. Inarticulate, a man who had many thoughts that were no more than a nebulous, cloudy mingling of impressions, half-memories, and emotions, Hughie was continually haunted by the knowledge that he could not express. When he was half-drunk he was possessed with incalculable sorrow for all the piteous strivings and battlings of humanity. For what? Something better than what it had. But what it was Hughie did not know. He only knew that there was implanted in his soul a fierce hunger for it, as there might be hunger for some beloved who had died a long time ago and left an emptiness nothing else could fill.

But when he was really drunk, Hughie grew six inches and put on four stone; he wore a uniform of red and gold and at the sound of his voice the crowds bowed down. Trumpets blew before him, and there were kettledrums rattling. If he met a respectable woman he hated the look of embarrassment or disdain on her face, and he said something filthy or disgusting to her just to see it replaced by another, no matter what it was; he gave dirty little goitrous kids pennies, because in his eyes he was distributing gilded largesse to beggars; he winked at prostitutes to let them know he was one of the boys; he even thought of rudeness to policemen as he passed their frowning presence on street corners. And when he got home he started in on Mumma.

He hated her then, because in her fatness and untidiness and drabness she reminded him of what he himself was when he was sober.

When Mumma heard his erratic feet stumping down the hall, her heart rushed sickeningly into her mouth and her face went yellow, not with fear, but with hatred and dread of the same old scene, the same old bellowings and crazy talk, the placatory words from herself, the brief spasms of anger, and Hughie's louder and more triumphant bellowings, and then the maudlin last stage when he cried into his food and threw it at the wall with melodramatic expressions of distaste.

And now there would be Grandma putting her spoke in, and getting abused, too, in words which made her achingly remember the same performance from her husband, long ago, and cry the hoarse painful sobs of the aged, not only from self-pity, but from nostalgia.

'I wish Thady hadn't gone,' wept Mumma suddenly. 'He would be fifteen. He'd be big and strong and look after me.'

At the thought of Thady she cried out loud, for the knot of pain in her breast which was his memory never left her, and only waited for such a moment as this to burst into agony.

'Thady, Thady,' she wept, with blinding tears, groping through the fog towards her mother, who held out her arms and cried, too, in sympathy.

Six

Mumma had always loved Christmas with a child-like love. It was like another world suddenly impinging upon her ordinary dull painful one; it was as bright-coloured and wonderful as a country road in the springtime, where even the shadows were full of light. It was mysterious, too – a unique mystery, for although when regarded in the abstract it was perfect, it was never quite that way in reality. Somewhere, thought Mumma, there was the perfect Christmas Day. They would be all together. Thady sitting opposite her with his little freckled face shining with soap and water, and his silvery hair fluffed up in a triangle off his brow; the dinner would be cooked just right, the pudding hot and rich, and yet not overheating, as it always was in Australia; she would feel well, and Hughie would be sober, and Grandma wouldn't choke on the solitary threepence in the duff. But it never happened that way. Dolour was invariably bilious, and Roie bad-tempered with the heat and the fatigue, and she herself so hot and worn out with cooking a winter's dinner at mid-summer that she was ready to cry with vexation. And invariably Hughie got drunk and spoiled things one way or another.

This Christmas was worse than ever. Hughie spent all of Christmas morning snoring, with intervals of staggering out to the lavatory and being ear-wrenchingly sick. When he recovered he was sullen and quiet, with black hollows under his eyes and a pallid look under his three-day bristle. He looked an old man, and he felt it.

'Gawd, how I hate Christmas!' he said, lying on the hot and lumpy bed and looking up at the ceiling, which was pitted and pockmarked with the plaster falling away. Once it had been a lovely ceiling, delicately ornamented with intaglio designs of grapes and leaves; but now it was clotted with dirt and wounded with age. The old house had perhaps been a good one in its time, way back in the 'seventies. Perhaps some rich or famous person had lived there, Mumma often thought, for she occasionally had the strangest feeling, as though someone delicate and fastidious and beautiful passed by her, said softly: 'This was my house. Have pity on it because it was,' and vanished away again.

'Gawd, I hate it!' snarled Hughie, the taste in his mouth as bitter as gall, and in his soul all the disillusionment of an opium-eater who runs out of his drug. He was all alone, for Grandma was asleep in her cubbyhole and Dolour and Mumma were at church, and Roie was getting ready to go out with Tommy Mendel. He could hear her at the sink, washing sketchily, banging a mirror down, clinking bottles of cosmetics.

'Roie!' he bawled. 'Make us a cuppa tea before you go!'

'Oh, damn! I'm in a hurry!' answered Roie angrily, but he heard the hiss and pop of the gas, and settled back on the pillow tranquil in the knowledge that she would make it. After a while she entered, a sullen look on her little face, her hair tousled and untidy, but her mouth as crimson as a poinsettia with lipstick.

'Ta, Ro.' She gave the cup to him silently, and turned to the mirror to comb her hair.

'Whatcher get for Christmas?' he asked, placatingly, to break the silence. Roie gave a little snort. 'Anyone'd think you weren't here,' she jeered. Hughie groaned.

'Ah, cripes, leave that to your mother, will you, Ro? I feel crook as hell. Come on, what did Tommy give you?'

Roie licked a finger and smoothed her thin dark wing-like eyebrows.

'He's a Jew. He didn't give me anything.'

'What, nothing at all? The little sheeny, eh?'

Roie's face flushed a faint red, and in the mirror her mouth looked sulky and cross. 'He don't believe in Christmas, Jews don't. You don't know nothing.'

'Betcha you gave him something,' grinned Hughie. 'Bet you put out some sort of sprat to catch a mackerel. So yer fell in, eh?'

'God, I hate you!' spat Roie, turning around and piercing him with a look of such fury that Hughie felt it enter his head and come sizzling out the other side. She ran out of the room and slammed the door. Grandma instantly awoke, and at the sound of her complaining voice Hughie pulled the sheet over his head and pretended to be asleep. But there was no fooling Grandma. He heard her clip-clop to the side of the bed, and then a hard old hand hit him in the stomach.

'Ah, hell' groaned Hughie, dragging the sheet off his face. 'Whyn't you leave me alone?'

Grandma, rubbing sleep out of her eyes, gave a wink. 'Do you know what Miss Sheily gave me for a present, Hughie lad?'

'No, I don't know and I don't care,' growled Hughie. 'What?'

Grandma fished in the musty folds of her skirt and withdrew a bottle.

'Cripes!' gasped Hughie. Life flowed back into his eyes, and he sat up. 'Cripes, Grandma! Come on, give us a nip.'

'First-grade Port,' read Grandma with pride, though she didn't have her glasses on, for she had read it before, and remembered. 'Now, they're all out, so we'll have a little drink, just you and me, eh?'

'God bless you, Grandma!' said Hughie fervently. 'You're a good woman, sometimes.'

He lay back and listened to the pop of the cork, and the rich trickle into two cups, and the expression on his face might well have been on the face of one of the Faithful who, having been slain but recently, heard the jingle of a houri's ankle bells, and smelt the attar of paradisal roses.

Roie clicked down the street on her high heels. She was angry and upset because Hughie's reference to a Christmas present from Tommy had come right on the heels of lively curiosity on the part of Grandma and Dolour and Mumma. To each of them she had replied the same, but it had been hard to keep her lips from trembling and giving away the hurt in her heart. She too had forgotten that Tommy was a Jew, and she was very disappointed that he hadn't thought enough of her to give her some little present. She had given him a pullover, bottle-green and shoddy, but costing far more than she could afford. She had three pounds saved up to buy her entire summer wardrobe, and the pullover had cost half of it. But he had been pleased. She remembered the look on his face like a kid suddenly presented with an ice-cream.

'Gosh, he's only young,' she thought forgivingly, with a hot gush of love in her heart. She loved him so much that she justified to herself his every fault; so much could be forgiven Tommy because he was so pitifully young, because he had never had any parents; because he was lame and ashamed of it; because he lived by himself in a dirty little attic room in the Haymarket district, and had to make his own bed and cook his food over a gas ring. Roie took him to her heart as she might have taken a sick bird or a lost cat; she fitted him into the vacant space, forgave him everything, as a mother might.

'Where'll we go?' she asked when they met. Tommy groaned.

'It's so hot, Roie. Can't we just go and sit in the park; find a cool spot and yarn?'

They walked down the burning, deserted Sunday-ish streets, and turned into Moore Park. The great English trees stood bushy and green still, their sap not yet curdled by the alien sun. They cast great umbrellas of shade that was dark and sharp-cut against the bright yellow of the sunshine. About their knotted arched roots there were bare, worn spaces of earth. Tommy spread out his coat, and Roie sat down. She was reluctant. She had wanted to go somewhere, on a ferry-boat, or to any place which was new and different, where they could really be alone. But she put the thought out of her mind quickly, and smiled shyly at Tommy. He was dull and discontented; he slouched beside her, picking out pine needles and building them into a little tepee. Then he lay back with his head on her knees and looked up into the chinks of blue sky that showed through the clotted green.

'I hate holidays,' he said. Roie laughed.

'I do,' he cried. 'I hate them because there's nothing to do and nowhere to go when you've got no money.' He thought of his friends, the horde of larrikins with whom he associated, always inferior to them and good-naturedly chaffed. Their life of pubs and billiard-rooms and two-up schools and endless filthy magpie chatter about women seemed to him to be unbearably far away from his.

'There's the beach,' said Roie timidly.

'Kid stuff. Give me the good old town. Lots of people. Noise. Rowdy trams rattling past. Tarts showing off their dresses. I'd like to go to the races with you, Roie, in a slinky black dress and a great big hat with lace round the brim, and a string of green beads.' Roie laughed again, because she did not know if he were serious enough. Tommy's eyes shone. 'With plenty of money to bet with. God, I'm sick of having no money. I'm sick of having a gammy foot. Where'll I ever get in life?'

'There's your Uncle Joseph,' suggested Roie shyly. 'Couldn't he help you to get a better job?'

'Uncle Joseph! That hook-nosed old scrub,' said Tommy fiercely. He turned over and buried his nose in her stomach. His voice came muffled. 'He don't care the flick of a nag's tail about me. He just has some old Jew idea about an obligation to a dead brother's child. I'm useful down there in the market, that's all. You smell nice, Roie.'

'Dolour gave me some lavender talcum powder for Christmas,' said Roie, delighted that he had smelt it. Then she flushed because she thought that perhaps the mention of Christmas gifts might hurt Tommy's feelings. He turned so that one sullen black eye was looking at her.

'I got something for you too. Bet you thought I wasn't going to give you anything,' he said. Roie flushed scarlet.

'Oh, Tommy, I never thought about it . . . I . . . I . . .' He fished in his pockets, first one and then the other, and Roie, her eyes sparkling, her heart beating like that of a child who stands outside the room where the Christmas Tree is kept, waited, overcome with joy and expectation. That old Dadda! Mumma and her mean suspicions! Dolour! She needed her face slapped! And Grandma and her nasty tongue about sheenies and long noses! At last Tommy hauled out of his pocket a little parcel wrapped in blue paper.

'I hope you like it. I bought it up Oxford Street last night, after I left you. I thought it was nice.'

Roie was undoing the parcel with trembling fingers. It felt hard and oblong, and there was something soft wrapped around it. Perhaps it was a little piece of jewellery in a box, or a bottle of perfume. Perhaps it was . . . oh, it might be almost anything. Roie fumbled the last piece of paper off, and there on her lap lay a cake of soap wrapped in a pink wash-cloth.

She was so shocked and abashed that tears rushed into her eyes, and she had to look away carefully so that Tommy wouldn't see them. At first she thought it was a joke, and he had a real present concealed in another pocket, but when she stole a swift look at him she saw that he had an expression of pleased expectancy on his face.

'Gee, Tommy,' said Roie gallantly, 'it's awfully useful. I mean . . . soap . . . everyone needs a lot of soap. And the wash-cloth is awful pretty . . . pink, I mean . . . I like pink things. Thank you so much, Tommy.'

It was terrible. Her heart hurt as though he had stabbed it with a knife. Soap and a wash-cloth; it was one of those nasty little gift packages which the chain store made up at Christmas and Easter and Mother's Day and sold for ninepence or a shilling. But oh, Tommy hadn't meant to be cheap or mean about it. The love within Roie rushed out to protect and defend him. He just hadn't thought. It wasn't the gift that mattered, Mumma always said, but the thought behind it. Roie fiercely winked away the tears. Tommy nuzzled his face into her lap and said happily. 'I couldn't think what to get you. I just didn't think of it until you gave me the sweater last evening. I wanted to get you something you liked.'

'I do like it, Tommy,' sobbed Robie suddenly, dropping tears and kisses indiscriminately on his face. 'And I love you with all my heart.'

As soon as she had said it she was panic-stricken, for although Tommy had often cuddled and kissed her, and they had gone steady for months, he had never said he loved her. Now she had done the unforgivable thing and said it first, which all the girls at the factory said was the worst thing anybody could do. The blood hummed in her ears. She wanted to get up and run away and never see Tommy again.

But he turned over and put his arms around her neck, and pulled her down clumsily and a little painfully. His soft boy's kisses fell warmly and ineffectually on her lips, and he whispered thickly: 'Do you mean that?' Roie nodded dumbly, ashamed. 'Gosh . . . Ro . . . nobody's ever said that to me before.' He whispered in her ear, with an excited voice: 'I love you, too.'

Now that it was out they were silent and embarrassed, each too timid to glance at the other, letting their warm arms lie slackly where they were. Finally they both glanced at each other and laughed ridiculously. Tommy rolled Roie over into the hot brittle grass and tickled her.

'Oh, Tommy, my dress . . . my hair . . . Oh, Tommy, don't! Don't!' she shrieked in a delighted whisper. They rolled about like two pups, relieved at the breaking of emotional tension. When they were tired and breathless they lay side by side, and Tommy breathed into her ear: 'Let me touch you.'

'What do you mean?' asked Roie, startled, shying away from his hand that edged itself softly down the neck of her dress.

'Go on, don't play hard to get,' he said, a little sparkle springing into his eyes. He had no real desire to fondle Roie, but he had heard his mates discuss it at length, and he wanted to experiment. When she refused he found himself growing angry, with an urgent wish to have his own way.

Roie flushed. Her quick temper rose. 'I never let anyone maul me around. I don't like it.'

'But I'm different,' pleaded Tommy. Roie sat up, sulkily, all the joy dying out of her. 'What good does that do anybody? It's . . . I don't like it,' she ended lamely.

'You'd want me to touch you if you loved me, like you said,' said Tommy roughly. He flung himself over on his stomach and began chewing a grass stem. Roie was left in the lurch. She began to feel that perhaps she had been too brusque, that perhaps she had hurt or offended him. Her heart went out in a great flood of tenderness towards Tommy's back, its slimness, his narrow neck riding out of the ill-fitting collar, his badly-cut clothes. He was only twenty. She felt much older and maturer.

'Ah, Tommy, don't be mad with me,' she pleaded. Tommy

shrugged a shoulder. Roie put a hand on it, and when he did not move away she felt encouraged. 'Tommy,' she said softly. 'Tommy, darling.' The boy looked up, and he saw the pointed pale face, so youthful, with worried eyes, and the mouth trembling a little, looking at him anxiously. He rolled over forgivingly and pulled her down to him.

'I don't want to maul you if you don't like it, kid.'

'Perhaps I wouldn't mind if it was you that did it,' said Roie, trembling, throwing all her moral teachings and inhibitions overboard in her anxiety to please her lover.

'I can't stop thinking about you,' he said sullenly. 'When I go to bed I dream of you, and I wake up and you aren't there, and I lie by myself in that old lonely bed and stare at the bedpost.'

'How can you if it's dark?' asked Roie.

He cried angrily: 'Because sometimes it's just getting light.'

Roie said, 'Oh.' Then she added: 'I guess it's just because I feel funny about doing that sort of thing, Tommy.'

'You're not like all the other sheilas,' he said, and she did not know whether the contempt in his voice was for her or them.

'There's lots of girls like me in Surry Hills,' said Roie stoutly. 'You don't have to be a rat just because you live in a hole. And besides,' she added resentfully, 'what do you know about other girls?'

'I don't know anything, except what other fellas have told me. Who'd ever look at me with my great clump of a foot?' he asked bitterly.

Roie hugged him tight. 'I would! I would!' she cried, her ardent heart burning with pity and love, and a maternally comforting feeling. The two slender bodies clung together, and so they were when a passing policeman leaned over the fence, tapped Tommy on the foot with his baton, and said: 'Hey, none of that in public places. You go and neck on your old woman's parlour sofa, young feller.'

'Garn!' snarled Tommy, jolted out of a half-doze. 'I was only cuddling her.'

'And very nice, too,' approved the policeman. 'But you go on out of here or I'll arrest you for loitering.'

77

They got up and fled, brushing the dried grass off themselves as they went, and the policeman looked after them and chuckled: 'Poor kids.' He sighed. 'Poor little rats.'

Roie and Tommy went up the street happily chanting under their breaths to the tune of 'A-tisket, a-tasket.'

'A flatfoot, a flatfoot, I lost me little flatfoot,' sang Tommy. He felt curiously triumphant. He knew that Roie would be more amenable next time he wanted to caress her. He squeezed her arm, and they looked into each other's eyes and laughed and trembled with delight. Roie felt words bursting their way out of her throat; she wanted to say something beautiful and memorable, for she knew that she had stumbled into some new and enchanting land. Life would never be the same again. But she could not shape her thoughts. Like mysterious flowers they bloomed and died without a soul to witness, falling into ashes in the mind that bore them.

'See you tomorrow, Tommy?' she asked. He nodded, started to say something, and changed his mind, for his voice was hoarse with excitement. Roie laughed and darted away with a coquetry that surprised herself. She danced into the hot dark hall of her home, and from its shelter watched him limp away down the street. Tommy! At the very name she shivered and hugged herself with delight. Then she remembered. She tiptoed upstairs, pricking an ear curiously to the cracked duet of Grandma and Hughie from the kitchen, as they socialized over another cup of wine.

'Ow! God blesser and keeper, Mother Machree!' cried Hughie, and Grandma sang in a monotonous treble:

> *Oh Brian O'Lynn had no britches to wear*
> *So he got him a sheepskin and made him a pair.*
> *With the skinny side out and the woolly side in*
> *Oww! It's warm in the winter said Brian O'Lynn!*

Roie let herself into her room. She went straight to the old powder-box where she kept her savings. There was thirty shillings left, which meant that she could get a new cotton frock . . . a yellow one . . . and a pair of white shoes. But Roie had other plans for her money. Wistfully she bundled up all her longings for a new dress, and hurled them out of the window. She scraped the shillings and the florins out of the box, which she kept shoved behind a rotten beam by the skylight. Then she tiptoed out of the room. Patrick Diamond's door was half-open. She peeped in to see him lying on his bed, his glasses jammed on his nose, and a puzzled frown on his brow. She stood in the doorway.

'Whatcher thinking of, Mr Diamond?' He glanced up at the girl poised like a butterfly in the doorway.

'Have a nice Christmas, Mr Diamond?'

'All by meself.'

'You should have come down and had Christmas dinner with us. We had a chook but it was as hard as a football.' Mr Diamond smiled, and there was something in his smile that made Roie want to rush over and kiss him, red nose and all.

'Families ought to be by themselves on Christmas Day.'

'But we've known you and Miss Sheily for so long you're almost part of our family,' argued Roie.

'I'll never be part of any pope-worshipping family, saving your presence,' said Mr Diamond, with what he considered extreme civility. Roie flared up like a heap of dry grass in mid-summer. She stamped her foot on the ragged linoleum and cried: 'All right, you can stick in your old room! And never think that I'll ask you to dinner again, because I won't!'

She rattled down the stairs as annoyed as if she had really asked him to Christmas dinner, and he had impolitely refused. She ran down the street to Jacky Siciliano's fruit shop. It was a heavily odorous place, with a luscious smell of over-ripe pineapples and rotting bananas. Half a dozen black-eyed little Sicilianos played in and out of the packing-cases which littered the backyard.

'Hello, Rosina. Merry Christmas, Gio. Hello, Tonetta,' said Roie. 'Your mumma in?'

'Yeah,' said Gio, jetty-curled, and with most of his brown frame projecting through his torn shirt and ragged pants. 'She's lying down with Pop.'

'Come on in, dearie,' called Mrs Siciliano from inside. Roie caught a glimpse of her through the fly-screen as she came through the door, pulling on a blouse over her petticoat. A second later her magnificent cow-eyes looked around the door.

'Good day, Roie love. Did you have a nice-a Christmas? Come on in, and don't-a mind my old feller. He is sleeping off the big-a dinner he had.'

Roie looked at the bed, and the mound of Mr Siciliano's stomach protruding pinkly from his unbuttoned trousers. His mouth was open, and his moustache gently rose and fell as he snored. He was the picture of a happy Italian man on Christmas Day.

'I'm sorry to bother, Mrs Siciliano,' explained Roie, 'but I thought I'd pop around and ask if you still want to sell that brooch you showed me last week.'

'Oh, my big-a silver brooch!' exclaimed Mrs Siciliano, clasping her hands together, and shaking them outwards in a pleased, expansive gesture. 'You want to buy him now?'

'Yes,' said Roie unblushingly. 'I just thought of someone I didn't send a present to.'

'Buona, buona,' exclaimed Mrs Siciliano. 'It will make a nice-a present for some lady. Antonetta!' she shrieked out the door. Tonetta, small and brown and beautiful as an angel, came running.

'Watcher want, Mum?'

'You run upstairs and get my mother's brooch, the silver one. It's in the cardboard box with my corsets,' explained Mrs Siciliano in rapid Italian. A few moments later Tonetta appeared with the brooch. It was two inches square, with a dark red and beautiful stone in each corner. Both Roie and Mrs Siciliano thought they were rubies, but they were really balas. The centre of the brooch was a thick metal web of silver filigree, and a row of tiny tarnished tassels hung from the lower edge.

'Is it not bella?' demanded Mrs Siciliano proudly. Roie took it reverently. There was no jewellery in her family at all, except Mumma's wedding ring and a horrible, gold-bound shark-tooth that Hughie had once bought from a New Zealand sailor under the drunken impression that it was valuable.

'I've brought the thirty shillings,' said Roie, and as easily as that it was done. The brooch was hers. She ran out jubilantly, rubbing it on the front of her dress to brighten it. The red stones shone like a white rabbit's eyes in the sunshine, and the minutest fairy twinkle came from the swinging tassels.

Roie ran into Number Twelve-and-a-Half just as Dolour and Mumma returned from church. Grandma scuttled into the bedroom with the empty bottle, and Hughie composed himself on the couch, trying to appear fragile, and endeavouring not to breathe when Mumma was close, so that she might not smell the rich perfume of the port. Mumma was suspicious, but when Roie showed her the brooch, everything else flitted from her mind.

'Wherever did you get it? It's real!' marvelled Mumma, scratching with a reverent fingernail at the silver. Dolour squeaked with most satisfactory awe, and Roie said proudly, 'Tommy gave it to me this afternoon.'

'Oh, he did not!' cried Dolour sceptically. 'Jews never give anybody anything.'

'All right, if you don't believe me,' flashed Roie, grabbing the brooch and glaring at Dolour. 'He was saving up for it for months and months, just so he would surprise me. You don't know how good and kind he is!'

Hughie, gawking shamefacedly from the couch, said: 'Well, I take back everything I said about him. It's a better present than I ever gave anyone.'

'You're telling me,' said Mumma with a scornful sniff.

'Oh, is that so?' cried Hughie furiously. 'You're a nice one to be talking that way, and you're not out of church ten minutes.'

'You mustn't mention anything about it to Tommy when he comes round,' said Roie anxiously. She blushed. 'He wanted it to be just a secret between us.'

Dolour whistled. 'You mean, like an engagement ring?'

'Maybe,' stammered Roie. Mumma nodded in a pleased way. She liked romantic secrets. Roie continued desperately: 'He thought perhaps people might think he was showing off giving me such an expensive present.'

'There's something in that, too,' approved Hughie.

Roie sat beside him and shook the brooch so that the little tassels rang. 'They're real rubies,' she marvelled, peering into the dark garnet depths of the balas. Rapture filled her soul. Her imagination was so strong that she could easily see Tommy giving her the brooch wrapped up in tissue paper and saying: 'This is a secret for us, like an engagement ring.'

Dolour cried: 'Crumbs, he must think a lot of you, Ro. Maybe he pinched it.' But Roie knew that she had won her point, that her family was admiring and respecting Tommy's generosity and taking it as a tribute to her own attractiveness. She felt warm and excited. It was almost as good as if it had really happened that way. Without regrets, she allowed the image of the yellow cotton dress, with a drawstring neck, to fade from her mind.

'What's that other parcel?' inquired Mumma. Roie said carelessly 'Oh, that's a nice cake of soap and a face-cloth that Mrs Siciliano gave me. I went in to wish her Merry Christmas, and she gave me that, funny old thing.'

So Christmas ended very happily.

The day after Boxing Day, Mumma did her shopping at Mr Jacky Siciliano's, a thing she never did, for Lick Jimmy was both closer and cheaper. But she wanted to thank Mrs Siciliano for being so kind as to give Roie a present. She had hardly ordered her weekend fruit before Mrs Siciliano burst out: 'You see the bella brooch I sell to Roie, eh, Mrs Darcia?'

Mumma's heart jumped in her shabby bosom. She waited a moment, then she answered quickly: 'It is a beautiful brooch.'

'I brought it with me all the way from Milan,' explained Mrs Siciliano. A tear sprang liquidly and brilliantly into her beautful eyes, and she thumped herself on her enormous breast. 'Ah, they are all-a gone now . . . the lace shawl, the turtle-shell-a combs, the white linen pantaletta, and the gold ear-rings with the little bells hanging. But I have to have the money. I am having another bambino, you see.'

Mumma expressed polite surprise, though Mrs Siciliano's habitual condition was such.

The Italian woman continued, 'Only thirty-bob-a. It was bargain! But Roie she look after it for me. No, she say she going to give-a it to someone who had not a present. Well, that somebody look-a after it for me.' Mrs Siciliano rapidly polished the air in front of her as though to wipe out the whole conversation and asked briskly: 'You want-a broccoli today?'

Mumma walked slowly home, laden down like a horse with two great kits of foodstuffs.

'Oh, Roie . . . Roie, my little girl.'

The innocence and naiveté of Roie made her feel both proud and sorry, for she had been the same herself until she learned that nobody could be naivè in such a world as this and not end up with a broken heart.

'I wish she hadn't fallen in love so early,' said Mumma sadly, for to her love meant sacrifice, and Roie's sacrifice both of her truthfulness and her thirty shillings was solid proof indeed that she loved Tommy Mendel.

Seven

The New Year was important in Surry Hills. It was really the great feast of the year, uninhibited by religious thoughts, and with a pagan finality about it. Those people, simple and primitive, but with a great capacity for feeling the abstract strong and vital about them, really heard the Old Year's faltering footsteps, and the clang of the door which sounded in the midnight chimes on December 31st. So they made it a feast, with lots of noise and ribaldry, as ancient peoples did when they were a little fearful, and wanted to frighten away their fear.

Where Coronation Street met Plymouth Street there was a rough rectangle striped silver with tramlines. Every year it was the custom to build a bonfire there, just out of reach of the trams, which rushed past in a fleeting crimson glow from the flames. The authorities always forbade it, and nobody ever took any notice of what they said, but went on lighting New Year bonfires just the same.

It was Thady's birthday on the last day of the year, and Mumma always approached it with a sadness she could not control. They all felt this sadness, in a ready emotionalism which made tears spring to the eyes at the sound of a familiar song.

Grandma always felt a cold wind blow over her, for who was to tell whether this was not her last New Year?

To Roie the whole sweet scroll of the year was there, unblemished and white as snow. Christmas had been enchanted, and the enchantment had driven her on to this day, which she felt, fatalistically, would be important in her life. She dressed herself with special care, washing her body all over in the tub in the laundry. It was only a little tub, and when she breathed most of the water flew out. But when she finished, warm and clean, and dried herself on the hard old scrap of a towel, she felt light and airy and indescribably precious, as though her body had all at once become significant. Roie was a modest girl; she stacked lumps of firewood against the laundry door so that Hughie or Patrick Diamond should not come bursting in. In the dim light she looked down at her slender form and wondered. How strange it was! She breathed 'Tommy!' and stretched out her arms longing to hold him and be close to him.

Dolour and Hughie were the most excited of all. Their childish souls looked forward with wriggling impatience and rapture to the bonfire, and the spuds they would roast in the red embers afterwards and all the yarning, and the camaraderie and the high jinks.

'You like flire!' asked Lick Jimmy of Dolour as she bought the potatoes. 'They bling flire bligade and put him out,' he prophesied gleefully, his satin ivory face breaking into ten thousand hair-fine wrinkles. Dolour scoffed: 'Just as though anybody would be such spoilsports. You're silly, sometimes, Jimmy.'

All the afternoon the kids were dragging refuse to the fire. Most of the mothers thought that it was a good opportunity to get rid of all the old clothes and newspapers around the house, and the kids took their trolleys and trundled all the afternoon, with shouts and jeers at each other, as they spied familiar articles. Harry Drummy, reckless as all the Drummys, brought a whole barrow load of paper which would have been sold to Lick Jimmy or Mr Siciliano for the price of at least two Saturday afternoons at the pictures. Dolour Darcy brought two old chairs, which Miss Sheily, in the height of rage, had suddenly hurled down the stairs to her.

'Take the foul things and burn them,' cried Miss Sheily. 'They've got bugs in them, and I'm sick of having my bottom nipped every time I sit on them. Caesar's ghost, a woman can't even sit down in this place without being injured.'

So Dolour bore them rapturously off. Mumma reckoned that they had little to burn at all, for they wore all their old clothes, and used their old newspapers as packing for their beds in winter, as newspaper is warmer than blankets and doesn't require washing.

By the time the clear blue of evening was in the air, the bonfire was twelve feet high, with a base like a redwood tree. It was going to be the biggest bonfire Surry Hills had ever had. Dolour was so excited she couldn't eat any tea, though it was her favourite mince pie with potato crust marked into little channels with a fork. A dozen times she ran down to the bonfire to see how it was getting on, and to exchange pleasantries with the small boys posted there to guard it against the inevitable drunken lout who would want to set it off before its time.

By the time the street lamps lighted into high, far, wire-guarded topaz globes, there was quite a crowd, sitting on doorsteps, squatting on kerbs, and leaning idly against walls. An air of satisfied expectancy was abroad. Father Cooley came out of the presbytery and pottered around amongst his parishioners for a little while, then tactfully went off. Sister Beatrix, on her way to chapel, stood on tiptoe and peered out between the grilles to see if she could spy the yellow spark of the fire.

Grandma had dressed herself as well as she was able, and put on an old cardigan with a huge hole in the elbow. She had brushed her white hair back very neatly, and was hanging over the gate, looking with bright-eyed curiosity at the passers-by, trying to pick out which ones were the prostitutes, the bash-gang men, and the cockatoos from the SP joint. Grandma's interest in sin was indefatigable.

Roie and Tommy wandered off early, into the shadow of the alleys, emerging to look astonished at the stars, so bright and enchanted tonight that they threw shadows. Once they came across, in a deserted street, a blind cat with opal-white eyes, walking around and around in a ceaseless circle, mewing pitifully. They stood and watched it moving in its endless darkness. Roie shuddered close to Tommy. A great gulp came out of her throat. Then a man came briskly out of a gate, seized the cat by the hind legs and thumped it six or seven times against a lamp-post. He threw the limp body into the gutter, and rubbed his hands down his trousers.

'Can't put up with that yowling all night,' he said cheerily to them as he walked inside again.

'Ah, God!' Roie and Tommy started to run. They panted down into Plymouth Street again. Tears streamed down Roie's face, and her throat ached with pain. Tommy held her face close to his jacket; he wanted to comfort her, but he did not know what to say.

'It couldn't see! It couldn't see!' was all Roie could murmur.

Suddenly there was a glad roar in the distance, and, startled, they looked up. Tommy, with glistening eyes, cried: 'It's on!' They forgot everything and pelted down towards the bonfire. They overtook Hughie, hurrying along with Grandma, very pigeon-toed, and discussing the whole thing energetically with her invisible familiar; Mumma waddled along behind, and behind her again came Miss Sheily, a look of supreme disinterest on her face, because she thought it beneath her to go to watch a bonfire. As they got there a long red streak of flame licked up the side of the pile, and sparkled across the surface of the scattered papers. A second later there was a yellow glare, as some old books which Mrs Siciliano had saturated with grease and kerosene caught the flame. Whoosh! A ragged blue tongue of fire spurted high into the air, and everyone sprang back and surveyed it with awed excitement.

'Bravo! Bravo!' yelled Jacky Siciliano, and he kissed his wife with pride because she had thought of the kerosene. And all the black-haired little Siciliano brats danced gipsy-like around the bonfire, yelling shrilly.

Roie looked awed at the rose-red tower of flame, and the little hyacinth-blue sparks that showed and vanished. A ruby glow was cast over every face, the good and the wicked, the old and the young – old women with their hair rosy with reflected light; little goblin children, dirty and hungry, with bony brows and big, shining eyes; even babies with grubby wrinkled faces, blinking painfully in the glare. Dolour jumped up and down with hysterical excitement. The Old Year hovered around them; he was like a shadow vanishing bit by bit under an onslaught of light; all his fears and terrors, his failures and monotonies seemed now something soon to be tossed away upon the stream of time, to be forgotten for ever. Dolour did not feel this; she was only glad that she was one year older than this time last year; that she was almost fourteen, and not a child any longer, and soon would be freed from school and allowed to go to work.

Hughie stood with a grin frozen on his red-lit face. He thought:

'New Year resolutions . . . kid stuff. I'll keep off the plonk, except on Saturdays, because it does a man no harm to have a bit of a gee-up now and again.'

Dolour dreamed: 'Perhaps this year I'll find a diamond ring which nobody claims, or a five-pound note, or get on a quiz-session on the radio and win three hundred pounds and a fur coat for Mumma.' She wanted it so hard that tears gushed into her eyes, and her face turned crimson.

Mumma meditated: 'Thady would have been sixteen today. He would have been a big feller, like my family, because boys take after their mothers. He had blue eyes, and his hair was fair and sheeny-looking. But it might have gone dark. He might have looked like that boy over there . . . or that one.' And her heart cried out achingly: 'Oh, God, where is my little boy? Wherever he is, don't let anyone hurt him.'

Miss Sheily, staring into the yellow tongues of fire, thought: 'Last year Johnny was here. He laughed, and then he was frightened, and crouched down behind me.' Nobody could have told from Miss Sheily's acidly cold face what she was thinking, but the people standing near her moved uneasily away, for they could sense the chill waves of desolation that emanated from her.

And old Patrick Diamond, his stiff white hair roughly brushed over his low brow, his ruddy skin paler than it had been the year before, thought: 'What is the difference? One more lonely year. A long and empty life on the outskirts of other people's families. And no joy in it for a lonely man.'

He felt the premonitory prickling in his vitals, and then his stomach filled with nauseous pain. His indigestion was growing worse. He moved away quickly and stood amongst the crowd, so that Hughie wouldn't see the look on his face.

Suddenly there was a roar of laughter as Lick Jimmy, bent almost double under the weight of a huge humped mattress, trotted bent-kneed down the road.

'Mlind! Make wlay!' he giggled, flashing smiles to right and left as he peered under the drooping mattress. From a rent in its side kapok fell in a snowstorm, littering the street. With a gigantic heave Jimmy tossed it on the fire. There was a white puff of stinking smoke that billowed out and almost obscured a passing tram.

'Hooray! You beaut!' cheered everyone, and Lick Jimmy, taking it as a compliment, shook his clasped hands at them and vanished into the darkness again.

Suddenly, as though the sound fell from amongst the frequent and glossy stars, came the goblin wail of far-away sirens, blowing, blowing, in loops and streamers of sound.

'It's the New Year!' shouted Mr Siciliano, and he blessed himself with great, vigorous thumps. Then he seized his wife around her huge waist, and they danced like two elephants. Hughie gave Mumma a timid, shamefaced kiss on the cheek. She was delighted. 'Oh, Hughie!' she said, and then he kissed her properly. The sound of bells commenced. With harsh, jangling sweetness they swung and clashed in some far-off church tower; they shook out their simple music from narrow slotted windows, and it ran into waves and concussions of sound all over the huge and noisy city.

'Happy New Year!' shrieked everyone, and down in the dirtiest part of Surry Hills two hundred people linked hands and danced like red-lit gnomes about the fire; they forgot everything except the pagan pleasure of dancing in a warm and lighted circle of company and safety, with the dark outside it.

Roie and Tommy broke away. They ran up a dark street and stopped panting by a doorway. Tommy's lips felt their way over her cheek to her mouth. He felt excited and strong but he still did not know how to kiss her. He just pressed his lips on hers so hard that she nearly suffocated. They trembled; their eyes shone and their blood beat fast.

'Let's go for a walk. I'm sick of yammering boneheads.'

'Mumma'll miss me.'

'She knows I'll look after you.'

Two shadows passed swiftly through the starlit patch that slanted diagonally past the huge black bulk of the church, and the street was empty.

Back at the bonfire Mumma was breathlessly trying to disentangle her hands from Grandma's dry horny one and Dolour's hot erratic paw, when all at once there was a loudening shriek, swooping down the distant slope of Coronation Street. It was the fire engine. Almost simultaneously a large policeman detached himself from the fence. 'Move along,' he commanded, authoritatively. 'Move along there. Break it up. Move along.'

'Here,' protested Hughie. 'Don't tell me them cows in brass helmets is going to douse our fire?'

'All fires forbidden,' retorted the policeman. 'You read it in the newspapers, and it's posted up on the post-office wall.'

Beefy-faced, solemn, he inspired instant hatred in the crowd. There were yells of: 'Ole wet blanket. Why the hell don't you go home and go to bed?'

'Trust the bloody coppers to break up a bit of innocent fun.'

'Feet like wash-tubs.'

This caught Mr Diamond's fancy. He was by now slightly drunk having withdrawn to the shadows to have a nip or three from the bottle in his pocket, just to ease his indigestion. He began to revolve on his own axis, quietly chanting: 'Feet like wash-tubs. Feet like wash-tubs.'

The policeman quelled a smile. He prodded Mr Diamond gently. 'Come on, get along home. You've had enough for the night.'

Immediately Mr Siciliano, round as a barrel and dark as thunder, rolled up to him: 'Here, you flatfoot. You leave my friend alone. He has-a done nuttin.'

Mr Diamond looked down his hooky nose at him. 'No friend of mine, you black smoke. Go on, outa me way.' He waved an arm, and it struck the policeman across his cap and forced it down over his nose. Immediately an urchin, sneaking between the legs of the crowd, bit the blinded representative of the law savagely on the calf. The policeman gave an involuntary yell, thinking he had been stabbed, and promptly blew his whistle.

The fire brigade stopped further up Coronation Street to put out a smaller fire. Now it came ripping down the road, and stopped in all its splendour of crimson and brass helmets. Its arrival coincided with that of Delie Stock, who had just sidled out of her alley and was standing on the outskirts of the crowd, her eyes sparkling with indignation. 'Can't let the kids have a bit of fun,' shrilled Delie Stock.

'Aw, stow it, will ya, ma?' called back one of the firemen. With a high squawk of rage, Delie Stock picked up a potato from the heap which had been put aside for roasting in the embers. She hurled it with unerring aim, and the next moment a perfect hail of potatoes fell and clanged about the fireman's helmet. The policeman, struggling in the centre of the crowd, was a man besieged. Half a dozen old women battered him around the waist, and the taller members of the crowd clunked him with anything handy. Nobody hit very hard, and the policeman's dignity was hurt more than his head. Grandma, with eyes glittering with excitement, and a red spot in each cheek, was making a great to-do about getting a suitable potato. She picked up two or three before she found a nice round solid one that fitted into her hand. She had her arm raised to throw it, murmuring: 'Great splaw-footed spalpeen,' and 'I'll send it clean through his brisket,' when the horrified Mumma seized it from her hand. Grandma was bereaved, for she came from a long line of wild boys and girls who had specialized in potting King's Men from behind hedges, in the insurrections. While they argued about the justice of the matter, the firemen, with potatoes bouncing resoundingly off their helmets, played their hoses on the fire.

Dolour burst into tears: 'And it was such a lovely fire, the old bastards!'

Hughie was appalled. 'You cut that out, or I'll skelp yer hind shoulders good and proper.'

'You can talk, you and yer swearing,' fired up Mumma in defence of her child. The water cut a glittering white arc, falling in a hissing torrent across the street. The children wailed: 'Awwwwwwwww!' and the struggle around the policeman began with renewed fervour, many trying to rescue him before some lout hit him with a broken bottle, and others trying to commit assault on his person. There was a shrieked colloquy among the firemen, and all at once the nozzles of the hoses were pointed right at the crowd. It was packed too tightly for any one of them to move away quickly. Grandma was torn from Mumma's restraining hand, and washed away, a rain-bowed spray of water beating against the back of her neck and blowing her white hair up in an enraged crest. Delie Stock was right before a nozzle, and the force of the roaring crystal stream threw her violently across the street. It was the first time she had had a bath for thirty years, and she loathed it. She lay in the gutter bubbling and spitting out curses in a half-drowned tone. As she pulled herself up to a sitting position another avalanche of water washed her further down the street, where she lay spreadeagled over a grating until somebody picked her up.

Grandma was shuddering like a tree in a wind, and talking rapidly to herself and everyone else in a voice which grew more Irish every moment. She had never had such a time in her life. Her enjoyment was so evident that Mumma was not only anxious, she was furious. She seized Grandma by her stick-like arm and marched her up Plymouth Street, Grandma pulling back and complaining, and dripping wet at every step, and finally bursting into tears of rage and over-excitement.

Hughie and Patrick Diamond, soaked to the skin, and muddy to the elbow from rolling in the drenched dust, heard the fire engine start and whirr away to some other fire. In the semi-darkness they looked sadly at the drenched black mess which had been their lovely bonfire. A dripping and shivering figure flew up to them. It was Dolour, her cotton frock clinging to every bone in her thin body, her hair plastered in dark rat-tails.

'You little chump, why didn't you get out of the way of the water?' demanded Hughie with angry anxiety. Patrick snarled: 'Why didn't you?' and then all three laughed. The crowd laughed with them.

'Well, we had our dance and our old langa-syne,' said Jacky Siciliano philosophically. He gathered up all his chicks. 'Come, Antonetta! Rosina, Amelia, Grazia, Maria, Violetta and Giacomo!'

Mrs Siciliano, who had been looking as though she were listening to some elusive sound, very distant, suddenly gave a shrill scream and bent over, clasping her hands to her abdomen. The whole crowd of Sicilianos, chattering and screeching amid groans and ejaculations of 'Dio Mio!' hurried down the road, Mamma Siciliano in the middle like a clumsy hen. Hughie, looking after them, shrugged: 'Ah, well, another one in the basket before morning.'

'They're going to call it Michelangelo,' remarked Dolour with bright, interested eyes.

The evening had ended in the sort of excitement Plymouth Street loved. The kiddies played in the pools of dust-streaked water, and the toddlers chewed bits of charred potato, and had to be dragged shrieking home to dry clothes and bed. The elders said they had never had so much fun in all their lives, and shouting gaily across the streets they straggled home. The New Year was here, and bright and shining it stretched before them, unblemished by any failure, unsmudged by sorrow or ignominy. They found it impossible to think of it in any way except optimistically.

Eight

Down in the park, in the dark spokes of shade which radiated from a phoenix palm, Roie and Tommy lay. It was one o'clock, and very quiet. Only a cricket chirped in the moonlight. It was hard to believe that they were almost in the centre of a great industrial city.

Tommy looked up at the sheaves of rich golden 'dates' which hung above him. He was so troubled he did not know what to do. Although he had received a normal education he had so few instincts of right and wrong that he was morally a savage. He was almost incapable of comprehending another person's viewpoint, or imagining the consequences of his deeds in another's life. So when he desired Roie, he thought nothing of Roie. He loved her only because she induced in him a sense of importance, and a sequence of pleasurable sensations. Most of all, he wanted to have an experience, which he could recount in lingering detail to his mates. They all boasted so much, and though he boasted, too, he always felt that they listened to his lies only through pity for his physical deformity. He knew that they knew he had never had a girl; there had been nothing worth boasting about in his life according to his standards. But he did not know how to go about making love to Roie. His desires choked him, and he did not know how to start the cycle that would release them.

He felt ashamed of himself, knowing that he did not have the forwardness or the coarse male pride that would permit him to take her by force, no matter how much she struggled. Yet, unknowing, his quietness and unease won her as force would never have done.

As he lay with his head on her little breast, a strange and delicate feeling stole over Roie. His soft hair was under her chin, so soft it was like a child's hair. She knew he was not the tender and masterful lover her dreams had built; he did not fit into the mould created by books and films; his words were ordinary, his body was slight and ill-formed, and his clothes were musty-smelling, rough to feel, and ugly to look at. There was nothing admirable, romantic, or even desirable about him. Deep in her heart Roie knew all this, yet she fiercely drove the knowledge back before the force of her love and pity for, and understanding of him. She deliberately shut her eyes to all that was weak or foolish, because in her mind recognition of it would be disloyalty to her love for him. She rubbed her cheek gently against his hair, springy and faintly warm. She said shyly: 'Darling.' He answered nothing, pressing his face closer, and trembling. It was queer; it was like the time when, in the country, she had come across a rabbit in a trap, and, running her finger along its silken side, she had felt the minute, continuous vibration of its terror.

She held him as a mother might an agitated child. 'Tommy, this isn't any good for you or me either. Let's get up and go home. It's time.'

He held her tightly and mumbled hoarsely.

'No,' she said, frightened suddenly. 'No, I can't.'

He snarled in a sudden fury: 'It's the same with all you sheilas. Giving a bloke the come-on for all you're worth, and then all at once, biff, it's turned off at the main.'

He put his head down on her breast again and she felt a tear fall on her skin. It was as though she were made of ice, and the warm tear melted it.

'Tommy . . . Tommy, darling, don't . . .'

'God, I wish you felt as I feel. I wish you were a man, just for a minute. Then you wouldn't say no to me again, ever.'

For a brief moment she had a wordless, almost uncomprehended glimpse into his mind; she saw as he did, his drab room somewhere, the chafings of his daily life, the disillusionments that had always been his; the surgings of manhood which distorted his outlook, broke into his sleep, and interrupted the flow of his whole existence. She felt such tenderness her heart nearly broke.

'Tommy, you do love me, don't you?'

He wanted to say 'Ah, hell!' but already he had learned that it was better to say yes.

'Roie, would I feel like this if I didn't? Ah, Ro, only once, I swear I'll never ask you again.'

It was too late to retreat. His breath on her face, his clumsy, uncontrolled kisses on her throat, Roie struggled for an instant. She wanted to yell for her mother. But the black panic which engulfed her became grey, and then faded into nothing at all. Did it matter? Did anything matter but to serve the blinding love and desire to please that possessed her?

'No, Tommy . . . please, Tommy, no.'

But she knew, all the same, as she had subconsciously known when she dressed that evening, that it was the end. The stars swung down, and were blotted out by his shoulder.

Afterwards, walking up the street, they were self-conscious and afraid to look at each other. Roie tried very hard to feel uplifted and thrilled, as she knew people in books and in pictures felt, but there was nothing in her heart but an ache and a terror of realization. She wanted to cry on Tommy's shoulder, but she knew bleakly that he wouldn't understand what it was all about. When they saw an empty tram swing around the corner, an illuminated red and yellow beetle, they were both so glad that they began to run.

'Feel all right, kid?' asked Tommy as she swung aboard.

She smiled. 'Sure, I feel fine.' Her lips trembled.

'I'll be around Wednesday.' He half-pushed her into the tram, and crying 'Goodbye, here's yer fare,' he shoved threepence into her hand.

Roie didn't say anything. She was afraid that the ache in her throat would grow and engulf her self-control. Oh, God! Was it like this with everyone? Disappointment and apathy and a let-down feeling worse than anything on earth? She sat heedlessly staring into the darkness, blotched with faint light, that flowed past the open door. Why had she done it? She began to shake, cold and prickling alarm enveloping her. Forgotten was that moment of pity and understanding for Tommy, and the tenderness which, like something out of heaven, with the dew still on it, had flooded her heart.

But the threepence hurt worst of all.

Crawling into bed later, Roie pushed the whimpering Dolour over on her own side with more than usual ferocity.

'Quit crawling all over me, will you?'

She glared down at the pinched mouse face of the child whey-white in the moonlight, her upper lip raised over two dry and shiny rabbit teeth, her eyelids heavy circles of sleep.

'Stop yer kicking,' wailed Dolour in a thick, sleep-sodden voice, which drifted away into a complaining mumble.

'Yeah,' whispered Roie with unreasonable savagery, raising her swollen face from the pillow. 'You just wait until it happens to you. You just wait until you find out what it's all about.'

Then she put her arm over Dolour and hugged her thin and bony little body close, vowing that she would never suffer as she, Roie, was suffering.

The next morning it did not seem so bad. It was so strange and unfamiliar a happening that it was almost unreal. Roie lived as though in a dream until Wednesday, when Tommy came around for her. They went to the pictures, treating each other with courteous attention, just like strangers. Roie made desperate efforts to recapture the thrill that had once been hers when she sat next to him, the brush of his fingers on her arm, the sound of his breath. But it was all gone. Strangely and mysteriously it had gone. Tommy looked at her, her lower lip thrust out sulkily, her eyes sombre, and thought with what fast turned to indignation, 'I suppose she wants me to crawl to her – tell her how wonderful she was to give in to me. Yeah, some chance of that. Just like any other sheila. It's true what the boys say . . . they're all alike when you've got to know them.'

He did not feel desire for her any longer. She might have been almost anyone. Any rate, she hadn't been so marvellous; discussing the incident in minutest detail with his mates, he had found out that other girls could provide much more excitement.

Outside the picture show he said, 'Saw my Uncle Joseph last night.'

'Yeah?' trembled Roie, trying to be interested.

'Yeah. He's getting me a job all right. Funny you should mention it the other day. He's getting me a job in a boot factory at Leichhardt; so I won't be seeing you so often.'

Roie instantly recognized the tone in his voice for what it was. She tried to be angry, hurt, almost anything rather than the apathy which possessed her.

'You needn't think I care,' she said, piteously defiant.

'Don't be bats. I'll come over as often as I can,' he said. He felt a little regretful. She was a nice kid; she'd looked pretty in that old red shawl. Even now he was half willing that they should continue their relationship.

'Sure,' said Roie.

She stood there for a moment, her lip trembling, not looking at him. There seemed to be nothing to say at all. All at once, almost violently, life returned to her limbs and mumbling something she did not hear herself, she ran away up the street. She did not want to see Tommy limping away, no longer the centre of her existence, but just an ordinary young man with untidy hair and the mark of a boil on his neck. She ran into the church, for her breath was beginning to come in sobs and she knew that at any moment she might cry. It was shabby and drab in there, but its silence thrust away the street noises until it was as though she knelt in an oasis of quiet and peace.

'Oh, gee,' she prayed, 'what did I do wrong? I tried to give him everything he wanted. But I'm not sorry he doesn't love me any more . . . that's the dreadful thing. I'm not sorry. I don't love him either. We lost it somewhere. Oh, God, why does it happen like that?'

Then her fear caught up with her, and she cried in a mental voice so full of anguish that she felt it would reach to the ear of God Himself.

'Oh, Lord, let me get away with it this time! I won't ever do it again. Don't let anything happen to me, for Mumma's sake. Oh, Lord, please don't!'

She looked at the altar, wishing a candle might miraculously light, or even a flower fall out of a vase . . . anything that would tell her that heaven, with an invisible stream of light, had opened towards her. But there was nothing but silence and the muffled orchestra of the trams in the far distance.

She said over and over again, 'I'm wicked, I'm wicked,' but no comprehension of the words came into her mind. She felt no weight of sin, and she was bitterly ashamed, for it was as though all the teaching she had ever had was gone for nought.

Roie entered upon a period of cruel and agonized waiting for reassurance. Every minute as it crawled by was filled with unutterable confusion. She found it impossible to hide it all, and everyone noticed that there was something wrong with her. Mumma put it down to the bust-up Roie had told her she had had with Tommy, but consoled herself with the thought that it was all for the best, for a Jew and a Catholic are not the best of religious partners. She slept restlessly, so that at last Dolour complained.

'She's still thinking about Tommy,' chuckled Grandma maliciously. Mumma flared: 'You shut up, with yer unkind remarks, Ma. It's more likely them bugs up there in that room.'

'It is, too,' said Roie fiercely, glaring at Grandma, 'chewing the feet off me every night.'

Hughie shrugged resignedly. 'They're in the cracks of the old dump. You'd have to burn it down before you got rid of them.'

'Then why can't we go somewhere where there ain't no bugs?' asked Dolour. 'Are there bugs in all the houses in Sydney?'

'How should I know? Have I been everywhere?' asked Mumma. Roie flung herself down at the table and looked at a newspaper.

'Look at this: "Beautiful Socialite Weds Visiting Actor". Bet she never got up in the morning dead-tired through being bitten to death all night. Bet bugs don't crawl out of her nightdress on her honeymoon. Dirty stinking things. I'm sick of them!'

'Well, what are you yelling about them now for? We've had them all our lives, haven't we?' asked Dolour reasonably. Hughie suddenly thumped the table.

'Let's declare war on the foul creatures!' he cried with enthusiasm. 'Come on, Dolour, go and get the kerosene, and Grandma, you can bring up yer pipe. It'd smoke anything out of its hole.'

'Hugh!' remonstrated Mumma, blushing. She put their dinner in the oven, and they all trooped upstairs, Grandma well behind, because she had had a bad cold since New Year's Eve, and felt a strange heaviness in her bones.

Hughie turned over the bed, and they pulled it to pieces.

'Ah, look at the cows!' he ejaculated. He held his nose, and his blue eyes looked over the knot of his fingers with a disgusted horror. For there were more bugs than could be believed. In every pit and screwhole, every joint and crack they clustered, so thickly that sometimes there were whole marshalled lines of them, hidden cunningly in a twist of the wire or a crevice in the iron. A faint filthy smell arose from them alive. Dead, they would smell overpoweringly, of mingled musk and ammonia.

'Every night's blood transfusion night for them,' said Dolour. 'Whee, lookut them run!'

'Why can't we get a fumigator in?' asked Roie querulously. 'We've done this a thousand times. Washed down the beds with kerosene. Burnt them out of all the cracks, and what happens? A month later we've got them worse than ever.'

'Well, it stands to reason you won't never have *no* bugs,' pointed out Mumma reasonably. 'Everyone's got bugs around here.'

'Why don't the Government do something about it? That's what I'd like to know,' said Hughie, lighting a twist of newspaper and running it deftly along the thick currant-like clusters. They shrivelled up under his eyes, and fell to the floor, a scattering of dirty little brown corpses. 'A gink from New Zealand was telling me it's a crime to have bugs over there. You get fined if they's found in yer house.'

'A fine thing that is!' said Grandma indignantly. 'As though it's a body's own fault.'

'The point is,' explained Dolour, 'if everyone had no bugs then nobody would have any bugs.'

'Say, you think that up yourself?' asked Hughie admiringly.

'Ah, shut up!' snapped Roie. She dabbed a brush in the kerosene and began painting the wooden parts of the bed. Everywhere before her brush rudely awakened bugs scurried away. Without distaste or disgust she crushed under her shoe the ones that fell on the floor. She was inured to their filthy smell; she had been squashing bugs all her life, for only in the coldest months of winter were the slum houses free of them, as it was then that they hibernated in half-dead transparent clusters in the walls and furniture. Roie could have told you all about them, the tiny white baby bug whose bite is the most vicious; the mature bug, brown like a woodlouse and marked in tiny ridges across the back, which feeds until it is so bloated it is shiny, and disgorges droplets of blood at every step. She could have told you that bugs rear up on their hindlegs in order to bite; that they are terrified of light and move with extraordinary swiftness; she could have described the way they tormented her whilst she was at work, for it is so difficult to find a bug that is adept at hiding under the narrowest seam. Bugs had dwelt with her since she was a baby, as they had dwelt with her parents and grandparents, and the people who had occupied Number Twelve-and-a-Half before them.

Cynically she watched Hughie's enthusiastic efforts, for she knew that nothing short of cyanide ever cleared them out of a house. Even then they were back again in a year or two, migrating from the house next door as soon as the poison died out of the timbers. And who would pay for a cyanide fumigation? Not the landlord; he got his rent even if his property were vermin-infested.

Hughie screwed up the bed again, and Grandma swept up all the corpses and bits of burned paper. Mumma felt happy and satisfied. 'There now, Roie love; you'll sleep better tonight.'

'Nobody cares how I sleep,' complained Dolour.

Hughie gave her a slap on the tail as they went downstairs. 'You sleep like a dead horse. I can hear you snoring every night, right through the floor.'

Late that night Roie lay awake, for the night was hot and stifling, and Dolour restless, kicking her savagely, and lying diagonally across her body and clutching her with feverish nightmare-ridden hands.

'Oh, God,' moaned Roie. 'If only I could have a bed to meself!'

She got up and leaned out the window. The backyard, shrouded in shadows, was beautiful, the white moonlight clothing ugly prosaic things with a milky vapour. A cat slunk, a padding shadow, across the white space, and she saw its eyes like glazy green circles in the darkness. Far away a tug hooted on Darling Harbour. But there was nothing of the sea in the air, only the rising breezes laden with the smells of the cooling earth; dry grass, and night flowers opening and the half-exotic odour of a great sleeping city.

She wanted to pray, but she could not. Her secret terror shook itself and awoke, filling all her body with a cold, prickling panic. What was the use of praying? God had hidden his face; the saints loathed her. There was nothing but confusion and darkness all around. Suddenly Roie heard a strange sound, a swishing, regular sound. And now and then there was a whimper, cut off short, as though it were jerked involuntarily out of someone. Roie's skin prickled; it seemed to be in the room, and then all at once a long way away. Could it be a ghost? For Roie believed most matter-of-factly in ghosts, and would not have been at all surprised to meet one.

Then she realized that it was coming from Miss Sheily's room, through the wall. She pressed her ear against the plaster, and it was much louder, a swish, a thud, a swish, a thud. What on earth was Miss Sheily doing? At first Roie thought of wakening Dolour, and asking her what she thought of it, and then she remembered the peephole.

The peephole was a tiny hole pecked in the wall at the end of the room. Long ago, when Roie and Dolour were children, they had discovered it, and had had a wonderful and illuminating time watching the squabbles and reconciliations of a young couple who lived there; Roie had learned more about the facts of life from the couple than she ever had from her mother's timorous teachings. Then one day Dolour and she had been discovered, and Mumma had blocked up the hole with putty and taken them both downstairs and lectured them for a solid half hour on miserable tom todgers who hadn't the honour to keep their sticky beaks out of other folks' privacy.

'It's worse than looking under the door of the lavatory,' Dolour had miserably confided to Roie later, after they had yelled their way upstairs, holding their wounded bottoms. But now Roie, without a thought of intruding on Miss Sheily's privacy, did something she hadn't thought of doing for years. She took a bobby pin and pecked out the putty and applied her eye to the hole. She could see a jagged piece of the next room, half lit by a bare electric light globe that had an old blue scarf draped over it. There was a dressing-table, and a corner of a shelf with a packet of cheese on it, and something that looked like half a loaf tied up in a tea-towel. And there was also Miss Sheily, kneeling down, her back bare, and her blouse hanging down around her waist.

At first Roie thought Miss Sheily was having a wash, and she was about to replace the putty when the swishing sound began again, and with a shiver of horror, her blood tingling with the shock, she saw that Miss Sheily was whipping herself.

'Oh, God!' thought Roie. 'She's gone mad!'

In her hand Miss Sheily had a bundle of knotted strings. They were tipped with something like sharp little screws of wire, and she was lashing her back with them. The whip flicked over her shoulders with regularity, falling with little thuds on her sharp shoulder-blades and the flat ugly back. And each time there was a thud, Miss Sheily's breath escaped in a little involuntary moan.

Roie was frozen with horror. She could never have imagined so bizarre a scene. She made wild gestures to the sleeping Dolour to wake and look, then she became aware that every time Miss Sheily moaned she moaned a word. It was 'Johnny'. The blood sprang up on her back in dark ruby beads, and a spiderweb of red marks slowly grew under the lash.

'Johnny! Johnny!' moaned Miss Sheily. Roie sat back from the peephole with a shudder of disgust and shock. She jammed back the little plug of crumbling putty and tottered over to the window, feeling sick.

'Oh, gosh,' said Roie. She was sorry she had spied, but only because she had been precipitated into such grief, and Miss Sheily's sour, bitter, determination to atone for the wrongs she had done her son.

Staring out into the desolate backyard, and the ebony channel of the alleyway, Roie wondered about life, and the strange way it revealed itself. Who would have guessed that Miss Sheily, so poker-faced, so consumed by bitter furies and hatred of everyone, was in secret whipping herself in an effort to . . . to what? Roie's conjectures fell short, though she was no stranger to the doctrine of atonement. She had been brought up on tales of saints who inflicted pain on themselves in an attempt to atone for the sins of themselves and the world.

'Poor Johnny,' sobbed Roie. 'Poor Miss Sheily.' The tears stung their way to her eyes, and she hung her head, so that the moonlight failed to find her in the slanting bay of the window. When she moved back to her bed, the moon had gone, and all was in darkness.

Nine

Saturday afternoon was the great afternoon of the week in Plymouth Street. The factory girls washed their hair and did it up in perforated aluminium curlers, put on old print dresses with sagging necklines and torn pockets, and sat on the peeling, cocoa-coloured balconies of the tenements, beating off the flies and saying: 'Gawd, ain't it hot!' Downstairs, on the pockmarked steps of the old houses and the drab boarded-up shops, old men sat, legs wide, their stomachs bulging open the top buttons of their pants, hats pulled down over their grey frowsy faces, and talked politics, racing, or lang syne.

Down into the mean canyon of the street the sunshine poured, like yellow wine, and under its magic there was a gleam and a glimmer over everything, so that shadows seemed furry and mysterious, and the iron lace around the balconies Moorish and exotic. Lick Jimmy came out, cleaned his window, scrubbed his step, his little black-clad bottom jiggling energetically as he did so. Then he went in and locked and bolted the door, and sat in his corner by the window, peering over the humped, comfortable back of his cat, which drowsed between two pineapples. Lick Jimmy, too, liked to watch Saturday afternoon in Plymouth Street.

Joseph Mendel came from between the concertinaed gratings which protected his front door from the blow-torch and the exploring hand. His round black velour hat clamped firmly on his white, intellectual head, he walked briskly off down the street. The skirt of his coat had a foreign look to it, different from the hip-hugging coats that the men of Plymouth Street liked to wear if they were young, or the baggy hand-me-downs that they had to wear if they were old.

Joseph Mendel was respectfully greeted as he passed, but there was no friendliness in the eyes which looked at him, for he held so many of the people there in bondage. There was something queer about him, as there was about his nephew Tommy, always a sly one in spite of his deformity, which should have taken some of the reticence out of him. They were both foreigners, Australian born, perhaps, but still with the black and antique seal of their ancestry upon them.

Hughie was asleep with the exhaustion of his heavy work and the heat, which had not ebbed for twelve or fourteen days of bush-fire and drought. Dolour was sprawled on the floor of her room reading movie magazines and chewing potato crisps. Roie was out for a walk. But after they had finished the lunch dishes Grandma and Mumma tidied their hair and went out and sat on the balcony, Grandma with her hair pulled back very tight and smooth from her bony freckled forehead and Mumma fatigued and yellow, her stockings wrinkling down into old dirty slippers, the heels of which had been trodden into pancakes. It was so hot on the balcony, yet there was air there, fresh with the breeze which played fugitive from Darling Harbour and came running over the city. The two of them sat there, rocking in the old, uncomfortable wooden chairs, the rush bottoms of which had poked through and were in the habit of pinching any unwary behind that sat upon them.

Grandma was not feeling very well; there was a drag in her feet as though an invisible anchor had attached itself to her heels. She asked: 'Where's that Tommy these days, love?'

'Oh, they had a fight. He'll come around again.'

'He's an unchancy one, that,' commented Grandma. Mumma took it as a personal slur upon Roie's good taste.

'A gammy foot's nothing in these days of trams,' she said crossly.

Grandma chewed rapidly for a few moments, for she was wondering how to broach a subject that was in her mind. Finally she said: 'You want to wise her up about men, lovie.'

Mumma flushed. She had a curiously pure and naivè mind and although every form of sin and obscenity had affronted her eyes while she lived in Plymouth Street she still cringed away from it as though it had been a beast, sly, lithe, and poisonous.

'Roie can look after herself, Ma. Anyway, Tommy ain't her first boy.'

'No,' said Grandma sagaciously, 'but he's the first one she's really liked, and that makes a difference.'

Mumma knew exactly what Grandma meant and because she did and had feared the same thing she became angry and tried to take it out on Grandma.

'Go on, you unnatural old sling-off, throwing mud at your own granddaughter,' she said heatedly. Grandma shrugged one shoulder and they went on rocking with determined rhythm, each intending that the other should see how utterly undisturbed she was. Then down the street came Chocolate Molly.

She was an Indian half-caste; she was a beautiful girl lost in a gigantically fat body. Magnificent eyes as lucent and black as glass flashed and flirted out of a face that was drawn in a succession of little curves, curved eyebrows and mouth, curved cheeks and chins. A green dress was drawn as tightly as upholstery over her bulges and her monstrous legs vanished abruptly into the tiny slippered feet of a fat woman.

'Lord look down on yer!' exclaimed Mumma. 'I wonder she's got the nerve to show her face!'

'What's she done now?' asked Grandma eagerly. 'Run off with someone's husband again?'

'Not her, the dirty little scrub,' returned Mumma, looking with unconsciously jealous eyes at the way all the men's eyes followed Chocolate Molly as she waddled up the street. 'Put the coppers on to Delie Stock's dope peddling, that's all. Fifty pound they say she got out of it. Delie managed to get out of it, but she'll be after Molly with an axe.'

Chocolate Molly was feeling nervous. She knew that pimping in Surry Hills rarely went unpunished. She was stupid and impulsive and had squealed on Delie Stock mainly because she had refused to sell her some wine at a decent price the day before. Still, she felt that little harm could come to her in an open street on Saturday afternoon.

She glanced liquidly at men on street corners draped against doorways and clotted in groups like flies before the pub doors.

'Hello, Teddy,' she called to a lank pimply youth who squatted in a doorway combing his long, oily hair. 'When you coming up again?' He winked and guffawed, jerking his head at the men around to draw attention to the conversation.

'What'll I get if I do?' he called.

'Why don't you come and see?' she shrieked across the street. Mumma blushed and looked away from Grandma, but Grandma chuckled like an old magpie and croaked admiringly: 'The dirty neygar.' Chocolate Molly, her confidence restored, waddled onwards. The lank young man, belatedly, shouted after her: 'You better watch your step, blossom. Phyllis and Flo are after yer.'

'What?' she shrieked. He made gestures, but they were lost on her. She drifted onwards. The young man shrugged, and went back to his rolling of a straw-thin cigarette. If Chocolate Molly chose to stick her fat neck out, why should he stop her?

All at once, just by the little dank alley which ran alongside the ham-and-beef shop, Molly noticed Phyllis and Flo. They were a strange pair. Phyllis was very young, about sixteen, with an oblong, solid face lined and grimed with guilt. She had been a prostitute since she was ten. Her eyes were currant-brown, furtive and rabbity, darting away from the onlooker's stare. Her body was thick and lumpish, as graceless as a bathtub. On the other hand, Flo was a tall, slender, elderly woman, with a face painted into the semblance of gentility. She wore a tight black costume, and her hair was set with steely rigidity into the most elegant of afternoon-tea coiffures. She even wore gloves.

The sight of the two was more sinister to Chocolate Molly than that of a man with a knife in his hand, for they were both employees of Delie Stock. She noted the gloating greed upon the moronic face of the younger girl, and the cruel, vulture-like expression in the yellow eyes of Flo.

'Why, hello, Molly love,' said Flo in her tight, genteel voice. Mumma felt quite sick. Her hand closed over the withered arm of Grandma, in order to take her inside. But Grandma let out a yelp of indignation and shook it off.

'What are yer, yer wet blanket, spoiling the only bit of fun I get?' she complained.

Chocolate Molly, cornered, attempted to brazen it out.

'What you want, eh? You get outa my way, you bag of bones,' she said, for she did not lack courage. Phyllis swore explosively. She was like an animal trained to maul and kill, and she was chafing at the bonds of Flo's restraint. Her pig-like eyes roamed all over Molly's luscious and defenceless frame, as though choosing a vulnerable spot.

'Yer stinking stoolie,' remarked Flo softly in her strange cracked voice. And beside her Phyllis jerked and reared like a tethered hound hungry to get in for the kill. Molly stood her ground.

'You touch me, and I'll tell the coppers,' she said loudly, glancing back at the men who stood watching.

'Yeah, if we leave yer lousy tongue in yer lousy head,' jeered Phyllis. Molly gave up all pretence of boldness. She gave a loud anguished squawk and tried to run, but Flo's long polished shoe shot out and she tripped headlong over it. She hit the ground with the squashy sound of a ripe fruit falling, and the men in the distance laughed. It did not occur to them to interfere, because in that district it is neither polite nor politic to get into other people's quarrels.

Not only did Phyllis remember the reward held out to Flo and herself by Delie Stock if they beat Chocolate Molly up. She was aching to slam into her for her own sake. In her ferocious and deadly unmoral little soul there was a love of violence. She threw herself upon Molly's quaking body and hammered her head upon the pavement. She rubbed it this way and that, grinding the brown girl's nose into the burning asphalt and making her squeal with agony.

'Go easy, love, you'll hurt her,' remonstrated Flo. Phyllis gave a strong heave and hurled Molly face upwards on the pavement. Her lips were purple, and her thick mouth open in a dark O of dust and blood. Phyllis punched her in the teeth a dozen times, then stuck one finger in her eye and wrenched it sideways. Molly shrieked 'Help! Help!' at the top of her voice, but nobody took any notice. Phyllis's face was a horrid, doglike mask of ferocity, her stained false teeth showing and her porcine eyes red with lust. She jumped to her feet and began kicking Molly in the stomach.

Mumma cried: 'Oh, oh, oh!' but Grandma merely murmured:

'Sure and she's got a boot on her, that one. She's wasting her time in this street. She ought to be on a football field.'

'They'll kill her! They'll kill her!' gasped Mumma, but she was too fascinated to turn her face away.

Then all at once Flo, who had been negligently leaning against the wall, took off her gloves and arranged them fastidiously upon the window sill. Then she sprang upon Molly's broad body, and holding on to the sill for balance, she began to trample her with her high heels, digging them deeply into her soft breasts and abdomen. Stamp! Stamp! She was like a savage tramping out the brains of his fallen enemy, and yet all the time there was a sort of polite smile upon her face. It seemed to Mumma that there was more cruelty in her action than in all Phyllis's wild beast attack.

When Molly was unconscious, Flo stepped daintily off, gave a few touches to her still perfect hair, and put on her gloves. She touched the reluctant Phyllis, and they moved off, to look for customers in Coronation Street. A drunk weaved up and hauled Molly into a laneway, where she lay for a long time. Hardly anyone else took any notice, for the pub was open, and so was the SP shop, Bert Drummy's. Grandma awoke to instant action. She dug eagerly in her skinny black purse.

'Run down with this and put threepence each way on Black Marlin for the third, will you, love?' she asked. 'Or maybe Dolour will do it.'

'I'll do it meself,' answered Mumma wearily; she would not have thought of allowing Dolour to go to Bert Drummy's, for he was the sort that liked to pinch the bottoms of his customers.

She shook a shovelful of coal into Puffing Billy's maw, pulled in a damper and moved up a slide, shook her finger at him when he started to cough, and went out, her old brown hat sitting on top of her screwed-up hair. The burning wind smote her like a blow, and on her way back she was glad to go into St Brandan's for a visit. She trotted up the hollowed sandstone steps into the quiet dimness. There was a scattering of people before the confessional, and now and then the door squeaked open, and someone tiptoed creakily in. Mumma drew a deep breath of the clean, faintly incense-scented air, which she loved. She cast an affectionate glance towards the altar, still a mass of thick flowers, with brass shining amongst them. Dolour had helped to polish that brass, she thought proudly; it was almost as though she had done something herself. She knelt down before the poor little Crib, lovingly fixed up by the sisters, but still a miserable plaster cave with thin-necked plaster cows and horses standing amongst the sprinkled straw. A brown-robed Joseph stood stiffly by the little cradle, and a goggle-eyed Mary knelt by the goggle-eyed, too large Child. But Mumma saw it with other eyes. It was all real to her; the little plaster Baby soon became her own lost boy, Thady. Lovingly she looked once more at his rounded limbs, the gentle paleness of his hair, and the way his eyes crinkled as he laughed, showing his little square white teeth with the spaces between them. Little Thady! It was hard to think that he had often come into this church with her, and once she had smacked him because he had cried during Mass. She knelt in a muse. What could have happened to him? How was it possible for any child to vanish into thin air, the way he had done? He was a big boy, she thought piteously. Six years old, and big for his age. Her mind ran over the well-worn track of ten years: murdered, kidnapped for some inconceivable bad house, stolen by a woman with no child, taken by gipsies for sale . . . how could he vanish?

She pulled herself back to consciousness with a start, aware that her heart was beginning to fill with the old mad tumult of grief, and that her face was showing it. She hurried out of the church, quickly, quickly, looking at the ground, so that people would not see her wild, anguished eyes. When she got back to the house, she went into the bedroom to take her hat off. Hughie was awake, staring at the ceiling with sunken dark-shadowed eyes. They turned and fastened on her.

'Where you been?' There was a forlorn sound in his voice, as in the whine of a dog which dumbly asks its master not to reproach it for continued failings. Mumma rushed over to the bed and flung herself down beside him.

'Oh, Hughie, I been thinking about Thady, and it's at me again.'

'Ah, Thady. Me poor little feller,' said Hughie. He held her tight against his thin, lank, middle-aged body, and felt her breast shuddering with unvoiced sobs.

'He was so little to be by himself somewhere,' breathed Mumma. 'Oh, Hughie, what will we do? What will we do about it?'

They clung together, and all the memory of his past transgressions was wiped out in his mind and hers, and they loved and comforted each other, while upstairs Grandma, chewing rapidly, and discoursing irately with no one at all, leaned over the balcony rail and wondered the fate of her threepence each way.

As Roie walked, she thought, her thoughts chasing each other round and round like white mice in a cage. It seemed impossible that a baby could come from the clumsy and ludicrous embrace under the phoenix palm in the park. Roie did not know what to think of it. Sometimes she shuddered away in guilt and shame from the memory of Tommy's slender warm body pressed on hers, and his hungry untutored hands that hurt and fondled in one action. And at other times she thought that it hadn't happened at all; that she'd dreamed it in a sinful dream.

Almost with astonishment she viewed the fact that almost certainly she was to have a baby. Sometimes she thought that it was only because she was so afraid that she felt so sick, but in her heart she knew that nothing in her experience could cause these strange feelings; the swimmy nausea if she turned quickly, the tiny achings in her body, and the swelling of her breasts. But still it seemed impossible. Lots of other girls had babies; lots of them in Plymouth Street had had illegal babies. But not she. Not Roie Darcy, who hadn't mucked around with boys since the time when she was little; who had always gone to Mass and her duty, who worked hard and paid her board and tried to be good. Roie recounted her virtues with urgent force to God, who seemed to have forgotten them.

'I'm mistaken, aren't I, dear Lord? You will please let me off it this time, won't you? You know I'll never do it again.'

But soon there was no mistake. Roie found herself in a blank terror. She prayed with frenzy that she might wake up and find she had died in the night. Yet she could not show any of this terror on her face. She went to work and came home and went to bed. She even went to the pictures with Mumma and Dolour and laughed. She lay every night beside her little sister and did not sob aloud. But deep down in her chest her grief racked her till her whole body ached.

What was she afraid of? Roie couldn't work it out. It wasn't the pain she was frightened of, nor of having a baby like Miss Sheily, to be a burden and a drawback all her life. She was afraid mostly of Mumma's finding out. It would have been different if Mumma had been like other women in Plymouth Street, bawdy and coarse and rough, even though they were kindhearted. She could have taken all the accusatory screams of a mother of that sort, and screamed back similar abuse. But she felt she couldn't face the shock on her Mumma's face when she told her. And Dadda. He'd go straight out to Leichhardt and get Tommy Mendel by the neck and beat him up, that's what he'd do. Roie felt that she couldn't bear that, either, the whimpering boy, and the sodden, infuriated father, and the ring of faces, and the dirty jokes of the crowd: 'He wants to take it out on the sheeny because he did his daughter in,' and the endless chatter from fence to fence until everyone who knew Roie Darcy even by sight would point her out, not always unkindly, but just with interest.

'It wasn't Tommy's fault,' sobbed Roie suddenly, and she buried her face in the pillow so that Dolour would not wake. 'It wasn't his fault. He was just being like all the other fellers. And I don't want him to know. I don't want to be married to Tommy.'

The horror of that idea became greater than the other. She imagined herself married to Tommy, who didn't like her any more. Perhaps they would have to live in the dark little rooms over old Mendel's shop, and Tommy would get drunk because he hated her, and knock her around, and her life would be the long misery of the unwanted wife's. And Tommy was a Jew; not a practising Jew perhaps, but still a foreigner. Roie nearly went crazy at the thought of marriage with Tommy. It was like looking through a prison gate and knowing that next year you would be looking through from the other side.

She remembered her talk with Dolour, long ago, and her saying, 'It's a wonder she didn't get rid of it,' and Dolour's naivè little voice saying, 'How?'

Roie pushed the thought from her, but again and again it returned. The baby wasn't alive yet; it hadn't breathed. She wouldn't really be killing it. Other women did it, most women. Didn't old Mrs Campion next door openly boast of her fifteen misses? She took something . . . Roie remembered giggles amongst the girls at work and whispers from machine to machine: 'She's in trouble. Bet she'll be getting into the Epsom salts.' And there were other things, too, that you could buy at dirty little chemist shops. They slipped them over the counter – packets of pills, and little bottles of bitter black medicine. Roie knew. But they didn't always work. Even Mrs Campion, who found it so easy, said that. And if she did do it, and it worked, she could be sorry and never do it again. It was really the sort of sin you could be sorry about, once it was all over.

There were places you could go to, as well. There was Rosie Glavich at the factory, she was in trouble, everyone knew it, for she had to leave her machine every so often to go to the cloakroom and be sick. Then one day Rosie turned up, as white as a sheet, and spent the day sitting down too scared to move, and she'd told some of the girls that she'd been fixed up. She was sick a long time, but she didn't have a baby. It was worth it, everyone agreed.

Roie was like a girl running down a long dark lane from some pursuing horror. There seemed nothing else to do. Then out of the recesses of her mind came the name of the doctor who fixed Rosie up. He operated at a queer old yellow house in Murphy Street; a house with a genteel row of hanging palms and ferns, so that you dodged under a curtain of depressed and livid green before you reached the blistered brown door. The doctor used to come in the back entrance, and left the same way, and he charged ten pounds. Once Roie had decided, things were a little better for her, and she gradually developed a cold, calm tranquillity. She felt nothing for the baby. It was only an uncomfortable little lump in the pit of her stomach that made her sick if she walked fast. It wasn't really a baby yet; she didn't feel sorrow, or shame, or anything for the baby, only for herself.

She became very crafty at hiding her sickness, and every morning she got up early so that nobody would see her face without make-up. She did a lot of overtime too, and in a couple of months she had put aside the ten pounds. It was not difficult to get some overtime, for the work was so hard at the factory that the girls were exhausted after the day's labour, and did not seek it. Roie did not tell her family she was working overtime, pretending she was going skating or dancing with her girl friends. The lies slid awkwardly off her simple tongue, but Mumma believed them all the more because of that, thinking that Roie was trying to forget Tommy in this unaccustomed gaiety and did not want them to comment on it.

On her way home from work she called in at No. 17 Murphy Street. As she raised the iron knocker her heart thudded sickeningly, and she was afraid that she might be sick there and then. There was an old chair placed at one side of the door, with a sort of sardonic implication that visitors to that house might require it. Roie sat down upon it and tried to control her sickness. When she looked up she found that the door had opened silently, and a face was looking at her out of the crack. It was a face of an elderly woman, cracked into a thousand fine lines, like an old piece of china. Sharp grey eyes looked at her, and then, as she was about to speak, a voice said with a poisonous sympathy: 'Feeling bad, dearie?'

And then Roie knew that she had come to the right place. The door opened wider, in furtive invitation, and she stepped into the tiny hall with a grubby carpet on the floor, and a pot plant sitting spiky and hostile in the corner.

'Is this where . . . I mean . . . does the . . .'

The woman nodded familiarly. 'Yes, dearie, it's here. And he does. I make all the arrangements.'

There was a cold dankness about the house, as though the sunshine had never crept within its secret walls. A depression settled over Roie's spirit, so that she felt dreary and fatigued. The woman gave her a chair, and pulling a thumb-marked notebook towards her, said with a professional air: 'Now love, how far are yer?'

'Four months,' faltered Roie. The woman clicked her tongue.

'Youghta come earlier. Three months is bad enough. But four!'

Roie gasped: 'I couldn't save the money before this. I . . .'

The woman said: 'Men!' Then she added: 'What's yer name, love?'

'Beryl Graham,' said Roie instantly. The woman nodded approvingly.

'Better'n Smith or Jones.' She wrote it down. She leaned over and said confidentially, 'The Doctor's a good 'un. Good as a Macquarie Street man. He likes to help poor girls outa their trouble, that's why he comes down here.'

'Does it hurt?' gasped Roie. The familiar woman shook her head.

'Nah, no more'n a toothache. That's if you keep still. Ah, it's a good thing there's men like the doctor ready to help us girls outa our trouble. It'll cost you twelve pounds,' she added suddenly. Roie's heart fell.

'They told me ten!' she hurried out. 'I could only save ten.'

The woman looked at her grudgingly, 'I'll speak to the doctor.'

Roie nearly fell on her knees with gratitude. 'Oh, you must make him. Please make him help me.'

'Ho,' said the woman, sniffing. 'Mighty snooty you are with "make him". The doctor won't be made by no dirty little tart who wants to get outa the trouble she got herself into.'

'I didn't mean that,' gasped Roie humbly. 'I didn't mean to . . .'

'All right,' said the woman, softening, 'you can come on Wednesday evening about ten.'

Roie went blinking out into the blinding sunshine. The door shut behind her with a stealthy click, as it had shut behind dozens and hundreds of other girls. The street looked the same as it always had, smelling of unclean gutters and the sharp pungency of orange peel and rotting cabbage stalks. Roie hurried away, hoping that none of the peering eyes behind the curtains of nearby houses had noticed her, for she was sure that No. 17 and its purpose was known to everyone in Murphy Street.

When she got home, so great was her relief that she felt much better than she had for months. It was almost as though she had already been fixed up, and she was as she had been before she met Tommy Mendel. But during tea Mumma said, 'You're looking peaky, Roie. I bought you a tonic. It looks fine and strong.'

She gestured to the mantelpiece, and Roie saw the bottle, raspberry red, with a surly dark sediment in the bottom, and a chemists' sticker proclaiming it was the tonic of the times.

'Gee,' said Roie abashed. 'You shouldn't have done it, Mumma. Medicine's too dear.'

'Cost me five and six,' said Mumma proudly. 'I had to save up for a fortnight out of the house-money.'

Suddenly all the mischief in Roie's chest came to the top in one great bursting sob. The thought of her Mumma buying tonics for her when she was guilty and deceptive and plotting dark shame in her soul was too much for her to bear. She gave a croak of anguish, and burst into tears.

'Whist-awhist!' cried Grandma, staring at her over her fork.

Mumma dropped her knife and reached over and patted her daughter on the back, as though she had choked on something.

'What's the matter with you, child?' Roie jumped up and fled from the room. Face down on the bed, she sobbed with such hoarse rhythm that old Patrick Diamond knocked irritably on the wall and inquired what all the waterworks were about.

'You shut yer big gob, Mr Diamond!' cried Mumma stoutly, as she panted up the crooked stairs. 'Can't a girl even have a bit of a weep without you putting yer big snout into it?'

She looked at Roie with real anxiety. 'Now tell Mumma, can't you, darling, and whatever you've done, I'm on yer side.'

For one wild moment Roie thought of telling her everything, and then she realized that it was impossible. She choked: 'It's just that I'm so tired, and I got into a muddle at the factory today and the foreman told me off.'

'Oh,' she felt her mother's breast subside, and the relief come out of her like a wave. 'Then you take yer tonic, lovie, and yer'll feel better. I know what that sort of feeling is, none better.'

Down the road that night, someone stuck a knife into a Dutch sailor, and everyone forgot about Roie's outburst. Murders were not uncommon in Plymouth Street; in fact, on the corner where the sailor was found lying, two bodies had previously been picked up. The sailor lay face downwards, curled up in a gutter, and all evening long passers-by had not given him a glance, for the gutter was a favourite resting-place of drunks. Then someone noticed that he had no hat or shoes, and they investigated, and found the broken-off blade of a knife like a little silver slit in the centre of his adam's apple. He was a young dark man with good teeth, and he had a good deal of money on him before he was murdered.

Hughie stopped and had a look at the spot on his way home from work. There were still a few sticky, fly-clotted black stains in the gutter, and the urchins were gleefully pointing them out to people who went past. Hughie felt sorry for the young sailor, particularly as he had been a mug and flashed a roll of deferred pay in a pub, Hughie considered. His knowledge that he himself would have had more brains than that made him feel doubly sympathetic.

'Come down here after a girl, I suppose,' he said at the dinner table 'and someone sees his dough and invites him in for a glass of plonk and then lets him have it in the gizzard.'

'Stop it afore yer turn me liver up,' protested Grandma.

'I'll bet it had something to do with Delie Stock,' said Dolour, holding up a sausage on a fork and consuming it piecemeal. Mumma scolded: 'Youghtn't to talk that way about Mrs Stock that give you the lovely picnic,' she said. Roie rose from the table.

'I'm going to the pitchers tonight. Is my pink dress ironed, Mumma?'

'It's going under the arms, love. But it's hanging in the cupboard. Who're yer going with?' inquired Mumma.

'Rosie Glavich,' answered Roie. 'I'm meeting her in front of the Palace.'

'Why doesn't Tommy call now?' teased Hughie coarsely. 'Scared I might take a shotgun to him?' Grandma tittered from the bedroom and Mumma went pink.

'Don't you dare talk like that to yer own daughter, yer piggy old fellow,' she remonstrated. 'Never you mind him, Roie love. He's got a tongue so long someone could tie a knot in it.'

'Someone oughter tie one in yours, and then we'd notice,' roared Hughie. 'Ah, the peace, the tranquillity!'

Roie got dressed, slowly. Because it was the gravest and most important night of her life, she put on her best underwear, her only pair of stockings without cobbles, and polished her shoes, which was a thing she rarely did. She cut her fingernails and brushed her hair carefully. Then she made up her face. Looking in the mirror was like looking at a stranger. She felt so much terror that it had all merged into a cold dreamlike numbness. She was like a woman committed to the guillotine and resigned to it, though in no way was her fear alleviated.

When she said goodbye to her mother, her voice was light and normal so that she marvelled at it. But as she went up the hall complete anguish seized her, and she shrank into the dark recess under the stairs where poor Johnny Sheily had played, so that he would not get in anybody's way. Girls sometimes died when they were fixed up. Roie couldn't imagine death for herself, but she could imagine her mother's face when someone, the slatternly familiar woman at No. 17, for instance, came and told her that her daughter had died in a dirty back room in Murphy Street.

But it was too late now. She walked out into the street. The bright autumn evening, lucently blue in the east, with stars sparkling and in the west the calmest, purest saffron, burst upon her with the shock of some lovely picture. The old plane trees, their boughs mutilated so that they had grown into crippled knobs of intertwined twigs, their bark splashed with white, their wide leaves yellowing, seemed to her to be old friends she was leaving for ever. She remembered those leaves tenderly, piteously green in spring, ready fodder for the ferocious burning winds of summer; she remembered the boughs wet and black and shining in winter. She put out her hand and touched a trunk as she went past; the wood was still warm from the daylong sunshine. It was almost like touching flesh.

She got in a tram and went down to the city, for she had three hours to kill before she went to No. 17. The city was full of life. In the day it had smelt of dust and petrol and heat; but now it smelt of coolness, face powder and wine. Crowds were standing outside the theatres, in gabbling queues which snaked untidily over the foot-path. Men were waiting on corners for buses or girls. Roie did not know where to go. She had thought perhaps that she could go to the Cathedral, but there might be benediction on there, or some other service in which she had no part when there was sin on her soul.

'But it's not sin for me,' thought Roie desperately. 'It's the only thing I can do.'

She went down to the Quay and pretended she was catching a ferry. Outside the Manly berth she leaned over the railing, and watched the Bridge outlined with golden lights, with the little twinkling beetles that were trams moving rapidly across it. She saw the dark glossy water, and the fiery chestnut of reflected light dancing upon the ripples. She thought how simple it would be for a brave person to slip into that water, and steadfastly die. She knew she couldn't. She'd kick and yell with panic, and before long some courageous halfwit would be over the rail to rescue her, and her name would be in the papers, and doctors would examine her, and then everyone would know.

With almost a feeling of relief Roie saw the hands of a clock pointing to half-past nine. She went up into the rattling bedlam of the tram station and caught one home.

'I'm not the only girl who has to face it tonight,' thought Roie, but the thought gave her no comfort. The tram journey seemed very short. She got off a stop or two before the usual one, and walked quickly into Murphy Street. She thought that if she hurried perhaps she would feel sick, and then she would be glad for it all to happen, as one panted for the dentist's coming when one had a really bad toothache.

The house was very dark. There were heavy blinds on the windows and the only glass panel in the door glowed dimly yellow like an old kerosene lamp. Roie tapped at the door, and silently it opened. She stepped in to the musty-smelling little hall. There was a faint odour of disinfectant somewhere. The familiar woman was waiting for her.

'Thought you weren't coming. Thought you got cold feet.'

'No,' quavered Roie. Her stomach was sickening already, and perspiration damped her skin.

'That's the kid. Wait in there for me, there's a duck.' She pushed Roie into a little room which opened off the hall. It had lavender-striped wallpaper, and a bobble-edged parchment shade on the light.

There was an unused feeling about the room, and Roie knew it didn't like her. She was surprised to see another girl there, a dark, oily-skinned girl with bold Italian eyes and an old food-stained coat pulled around her already prominent stomach. Roie and she looked at each other furtively for a while, then the other girl grinned, showing bad teeth.

'God, I'm scared, ain't you?'

Roie nodded feebly. She was so terrified that she could hardly sit straight in the chair.

'But it's not so bad when it comes to the point. You've always got more guts than you thought,' said the other girl. It was a relief to hear another voice in that secret, hostile room. Roie faltered: 'I'm four months gone. How long are you?'

'God, I'm four and a half,' she boasted. 'I got stuck into the dope, but it didn't work. So here I am again.'

'You mean, you've been here before?' asked Roie.

'Cripes, this is me fourth miss, if it comes off. Somehow I'm always falling in. Course, I'm married. But don't you be afraid, love. It only hurts for a little while. Just put yer hanky in yer mouth and bite on it to stop yelling. It's getting home that's hard.'

'Why?' trembled Roie. The other girl looked at her amazed.

'Hell, don't you know anything? Well, if you ain't got no one to take you home in a car, like the flash tarts have, you gotta walk, and things often happen on the way.'

'Things?' Roie just had to ask, although her terror of the answer was almost too much for her to bear. The other girl leaped at the opportunity to tell her, and in a low, greedy voice she gave Roie all the loathsome details of abortion. She had hardly finished before the familiar woman stuck her head in the door and said: 'You next, Stell.'

Stell swaggered to the door, turned, and patted her stomach with a jolly wiggle of her hips. 'Don't take it bad, love. Look at me. In another fortnight I'll be wearing me red dress with the bead flower again.'

'Yeah,' put in the woman with a wink at Roie, 'and six weeks after that you'll be right back here again.'

The door closed. Roie sat on the edge of the chair, trembling like a rabbit in a trap. It was worse than a nightmare. Her mind, shocked almost to the point of insensibility with the information she had just received, was incapable of forming a conclusion about anything. She stared at the wallpaper, until its pattern, a long chain of faded purple diamonds, was imprinted on the air when she looked away. She did not know how long she sat there. She was only aware of her knees joggling under her hands, and the sweat staining the sides of her stockings where they touched each other. Then all at once there was a rapid shuffle of feet upstairs, and she awoke as though from a dream. Opening the door, she listened. There was a low mutter of a man's deep voice; the sound of metal clinking on china; and a horrible gagged scream which diminished into gurgling moans. Feet sounded on the stairs, and Roie nearly collapsed against the door, for she thought that it was the woman coming to get her. But the feet ran on into the kitchen at the back, and Roie heard the hiss and pop of gas, and the sound of something trickling into a glass. There was another hoarse shriek, cut off short as if someone had suddenly jabbed a gag into Stell's mouth. Feet ran up the stairs again. The whole atmosphere of that dirty old slum house was instinct with mystery and evil. It seemed to gloat, and hold to itself all the murders that had been committed within its walls. The smell of blood was there, and the miasma of cowardice and stealth and cruelty.

Roie gave a stifled little groan. She ran at the front door and struggled with it until she wrested the bolt from the socket and pulled it open. Crazy with terror, she slid it back and ran out and down the path. She did not look back, nor did she hear any sound. The street was dark now, save for the pools of topaz lights under the lamps. And there was a cold wind blowing, sweeping up the fallen leaves and whirling them forlornly away. Roie raced down the street, little muffled sobs bursting from her chest. It was then a nightmare; there was no longer any control of her thoughts. She pictured the familiar woman, grown to delirious proportions, with bulging forehead and strange receding chin, coming after her; and the doctor, a faceless, bodyless creature that was nothing more than a low mutter, and the sound of metal on crockery, and a hoarse strangled scream, seizing her and vanishing her out of her familiar world the way someone had vanished her little brother Thady.

Then she was out of Murphy Street and turning into the long dark channel of Coronation Street. Roie slowed down, stumbling with fatigue. Almost immediately she was aware of several men lounging in the shadows of a shop verandah. As she drew abreast, one of them snatched her arm. He was a short sturdy man in a blue overcoat; his fair bristly hair stood straight up from his forehead. There was a smell of gin, and his fingers made no attempt to be gentle.

Roie was too breathless to speak. She wrenched her arm away from the man and started to run again, sobbing under her breath. But another stepped in her path, and a thick and rhythmic voice chanted: 'Good efening, good efening, good efening.'

There was a mutter of drunken foreign babble around her, and Roie, astonished, looked through her tear-blurred eyes at the dark ribboned hats most of the men wore. Some were dark-featured, like Indians; others blonde, with pink cheeks, like dressed-up children.

It was the violent conclusion of the nightmare. Screaming, she fought, beating at their strong arms, their chests, their faces. She was dragged into the deep dark doorway, and a strong and violating hand groped over her.

'No, no,' choked Roie, 'I want to go home. I feel sick. I'm going to have a baby. Let me go home to my Mumma! Mumma! Mumma!'

She was dragged from one to the other; bristly chins rubbed against her soft chin, her dress was ripped from her shoulders. A rough torrent of Dutch poured back and forth over her head, drunken, violent, and savage. As she was slammed against the shop door, a window was flung up overhead, and an alarmed voice yelled: 'Hi, what's going on down there?'

There was a sentence of strange words, and one of the sailors ran into the road, plucked a knife from his sleeve and hurled it at the window above. There was a shocked silence, and glass fell with a loud soprano tinkle on to the iron roof. The shopkeeper began to yell at the top of his voice: 'Help! Help! Police! Where are the bloody coppers? He nearly got me with a knife! Help!'

There were no patrol men within hearing, but the black car of the Vice Squad, cruising slowly along Plymouth Street, silently accelerated. It drew in beside the kerb even as one of the sailors threw Roie to the ground.

One boot grazed stingingly past her ear; the other did not miss. She felt a flood of pain unlike anything she had ever experienced. It was so great it made her eyes blur, go bloodshot and lose their focus. She rolled like a kicked football before the feet that stumbled over her as the sailors raced away up the street. There was a deafening babel of noise, shouts, a shot which echoed up the empty roadway like a whiplash, screams, upflung windows, and vanishing footbeats. She dragged herself up to a sitting position. She could see nobody. The squad car was gone; the men were gone. There was no one to help.

'Mumma! Mumma!' she moaned. She scratched feebly on the peeling door of the shop. There was no sound.

'What'll I do? What'll I do?' she moaned. 'Oh, Jesus, help me. Oh, Jesus, come and help me!'

She lay there for half an hour in utter agony. Finally a drunk came along, picking his way with infinite care from one side of the pavement to the other. He sang in a low, happy voice: 'Flowers all dripping with dew! And they join in the chorus of . . . Gawd, what you doin' in there? You been at the meth, sister?'

Roie gasped, the effort bringing sweat to her deathly face: 'A man kicked me. I've got to go home.'

The drunk came closer, looked at her with owlish eyes. 'I'll go and get a doc.'

'No, get me home. Please, get me home,' she begged in a whisper. He gave a foolish shrug. 'Okay!' It was a gay little chirp. He was a tall, strong man, middle-aged, with a labourer's bullocky shoulders. He lifted Roie easily, and held her against his beer-smelling shirt.

He weaved off down Coronation Street, still chanting under his breath: 'Flowers all dripping with dew, and they join in the chorus . . . loverly song . . . loverly sheila on the meth. Where you say you live, miss?'

'Fourth house around the corner in Plymouth Street,' breathed Roie out of the black mist of unconsciousness. 'Fourth house.'

'Okay!' She felt nothing but the jolting of his slow walk, every movement of which was a delicate and subtle torture.

'Here y'are,' said his voice suddenly. It seemed remote, miles away.

'Carry me down the hall,' breathed Roie. He was a little indignant.

'Charge you taxi rates, miss. No, I won't. It's a pleasure.'

He thrust open the green door with one shoulder, and trod heavily down the hall. He had not gone half-way before Mumma came running to the kitchen door and cried: 'Who's that? That you, Roie?'

At the sound of her voice Roie lost her head. She beat on the shoulder of her rescuer and shrieked: 'Let me down, let me down! I want my mother! Oh, I want my mother!' Then she fell deep into the darkness that was full of strange noises and monstrous, bulging faces, and voices that said: 'Good efening, good efening, good efening.'

Ten

It was three hours later, and Hughie, with scarlet face and eyes that watered, so intense was their glare, was saying to Mumma: 'I'm going to get the quack.'

Mumma's mouth closed into a thin line. 'Keep yer voice down, can't yer? Don't yer know old Diamond's got his ear plastered to the crack in the floor? Keep yer voice down.'

'I'm going to get the doctor,' Hughie shouted in a whisper, like the croak of a magpie.

'You will not.' Mumma's face was as white as paper, with a yellow look around her mouth. 'It's not only a kick in the stomach she got.'

'What d'ya mean?' Because he was frightened, Hughie's voice was rougher than usual, his demeanour fiercer.

'She's losing a baby.' Once Mumma said it, her face crumpled up like newspaper in a fire, and she sat down on the bed and pushed her knuckles into her eyes, with a childish piteous gesture. Hughie was stunned.

'You're mad.' Mumma said nothing, and he repeated, more fiercely, but with a pitiful question in his voice. 'You're mad.' Her silence answered him. 'Cripes,' he whispered. 'Ro! Who'd a guessed it?'

'Nobody ain't going to guess,' replied Mumma, with white-hot determination. 'Whatever Ro's done she's had a reason for it. And nobody's going to know about it but us, see?'

'It's Tommy Mendel, the dirty little swine,' cried Hughie, flaming-eyed. Mumma put her hand on his arm.

'Whoever it was can wait. Roie's very sick. You've got to help me.' Hughie looked at her obediently.

'What'll I do? You tell me.'

Mumma's emotion had subsided. 'Put some hot water on. Get those old sheets out from the port under the bed. Get the bucket and scald it out. Yes, and the couch . . . put the blankets on it off our bed, because I'm going to bring Dolour down before she gets wise to what's happening. And for God's sake, if Grandma wakes up, tell her it's nothing, and give her a pipe and send her off to sleep again.'

Hughie, mumbling over the orders, rushed off to the gas stove, and Mumma returned up the dark stairs to Roie.

The light in the room was burning bare and glaring. Dolour, her face like parchment, perched shivering with terror and cold on the broken-legged chair at the end of the room. Her eyes were glazed with fright.

'Is Ro going to die?' she whimpered as her mother entered the room.

'Don't be silly. Them Dutchmen knocked her down and hurt her, that's all. Now I want you to go downstairs and sleep on the couch for the rest of the night. And take yer rosary with you and say a Pater-n-Ave for my intention.'

Dolour scampered off, tears streaming down her cheeks, her bare shoulders sticking out of the rents in her grubby nightgown.

Roie's fine dark hair was matted into long rat-tails. The side of her face was plum-purple, and her lips were swollen. She groaned: 'I am going to die, aren't I?'

'No, darling love. Don't think about that. Mumma won't let you die. Mumma's looking after you,' soothed her mother. Roie forced her drowsy eyes open.

'Mumma, you know about me?'

'Yes, darling.'

'What's going to happen?'

'You're going to be all right. Everything will be all right.'

In a frenzy Roie beat on her mother's shoulders with feeble hands.

'What's going to happen to my baby? What's happening to my little baby?'

'There isn't any baby now, Roie.' Mumma was pulling Roie's torn garments off, and wrapping a sheet about her slender body that was bruised to the colour of a grape. Roie turned her head away and the bitterest tears she had ever known crept from under her eyelids and slid slowly down her stinging cheeks. Until now she had felt no real moral wrong in what she had done or what she had contemplated, but now, as though she had walked into a great shadow, the world was different. It wasn't that she had been going to have a baby that made her sink down to the lowest depths of grief and shame but the knowledge that she would have murdered it, if it had not been for her own cowardice.

'I killed it, Mumma.'

'No, darling. The Dutchmen killed it. And it wasn't alive. It didn't miss anything of life.'

'I killed it,' repeated Roie monotonously. 'I killed it because I didn't want it. That's why God punished me this way. I want to die. Mumma, let me die.'

'Lie still now,' cried Mumma in anxiety. 'Mr Diamond will hear you. Miss Sheily will hear you. Don't talk like that. Oh, Roie, don't talk about anything until you get better.'

'I got to talk about it. You don't know how bad I am. Tonight . . . I didn't go to the pictures with Rosie Glavich. I went to that place in Murphy Street where the doctor comes.'

Mumma's face went yellow-white again. She stared at Roie with her mouth hanging open, and nothing on her face but blank shock.

'You mean . . . is this the result of . . . you mean . . .' she quavered.

'No, I ran away. I wouldn't let them touch me. But it was only because I was frightened when that girl screamed. I didn't have the guts to face it for myself, but I was going to let them kill my little baby.'

Mumma went to the window. She looked out into the chalcedony-blue sky of the early morning, and the great, glossy stars. The wind blew pure and salt-laden from Darling Harbour, with no hint of the dirty alleyways, and fetid lavatories and the rotting garbage it blew across. She felt as though she were a different woman from the one who had climbed the steps only a few minutes before. Incapable of comprehending the dark recesses in others' natures, to her Roie's confession had come as a deep and abiding shock which was never altogether to leave her. She turned her face into the wind and said: 'Dear God, help me to be strong as mothers ought to be.'

Then she came back and said: 'Such thoughts do nothing but harm, Roie, love. You're my little girl, and whatever you've done, it's over now and nothing to you but the past.'

She leaned over Roie and pressed her head close to her breast, and the poignant pain which had been hers when first she had felt Roie's little downy head at her birth went through her again, and she knew that her feeling was no different.

Eleven

Dolour huddled on the couch downstairs. It was very uncomfortable. Her dirty little heels slid up and down the shiny leather until a clean pink patch was worn on each. She looked at the dim speckled globe burning up near the ceiling, and said a Hail Mary in a drowsy way as though to convince herself that she wanted to go to sleep. But she didn't. She was wide awake. She could hear with sharp distinctiveness the dripping of a tap in the scullery, the creaking of a clothes-line in the yard, and, upstairs, mysterious rustlings and mumblings and footsteps passing back and forth.

'Ah, gosh, I wish Dad would come down,' wailed Dolour. Tears, hot and sticky with lack of sleep, squeezed themselves out of her eyes. Suddenly Grandma, who had been creaking uneasily for the last five minutes, called out in a tired, wheezy voice: 'What's bothering yer out there? Have yer the toothache?'

'Oh, Grandma!' bellowed Dolour, leaping off the couch and running in. She jumped on to the bed beside her Grandma's little humpy form, and the stretcher dipped and quivered. Grandma's vexed sunken face yapped at her:

'Be careful, you big ellafump. Just about shook the kidneys outa me, you did. Time you were in bed, anyway.' She closed her eyes and sank back, chewing rapidly. Dolour bawled: 'But I'm supposed to be sleeping in the kitchen, and Dadda and Mumma are upstairs with Roie.'

Grandma opened her eyes instantly. From a filmy grey they changed to a sharp and discerning blue. 'What are you gabbering about?'

'Roie's awful sick. I think she's going to die,' sobbed Dolour. 'Oh, Grandma, I think she's going to die.'

'What happened?' squawked Grandma, levering herself painfully upwards, and wincing as the rheumatics stabbed her in her slow joints.

Dolour wiped her nose on the sleeve of her nightdress. 'It was them Dutchmen . . . them that came down to Surry Hills looking for the fellers that murdered their mate.'

Grandma had already heard all about the Dutchmen, for they had kicked in half a dozen shop windows and kicked old Bert Drummy's head half in, as well.

'Glory-lory-ory!' she whispered. Dolour nodded.

'They were all drunk, everyone thinks, and they attacked lots of girls, too. They caught Roie when she was coming home from the pitchers.' She dissolved into hiccuping sobs. Grandma asked:

'Has your Mumma got the doctor to Roie?' Dolour dumbly shook her head. Grandma gave a sigh of relief and lay back.

'Then Roie's not going to die, acushla. Lie down with yer old gran and go to sleep.'

Dolour felt as though a huge weight had been lifted from her shoulders. She complained: 'There ain't enough room.'

Grandma snorted. 'Don't then. Go and freeze, you ungrateful young tom todger.'

Dolour snivelled. 'I'm sorry, Grandma. I would like to come in with you.'

Grandma's eyes opened, with a wicked glint in them. She shuffled further over in the bed and left about four inches space. Humbly and gratefully Dolour climbed in beside her and wiggled down under the blankets. Grandma smelt of tobacco, old clothes, and plain old age, but Dolour soon got used to it, and she put her head on the old woman's thin flat chest and asked: 'Tell me about when you were a little girl in Ireland, Grandma.'

Grandma answered drowsily: 'When I was a little girl in Ireland I lived in a house with a fine shaggy roof on it. Our house was right in the middle of the shaky, quaky bog, and there was pools of brown water, for all the world like coffee, right at the back door. When you stamped very hard on our front door sill the whole bog shivered all over. It did so. And one day when I was digging with a stick in the mud I found a golden coin shaped like a shell, with a strange lady's face on it.'

'Was it a sovereign, Grandma?' whispered Dolour, as she knew she was meant to ask, for she had heard the story a hundred times before. Grandma snorted triumphantly. 'It was not. It was a coin of the fairy times, long before any people at all came to Ireland. They was great goldsmiths, them fairy people. And my Dadda took the coin into the town, and he came back with a brown pony and a little wagon with red spokes to the wheel. And it was called "Eny's car", for my name is Eny, though the dear Lord knows what use it is to me, who's always been Ma and Grandma for sixty wearisome years.'

Here Grandma got annoyed, and refused to talk any more, and they both went to sleep. A little while later Hughie came down from the upper bedroom. He lifted a candle and peered around the sheet which curtained Grandma's cubbyhole from the rest of the room. He exclaimed silently when he saw the two faces, both sharpened and yellowish with fatigue and sleep, on the grey pillow. Dolour's two arms were linked about Grandma's neck, and her mouth was open, so that her two front teeth showed over her lip.

'God forgive me, Grandma, that I've often been so hard on yer, yer old skunk,' breathed Hughie penitently. He set down the candle and slipped off his trousers; in his patched underpants he knelt down by the side of the bed.

'Hail, Mary, full of grace, don't let me little girl die. And don't be too hard on her. Hail Mary. It's only the one mistake she's made, and she won't never do it again. And God put fire into the belly of the foreign swine what did it.'

The next day everyone knew that the Netherlands sailors who had beaten up Bert Drummy, and assaulted Kitty Gall and Connie Lock and goodness knows how many other girls that they had met in their vengeful progress along the dark and unpoliced slum streets, had kicked Roie Darcy and hurt her bad. Mumma had decided that it was useless trying to keep it quiet, for it was certain sure that Miss Sheily and Patrick Diamond had heard all the commotion, and would be sure to drop a word or two amongst the neighbours.

'Besides, don't you see, Hughie,' she argued wearily, her eyes swollen with sleeplessness, 'it's a good excuse for Roie being so ill, and nobody need know about the other.'

'How is she now?' asked Hughie. Mumma shook her head.

'It's over now, but she's still bad, and sort of delirious. Moaning, she is. I can't keep her quiet.'

A cold wind swept up the street, lifting the tatters of paper and the crackling leaves. Lick Jimmy was in his window, busily mixing up mandarins and tomatoes, with a few parsnips added for effect. He waggled a finger at Hughie as he slouched past: 'Plenty blad blisnis last night, misser! Dlirty folleners!'

Hughie grunted surlily, but his expression lightened. For once he was in the news. He wasn't just Hugh Darcy, home from work; he was Hugh Darcy, home from work because his daughter had been beaten up by sailors. He hastened his step, and when old Delie Stock hailed him from her doorway in Little Ryan Street, he went across with alacrity.

'Didja hear about poor, stinking old Bert?' she inquired. Hughie nodded. He rolled a starveling cigarette.

'Stinking foreigners,' she said. There was real indignation in her voice. Her parchment face, broken into so many minute hair-like lines that it looked like some strange mosaic, filled with sympathy at the thought of Bert Drummy.

'And them poor girls,' she added. Both Hughie and she forgot entirely all the things she had done to girls in her time, and the old buffers like Bert Drummy whom she had had ruined, bashed-up and occasionally murdered. Hughie's blue eyes sparkled. His news would set her back a step, the old lizard. He put his cigarette in his mouth and drew on it carefully.

'Me girl Roie nearly got murdered, too. They grabbed her as she was coming home from the pitchers.'

'Yer don't say!'

'Yeah. Kicked her in the stomach. Face all out like a balloon. Clothes torn off her.'

'You mean they . . . ?'

'No,' added Hughie hastily. 'Vice Squad came along, and they left her. By God, if I could get my hands on them square-heads I'd strew them all over the street.'

'Yeah,' agreed Delie Stock. 'What I say is, they ain't got no business allowing foreigners in this country. Chows, yes. Nobody can wash a collar like a Chow. But not blasted Dutch. Anyone with corners on their head is next best thing to a German, I always say. Cripes, Roie, eh? Here,' said Delie Stock. She fished down the baggy front of her dress, and pulled put a greasy little cotton bag. Hugh tried to look somewhere else, but he couldn't, because the bag was so full of money. Delie Stock pulled out a couple of notes haphazardly, and stuffed them into Hughie's resistless paw.

'Here, you see that kid gets all she needs, Hugh Darcy, and if you're hard up, come around here and get some more. There's plenty where that came from,' said Delie Stock, giving herself a spank on the chest.

'Yere!' protested Hughie feebly. 'What's this? Cripes, I can't do it.'

'Go on, go on,' croaked Delie Stock. She was so overcome by her own generosity that she almost cried. She was a character, if ever there was one, she reflected, her the worst woman in the Hills, and giving this old goon a handout when he needed it most.

Hughie tottered off, looking at a fiver in one hand and a tenner in the other. Beautiful, priceless money! Food and beer and a bottle of good wine, and a baked chook, and new shoes for Dolour and a bit off the arrears of rent! He ran across the road, stuffing the money into his inside pocket as he did so. Mumma'd jump out of her skin. But she mightn't take it if she knew it had come from Delie Stock, for, in spite of her steady squashing of Dolour's criticism of the old girl, he knew that Mumma still feared and hated Delie Stock's profession. All right, then, he'd say he found it. But then she might think he'd pinched it. To make up his mind in a little peace and quiet, Hughie turned in at the open door of the Foundry pub. It was quiet in there, with a bit of water sluiced over the floor, and some clotted sawdust, and the handyman sweeping the two together out the door. The sunlight fell amber and warm on the polished counter and the many bottles. Flies buzzed about the threadbare backs of the two steady drinkers who leaned on the end of the bar.

'Gawd,' remarked the barmaid, winding tow hair around her thick glittering finger before the mirror, 'how's yer poor girl? Pat Diamond was in here telling me about it not ten minutes ago.'

'Pat Diamond had better keep his great gob shut or I'll stick me hoof fair in it,' snarled Hughie. Never before had he felt so big or important. He slapped the fiver on the bar. The steady drinkers at the other end shuffled closer, prepared to listen for as long as Hughie cared to talk.

An hour later he came out into the bright sunlight, blinking like an owl. There were many people about now, frowsy women with their hair in pipe-cleaners, and shopping kits in their red hands; little children with transparent skin and large bright birdlike eyes looking through the grime. Hughie barged through them all. He was wearing his idealistic red uniform again, and was six foot high and was accompanied by the grave and pompous rattle of a drum. Hardly anybody looked at him, though drunken men in the morning were not common. They just shoved him good-naturedly away as he lurched into them, with a laugh and 'Push off, mate, yer off yer course,' or 'Garn, get outa me way, you old crackpot.'

Hughie passed Jacky Siciliano's fruit shop, and Bert Drummy's ham and beef, and the second-hand dump and the fish shop. And there was Joseph Mendel's hock joint, with three brass balls swinging like monstrous grapes from the verandah beam. The window was crammed with old jewellery, coarse garnets and peridots and turquoise matrix set in brassy rolled gold; pewter shaving mugs, tarnished silver buckles, cigarette cases with cameos of coursing dogs and girls' profiles; crystal powder bowls with every facet grimy with dust, diamante inlaid hair slides, gold-rimmed spectacles, naked sets of chipped false teeth, brooches with MOTHER in gold wire, bracelets of square topazes, and little phials full of opal nobbies, like drab pebbles with rainbow veins.

Hughie snorted, and lumbered in through the grille gate. Old Joseph Mendel, his white hair brushed straight back from his sloping forehead, his beak of a nose magnificently jutting, his lips classically curved in the eastern way, looked up from his ledger.

'Good day, sir, what can I show you,' he said automatically, though he instantly noted that Hughie was drunk, that he was truculent, that he had something serious on his mind. Hughie leaned over the counter and blew a gust of wine-sodden breath into Joseph Mendel's face. The old man's expression did not change. He did not even bother to slip his hand along under the counter to reassure himself that the metal-bound cudgel he kept for self-protection was still there.

Hughie exploded into a torrent of filthy abuse. It was filthy mainly because he did not have much vocabulary. He did not have a particularly obscene mind, but the words he used seemed to have the necessity of adjectival qualification, and so he fitted the expressions he knew into the vacant spaces. With hardly an expression save that of polite interest, Joseph Mendel listened until Hughie, sputtering and scarlet and flaming-eyed, had paused for breath. Then he said: 'Be that as it may, what can I do for you?'

Hughie was doubly enraged. The coolness of the man he abused seemed to be a reproach, and to prevent that reproach from being any brake upon his self-confidence, he broke into further abuse.

'That little sneaking swine of a nephew of yours has ruined my girl,' he said thickly. Joseph Mendel inclined his head.

'I would not be at all surprised,' he replied courteously.

Hughie bellowed: 'You mean he's done it to other sheilas!'

'Not that I know about,' answered the old man amiably. 'But he is twenty, I believe, and most young men of twenty are seducing young women, either in fact, fancy, or desire.'

Hughie did not comprehend, so he bellowed even louder: 'What are you going to do about it?'

Joseph Mendel registered polite surprise. 'What can I do about it? What is done is done. It is nothing to do with me. Tommy is not even one of my employees any longer. If you wish anything done you had better see him.'

'I'll break his stinking little yid neck,' roared Hughie.

'Perhaps that would be the best plan,' remarked the old man placidly. Hughie, baffled, tried another tack.

'I'll take it to court.'

Joseph Mendel smiled. 'Paternity cases cost money, and you will need considerable proof that Tommy is really the culprit. You forget that you come from a street with a very bad name, where the general standard of morality is low.'

Hughie's eyes flashed. 'You insinerating that my girl is on the town?'

'I am insinuating nothing, my dear sir, I am merely stating public opinion. You are perhaps aware that a Surry Hills girl finds it difficult to obtain a position in the city. She may be educated; she may be more highly moral than similar young ladies in more prosperous suburbs, but her address is against her. Most Sydney people persist, somewhat biasedly, perhaps, in thinking of Surry Hills in terms of brothels, razor-gangs, tenements, and fried fish shops.'

Hughie, abashed, said: 'Swallered the dictionary, ain't yer?'

Joseph Mendel straightened his shoulders. His black eyes gleamed as opaque and stony as jet.

'I am well aware that you came to me this morning hoping that I would, on behalf of Tommy, attempt to buy you off, so that your daughter's questionable honour might be salved. But you might as well know that I do not care the price of one of those leaden trinkets whether my nephew Tommy fathers a dozen come-by-chances.'

'I don't want any of your stinking Jew money,' yelled Hughie, defeated and enraged. He flung the remainder of the fifteen pounds on the counter, and gathered it up again quickly in case Joseph Mendel should pounce on it. 'I can make that any week in the year, if I work a bit overtime,' he boasted. 'Honestly, too, not by squeezing it out of poor old tarts with nothing between them and starvation but a ring or a brooch to pawn.'

'Indeed,' Joseph Mendel bowed slightly and stood at courteous attention waiting to hear the rest. But for some reason Hughie had nothing more to say. He had pictured the old Jew cringing before him . . . he who was six foot high, and wearing a red uniform, and was accompanied by the noise of drums. He had pictured him offering him the shop if only he'd keep his trap shut about his nephew's misdemeanours. But somehow it had all come out wrong, and Hughie couldn't imagine why.

Tears stung his eyes, and angrily and savagely he turned and blundered out. He couldn't go home, for Mumma would be furious with him for getting drunk on a day like that when he was needed; he couldn't stay in the street, for a cop might pull him up. So he went back to the Foundry and 'shouted' everyone, and in their applause and warm good fellowship he forgot his misery and hatred of those who always put it over on him. When closing time came they threw him out into the gutter, and he lay there a long time before one of his mates came along and helped him home. And when he went through his pockets, of course, there was nothing there, for someone else had been through them first.

It was just after this that Grandma got sick, too. She had been a wonderfully healthy woman, with a wiry, whalebone body, and a constitution which had repelled all the bacteria which had assailed it from the moment she was born. Although she had spent her childhood in a damp mud hut on a bog island which was surrounded by poisonous vapours for half the day and all the night – although she had decided at the age of eighteen to leave Ireland for a better land and had embarked on an emigrant ship which carried its free passengers between decks in evil-smelling, airless little cupboards lit by oil lamps, she had survived. She had survived measles, scarlet fever, and finally the cholera which had broken out on board. When she arrived in Australia, still eighteen, and not much wiser than when she had left, she married an ex-gold-miner with a splendid square-cut beard and a watch-chain of little nuggets. He gave her eleven children in as many years, and she brought them all up with the money she earned scrubbing out other people's boarding houses. But somehow all but two died before she became an old woman, because they did not have the constitution to face the rigours of existence, as she did.

But now, after eighty-five years, Grandma's body suddenly went tired. She wasn't ill, and she wasn't fatigued. She was just negative where she had always been vigorously positive. It started when she said: 'I think I'll have me dinner in bed today.'

Mumma burst out. 'Don't be loony! And me with Roie to look after! When am I going to get the time to come running in and out to you like a sick hen, with the salt one moment and another cup of tea the next?'

To her astonishment, Grandma, who never cried, burst into tears.

'Holy Mother,' cried Mumma, aghast at her own cruelty in refusing a cup of tea in bed for her own mother who had done everything in the world for her until she was old enough to do it for herself. 'It was only a joke, now, Ma, and you can have yer dinner in bed any time you want it. Sure, it was only a joke, and you're the old blockhead to be taking it serious.'

Whereupon Grandma said: 'I'm not crying because you wouldn't give me a bite in bed, dotie; I'm crying because I want it.'

Mumma instantly understood what she meant, and a stab went involuntarily through her heart. Because she was upset she became cross:

'Don't be talking such tripe, Ma. You're a silly old goat if ever there was one.'

Grandma grabbed her hand with her knobbly old ones and asked: 'You do think so, lovie?'

'Of course I do, Ma,' Mumma soothed.

Grandma relinquished her hand. 'Ah, it's a frightful liar you are, dotie. When I've got time, ask me to tell you how to tell a lie. You just haven't got the knack.'

Mumma went out into the scullery and cried, stirring the stew vigorously all the time. She cried because she was worn out with lack of sleep and worry for Roie, and the deep abiding shock which the revelation of her daughter's escapade had brought her. She also cried because the stew had burned a bit at the bottom and she hadn't enough custard powder to make a pudding without going out and getting extra. And she cried because at last old age had caught up with her sprightly and wicked little Ma, and would never be defeated any more.

'Dear Lord,' said Mumma, looking up at the greasy, dirt-stained ceiling and seeing nothing but vast azure expanses with bright slits through which she could glimpse the cool avenues of paradise. 'Dear Lord, don't let go of me hand now, there's a good Lord.'

Grandma did not often get up again. The slow winter weeks went by and the roof leaked, and the great map-like stain on the bedroom wall grew into a continent. Near the roof above the wardrobe, fungus sprouted blue-green and exotic. Then came the spring, and sudden heat. Number Twelve-and-a-Half baked and simmered, for it had an iron roof, and concentrated the sun's rays like a magnifying glass. But Grandma did not seem to mind. She lay in her little dark cubbyhole, so smelly, and uncomfortable and devoid of all the peace and tranquillity that should surround one's last days. The sweat lay in heavy drops upon her ridgy forehead, and the old corded arms that projected from her torn nightdress. Now and then she was chirpy, and had short spats with Hughie when he came in unnecessarily drunk, or with Dolour when she persisted in yapping out in the kitchen without sticking her head in at intervals to explain what the conversation was about. But most times she just lay, her eyes staring at nothing at all, talking to herself. Mumma rarely had time to sit with Grandma, for all her energy was taken up with Roie, just crawling into health again. But Dolour loved to sit beside her and listen to the things she said.

To Dolour Ireland was inconceivably far away. It seemed strange and enchanting that her own Grandma had come from that land; it was almost as though Grandma were an old fairy woman from another and more fantastic world. Dolour's own half-digested reading about it had been reinforced by the loyal Irisholatry of the nuns at St Brandan's, who were Australian-born to a woman, and yet kept the memory of their surnames vivid in their hearts. Phelans and Flanagans and Dunnes and MacBrides there were at the convent, and old Sister Beatrix had been a Mullins born. And then there was Father Cooley, with a honey of an accent, and yet Australian too, as though he wore a buckled shoe on one foot and an Australian 'laughin'-side' on the other. They had all helped to make Ireland very real to Dolour, even though it was so fantastic a place.

Grandma had fights with people Dolour couldn't see: 'Keep yer tongue in yer jaw and yer toe in yer pump or it'll be the worse for yer,' she would say, or 'I never did like a bone in yer skin, yer crooked ould disciple.'

And another time she drowsed: 'He was a little queer man in a red, square-cut coat, and he came up to me jiggeting on the toes of his shoes and crying as though the heart of him would be broke in three halves.'

'Who was he?' asked Dolour eagerly, and after repeating the question three times, her grandma opened her eyes and glared: 'You'd talk the leg off an iron pot, Dolour Mary Darcy. Go off and don't be bothering me head.'

Other times Grandma really talked to Dolour, and into the child's soft-moulded mind went unique phrases, strange bits of grammar, and a smattering of old songs which Grandma had learned at her grandmother's knee, and which went back into the dream-days beyant Napoleon.

One day at school Sister Theophilus called Dolour aside and said: 'How's Roie getting on, dear?'

Dolour did not know what to say, because Mumma had told her never to answer any questions about her home life, if she was asked. Then she replied: 'She's getting on all right now, thank you.' She turned her eyes away from Sister's beautiful brown ones; clear, they were, like a bush pool with sunlight on it, or a setter's eyes, freckled with gold.

'We've just finished a novena for her. Do you think your mother would mind if Sister Beatrix and I came around after school this afternoon for a little visit?'

'No, no, I don't think so,' stammered Dolour, overcome with delight and fear because she didn't know what Mumma would think about it.

'Then run away home, Dolour, and we'll be around about four.'

Dolour rushed up the street very fast. She did not even stop outside the fish shop, as she usually did, to look fascinated at the beautiful blue eyes of the giant pink prawns. She burst into the kitchen, where Mumma, with furrowed brow and soot-freckled face was jamming coal into Puffing Billy's scarlet-lit throat.

'Mumma, Sister's coming round. She wants to see Roie.'

Mumma gave a shriek of alarm. 'Not today? Not today when the house is in a frightful mess and me hair hasn't even been done yet.'

'They'll be coming at four,' gasped Dolour. 'Crumbs, I didn't know what to say.'

'You should have said that Grandma had smallpox,' cried Mumma. 'Anything to keep them away.'

'Don't you dare be saying I've got smallpox, the filthy disease,' yapped Grandma from the bedroom.

Mumma sighed: 'There now. You've got her awake with yer loud tongue!'

'I didn't say it; you said it!' expostulated Dolour.

Mumma gave her a light skelp on the ear. 'There now, get the broom and start sweeping the upstairs room. I'll get a basin of water and clean Roie up.'

Dolour rushed upstairs, falling over the treads in her haste. Roie was half asleep; she was hardly recognizable, with her face waxy pale and sunken, and her eyes smudged dark and purplish and extraordinarily empty. Her hair was ragged and tousled; even her teeth appeared brittle.

'Wake up Ro!' cried Dolour excitedly, beginning to whisk all the litter of papers and hairpins and dust under the dressing-table. 'You're going to have visitors!'

Roie gave a sick gasp: 'Not Tommy!'

'Don't be mad,' said Dolour scornfully. 'That flip. Fine sort of mug he turned out to be, not even coming to see you once.'

'We had a fight. We aren't friends any longer,' said Roie. Then she pleaded. 'I don't want to see anyone, Dolour. Who is it?'

'It's Sister Theophilus, that's who. And Sister Beatrix.'

'But me nightie's awful, and . . . and . . . my hair . . .' Roie's eyes, which had shed so many tears those past weeks, filled again.

'We'll fix that,' said Mumma briskly, marching in with a bowl of hot water and a bundle under her arm. 'Here, I got an idea.'

'My nightie,' wailed Roie. Mumma whisked open her bundle. In it was a pale pink cotton blouse with a draw-string neck. 'Here's yer new cotton blouse. What say you put it on and keep the blankets well up, and they'll never know the difference.'

'Yes, all right,' wailed Roie, 'but . . .' Weakly she levered herself up, and Mumma quickly divested her of the old locknit nightdress. Dolour gasped open-mouthed at the emaciation of her sister, the scrawny yellowish arms and the chest which no longer had the sweet soft eminences of breasts, but only the curving ridges of ribs. Mumma caught her staring, and said sharply: 'What are you gawping at, yer big gawk? Go on, get downstairs and give me a hail when they're coming.'

She slipped the blouse on Roie. The girl fingered it softly: 'Gee, it's pretty, ain't it. I wonder if I'll ever wear it?'

'Don't talk like a goat, lovie. You'll be wearing it before this summer's through. Only you'd better not let Sister see you wearing it in the street.'

She looked for a laugh from Roie, but only the ghost of a smile flitted over her lips. She lay down again, exhausted.

'Now, let me do yer hair.' She carefully brushed the long straggling dark locks into some appearance of tidiness and knotted them back with a bit of brown wool. Then with brisk efficiency she rubbed a hot face-cloth over the girl's face. 'Anyone would think you were a baby, getting your face washed.'

Roie winced, and mentally Mumma kicked herself for putting her big foot in it. Oh, wouldn't Roie ever forget that little baby that had never come to anything but a heartache?

'Now, I thought we'd put this over the blankets.' Mumma unfolded the rest of the bundle, which turned out to be a clean patched towel, and the red silk shawl that Roie had bought at the markets. It glowed like a deep ruby in that drab and squalid mousehole of a room; its embroidered jade and turquoise were as beautiful as sea-colours. Roie wouldn't look at it for a moment. She shrank into herself in case she should hear in her mind a voice saying: 'Oh, rose of all the world.' But nothing happened. The memory was dead. She felt grief that it was, the only beautiful thing that anyone had ever said to her. But it was dead; it was dead like the baby it had begotten.

There was a sudden shriek from Dolour up the stairs: 'They're coming! I seen them turn the corner!'

Mr Diamond popped out of his door on to the landing. 'Who's coming, my girl?'

Mumma popped out of hers: 'The good sisters are coming to see poor Roie, and one yip outa you about Popish mummery, and so help me God I'll ram yer false teeth down yer orange throat,' she hissed with such extreme malevolence that Mr Diamond backed into his room and closed the door with extreme gentility.

A few moments later there was the sound of Dolour awkwardly greeting someone at the front door. There was also the stealthy sound of Miss Sheily's door opening, and being left ajar. Dolour fell over the bottom step, giggled hysterically, and said: 'I'm afraid it's dark.'

'Just as though they can't see,' hissed Mumma irately to Roie. 'Go on, pull the blanket up and don't be showing yer stomach.'

There was a gentle jingle of rosary beads, the sound which the world over heralds the approach of a nun. A light step on the landing followed, and into the shabby room came tall Sister Theophilus. Behind her came red-faced little old Sister Beatrix, whose spectacled black glances skipped with facile observation before they came to rest on Roie, who sat, stiff with embarrassment and fright, against her pillow.

'My dear Mrs Darcy!' said Sister Theophilus, warmly. 'And my poor little Roie!' She moved gracefully towards the bed and kissed Roie on her damp forehead. Sister Beatrix unsmilingly shook hands with Mumma, who, hot and flustered, and not knowing whether to smile or imitate the dignity of the nun, waved her to a chair. It was lame on one corner, and squawked reproachfully when Sister Beatrix gingerly put her weight on it. Sister Theophilus patted the bed.

'May I sit here, Roie?'

Roie nodded voicelessly. Sister raised one corner of the lovely shawl.

'What truly beautiful needlework. Yours, Mrs Darcy?'

'Good life, no,' cried Mumma, blushing. 'I can't even put a patch on Mr Darcy's pants without getting it skew-whiff.'

Roie did not say a word. Somehow, with Dolour and Mumma around, all her illness and the disillusionment of her knowledge had seemed bearable. Sometimes she even forgot that her room was a poor attic, bug-ridden, damp and malodorous. But now it looked what it was, the poor bedroom of a poor girl, each as soiled and hopeless and unexquisite as the other. All at once tears rolled effortlessly down her face, and she turned her head into the pillow and sobbed. Sister Theophilus looked in alarm at Mumma.

'She's not herself yet. She's very weak. It's a hard time she's been through,' said Mumma apologetically, longing to run to Roie, and yet not knowing whether that would be a polite thing to do. Sister Beatrix got up and stumped over towards the bed. She was mushroom-stout, little and dumpy, her white chin-band probably hiding a multitude of chins, the leather belt girding her waist so tight that the top of her wooden crucifix prodded her in the chest. She had a reputation for hardness, and many was the time her gimlet eye had pierced Dolour to the very marrow. Dolour would not have been in the least surprised if Sister Beatrix had given Roie's shoulder a good shake and said sharply: 'Rowena Darcy! Stop that ridiculous snivelling at once! Get up and dress yourself and go and help your mother to get the dinner ready.'

But instead Sister Beatrix said: 'God has his own ways of giving us experience, Rowena. Don't regret all the pain you have suffered. You will learn in the long run that it gave you wisdom of strength. Lift up your heart, as Father says in the Mass, and be glad that God thought you worthy to go through this trial for his sake and your own.'

Mumma and Dolour listened with the rapt expression of those who see visions and hear things they do not understand. When Sister Beatrix turned to Mumma and said: 'You mustn't worry any more, Mrs Darcy. Roie will be all right.' Mumma nodded as though hypnotized.

As they left the room, Sister Theophilus gave Dolour's arm a little squeeze, and a kind look out of her lovely eyes. Sister was always kind, even when Dolour's arithmetic was a disgrace to her, but never before had she seemed so utterly gracious. Dolour resolved on the instant that she too would be a nun, and learn how to be adored by her pupils, and would die and become a saint and in time be canonized and known as St Anne of the Seven Dolours. She had concluded this dream by the time Mumma had taken the Sisters to the bottom of the dark steep stair, and she was instantly awakened from it by hearing a familiar voice say: 'Blessed be God, Sister dear. Now come into the kitchen where I can get a good look at you.'

'Grandma! Oh, gosh! Oh, jeepers!' wailed Dolour, pelting down the stairs, for she was fully convinced that Grandma in her hearty hospitality, had climbed straight out of bed and gone to welcome the Sisters in her old flannelette nightdress and faded pink cardigan with no elbows in it. But Grandma had made a determined effort to get dressed. Her legs were bare, and she wore old flapping slippers spotted with candle-grease, but she had put on her best dress, and over it 'me tippet'. The fur collar stuck up with ridiculous pomp around Grandma's uncombed head, but the expression on her face was warm and delighted, and there was no doubt that Grandma was really glad to see the Sisters. In face of Mumma's anguished gestures, she drew them into the disordered kitchen, from which the volcanic upheaval of the bedroom could be seen.

They sat down, smiling, on the rickety kitchen chairs.

'You must pardon my mother,' babbled Mumma. 'She's not very well. She . . .'

'Ah, hold yer tongue, darling,' broke in Grandma determinedly. Sister Theophilus patted her veined old hand.

'It's lovely to hear a real Irish voice again,' she smiled. 'I haven't heard the real brogue since my father died.'

Grandma was delighted. She flashed a look of aggravating mischief at poor Mumma. 'And what was his name, if I may be so bold as to ask a Sister?' she inquired, with every confidence of being answered. Sister Theophilus blushed and confessed: 'Matthew Nolan. He came from Kerry in, . . . I think 1880.'

'God be praised,' exclaimed Grandma, lifting her hands to heaven. 'If that wasn't the year I came out meself. Matthew Nolan! He didn't come out on the *Fair Isle*, did he?'

'No, the *Stratford*, I believe.'

'Ah, I came on the *Fair Isle*. Matthew Nolan. I once knew some Nolans on a farm. Outside Tralee, it was.'

'But I had an uncle near Tralee,' exclaimed Sister Theophilus, delightedly. 'The farm was called Knock-na-gree.'

'Glory be!' marvelled Grandma. 'So it was. There was one by the name of Michael, I think.'

'My Uncle Michael!' Sister Theophilus looked at Grandma with shining eyes. 'I often heard my Dad speak of him. What was he like, Mrs —?'

'Mrs Kilker. Oh, he was a fine man, with black hair that stood up like a wall. A real, elegant Irish face, and blue eyes like glass marbles.'

'My father had eyes like that,' said Sister Theophilus dreamily.

'And the cut of him! A real gentleman,' added Grandma. 'Now that I'm looking at you I can see you've got the Nolan chin. So I can. It's as plain as the nose on your face that you're a Nolan, begging your pardon.'

Sister Theophilus rose reluctantly, glancing at the clock which stood on the shelf. 'I'm so sorry, but we'll have to go, Mrs Kilker. That's a really Irish name, too, isn't it?'

'Me old man, God rest him,' said Grandma proudly, 'was Johnny Kilker the iceman. But me maiden name was Mullins.'

'Was it?' asked Sister Beatrix with interest. She blushed a little, for Dolour was listening, and she did not believe in the pupils knowing their teachers' pre-profession names. 'My name was Mullins, too.'

Grandma gave a crow of excitement. 'Mullins, is it? Would it be the Cookstown Mullinses, or the Kerry Mullinses, or the Mullinses from Dublin?'

'From Dublin,' said Sister Beatrix. She gave a sigh. 'My father was from Coleraine Street, Dublin. He owned a livery stable there.'

Grandma tck-tcked sympathetically, for she could tell that old man Mullins was no more. Then Sister Theophilus interposed: 'Well, you and Mrs Darcy must come to afternoon tea at the convent one afternoon, Mrs Kilker. I am sure all the other Sisters would love to hear some of your reminiscences of Home.'

She extended a hand, and Grandma bobbed in what Dolour thought must be a curtsy. Then the nuns went. As soon as they had gone, Mumma fell into a chair and fanned herself with her apron. 'Ah, bless them, they're nice, but me heart's racing fit to burst. Run up and see how Roie is, there's a good girl.'

As Dolour disappeared, she turned to Grandma: 'A fine one you are, Ma, coming out in that terrible rig and talking so forward to the Sisters.'

Grandma pulled up the collar of her tippet like a proud old parrot. 'Yer only jealous, dearie, 'cause I made meself felt.'

Mumma gazed at her in admiration. 'You certainly did that. There's no beating the Irish, no mistake. But wasn't it the strangest thing you knowing her uncle?'

'Uncle me foot!' scoffed Grandma, wetting her finger and rubbing at a spot on her black dress. 'Uncle me foot! I only used the brain God kindly gave me.'

'You mean to say . . . you mean to say you didn't know him?' gasped Mumma in horror. 'You unnatural old liar.'

'It was a lucky guess and me own reasoning,' confessed Grandma, her filmy blue eyes dancing. 'But sure it gave the poor locked-up soul pleasure, so there was justification in it.'

'You're a wicked old article,' stormed Mumma, 'but I don't believe it. You described him as though you'd seen him with yer own eyes, and it was right, too.'

'Oh, that,' jeered Grandma. 'All Irishmen look alike. I just described your dadda, that's all, God rest his ashes. And now, help me back to me bed, will yer, darlin', because me legs are aching, something cruel, and I need a pipeful.'

'Shame on you, Ma!' said Mumma crossly. Then she started to laugh. Grandma's high cackle joined in, and Dolour, coming down the stairs, frowned at such unseemly mirth. She had her hands folded in her sleeves, and she was busy being St Anne of the Seven Dolours.

Twelve

Grandma got worse after that, almost never leaving her bed, sinking into a drowse of old age and weariness. It was hard for Mumma, running for ever between Roie and Grandma, sitting with one in the hot and prickling darkness and hearing the feeble cry of the other. Dolour was still sleeping on the old lumpy couch and often when Mumma was getting Hughie away to work in the morning they would stay for a moment in their frantic hurry and look at her mousy exhausted face, yellow in the pure light of early morning, drooping upon the curved shiny back of the sofa.

'Ah, it's tough on a kid, this life,' was all Hughie said, and Mumma turned away to Puffing Billy and stabbed a sausage with her long fork, trying to prevent the scalding words from coming up her throat. For it seemed to her that if Hughie had been a different man, a man who hadn't sat down and allowed life to defeat him, then things would have been better for them all.

Grandma had no teeth, having had them all out when she was twenty. In those days you just sat down on the blacksmith's stool and he pulled them out with his blackened pincers, giving you a swallow of brandy when you were near fainting with the blood and the pain and the horror. So Grandma's purply-pink lips were tucked in under her nose and her chin looked very long and pointed. She lay now with her head turning restlessly from side to side and her long, coarse, shiny white hair, like unstranded rope, lying over the pillow.

Mumma sat by her, smoothing her knotted hand as Hughie came in.

He looked down at the old lady, bending his fearsome black eyebrows at her.

'What's the matter with yer, you old devil?'

Mumma said: 'Hush yer gab, Hugh. She's asleep.'

But a thin thread of a voice came from Grandma: 'It's mortal sick I am, Hughie. Mortal sick.'

'Gah!' scoffed Hughie. 'Here, I'll fill yer pipe for yer and see if that puts some ginger in yer.'

He stuffed some tobacco in the little brown-stained clay cutty that lay on the counterpane, but Grandma, with the whisper of a gesture, motioned him away.

'Don't be sending me to a home, Hughie boy, whatever yer do. Say yer won't.'

Mumma blotted up a tear. 'Ah, don't be talking such rubbidge, Ma. As if Hughie would. Now try and sleep and you'll feel better when yer wake up.'

She pulled the blankets up to the ruffle on Grandma's nightgown and they left the room, walking heavily and wearily, for they were both worn out with the work and the heat.

Then one night Grandma ran away. It happened when Hughie came home a little happy, content to have his boots taken off and his bemused and wary body shoved haphazardly into bed. Roie had delirious nightmares that night, sitting up in bed and screaming in a thin squeal that made Miss Sheily thump against the wall and demand what the matter was. Mumma sat beside her, holding her poor tousled head against her breast and hushing her to and fro like a baby.

'There, there, it's all over, darling. Never again. Never again,' she murmured. When the girl was quiet again she went downstairs and found instead of Grandma an empty bed.

Mumma gave a great cry and ran out into the passage where a light blue oblong showed the dawn stealing through the open door. She pounded out to the verandah, looking up and down the street in anguish. But although the wind blew bits of paper along the gutter and a dog slunk from an upturned garbage can on the corner there was no more movement.

Mumma screamed and screamed, beating her hands on the bosom of her nightdress and not caring about the people who came grumbling and alarmed from their bedrooms, Miss Sheily in an old tweed overcoat of Johnny's, Mr Diamond with his gingery bare legs sticking out of an old ragged pair of pants which he obviously used as pyjamas, and Hughie frankly in his shirt, rolling from the bedroom in a fury of fright and bellowing what the matter was.

They found Grandma a long way down the street, sitting on the kerb in her nightgown, with blood all down her face and staining her hair, for she had fallen over several times. Beside her squatted a large, caped policeman, trying to get some sense out of her for his notebook. But Grandma was so frightened to wake up and find herself out on the street that she couldn't say a word.

'You ought to be ashamed of yourself, a hulking big fellow like you, tormenting the life and soul out of an old granny!' exploded Hughie, so relieved he found it less embarrassing to burst into passion than into tears. 'Go on, be off with you! The poor old soul's wandering in her head.'

'Then she shouldn't be wandering in the street in her shimmy,' expostulated the policeman.

Hughie gave the policeman a wink. 'You needn't worry, constable. It's into a home she's going as soon as I get me wife's consent. Sure, she's had a good spin, the poor old girl, and I've done me duty by her, mother-in-law and all as she is.'

Mumma cried bitterly as she put her signature to a paper which took Grandma away into a home for the aged and helpless.

'I'd never do it as long as I'd breath in me body,' she sobbed. 'But I can't tie her up, and if she's going to go wandering away, I'll never get a wink of sleep, and I'm that worn out already with looking after Roie as well.'

So Grandma went away, and all the street turned out to see, for it was a great event when the ambulance drew up before Number Twelve-and-a-Half, and Grandma, very shaky, but all dressed up in her tippet, and her tucked black hat with the jet hatpins, was lifted in. She was tremulous with joy, for she thought she was going for a ride in a bus, and she had always loved buses. By the time they reached the hospital, Grandma had forgotten all about her home, and Roie and Dolour and Mumma and Auntie Josie had drifted back into the past, as insubstantial as figures out of a book she had read long ago. Even Hughie looked strange to her. She asked him doubtfully: 'Do you belong to me?' and he had nodded and smiled, and kissed her cheek like soft chamois leather before he left.

'Stop yer whining,' he bellowed exasperatedly to Mumma when he reached home. 'It's a place like a mansion, and she's fine. She's got a little bed, with an elegant white counterpane on it, and there's a cabinet beside it with a bunch of flowers on top. And nurses everywhere. She's lucky, I'm telling you.'

'I know she is,' said Mumma forlornly, and she bent over Puffing Billy again, and prodded him in the stomach with the poker and rattled some coal down his gullet, so that he hiccuped smoke into the kitchen and spat a little shower of soot from the crack in the flue. And Dolour knew that Mumma somehow felt that she had betrayed Grandma's trust and helplessness, for there was no doubt, even if the Home was like a mansion, if Grandma had been in her right sense she would have bashed the nurses over the heads with her handbag and walked all the way home again.

Almost straight away Roie began to get better. She looked like a girl painted in blue and white crayon, her bones like shadows showing through the skin. At first she wouldn't look at anyone, turning away her face and looking somewhere else as she answered questions, but after a while as the blood became redder and her heartbeat stronger, she seemed to forget what had happened. It was almost as though she had gone to the brink of madness, and come back again, without the burden that had sent her to the brink.

In some ways Hughie understood her better than Mumma did, for always in Mumma's heart there lay the memory of that awful night when she realized that Roie was almost a stranger, with distinct and individual experiences and troubles. That realization, in some strange way, was almost worse than the knowledge of her daughter's sin and tragedy.

But Roie hadn't forgotten anything. It was just that now, in the apathy and languor of convalescence, she could drift away from all her memories. She could not even remember the faces of girls at the box factory. Even after she got up, sitting out in the backyard soaking up sunlight, and crawling around the house, she kept up this pretence, until at last it was a habit, and nothing shook her apathetic calm but some fleeting thought which she pursued and threw violently from her.

All the pitifully hard shell which the slums had taught her to build about her gentle, timid nature had disappeared and was never to grow again. She had no defences now.

Her first outing was to see Grandma. It was like stepping out of a dream to see the narrow sweep of Plymouth Street again, the plane trees with their white-pocked trunks, and the familiar houses crammed against their sooty iron-railed fences. Roie saw with astonishment that the trees were heavily leaved, and the starlings squabbling in the gutters were young, with faint rainbows on their dusty feathers.

'Why, it's summer!' she cried.

'Of course it is,' said Mumma. As usual, it had crept up on her, and she was still in her hot winter dress, rough and chafing around the neck and under the armpits, so that she was in a continuous state of discomfort and uneasiness. Mumma had already been to see Grandma several times, timidly attempting the trams, of which she was nervous, and returning home in the flushed and nerve-wracked state of one who has narrowly escaped death. She had said little about Grandma, save that she was well cared for, and seemed to be happy.

'Of course she is,' answered Hughie heartily, 'who wouldn't be, with a nice clean hospital to lie in, instead of a bed full of bugs, like she had at home.'

'It was the best I could give her,' glared Mumma, 'and you couldn't expect poor Josie to take her back again.'

'Who said it wasn't?' demanded Hughie. 'But it's poor fare when you're old and cracking up.'

'It might have been better if you hadn't guzzled every shilling we had to spare, and a lot more beside, these last few months,' said Mumma, her lips cold and stiff and straight.

A crunchy red gravel path ran up to the hospital, and slim-legged flowers swayed beside it. Dolour was in great delight. The smell of disinfectant did not bother her; the hospital was like some great and romantic house out of a novel or a film. It did not enter her mind that within that great white colonnaded building there was suffering and loneliness and death, and the lingering misery of sick old age.

They creaked self-consciously down the ward, looking from left to right at the sunken old woman faces on the glittering white pillows. And, after a while, there was Grandma, so small, so thin, she hardly made a hummock on the bed. Her hair had been clipped off short, and it was neatly brushed. Her corded, sagging neck emerged from the ruffle of her nightgown. She was frightened when they all stood around her bed and stole a look at Dolour who stood stupidly, open-mouthed, staring at her minute and sunken face, the soft skin of which was now mottled with red, and the long, long hands which, like a skeleton's, lay aimlessly upon the frosty counterpane.

But the worst thing was that she didn't know any of them. It was so strange, to look into her familiar eyes and see no recognition there. It was almost as though they had become invisible.

'It's no good,' said Mumma. 'She'll never be any different. The doctor said her memory's quite gone.'

Hughie felt his temper rising in a sparkling, reviving tide. Borne on the surges of it, he said in a loud voice, for he was appalled and shocked at Grandma's condition. 'Do you mean to tell me you knew she was like this?'

Mumma nodded dumbly. Tears were in her eyes. 'I didn't want to tell you. I didn't want you to know.' Hughie understood quite well that Mumma's grief for this, Grandma's final stage in life, had tied her tongue. 'I just couldn't tell anyone, Hughie. It seems so strange. But it's for the best, Hughie. If she knew she was in a place like this she'd die.'

Hughie said foolishly: 'I wouldn't have allowed you to put her in here, if I'd known they'd do this to her.'

Roie whispered: 'Oh, Dad! It's only because she's so old.' She sat down by Grandma and held her hand. 'It's me, Grandma darling. It's Roie. Don't you remember me?'

But Grandma only looked at her with sad, wistful eyes, not knowing what to say to a stranger.

Hughie said slowly, the fire in him dying out: 'It's a fearful thing.'

It was just as though he could see Grandma's memory, like a stretched piece of cloth, and it fraying into holes, little useless tatters. He felt a lump in his throat and turned away, frightened that he might break down and disgrace himself before all the other old people, who were so close to the brink of death themselves.

Grandma crooked a knobby finger at Dolour, and trembling, the child went closer.

'Tell me what I'm doing in bed, Kathleen dear? Am I lazy, or is it the sickness has got me?'

Dolour stared. 'She called me Kathleen, Mumma.'

Mumma thought for a moment. 'Kathleen was my sister. She died a long time ago, when I was a little girl. Say something, Dolour.'

Dolour held Grandma's hand, piteously fragile, and feverishly hot. She opened her mouth to say something, but before she could frame the words Grandma was asleep, her mouth fallen open, and her sunken eyelids heavy.

So they went away, the two girls avoiding each other's eyes, and Mumma unnecessarily severe with everyone, because she was frightened she would burst into the tearing sobs which were knocking at her breast.

In bed, in the night, Hughie said shyly: 'Are you awake, dearie?'

Mumma answered thickly, for she had been soundlessly crying: 'What is it, Hugh?' He slid over and put his head down on her shoulder almost as if he were a boy, and soft with love again.

'Would you like us to bring Grandma back here again?'

'It was you who wanted to put her away, Hughie, in spite of what you said today in the Home,' she answered.

'I was wrong then, darling. Sure, it's her home here too. It's empty without her being in the old stretcher and yelling for a new pipeful every now and again.'

She turned to him and held his head closer, his dear, wicked, wasteful head that she loved so much, and it seemed in that enchanted instant that her breast was slim and eager again, and his hair soft and curly, and there was nothing more in all the world that she wanted.

So it was decided and the next day Hughie went back to the Home. The doctor was a strangely cubic being, with his white jacket falling in still perpendicular folds, and his nose and cheeks all following the same straight up-and-down pattern. His glasses flashed disapprovingly as he said: 'I don't deny that I'm against it. It's on your own responsibility that you do this.'

Hughie, a bright spark shining in his blue eyes, brought his eyebrows together with an almost audible clang and replied: 'We're doing the right thing, thank you kindly,' and added the rest under his breath.

So Grandma came home. It was almost a triumphant procession. Plymouth Street lay drowsy and golden under a heavenly flood of Christmas-month sunshine. You could not notice the smell of garbage and old, old timber, for the sunshine itself had an odour, of the hot acres of the hinterland, and flowering gum, sweet and sticky. Everyone, gossiping over fences, waddling home from the marketing, waiting for the tram, turned and looked when the taxi bearing Grandma pulled up in front of the house. There was a brief painful scuffle as Hughie hauled and lifted her out of the taxi, for Grandma wanted to continue her ride.

Dolour was pleased, excited. She had told her friends of Grandma's departure and her own visit to the Home. Most of them had grandmas of their own, but very few had relations in homes for the aged. It gave Dolour an aloof and important air. So at Grandma's return, as a special favour, Dolour brought Phyllis Gall and Gracie Drummy along to watch. They stood giggling explosively at intervals, in the shadow of the stairs. Mumma was so happy to have Grandma back that she did not even notice, and after a while Dolour became sorry that she so pandered to public curiosity, and coming out of the kitchen, spoke sharply to her friends, telling them that they ought to know better than to hang around where there was someone so sick she was nearly dead.

'Crumbs, Dolour!' they gasped, their eyes big, and Dolour felt an overwhelming sense of importance, so that she went back to the kitchen on tiptoe, as though walking in a solemn procession.

Hughie was on top of the world. His was the feeling of pride and joy which one feels when one has performed, against violent opposition, a purely charitable action. He basked in the adoring glance of his wife, who had in a single instant forgotten all his transgressions of the past, and loved him for what he was, a husband who had brought his old mother-in-law home so that she could die in familiar surroundings.

Nobody thought to ask Grandma what she thought of the change. She lay in the narrow sagging bed, looking at the light with her filmy blue eyes, her puckered mouth tight-shut against food, drink or medicine. Grandma was not in that room; she was walking in some long ago year as another might walk in a meadow. Days and nights filled with swift passions and griefs of youth lay around her feet like the pages of a discarded letter; hours and minutes of memory and sensation brushed her brain like the wings of moths.

Roie came and looked at her there, so tiny that she hardly interrupted the even flow of the quilt. It was hard to believe that from the little worn-out body had come eleven children; it was as though Grandma were a tiny gate in the great wall of life, and through her had flowed being itself.

Roie thought: 'If it hadn't been for Grandma, I wouldn't be here, or Dolour, or any of our cousins. My baby wouldn't have lived or died.'

Grandma began to mutter, and frightened, Roie called her mother. They all came in, Dolour and Hughie and Mumma, and sat about the bed in the intolerably hot room, Hughie breathing aromatic fumes.

'Stevie,' said Grandma; her voice was as tiny and hoarse as the voice of an old gramophone record. 'Stevie agrah, wait till I undo my stays.'

'Who's Stevie?' asked Hughie in a shocked whisper.

'I dunno,' said Mumma, holding Grandma's hand tight between her own. 'Me father's name was John.'

Grandma's face seemed to fade under their very eyes; it was the colour of yesterday's milk, and smaller than they had ever seen it. She looked straight at Dolour and said: 'Stevie, it's wicked you are, and there's hellfire under me feet, but I love you, Stevie. Ah, Stevie!' There came the ghost of a giggle from Grandma, and Hughie rose to his feet and gestured Roie and Dolour from the room.

'It isn't fitting for girls to be here, when there's talk of this nature.'

'Ah, Dadda!' whispered Roie.

Dolour gave a wail, but Hughie was not to be baulked. He gave her a push, an angry, frustrated push, and Dolour, furious, ran out of the room, flung herself down on the mat and listened at the crack, for she knew that Roie was not likely to tell her all that the delightful and scandalous old Grandma said. But all she heard was the mumble of forgotten love-words, and phrases with no more sense to them than the babble of a magpie. Then, all at once, Grandma opened her eyes wide, and said in a clear voice to Hughie: 'Don't be breathing on the candle, yer tom todger, or you'll have us all blown up.' Then she smiled at Mumma and closed her eyes and went to sleep.

Dolour couldn't believe it when the silence came over the room and the house, just as it does over the land between the still and the turning of the tide. Then, as she heard her mother cry out, hoarse and anguished, she ran out of the door and screamed up the stairs: 'Miss Sheily! Miss Sheily! Go and get the priest, for Grandma's dying.'

She waited long enough to hear Miss Sheily's alarmed feet thudding down the stairs, then she ran inside again. Roie, pale-faced, met her. Dolour tried to say: 'I've sent for the Father,' but she could not, for she could see the words already forming on Roie's lips.

She gave a little squeal and ran out in the yard, hiding herself in the great jagged shadow of the phoenix palm and looking up at the cool sky and its wind-washed purity of light and colour.

'Grandma!' whispered Dolour. 'Oh, Grandma, where are you?'

Chained to earth, shackled and bound by her own body, she strained to get some point of contact with that flying timeless spirit which had just been released. The soft air touched her cheek, melting as it touched; the pure light flooded down into her eyes, but Grandma was nowhere, nowhere at all.

Thirteen

There was a man who used to go around Surry Hills with a barrel-organ in a pram. The organ was no more than an oblong box, with a fluted and gilded facade, and sides that were painted with gaudy pictures. When Dolour was very little she loved to stand and look at them . . . there was one of a Florentine blue lake with a snowy mountain behind it, as triangular as a moth's wing, but much whiter; there was another of a gipsy man in a yellow shirt sitting by a stile while his dappled horse grazed, and another, her favourite, of a little boat with a red sail, gliding for ever to a distant blue shore where a dusky castle stood. And, all the time, there would be in her ears the haunting wheeze of 'Come Back to Erin' or 'Land of Our Fathers' or 'Swanee River'.

The man who owned the barrel-organ, and presumably lived on the pennies its music brought him, was an elderly clean fellow with a lot of tidy white hair around his ears and a square, sturdy body. He spoke with an accent that puzzled everybody: Irish they knew, and Italian and Greek, but not his.

'What makes you talk like that?' Roie had asked him when she was ten, and he became cross and sparkled his bright light blue eyes at her, and moved off, playing 'Beautiful Dreamer' very fast.

The morning Grandma was buried, he happened to be coming up Plymouth Street. He wheeled his pram to a stop before Bert Drummy's ham-and-beef, and with tranquil slowness moved the lever and began winding out 'Come Back to Erin'. The music jingled like a harp with a broken string, but sweet and clear it drifted down the road to the church, where a curious sprinkling of people had gathered to watch the tail-end of a poor funeral. There was a strange

159

deep satisfaction in watching a funeral; it made them feel almost smug that they were still alive; that someone else had fallen before the Reaper, while they still stood, not only alive and kicking, but with a good chance of winning the double on Saturday.

There was a chitter of hushed talk: 'Old Mrs Kilker. Her that stayed with the Darcys.'

'They say she was eighty-six, poor old thing. Well, she's better off than the rest of us, that's what I say.'

'Yeah, that's her granddaughter, that was knocked around by them Dutch bastards. Don't she look pale and sick, poor thing.'

'I'll bet Hughie's got a few under his belt. Ain't like him to carry a pall without getting in a few stiffeners first,' chuckled someone coarsely.

Mumma, awkwardly dressed in someone else's new brown coat and with a stiff, unbecoming black hat wedged on her head, her poor, swollen face averted from the inquisitive glance of her neighbours, climbed into the taxi. As she settled uncomfortably into the corner, the sweet tinny strains of the barrel-organ floated through the open door. Hughie slammed it with a muttered blasphemy.

'Nice time to be playing that now.'

'It's true, though,' choked Mumma. 'She was always wanting to go back to Ireland, and now she knows all about it. Oh, Ma, I miss you so much!'

She collapsed into tears, leaning her wet cheek against the smudgy window of the taxi. Hughie sat gazing mournfully at the pockmarked red neck of the driver and the way his hairy, capable hands gently caressed the wheel.

'Sure, I might have let her make the Christmas pudding without all the fuss,' he said suddenly. Mumma gave a snort of assent. 'And there's many times when she called out in the night that I could have got her a little nip of brandy, and no harm done.' In the depths of his grief, which was nonetheless sincere because it was ephemeral, Hughie searched for more damning statements. 'I had many hard thoughts of her, and said hard things, and now she's gone for ever, and I can't say beg pardon.'

'I wish we could have got a priest in time,' sighed Mumma. Before her eyes marched a succession of little pictures of Grandma . . . Grandma young and vigorous, and skelping kids left and right; Grandma clouting a travelling salesman with a frying pan; Grandma getting tipsy at Christmas time, and having knock-down, drag-out fights with Pa; Grandma telling lies, being proud and hard with sinners, maliciously witty with the unfortunate. It seemed to her that she couldn't remember Grandma when she wasn't committing some sin or another. Then she said, with piteous defiance. 'If I could love her, the good Lord could, and he won't be too hard on an old lady who didn't have an easy life.'

'That's true enough,' admitted Hughie. He put his hand shyly on the sleeve of the ugly brown coat. 'That's an elegant coat you're wearing.'

'It's Miss Sheily's sister's,' said Mumma, comforted. 'It's good cloth.'

The little funeral passed slowly through the crowded streets. More men raised their hats to Grandma dead than ever had while she was alive. Hughie and Mumma felt a little happy because of this. It was almost as if for once she had commanded other people's consideration and respect.

When the funeral left the church, Miss Sheily, spare and white and emaciated in her tight black costume of another generation, trotted hastily down the street with determination in her heels. As she approached the barrel-organ man she said hastily: 'Fine time to be playing, with a funeral only a few doors away! You ought to be ashamed of yourself. Caesar's ghost! Isn't there any decency left?'

The barrel-organ man stopped playing right in the middle of an arpeggio and a tide of red flowed up from under his collar and swamped him even to his bald patch. He stammered: 'I didn't know. I am short-sight. Please pardon. I go.'

'You'd better,' shrilled Miss Sheily, in her high, cultured, birdlike voice. He looked at her out of round crystal blue eyes, sea-blue they were, with simplicity and naiveté in them. He gave a duck and a tug at his suddenly assumed round felt hat, and hastily trundled the pram away.

The next day he arrived at Number Twelve-and-a-Half, having

inquired in the meantime where Miss Sheily lived. Dolour was surprised and delighted to see the barrel-organ in the pram come jolting over the flagstone path.

'Hello, you come to play us a tune?' she invited thoughtlessly. The barrel-organ man shook his head.

'I come to see lady; the lady whose funeral it was yesterday.'

Dolour understood at once. 'Oh, you mean my Mumma. All right, I'll call her.'

Mumma, swollen-eyed, and melancholy-faced, came to the door. When he saw her the barrel-organ man said timidly: 'I come to say I sorry I played so loud yesterday while the funeral was on.'

Mumma said: 'Oh, that's all right, and it was very civil of you to call.'

'Mr Gunnarson my name,' said the barrel-organ man.

'Mr Gunson,' muttered Mumma embarrassedly, for she could smell something burning in the kitchen, and beside, any mention of Grandma and she knew tears would gush into her hot and stinging eyes.

'No,' said the barrel-organ man. 'Gunson not right. I am Gunnarson. It is Swedish name. Please, I would like to speak to lady with black dress, white face, who say "Caesar's ghost!"'

Dolour gave a spurt of laughter, and Mumma, frowning, said: 'Oh, you mean Miss Sheily. She doesn't belong to our family. She just has a room.'

'She's upstairs, on the landing. First room on the right,' added Dolour.

Mr Gunnarson replaced his hat neatly. 'Thank you. I go.'

He slipped past Mumma and Dolour, who looked at each other in dismay. His outward pointed boots clip-clopped down the hall. He looked up the dark crooked staircase and without any hesitation ascended it.

'Gosh!' remarked Dolour. 'Bet she pushes him down the stairs.'

'Sssssssh!' said Mumma. For the first time in a week a little smile tweaked at her mouth. Upstairs there was a brisk rat-tat on Miss Sheily's door.

Dolour and Mumma heard an irate squawk from inside. 'Very

well, I'm coming. Don't knock the door down,' and Miss Sheily's sharp skinny shoes squeaking across the floor.

'Well?' they heard her say. Mumma rapidly waddled down towards the stairs, and crouched tittering, in the shadows. Dolour's face went scarlet with the effort of keeping her giggles under control. They heard Mr Gunnarson's tranquil voice explaining his sorrow at putting his big hoof in it on the day of the funeral. Then Miss Sheily said: 'Well, what about it? It's all over, and it's Mrs Darcy you want to rub your nose in the dirt to, not me.'

'I'm a lonely man,' explained Mr Gunnarson, 'and I like you. You are a lady, you are not married, and I like to come and see you then and now.'

'Pooh, you dirty old man!' exploded Miss Sheily. 'Using a funeral as an excuse to pick up a woman. It's ghoulish, that's what it is, you dirty old disgrace. Now be off before I push you down the stairs.'

'There you are, I told you,' triumphed Dolour, and Mumma pinched her tail threateningly.

'I do not try to pick you up,' protested Mr Gunnarson. 'I am a man with a good business. Here, I have my bank book. You read. And I am not dirty. I wash my hands many times a day. You look.'

There was the sound of a door jarring on an intercepting shoe.

'Go on, take your foot out of there,' cried Miss Sheily angrily, and they could just imagine her white face distorted with fury and her black eyes snapping and sparkling above her beaky nose.

'I go,' agreed Mr Gunnarson, 'but I come back. I like you. You have kick in you.'

'Caesar's ghost!' yelled Miss Sheily, and there was the crisp sound of someone kicking someone else on the shin. 'I've got kick in me all right.' The door slammed. Mr Gunnarson quietly descended the stairs. When he saw Mumma and Dolour he said: 'I like her. She is Miss Sheily, yes? One day she will be Mrs Gunnarson, no? You see.'

He raised his hat, and his innocent blue eyes, as round as a child's, smiled naively: 'You think I am angry because she kick me in the shin? No, I like woman with fire.'

He slid past down the narrow passage, and Mumma and Dolour turned their heads like one woman. As he trundled the old pram down the road he started to play and the tingling, jingling strains of 'Pop Goes the Weasel' filled Plymouth Street with music.

Down in Hughie's work the men often ran a syndicate in a lottery ticket, a bob in per man, and Hughie always refused to join in. The Government, he said, had enough dough without him sticking in a bob for nothing. And as it had also happened that nobody amongst these faithful gamblers had ever won a fiver, he firmly continued in his belief that the whole thing was a rook.

When at last Roie was well, Hughie was so pleased that he paid a visit to church on his way to work. Hughie was a stranger to his religion. He would have knocked down anybody who announced that it was not the true one, but he never found time to attend to it, personally. He had not been to confession since the day, six years before, when he had been nearly run over by a tram, and in a burst of thankfulness had shed his sins.

Hughie left for work very early; the narrow streets were full of shabby girls hurrying off to the factories that hummed in every alleyway of the district. And there were men in navy work shirts and good tough tweed trousers; men with hard, cracked hands that they were proud of, for they were the symbol of their contribution to labour, and the commerce that made Sydney what it was. Inside the church Mass was proceeding; there was a sprinkling of people in the dusky brown pews, mainly very old or very young, for the middle-aged were engaged either in getting breakfast or in eating it preparatory to leaving for the day's work. Hughie stood awkwardly in the side doorway before he creakingly knelt and prayed:

'Lord,' he said, in a mental voice which seemed to him to be rough and manly, but straightforward and easy to listen to, 'Thanks for making Roie better, and don't ever let her do it again. Lord, I forget how to talk to you; you'll have to excuse me. When I get drunk keep me tongue outa the dirt, will yer please. And for God's sake give me some encouragement so that I'll have something to live for, me and me wife.'

Instantly and mysteriously, there shot into his mind the idea: 'Why not buy a lottery ticket?' It was like seeing the roof of the church split apart, and heaven itself peep through. Nothing could have convinced Hughie that it was not a thought straight from God himself.

'Christ!' he muttered, awed, and hastily changed his tone to a prayerful reverent one, repeating: 'Christ!'

He got up and clumped out on feet that refused to adopt a tiptoe stance, and from the door he looked at the altar and gave that familiar sideways jerk of the head which the man in the street always uses to greet or farewell a friendly acquaintance.

He did not think of the first prize; his imagination went no farther than the hundred pound prize. It seemed to him to be the limit of all wealth. He spent the day in a fever of impatience till he received his pay, for who was to tell whether or not some other clunk, perhaps even a wealthy clunk, was not buying the ticket which had the signature of heaven itself upon it?

When finally his money passed over the counter, and he received the jade green slip into his horny hand, Hughie had a conflict of sensations in his heart. He believed so sincerely that it was the lucky one, and yet at the same time he mentally prepared a speech of denunciation and contempt for God, if it should prove to be otherwise. The days passed slowly by, bringing more excited anticipation with them. It was like being a kid again and looking forward to Christmas, or a birthday.

Yet, finally, when he stood on the verandah, with the newly-arrived paper in his hand, he was too scared to open it.

'I don't ask for fifty, Lord. Maybe that was high-flown of me. Just ten, or even a fiver would ease things up a bit.'

Dolour came prancing out. 'That the paper, Dad? Let's have the pitcher ads. Roie and me are going to the Palace tonight. I earned our fares doing some messages for the Sisters last week.'

'Garn, hop it,' growled Hughie. He opened the paper with tremulous hands. The print blurred. He couldn't read it. Dolour said impatiently: 'Watcher looking for? I'll find it for you.'

'Leave me alone, willya?' yelled Hughie, and to Patrick Diamond, who clumped past just then, he complained: 'Blasted kids. Always around like flies around flypaper. Can't let a man have a peaceful read of 'is paper!' he finished, bellowing the words at the surprised Dolour.

'Oh, okay,' she said, skipping inside again. As Mr Diamond vanished through the gate, Hughie opened the paper again. He forced his eyes to the column headed 'Lottery Results'. The blood drummed in his ears, then faded away to a quiet humming sound. Hughie sat down suddenly on the gas box. For there was no doubt. The print plainly stated, 'First Prize (£5,000) to H. Darcy, Surry Hills.'

'Heaven look down on me,' whispered Hughie, brushing away the little black stars and moons that swung before his dazzled eyes. He looked at the print, and it still said the same thing. He could even read who won the second prize – 'Can't be Me,' Rozelle. Hughie poked his head out between the mealy vines that cloaked the verandah, and looked up into the infinitely high, infinitely clear blue-green sky.

'You're a good man, Lord, you are that. Never would I have believed, disbelieving old bastard that I am. You don't hold any grudges for all that I've been to you. Ah, it's a good man you are, and I'll never forget you for it.'

He withdrew his head, and there was Dolour looking at him. 'Whatever are you gabbling to yourself for, Dadda?' she inquired. 'You look like an old looney.'

'Looney, is it?' cried Hughie hysterically. He burst into a roar of laughter. 'I read a joke,' he explained. 'Here, take yer pitcher ads.' He flung the butterfly of newspaper at her, and she pored over it in the yellow light of the street lamps. He thought he'd tell her then and there; then he changed his mind. It might be better to tell them all together. He rushed down the hall, then paused. How much better to get the money first, and shower it all around the room! Five thousand lovely quids, representing a motor car, a new house, and endless bottles of wine! Or should he go out and buy a fur coat for Mumma, and come in and say he'd found it. Hughie found himself so besieged with delightful ideas that he had to go out and sit quietly in the laundry amongst the smell of soap and wet wood, while he marshalled his thoughts. Sometimes he felt as though he were dreaming it all; people in Erskineville and Mona Vale and King's Cross won the lottery, but never anybody in Surry Hills. Particularly never anybody named H. Darcy.

In the mornings Mumma usually had a job to wake him, for he was much too old for the work he did, and sank into exhaustion every time his head touched a pillow. She hated the sight of him in the mornings, his false teeth sitting on the dusty table beside his bed, and his gums tucked in like an old man's, his exhausted eyelids too sodden with sleep to lift. He looked like an old grandfather, and in some inexplicable way it hurt her, so that often she said, 'For God's sake, Hugh, won't you be getting yer big frame outa the blankets!' and turned away with a tear of love and pity in her eye for him.

But to her astonishment and alarm the next morning she awoke to find the bed empty. She got up hurriedly and clumsily, putting her old coat over her nightdress, and waddled out into the kitchen, twisting up her hair at the same time.

'Hughie!' she called sharply. 'Where are you? What are you doing?'

'Getting some of the scrub off,' called Hughie from the scullery, and there she beheld the unprecedented sight of him, at six in the morning, scraping the stubble off his face.

'Are yer mad, Hughie,' she cried.

'No, I'm shaving,' replied Hughie, unaware of any witticism. Mumma was so angry, she put her hands on her hips and stared at him belligerently.

'What are you shaving for on a workday?' she demanded.

'To get me face clean,' answered Hughie patiently, pulling a long lip and snicking out the hairs in his nostrils with harsh rasping sounds.

'What for?' cried Mumma exasperated. Hughie wiped his razor and turned to her, a white ruff of suds around his mouth and under his chin.

'Because I ain't going to work this morning, that's why, sticky-beak.' He pecked over suddenly and kissed her on the cheek. 'Because I got some business to do. Now, don't be asking me,' he winked mysteriously. Mumma, shutting her mouth tight, stamped off. The next moment he heard the pop of the gas ring, and murmured dreamily: 'All electric.'

All through breakfast Mumma was deeply troubled. What did he mean, business? Was he perhaps buying a present? It was Christmas soon. But Hughie never bought anybody any presents. The only thing he had ever bought in his life had been her wedding ring, and he wouldn't have bought that except that everybody seemed to expect him to do so. She was so baffled and frustrated that she hacked into the loaf as though it was Hughie's neck, so that by the time Dolour wandered down it was the shape of a scallop, with strange fluted edges.

'What's the matter, Mumma?' asked Dolour, sleepily.

'It's '*im*!' cried Mumma, pointing the knife into the bedroom where Hughie, in his grey undershirt, stood deliberating. He had two shirts, the khaki one with the holes under the arms, and the blue one with the frayed collar. In her clumsy way Mumma had patched them, and then patched the patches, and now they were beyond all human aid. 'Six white silk shirts with dandy stand-up collars,' murmured Hughie.

Mumma continued to fulminate to Dolour against Hughie.

'Don't ask him,' cried Mumma. 'It's business. He ain't going to work this morning! Just as though we can afford to lose the money. Oh, no, he's the gentleman this morning. Shaving, if you please, and now putting on his good blue suit and his red tie as though he had nowhere to go but to the King's palace itself. And he can go, for all I care!' With that she made a slam with the bread knife, and rushed out into the laundry.

'Gee, Mum,' wailed Dolour. 'You know I'm practising to be a quiz kid. I need nourishment. Where's my breakfast?'

There was a snort of repentance in the laundry, and Mumma came in, flushed and tousled, but ready to prepare breakfast. She did not spare another glance for Hughie as he marched with unbearable casualness to the door. 'I'll be seeing yer,' he offered.

'If you're lucky,' said Mumma rudely. Hughie's temper rose.

'I'm telling you you'll be glad to see me, when I come back!' he cried. Mumma went over and put her arms around his neck.

'I'm always glad to see you, you old tripehound, and you know it,' she said. 'But I wish you wouldn't tease me.' Hughie closed his lips tight and smiled at her mysteriously, so that she nearly swatted him. Then he closed the door and went off.

He took a tram to the city. How lovely Sydney was, all newly washed by the night rain, with her narrow streets brimming with people, and the sun cutting great yellow swathes out of the shadows that still shrouded the tall buildings. Hughie walked in a sort of dream, past the great pillars of the Post Office, and the little stalls with their striped awnings, and the flowers that the vendors were unloading from barrows. Nameless flowers they were to Hughie. Flamboyant bucket-shaped pink things and dark ruby rosebuds, tightly furled, and exquisite sprays of white flowers, with golden middles, and dew carefully applied from a syringe. Hughie thought: 'I'll take her home a quid's worth. Only I'll go in a taxi, in case I meet someone I know.'

He was outside the lottery office as it opened. The clerk smiled the smile he had tried out on a hundred other prize-winners, and hazarded: 'Five thousand?'

Now that he actually heard someone else say those magnificent words, Hughie's spirit began to tremble, and he went red and stammered: 'I'm H. Darcy, Surry Hills, like it said in the paper.'

The clerk was all politeness and congratulations. 'Excellent, sir. Fine. Fine. Now, may I have your ticket?'

Hughie fished in his pocket and got it, faded sea-green now, but more precious than Aladdin's lamp. The clerk took a glance at it, wrote a little in his ledger, and then compared the numbers. A strange look flashed over his face; his spectacles glittered ominously as he raised his eyes.

'Have you another ticket, Mr Darcy?'

Hughie gasped: 'No, have I gotta have two?'

'I was just wondering if you'd bought another ticket and put the same name on it,' explained the clerk. 'You see, the numbers are entirely different.'

Hughie, his face pallid, and his tongue swelling so that he could not even grunt, took the ledger that the clerk reversed for him. There was no doubt. There were only nine usable figures for a lottery ticket, but the ones on the ledger and those on his ticket were so different they looked like words out of different languages.

Hughie cried: 'It's down wrong, that's what.'

The clerk shook his head sadly. 'No, sir. No possibility of a mistake. Didn't you check up with the number in the paper?'

'I was too busy keeping it from me wife,' stuttered Hughie. He felt so sick he wanted to go out in the fresh air and sit down on the steps. But the clerk was inexorable in his sympathy. He took Hughie upstairs so that they might compare the signature on the winning ticket. Hughie was a man in a dream. He did not think to pray any more; he was a miracle man whom God had deserted in the middle of a miracle.

The clerk looked over another file of ticket butts. 'Here you are, sir.' He showed Hughie the line of writing. It was inscribed shakily in black ink. 'H. Darcy, Clarion Street, Surry Hills'.

Hughie barged home like a blind man. He did not even think to take a tram. Numb and light-headed with anguish, he headed towards the maze of alleys and laneways of Plymouth Street. Then he realized that he couldn't go home and face Mumma, so he turned towards the works. It was very late, but the foreman, seeing his good clothes and surmising that he had attended another funeral, was non-committal instead of abusive. And Hughie's mates, who had been straining at the leash for a conversation with him, said nothing more than: 'In the family, Hughie?' He nodded. One of them whispered to another: 'There you are. I told you it wasn't him. The old coot doesn't believe in gambling. Never had a ticket in his life.'

'H. Darcy, Clarion Street, Surry Hills.' It was written on the bench before him; it was written on his soiled hands and his polished boots that were already dulling before the dirt and slime.

'Oh, God!' cried Hugh in his heart, and no more anguished voice had ever risen to heaven's implacable gates. His life seemed almost too much to bear. As soon as the whistle went he took his coat and ran away. His mates watched him go, astonished: 'Musta hit the old boy hard, eh?'

He clumped into the church, looked sourly at the altar. 'All I got to say is,' he remarked, 'you're a poor sport,' and the voice of Judas could have been no bitterer.

He couldn't face his home. He hated Mumma, he hated Dolour, he hated Roie with her fragile face and little bones that cried out for a holiday and a rest in some luxurious place where he could never, never take her. He thought of going to the pub, but he had no money; he hung around the door for a while, longing to ask someone for the price of a drink, then he spat in the gutter with contempt for himself and hurried along to Clarion Street.

It was not much better than Plymouth Street, strongly ammoniacal with the smell of the nearby brewery stables, but Hughie was not cheered with the knowledge that someone badly off was receiving the pot of gold. It made him feel worse that anyone in such poor circumstances should be so ruddy lucky. He hailed a fat woman leaning over a gate.

'Excuse, missus, but where's this Darcy feller live?' It seemed strange to be saying his own name and knowing that it belonged to a person he had never seen. The woman winked.

'You got it wrong, pal,' she said. 'It's Miss Darcy. Miss Helen Darcy. You 'eard the news, I suppose. Ain't one of these reporter fellers, are yer?'

Hughie recovered enough to gesture vulgarly. The woman snorted with laughter. 'They been around all day, like flies after a dirt-box. But she ain't seeing no one. She's that stuck-up, the old cow. Wouldn't chuck a few sixpences out into the gutter for the kids to fight over. Not 'er.'

'Well, I wanter see her,' explained Hughie, bringing his eyebrows down grimly. The woman shrugged. 'Betcher got to crawl through the keyhole, then. She lives in the house with the washing out.'

Hughie went to the little down-at-heel cocoa-coloured house that was squashed between two towering tenements. A string of depressed greyish washing hung from the upper verandah. He knocked at the door, and a curtain was agitated at the window. He knocked louder.

'Come on, open up,' he cried jovially. 'I ain't going to hurt you.'

A little voice breathed behind the door: 'Who . . . who is it?'

'Name of Darcy,' answered Hughie. The little voice hardened perceptibly.

'I ain't got no relations name of Darcy,' it replied. Hughie's mouth formed words, horrible, soul-searing words, but he said nothing.

Then he cried: 'I ain't trying to borrow nothing. I want to show you something. Look, I'll shove it under the door.'

He pushed the lottery ticket through the crack. It twitched out of his hand, and he waited patiently, hearing the click of a spectacle-case, and then a silence. The door opened a fraction, and a long nose strangely reminiscent of Grandma's poked through. A timid, faded eye surveyed him. 'I hope you ain't drunk or nothing.'

'Sober as a judge, Miss Darcy,' answered Hughie with bitter truth.

'Well, you can come in, but I'm all of a fumble with people knocking on me door, and the reporters from the papers, and everything.' Hughie slid through the narrow space. The hall was dark and dirty, and smelt of cats.

Miss Helen Darcy was a tiny bent old woman, at least seventy-five. She matched the house in its neglect and grime. One felt that her old fingers found it too long and difficult a task to do her hair properly, or to wash the once-white collar that shrank miserably on her old dark dress.

Hughie explained the position, hope springing in his soul as he did so. He felt sure that he was good for a fiver at least, although his only motive in coming down to Clarion Street was to pour more acid into his wound. What would this old haybag do with five thousand quid? She probably required no more than her pension; she was too old and shaky to enjoy even fifty pounds.

'It was a bad disappointment,' explained Hughie meaningly. She looked at him vaguely. 'You aren't related to the Lismore Darcys?'

'No, I said I ain't.'

'Then I can't think who you might be.'

'I ain't no relation. It was just the funny coincidence,' explained Hughie patiently. 'I thought it was me . . .' Once more he launched into the tale of the lottery ticket, and Miss Darcy listened, her eyes roving into space, and her thoughts obviously somewhere else.

'I'm a poor man, and it came a hard blow,' said Hugh once more, giving her a plain cue.

'I don't know whatever I'm going to do with it: I never thought I'd win. Five thousand pounds; it's an awful amount of money. People'll come bothering me about tax. They've been trying to borrow all day, too. That Mrs Bainter . . . and besides, all them religious people'll be around asking for donations for bazaars and things. I'll never have any peace.'

'You could give a bit of it away,' suggested Hughie roguishly, but she did not hear. She looked at him timidly: 'Not related to the Lismore Darcys, I think you said?'

'No!' bellowed Hugh. She doddered to her feet, pottered out of the room, and recollecting, came back and ushered him to the door.

'We must take a ticket in the lottery together, some time, Mr Darcy,' she said. She put out her hand, and then pulled it back.

'You needn't think I'd pinch it,' said Hughie bitterly, brushing out into the street. Every gate was decorated with a bystander; they all wanted to know if he'd succeeded in borrowing anything.

'How was yer luck, mate?' called the fat woman. Hughie scowled and bitterly humiliated, went home. He was very late for tea, and Mumma was cross and childishly vindictive, giving him the too-hot plate, and the leathery egg, and the dribbling old cracked cup. She had not yet forgiven him for his mysterious goings-on that morning, and though longing to ask him about it, would not give him the satisfaction. Also, he had grease on his good trousers, and hers was the job of cleaning it off.

Dolour and Roie went to the pictures again. Roie was excited, and a pink light shone in her cheeks. It was so long since she had been out anywhere. After they had gone, and Mumma sat sulkily reading the paper and slamming the creases savagely out of it, Hughie said: 'It's a fool I am, dearie.'

'You are, and that's a fact,' answered Mumma composedly, though her heart sank. Suddenly, to her amazement, Hughie put his head down on the table and began to cry. It was the first time she had known him to do so, apart from a few drunken tears. All the nervous strain and disappointment of the day opened like an abyss before his mind, and he sank into it.

'Darling, darling, my boy! My lovie! Were you hurt today. Hughie? Were you sacked? Never you mind. We'll find another job. A better one.'

She pressed his head against her bosom, and comforted him. A wave of tenderness filled her with such panting desire to shield him from the hard corners of the world that she felt quite faint.

He told her the story. It seemed funnier and less tragic when he told it all, his efforts at secrecy, and Miss Darcy's refusal to see the important point. But Mumma's eyes shone: 'Oh, Hughie, a fur coat, and an electric stove!' She was just as delighted as if she had really received them. Hughie felt proud of his generosity, and expanded visibly.

She fussed about him, got him a cup of coffee and a piece of the cake she was saving for Dolour's lunch. Then they went to bed, and he fell asleep in her arms completely comforted. He did not feel the heave of her breast, or the heartbroken sobs that struggled to free themselves from her hungry and disappointed heart.

'It's not for the likes of us,' she breathed. 'Not ever.'

Fourteen

A long time before Dolour had applied for a chance on the 'Junior Information, Please' quiz session from 2MB. Her family had laughed at the time, and Sister Theophilus had looked at the child with misgivings. But Dolour felt that she knew quite a lot. Bits of information of little use to her or anyone else stayed obstinately in her brain, and often she could have answered questions at school very well, if only Sister had given her enough time to find words to wrap up her knowledge.

When finally the letter accepting her application arrived at Number Twelve-and-a-Half, Hughie became so frightened on her behalf that he jeered abusively, trying to shake her out of the idea. Nothing in all the world would have persuaded him to step before a microphone, and for Dolour's sake he suffered more nervousness than he would have believed possible.

'You'll be making fools of us all, showing your ignorance, and the whole world listening-in,' he said angrily. Mumma poked her heated red face out of the kitchen.

'And if the whole world's got nothing better to do than to laugh at a little child's ignorance, then it's time it was boiled down for glue,' she cried. 'And what's more, I'm going down to the radio theatre to see her go on, and if nobody else claps, then there'll be a good one from me.'

'And I'm going, too,' added Roie. 'I'm going to say aspirations all the time that she answers the question.'

'Is that going to help her remember how far it is from here to Perth?' bellowed Hughie.

'Is it scoffing at God now you are?' cried Mumma vengefully, and

Hughie remained silent, smarting, for he had not forgotten the lottery, and he felt that much talk about God would lead him to say things both libellous and scandalous.

But when he went to work the following morning he boasted to his mates about his girl who would be on the air from 2MB that night, and showing the big pork-barrel of an announcer that there were brainy kids in Surry Hills, just as there were in Manly and Potts Point.

Mumma was worried, for Dolour had nothing to wear except her school uniform, which was old and faded. Dolour herself thought nothing of this, for she had not quite reached the age where the clothes become more important than the person they cover. The tunic was good enough for school, and she could not see why it was not good enough for a radio session.

'You can wear my new blouse,' offered Roie. Mumma was pleased. The incongruity of a pink draw-string cotton blouse with an old serge tunic did not occur to her. It was a good garment, and Dolour would look nice in it, and that was sufficient.

All during tea Dolour was as chirpy as a sparrow. She felt excitement comparable to that of a girl who has tasted champagne for the first time.

'I'll knock 'em all down,' she boasted, and Mumma surveyed her geranium-red cheeks and glistening eyes and privately thought she would end up in a storm of tears just before she wás due to go on the stage.

Hughie was sulky, because Dolour had taken no notice of his warning, and proud, too, because she hadn't. He sat on the couch and pretended to read the paper, glaring over it now and then at Mumma, who was dressing. First she tried on her old coat that had tomato sauce down the front in a huge ragged stain; then she put on her navy dress. But it didn't seem 'dressy' enough, so she added her red cardigan with a hole in the elbow. Roie hastily cobbled the hole, and by adroit wrinkling of the sleeve they managed to hide the darn satisfactorily. Then came the question of shoes. Mumma was in the pernicious habit of unpicking the side seams of her shoes, just a little, to allow her bunions breathing room, and all her shoes had this peculiarity.

'You can wear my school ones,' suggested Dolour desperately. She was already dressed, the rims of her ears shining scarlet from soap, and her hair combed back with a wet comb into a slick, raggle-tailed mop.

'Think I'm going to be seen in them great canal boats,' said Mumma angrily.

'My feet are no bigger than yours,' defended Dolour. Mumma scolded, and began picking over the heap of dead and gone shoes once more. Roie seized a comb and cried: 'For goodness sake, Dolour, come here and let me do something about your hair. It looks downright frightful.'

'It'll do me,' answered Dolour, shying away. 'I don't want any old sissy curls and things.' But all the same she went, and stood docilely while Roie, her hand trembling a little with the weakness she had never shaken off since her illness, combed her hair into little tendrils which dried into featheriness.

'I can't find none!' cried Mumma in a panic, and stood, a forlorn figure in her mended stockings, her face red, her hair unkempt, acutely aware of the clock inexorably ticking away the too short moments.

'We're going to be late,' moaned Dolour, feverishly rocking from heel to toe. Hughie jeered: 'Best stay here with me, rather then see her bring disgrace upon everyone.'

Mumma instantly straightened her lips, and jammed her feet into Dolour's school shoes, scuffed and slanting of heel. They were a little too small, just enough to remind her in an exquisitely subtle fashion that her bunions were still there, and full of vigour. She crammed on her hat, rubbed a powder puff over her hot damp face and pronounced herself ready.

'Ho!' commented Hughie, with a derisive shake of his paper, as he subsided behind it and all they saw of him as they went out was a cloud of smoke and a pair of stiff defiant legs protruding underneath the white butterfly of the paper.

Dolour hesitated at the door. 'Ain't yer going to wish me luck, Dadda?' she asked expectantly. Hughie flung the paper down.

'You'll never win any quiz session when you say ain't,' he

bellowed, and beckoned her over and gave her a smacking kiss on the cheek. 'Good luck to yer, darling, and be sure to show them smart aleck announcers that yer not afraid of them.'

As soon as they had all disappeared from sight, Hughie leaped into action. He rushed into the laundry and rubbed the wet end of the towel around his neck and face, then hurried into his good clothes, swearing at the big toe that popped through the end of his sock as soon as he donned it. He rubbed the toe of each shoe on the back of his trouser-cuffs, and in less than ten minutes was pounding down the hall.

'Where yer going, Hughie, in such a ramtam?' inquired Mr Patrick Diamond, who was leaning over the banister.

'Me girl Dolour's been picked for the junior information session,' cried Hughie proudly, 'and it wouldn't be me to let her go to such a place without the support of her dad.'

Hughie arrived at the radio theatre not twenty minutes after his womenfolk. He sought high and low for them in the crowd, and at last caught sight of Mumma's red cardigan, and Roie's neat black head and white collar, near the front row. He was extremely annoyed, for it seemed to him that if he had been encouraged more he would have gone with them and thus not be forced to sit in the back seat.

He pushed past a dozen knees to a seat in the centre and settled himself against the soft overflowing bulk of a fat woman. Craning his neck, he saw Dolour on the stage, her knees very close together, and her ankles apart. Hughie groaned in spirit when he saw her. Only fourteen, and undergoing this torture. He suffered acutely, and the fat woman, annoyed by his agonized writhings, turned and said: 'Can't you keep quiet?'

'I could if you'd keep yer fleas to yerself,' retorted Hugh vengefully. The fat woman's temperature went up three or four points; he could distinctly feel it. He jammed the soft flesh of her arm against the side of the chair.

'Lout,' murmured the fat woman.

'Tub of lard,' hissed Hughie.

The compere appeared and gave the audience their instructions. They were to clap when he held up a large board with the word

'APPLAUSE' printed on it. Otherwise they were to be silent. He was a glittering individual in a white dinner jacket; his spectacles flashed semaphore messages of hope and cheer to the farthest corners of the theatre. Hughie hated him on the spot; he was just the sort of man to tangle up a kid with some frightful questions on general knowledge, sport or music.

Down in the front row Mumma's lips moved steadily as she murmured Paters and Aves to herself. Roie jammed her hands between her knees to keep them from shaking, and tried to draw Dolour's attention, which was hypnotized by the microphone.

For Dolour had lost all her *savoir faire*, her nonchalance, and her champagne feeling. The marrow had drained out of her bones, and her toes were so cold she could not have sworn that she had any. The other contestants looked much the same, some red-faced and prone to giggle, nudging each other and pushing handkerchiefs into their mouths; others waxy with the paralysis of stage-fright. Every one was wishing he had not been such an idiot as to enter this ridiculous contest.

The announcer, in milky tones, rolled out the commercial; it was all about some sort of washing powder that made laundry days a mere frolic in the backyard. Mumma's raspy red hands twisted in her lap. She muttered the more rapidly. There was a brassy blare from the orchestra, and the session commenced on a high note of jollity and suspense. One by one the contestants went before the microphone, and the compere mowed them down with the simplest questions. It was not that they did not know the answers; they were too frightened to think. But here went a ten shilling prize, and there fifteen shillings, and one terrified boy, potato-pale, walked off with five pounds. Before they knew where they were, Dolour was standing in front of the microphone, a thin, badly-clothed child with bony legs and a sliver of white petticoat showing above them. The pink blouse looked ludicrous. Roie blushed for shame. And Dolour's mousy whey-white face looked even worse.

'Closer, please,' said the announcer. Dolour stayed still.

'Closer, please,' he said, and on faltering footsteps she moved towards the little soapdish which stood there, looking at her with its single evil eye and sharpening its every wit to catch the least and slightest syllable.

'Now,' said the compere pleasantly. 'Will you have sport, music, history, or general knowledge?'

'Eh?' squeaked Dolour faintly.

'Don't say eh, say wot,' cried some jokester from the audience, and Hugh, fighting his way out of the folds of soft flesh that billowed upon him, shouted: 'Shut yer big gob and give the kid a chance.'

In an instant an usher with a torch was at the end of the row, flashing it up and down, but Hugh, sinking down behind his fat companion, was invisible. Meanwhile the announcer, with a humorously despairing shrug at the audience, had repeated his question. Dolour whispered: 'General knowledge.'

The announcer looked up and down his list of questions. The jackpot was three pounds, and he did not want to lose it to this trembling child, but rather to one of the pert, red-faced adolescents who would be good for a bit of repartee and slick gaggery. He found a nice, simple-appearing question, and put it to her bluntly: 'What is a Dead Sea apple?'

His voice was as far away to Dolour as a cricket in the grass. She stared at him uncomprehending, conscious of the microphone with its greedy mouth wide open to catch her trembling reply.

'Come now, have a guess,' suggested the announcer pleasantly. There was another dead silence which seemed to stretch into interminable minutes. Hughie was overcome with torture for his poor child; he tried to send her telepathic messages . . . 'Come on kid, kick 'im in the belly and come back here to Dadda.'

The announcer repeated: 'Just a guess, that's all we ask for,' and winked at the crowd. All at once Dolour woke up. What was the matter with her? She knew that question. She'd read it in a book once. Things flicked back into focus. She said firmly: 'It's anything that looks nice on the outside and is nasty inside. A real Dead Sea apple is fruit with a lovely red skin and a whole lot of slimy stuff inside it.'

'Wow!' cried the announcer, giving the audience the wave to clap. The crowd cheered, and Dolour, clutching the money like a bouquet, walked off the platform. There was another commercial from the announcer, who infused the most innocent sincerity into his voice; a lot of rowdy music, and the audience rose and clumped out, reassured by the green slot of light over the door that the sound of their feet would not deafen half listening Australia.

Hughie turned and clapped the fat lady on the shoulder. He loved her. But she jerked away from him and glared.

'Sorry if I annoyed you, missus,' said Hughie placatingly, 'but that was me little girl. I was scared stiff she'd burst into tears or sumpin.'

The fat lady tried to glare again, but her curving cheeks and tiny fluffy brows were not made for frowns. She melted into a smile which involved a dozen dimples and four chins.

Hughie was a different man. It was not quite as ego-inflating as being drunk, but well on the way. He grew three inches, and all the mediocrity of his being vanished. He knew that people were looking at him, with tolerant grins, so he spoke extra loudly in a ringing voice, so that everyone might know that Dolour was only fourteen, and the smartest kid in Plymouth Street.

Mumma's pride was silent. She gave Dolour a squeeze, and cast around shy eyes to see if other people were noticing. Roie as though to redeem the disloyalty of her first thought about that frightful pink blouse, lied gallantly: 'You looked as cool as a cucumber. Nice, too.'

Dolour was too breathless to speak. She held up her hand and showed them money crisp and starchy; it was the first she had ever possessed. Together they turned into the retreating crowd, all struggling to reach the door first. Somehow Roie dropped behind. She could not see Mumma's hat anywhere, or Dolour's bobbing head. To make it worse, she was feeling dizzy, with cold pricklings at the base of her spine and perspiration damping her hair.

'Ah.., ah, gosh,' murmured Roie, desperately trying to get past the mass of people into the fresh air. But it was no good. Her knees melted, and she would have fallen, if it had not been for the fact that she was wedged upright in the crowd. Perspiration streamed down her back. Terror of falling, and fear of drawing attention to herself filled her. Noises were already fast fading into a babble of sound. Then a voice said: 'What's the matter? Are you feeling sick?'

It was a hollow, echoing voice like thunder on a heath. Roie tried to answer it and couldn't. It sounded again, frightening her a little, then she felt someone lower her into a seat. She sat there with her eyes closed. After a while the feeling passed, leaving her limp, but singularly clear-minded. She glanced at her companion.

'How do you feel now?' he asked. He was young and dark, his white shirt collar over the grey one of his coat. Roie said with surprise: 'Your voice sounded so queer. But it doesn't now.' He laughed. Roie hurried on. 'I'm awfully sorry. It was just the heat . . . and the crowd . . . I've been sick . . . I'm so sorry.'

'It's not your fault,' he said. 'Are you by yourself?'

'Oh, no,' said Roie. 'My mother is somewhere in the crowd. And my sister. She was the last contestant, the one who won the three pounds.'

'Well, we'll go and look for them when you feel better.'

'I'm fine now,' Roie assured him. She rose to her feet, still shaky and together they moved up the aisle. Unselfconsciously he took her arm, and unselfconsciously she leaned upon his firm hand.

'Did you enjoy the show?' Now she realized that there was something different about his voice, a soft breathiness that was not in other men's.

'Oh, I did. I thought it was fun.'

They found Mumma and Dolour outside, together with Hughie, who had waited for them. Mumma was offended with Hughie for misleading them so, and delighted too that he had been there to witness Dolour's triumph. Dolour was rushing around amongst the people like a wet hen, searching for her sister.

'Oh, there you are, Roie!' said Mumma. They all stared in embarrassed amazement at the young man, his height and darkness, and the yellow clearness of his eyes. Who was this stranger? Roie stammered: 'I felt a bit sick in there . . . and he brought me outside.'

Mumma was blushing: 'It was very kind of you, son.'

The young man said unsmilingly: 'It was nothing. I hope your daughter will be all right now. Good evening.'

'Indeed, and you can't be going like that,' said Hughie beaming. He rolled up to the stranger and clasped him by the hand as though he were an old friend. 'Come on home with us and have a cup of tea.' He winked. 'Or I might find a drop of muscat in a bottle I've got stowed under the bed.'

Roie pulled at her father's arm, anxious to shut him up before he shamed them all. 'He doesn't want to . . . he's got somewhere else to go . . . please, Dadda!'

'Where's yer hospitality!' demanded Hughie irately, shaking off her clutch. Mumma added quietly: 'If you've nothing better to do perhaps you'd like to call in some evening and we could have a little supper and a listen to the radio.'

'I'd like to do that,' answered the young man. He and Mumma looked at each other as though they were old friends.

Dolour chirped. 'We live at Number Twelve-and-a-Half, Plymouth Street, Surry Hills.'

He smiled at them all, and vanished down the street. Mumma eased her heel out of her shoe, which had been giving her jip all evening. Her face screwed into awful lines of agony as she tried to slip it back again. Hughie said irately: 'What you looking like a gargoyle for?'

Dolour waved the money. 'I'll buy you a new pair tomorrow, Mumma. Sixes. So your feet won't ever hurt again.'

Hughie felt this to be a reproach to himself, so he digressed by staring off down the road and proclaiming: 'We won't never see that young sprout again. And he looked a good sort, even though he did have a bit of tar in him.'

'What do you mean by that?' asked Mumma sharply. Hughie glanced at her in surprise.

'A bit of Aboriginal, that's what. Couldn't you see it looking out of them eyes? And them long strangler hands?'

'No, I couldn't,' said Mumma shortly. She fell into silence, and not even the hysterical chatter of Dolour, recounting all the other questions she might have answered just as well, brought her out of it.

Into Roie's timid and cautious mind, so frightened now of anything new or out of the domestic rut of her life, came gentle thoughts of the young man. She had liked his warm hand, and his dark, tranquil glance. She did not want to see him again, but something strange and unusual in him made her wish, almost ashamedly, that their meeting had been more prolonged.

For a week there was no sign of him, and Roie had almost put him out of her mind, when one evening he came, strolling up the flagged path as though he had often done it before.

'Hello,' he said to Roie, who sat drying her hair on the verandah.

'Hello,' she answered breathlessly, looking shyly at him from under its dark fall.

'Sorry I couldn't come before. I've been put on night work. Mind if I sit down?'

'Oh, no,' gasped Roie, moving along the step a little. He sat beside her.

'You've got pretty hair.'

Roie blushed. 'Oh, it's all tangled and untidy now. I'll go and fix it in a minute. Where . . . where did you say you worked?'

'Down in Coogee Street. At the Clarkson printery. I'm a machinist.'

'Oh,' Roie was silent. She had never learned anything about making conversation. She was at first awkward and uncomfortable, but imperceptibly her unease vanished, and she had no desire to talk, or to do anything but sit there. He was a strange restful person. He made her feel remote from the usual muddlement of her thoughts, born of shame and sickness and a terror of the long unknown future.

'What's your name?' he asked after a while.

'Rowena Darcy . . . Roie. What's yours?'

'Charlie Rothe.'

'That's an unusual name.'

'It's Irish, just like Murphy.'

'Darcy's Irish, too.'

'I can see that.' He smiled at her, and it was as if he acknowledged in that smile the extreme Celticism of her dark blue eyes and milky skin, clouded around the eyes. He touched her hair lightly. 'You have got pretty hair.'

'Have I?' Roie melted into smiles. She was happy that he liked it. He saw the ghost of a dimple in her thin cheek, and a delectable crease at the side of her mouth. Almost then and there they fell in love.

Fifteen

Falling in love with Charlie Rothe was different from falling in love with Tommy Mendel. Had she really been in love with the Jewish boy, so shallow, so emotionally brittle, his mind clouded with the selfishness engendered by his deformity? Yes, yes, cried Roie passionately, as she remembered the subtle sweetness she had experienced at the touch of his hand, and the longing, yearning way she had tried to cover up his defects. But there was nothing left of it. It had all been killed that night in the park. Until then she had successfully fitted him into the mould her dreams had created, but her love had been too fugitive, too insubstantial, to survive that experience. She knew that she would never think of him again, other than as a stranger. But surely, surely, thought Roie piteously, all love isn't that, fading in a season, like a rose?

So she said farewell to first love, that had bloomed so swiftly, and died so pitifully soon. There had been pity in her heart for Tommy, his loneliness and despair and youth; but there was none for Charlie. Tommy had brought out maternal instincts; she had wanted to shelter him, to do things for him. Charlie brought out the lover in her; she wanted to be sheltered by him. He was one of those rare people who meet life with a non-derivative mind. He watched it go by with a patient and humorously impersonal eye; observing, he created his own opinions, and acted on them. Charlie would never be a great or famous man; he was not the sort that goes into politics and finally dies and is epitomized in the words, 'Slum Boy Makes Good.' But he had the sort of heart that great men have, straightforward, undeviating and tranquil.

Roie often looked at him speculatively, and wondered what he was thinking about. He had an interesting face, very brown of skin, with uneven eyebrows, one peaked. His eyes, so hazel they were translucent, rarely clouded or altered from their calm expression. His hands were broad and long, large capable hands with rough stained patches from his work.

Mumma had clucked sympathetically when he told them that he had no parents.

'They died when I was about seven, I think.'

'Don't you know?' asked Dolour curiously. He shook his head. 'I was adopted about that age. That's all I really know.'

'By kind people?' asked Mumma.

'By a bagman. He just picked me up. I was sitting by a fence yowling my head off, and he asked me to come along with him, and I went. He was good to me, old devil that he was.' Charlie's eyes looked back into the past and saw the endless dusky, dusty roads of New South Wales, linking station to station, and hamlet to hamlet; always the brazen sky above, and the sense of great unfathomable spaces all around, when not even the wind found a barrier for hundreds of miles. He said quietly: 'When I was fifteen we came to the city. We had a lodging together. He apprenticed me to the printery, and said that he would give up the road, and I could support him for a change. I would have been glad to do that, but after a week he disappeared. I've never heard of him since. That was nine years ago.'

'Twenty-four,' added up Mumma mentally, and a dread filled her soul. 'He's just right for Roie. I hope they don't get interested in each other.'

She was desperately frightened that a second love would be as disastrous as the first, and yet she was anxious for Roie to marry, so that the girl would forget the quicker. The stress between her two desires was so great that she became quite cross and upset with everyone, and, leaving the dishes to Hughie and Dolour, she went to Benediction to think it over.

But she received no help there, either. She felt that Our Lord was smiling at her enigmatically, as though to say: 'Now, Mrs Darcy, use your common sense, and no more of this running to me like a foolish child, big fat woman that you are.'

And it was no better when she got home, or during the following month, for Roie went round the house quiet and absorbed, and regaining her health at so rapid a rate that it was almost as though the strong heart that beat in Charlie Rothe's breast pulsed life and vitality through Roie's own body. Once again they heard her little voice, as fugitive and uncertain as the voice of a sparrow on a chimney-ledge, singing in the upper room. This made Mumma angrier than ever, in a muddled, anxious way. She hurled a mouthful of coal down Puffing Billy's maw and went up to tackle Roie herself.

She came to the point at once. 'Roie love, I'm worried about Charlie. You aren't getting serious about him, now?'

Roie instantly flew at her, her eyes as wide as a cat's with alarm.

'Mumma, you wouldn't tell him about me and Tommy?'

Mumma's heart sank. She sat on the bed and began rubbing her thumb over the smooth iron rail. 'Ah, Roie, I wouldn't tell a soul. You know I wouldn't tell him. But . . . are you in love with him, Ro?'

Roie's face suffused with relief, and a shy delight filled her eyes. 'Oh, Mumma, I am. And he loves me too,' she added with a delicate pride that tore her mother's heart.

'Did he say so?'

'No, he hasn't yet. But he will.'

'He's not like that Tommy,' warned Mumma, 'Charlie's a man. He's a grown man.'

Roie sat down beside her mother. 'Oh, Mumma, I know. I know that Charlie's quite different. Aren't people queer, Mumma?'

'Why, darlin'?'

Roie couldn't find words. 'People going along, each one like an island, quite separate from all the others. Then you meet someone going the same way, and you find that you don't want to be an island any more.'

Mumma said desperately, blurting out what was in her mind. 'Roie, you aren't ready for marriage yet. That illness, you don't know what it might have done to you. Maybe you'd get worse after you were married.'

Roie laughed. 'Oh, Mumma, I won't. And I do want to get married to Charlie. I do, so much. Isn't it funny . . . a little while ago I was so frightened to think about getting married that I wanted to die. But now it's different. Everything's different.'

'Maybe Charlie won't ask you,' said Mumma brutally, but Roie only looked at her wide-eyed and laughed: 'Oh, Mumma, of course he will!'

'How do you feel about him?' asked Mumma. Roie thought for a long time before replying: 'I want to be with him all the time. I want to do things for him.'

Mumma gave a silent groan, for she knew so well that the sort of love which wanted to serve the beloved was the sort you never escaped. It was around your neck, a silken cord of inconceivable strength, till the moment you died, and probably afterwards.

She went away, and brutally punished Puffing Billy all the afternoon, till Hughie came home, when she started on him. He was in a particularly good humour, having bested someone in a political argument down at the pub, and this irritated Mumma all the more. She had a teasing masochistic desire to precipitate a quarrel between herself and Hughie. She said sharpened things, and when he answered only with amiable chaff, made them sharper. When he finally turned on her and told her that if there was one more crack out of her he'd flatten her out, she subsided, satisfied. It was a good lead up to a timid, apologetic remark that she was worried, and it was a pity she couldn't get any help from him in this matter, which was beyond her powers to solve.

Hughie instantly melted into sympathy and self-importance.

'It's this Charlie,' said Mumma, helplessly. 'She's in love with him and talking about marrying.'

'And why not?' demanded Hughie warmly. 'She's a very pretty girl, our Roie. She wouldn't be my daughter if she had the bent nose and scraggy hair of some I could mention. And Charlie's got a good job, and a fine pair of broad shoulders too.' He saw the look on Mumma's face, and went on, even more warmly: 'And if you're thinking of her little slip-up with Tommy Mendel, then you can forget it, for there's many a girl who has made the same mistake and no worse for it. You would have made it yourself, if I hadn't been the gentleman.'

'Fine sort of gentleman, you with the hands that needed to be slapped every blessed minit,' declared Mumma. Then she blew her nose on her apron and looked at him red-eyed and told the truth. 'It's because there's nigger in him, Hughie. I'm scared of it, and no mistake.'

Hughie said defiantly: 'It's better than Chink. It's real Australian and no matter how bad that is, there's none better.' Then he lapsed into silence, seeing the same picture that haunted Mumma, of himself out on the verandah nursing a sooty grandchild.

He said grimly: 'I'll speak to him about it when he comes this evening,' and immediately fell into a state of nervousness in case his impulsive tongue offended Charlie and ruined Roie's chances.

That night Charlie instantly sensed the awkwardness and worry that was behind Hughie's greeting. His mind ran over one possible reason after another. He looked at Mumma, rushing off to the pictures with Dolour, and at Hughie's red creased face that was making every effort to be as garrulous and hospitable as usual, and yet plainly showed in every line the turmoil its owner was feeling.

Charlie quietly manoeuvred Hughie into a conversational position where he had no option but to ask the question that was bothering him.

'You won't get rumbustious now, Charlie boy, because there's no offence meant, and heaven knows I'm not the one to skite meself, having a hangman in the family, but could you be telling me where the dark blood in you comes out?'

He sat panting, fiercely swiping at mosquitoes, for they were sitting out on the verandah in the shadow of the hanging vine.

Charlie said: 'It comes out all over me, I guess,' and sat courteously waiting.

Hugh blurted: 'I mean, where it comes from?'

'Well, my grandfather was white, and my grandmother was white, so it must have been long before that. It's funny how it shows long after.'

'It is that,' agreed Hughie, baffled, pulling at his pipe and sliding the worn stem up and down a little nick in his teeth. After a while he tried again: 'Perhaps I'm rushing things a bit, Charlie, and no offence meant if I am, but what about the children?'

'You mean my children?' asked Charlie. A soft red crept into his brown cheek. 'Then you think Roie would marry me?'

Hughie said embarrassedly: 'There, now, I can't be telling on me own girl, can I? But it's my belief she likes you well enough, and that's saying it fairly.' He looked carefully at a vine leaf that had fallen near his hand and asked again: 'And now, what about the kids?'

'What do you think?' asked Charlie. Hugh didn't like staring at him, but he did, his own face going red meanwhile. And it seemed to him that Charlie spoke and behaved like a white man, and looked like one, too, except to the wise eye of a man such as himself, who had been in the outback more times than he could remember.

'I reckon they'd be white,' he declared.

'Who would?' called Roie, clattering down the stairs in her high heels.

'Our children,' answered Charlie. Roie gave her father a startled glance and fled past him into the blue dimness. Charlie followed her and, in the shadows away from Hughie's eyes, pulled her close and kissed her, stopping her whispered protests with words of his own.

'What did Dadda say? He's an old devil. He didn't mean it . . . whatever it was.'

'When can we be married?'

'You're making fun of me, and I'm not going to stand for it.'

'Will it be next month, or next week?'

'I'll kill Dadda. What did he say about children?'

'Only that ours will be white.'

Roie stopped, open-mouthed, and tried to walk away from him. He caught up with her, and they went swiftly up the street. Roie stole a sideways glance at Charlie's face.

'You don't mind, do you, Roie? I mean, me having a bit of dark blood in me?'

Roie said scornfully: 'Of course I don't. It's such a long time ago, and it wouldn't matter to me if it was only a generation ago. There are lots of lovely dark people. Even Dadda says that, and he often worked with them.'

Charlie realized that there was no black-white problem with Roie. Either people were nice, or they were not. Her wisdom had deeper roots than that of the people who put colour before character. Laughing aloud for exultation, he stopped her under a street lamp and stood tall and shadowed amidst the yellow circle of light.

'You haven't answered me, Roie. When can we be married?'

She blushed and hid her face on his coat. 'Could it be tomorrow?'

'As soon as that?' he teased. She held him tight around the waist and hugged him.

'I just want us to be together all the time, that's all,' she answered softly.

Something made them laugh, staring into each other's faces with joy and triumph pouring into their minds. The night was inconceivably bright and glamorous, and the saffron flood in the western sky like a reflection from the doorway of paradise. Hand in hand they ran down the street and vanished into the dark maze of alleys that led to the city.

Hughie, who had been watching their light-limned figures from his distant gate, shook his head and wandered slowly indoors, muttering: 'He ain't a buck nigger, and he's got a good job; but it's funny to think of little Ro married.'

A slow hurtful feeling was taking possession of him; he felt old. A man who had spent his whole life in pursuit of the satisfactions of the body, as far as was compatible with the wages of a poor labourer, he viewed with fear and mutinous feelings the approach of age. He was a strong healthy man, and all the gallons of rough wine he had poured into his stomach had not done more than sharpen his temper and slow down his digestive process. When he looked at Mumma, so fat and clumsy, he felt slight and young and superior, and he did not hesitate to tell her so.

But with the prospect of Roie's getting married, he felt worse, as though the shadow of old age and eventual death had become fleshly and well-established beside his daily path. He remembered Roie so well as a dirty, startled-faced little brat who scuttled under the kitchen table at his drunken approach; he remembered her howling on her first day at school, and his bribing her with a penny, the way she had doubled one fist upon the other, and looked at him with grey tear-streaks down her cheeks. And that other time when he gave her a belting for stealing biscuits out of an open tin at the grocer's; he had only done so because the grocer complained, and not because he thought it was right, for who but a bonehead would leave an open tin within the kid's reach? Many, many pictures of Roie, nostalgic and painful in some incomprehensible way, filled his mind, and merged into the picture of the girl she was now, thinking about getting married.

He went upstairs to see Patrick Diamond, wondering whether his friend had a half-bottle that would drown his unease. Patrick was lying on his bed, groaning.

'Now, what's the matter with you, mate?' asked Hughie irritably, sorry that he had come up. Patrick looked up at him with the eyes of a sick bloodhound, drawn down into great sallow pouches.

'It's me bloody indigestion. God, it gets me day and night like a chaff-cutter in me guts.'

'Why don't you go to a quack?' Hughie cast a furtive look under the bed. Yes, there was a bottle, amidst all the clotted dust and kapok from the corn tick. A warmer feeling for Patrick's suffering filling his soul; poor old coot with no one to look after him. Patrick Diamond cursed savagely, clutching his stomach, and rolled over into the pillow.

'It was them that guv it to me when I got me ulcer fixed. Bloody students mucking about with me organs as though they was a bunch of offal from the butcher's.'

Hughie tck-tcked sympathetically. 'What can yer expect in a free hospital? You've got to have a specialist or you come out worse than yer went in. Dirty quacks making a potful outa the sufferings of the working-class.'

'Get me some hot water, Hughie, willya?' groaned Mr Diamond. Hughie rose with alacrity and put the kettle on the grease-clogged gas-ring. The gas shot out in a fanning ring of blue crocuses, hissing and roaring.

'Why don't yer get married, Patrick, boy, and have a bit of comfort in yer old age?' he suggested. Mr Diamond's face showed even more agony.

'And have some old slut up here messing around with me things and making more work than enough? I hate women,' said Mr Diamond bitterly, for well he knew that he was far past the age when any woman, however hard up, would look at him twice.

Hughie shook his head. 'They're a comfort sometimes, Patrick. But not so much of a comfort as a good bottle of spirits,' he added meaningly. Mr Diamond shot him a look and sighed. He knew Hughie had spotted the bottle, and he said hopelessly: 'Go on then, yer old booze-artist. But for God's sake leave me some for when me stomach's better.'

'Indeed I will, Patrick,' came the amiable voice of Hughie from under the bed. 'Pooh, it stinks under here. Why don't you sweep it out?'

'Because I don't want to,' snapped Mr Diamond, wild-eyed. 'Now get me the hot water, Hughie, for God's own sake.'

Hughie lingeringly poured himself a cup of wine, and Mr Diamond a cup of rank hot water from the kettle. Mr Diamond sipped it, haltingly, while Hughie let the stinging aromatic turpentiny flavour of the wine roll around his tongue.

'Ah, there's comfort in the sup, as Grandma used to say,' he remarked dreamily.

There was a slow, steady, clip-clop on the stairs, as though an ascending horse were approaching.

'Hello, now, who's that?' wondered Hughie. Mr Diamond snorted into his cup, and came out wiping his whiskers.

'It's '*im*. Miss Sheily's boyfriend.'

Hughie began to roar. 'Don't tell me. That old hag? Who's the mug?'

Mr Diamond gestured towards the door. 'Go and have a look if you don't believe me. No, put the light out first, you fool.'

Hughie did as he was told, opening the door a crack and peering through. And there was Mr Gunnarson, his round grey felt set firmly on his head, and his bright eyes shining milky-pale in the dim light from the infinitesimally small globe the landlady provided to light the stairs. He was dressed most precisely, with a salmon pink bow tie butterflying from his stiff collar, and under his arm was a long, odd-shaped parcel. Hughie sniffed. He smelt fish.

Mr Gunnarson, unaware of scrutiny, knocked on Miss Sheily's door. After a little while there was a furtive scurry inside the room, and Miss Sheily's cracked voice called: 'Well, who is it?'

'It is I, Mr Gunnarson,' replied her visitor, smiling tenderly at the door. There was an irritated mumble from beyond it, and the sharp stamping about of Miss Sheily's wooden heels. Then it creaked open.

'Oh, it's you. Well, what do you want, you old pest-house?'

Mr Gunnarson removed his hat. 'I come to see you, Miss Sheily.' He stood humbly, waiting. Hughie could well see that Miss Sheily was dressed up more than usual, with a bit of yellow lace sticking out from her collar. But her manner was even more acrid.

'I'm busy,' she said. 'You can't come calling on me at all hours. I'm just going to bed.'

'I bring you a little present,' said Mr Gunnarson, tendering the odd-shaped parcel, devotion oozing from his every word. Miss Sheily snatched it from his hand. 'It stinks,' she stated briefly. 'What is it?'

'Lobster,' breathed Mr Gunnarson; Miss Sheily gave a shriek, and dropped the parcel. Hughie, drooling with desire, watched it slide into the shadows, but alas, Mr Gunnarson went after it and picked it up.

'Don't you come around here bringing your off-colour fish with you,' shrilled Miss Sheily, and as the expression on Mr Gunnarson's face grew more and more lugubrious, she suddenly spat: 'Caesar's ghost! Come inside, you poor old half-bake!'

Mr Gunnarson shuffled inside, and the door shut. Hughie, over-come, went back to Patrick, who, his pain ebbing, was now sitting up in bed.

'Who'd believe it?' marvelled Hughie, looking suspiciously into his cup, for the level of the liquor was much lower than when he had left.

'I tell you, he comes nearly every night,' said Patrick Diamond.

'And the poor coot thinks the world of her. He'd give her the eyes out of his head to play marbles with.'

'And she'd do it too,' agreed Hughie, 'for she's just like them old dames who used to sit around the guillotine waiting for the heads to fall so that they could cart them off to make soup of them.'

'Now, you're wrong there, Hughie man,' protested Patrick, to whom the breath of life was returning. 'Sure there's no one in this world, not even the French, who would make soup of a human being's nob.'

'Miss Sheily's that sort,' said Hugh decisively. Patrick gave a sigh and reached for the wine bottle, then he settled back comfortably, warmth stealing over him, and the awful loneliness which severe pain brings fading into the dimmest of memories.

Sixteen

Mumma cried like anything when the shining-eyed Roie told her that she and Charlie Rothe were to be married, but she did not allow Roie to see her tears. She kept them for the night, robbing Hughie of sleep, so that he spent hour after hour explosively swearing and thanking God audibly that he had only two children to get married off with such fuss and clatter.

'I wish Grandma was here to advise me,' wept Mumma.

'She'd tell you to stop roaring like a runover baboon,' cried Hughie furiously, sticking his cockatoo crest out of the blankets. 'She had six daughters, all married, and I'll bet she didn't howl over one of them.'

'I'll be losing her,' wept Mumma. 'She'll go away and I'll never see her any more. And marrying a nigger, too.'

Hughie sat up and glared at her, and Mumma tentatively moved away, for he looked as though he were going to thump her. 'Now, none of that talk,' he said decisively. 'If Roie's picked her man, then she's picked him, black, white or brindle, and we can't talk with a hangman in the family.'

'The hangman's in your family,' bristled Mumma. 'Never was a Kilker to make a living by other people's necks.'

'Be that as it may,' said Hughie firmly. 'There's no talk about niggers. The boy's good and solid, and I'll have nothing said against him.'

He lay down, mumbling to himself, and Mumma jerked the blankets up and tried angrily to go to sleep, saying prayers very rapidly until in the end they were nothing but words that not even her own ears heard.

Hughie said: 'Hey.'

'What yer want?' snarled Mumma. He turned over, and she could feel his stomach, warm and placatory, against the small of her back.

'We'll have to get you a nice dress for the wedding. A nice red dress.'

'Sure, I'd look like a house in red,' protested Mumma, secretly pleased that he had suggested such a bold and flashing colour. 'Black's right for stout people.'

'Not black,' cried Hughie. 'I won't have my wife looking like a morepork's widow.' This pleased him, and he lay there chuckling for some minutes, repeating 'morepork's widow'. Mumma's rage had subsided entirely, and a calm filled her mind.

'Perhaps a nice, elegant maroon, then, Hughie love,' she suggested, and had an instant vision of herself in elegant maroon silk, with tucks here and a few bits of ruching and fancywork there; with navy shoes that didn't hurt, and a nice hat with a flower. Her heart filled with gratitude towards her kind husband who had promised her a new dress for the wedding and she turned and flung her arms around him.

'Four pounds would do it all, Hughie,' she said. 'And I'd be proud to come right out at Roie's wedding and look decent for once in my life.'

'Of course, the question is where the four pounds is going to come from,' reminded Hughie gloomily. Mumma tossed that off lightly.

'We won't pay the grocer,' she said.

'Oh, well,' acquiesced Hughie. 'He's got more money than we have,' and snuggling against Mumma he went to sleep. But before he did he said: 'Betcher we'll have Miss Sheily off our hands, too, before long.'

But Mumma was already asleep.

Dolour was so excited when Roie told them she was engaged that she didn't know who to inform first. Usually girls in that district didn't get engaged; they just went steady with someone and then got married. But Roie even had a ring, a queer little turquoise, rather lumpy on one side, that Charlie had paid six times too much for at a refugee jeweller's in town.

'It's a real precious stone,' said Mumma, awed, looking into the opaque milky blue face of the turquoise.

'I like diamonds better,' said Dolour dreamily, and was amazed when Roie said sharply: 'Well, I don't. Flashy things, they look vulgar. I like little green and blue and red stones. I like them best.'

'So do I,' said Mumma, though when she was young she would have given ten years of her life for an engagement ring with a diamond in it. She thought regretfully of the pink cameo brooch Hughie had given her, and pawned a few years later, to pay for Roie's birth. That was what Roie had cost, a pink cameo brooch. And Thady had cost his father's gold tie-pin, and his silver watch-chain, and Dolour had been free, as all the assistance Mumma had had was that of the woman next door.

Dolour told Sister Theophilus: 'Roie's getting married soon.' Sister's eyes sparkled. She loved weddings, real white ones. She loved all the flutter and excitement of a marriage, and there was in it no vicarious happiness at all, just joyous faith that here at last was a couple who were really going to be happy ever after. She began at once to say prayers for Roie and Charlie, without the faintest doubt that they would be answered. She had the strange blithe childlike soul that is found so often in convents. Once when caught in a rainstorm she prayed that she might not get wet, and when she found no more than a sprinkle of raindrops upon her habit she was not at all surprised. She lived not in the shadow of God, but in his light. It was as warm and familiar and comprehensible as firelight. So when Sister Theophilus prayed for Roie, grace as impalpable as light itself stole ahead into the girl's life and made the rough smooth, and the smooth pleasant beyond doubt. She was like a magician weaving spells for Roie and Charlie, with complete faith that they would come true.

She also started to work on a gift, a white silk petticoat with handmade lace on it. She copied the design from a picture in the newspaper, blushingly, for Sister Theophilus's own petticoats were made of black material, and had sleeves in them. But she made up the lace out of her own head, with lovers' knots and grape leaves, crocheting with darting swiftness as she walked about the playground.

When she had finished she wrapped the slip up in tissue paper, slipped in a holy picture of St Anne with the child Mary at her knee, tied it with pink ribbon, and gave it to Dolour.

Dolour ran all the way home. She had two pleasures in store for her. Roie's excitement, and the praise her dear Sister Theophilus would be sure to get.

'It's my first wedding present,' breathed Roie, scarlet fluttering in her cheeks. She held up the slip. It was much too long, for Sister had measured it against herself, forgetting how small Roie was.

'I'll have to cut the lace off,' she cried in distress. Mumma was indignant.

'A fine way to treat Sister's lovely present,' she cried. Roie looked at the slip helplessly. 'I'll have to turn it up, then, and I can't sew.'

'Anything rather than cutting the good stuff,' said Mumma, who couldn't sew either beyond putting patches on. So Roie wore the petticoat to her wedding, the hem roughly cobbled up with pink cotton, so that it showed bulky under her skirt. But it made her feel happy, and that was all Sister Theophilus had wanted.

A little while after Roie had received her first present Charlie came in. His broad figure made the room look smaller and more congested, but he was not conscious of his surroundings, for he had lived in such nearly all his life. Dolour had never taken much notice of Charlie, beyond thinking how extraordinarily old he was, but now she was conscious of a feeling of resentment against him. It was almost as though he were an interloper at the wedding, that it should have been a family affair, and he was a stranger with no place at it. She thought that he touched Roie so frequently just to make them feel his new possession of her sister; the arm around her shoulder, the hand on her arm, the kiss as they stood wiping the dishes in the scullery, all annoyed her, incomprehensibly, so that after a while she found her self snappy and close to tears.

After they had gone out, Mumma found her sobbing in the laundry, a miserable bowed figure huddled in the soapy-smelling shadows of the tubs.

'What's the matter now?' she asked irascibly, for she was tired and overwrought herself.

'Roie doesn't belong to us any longer,' hiccupped Dolour. Mumma swallowed hard, for she had felt the same thing herself. She gave Dolour a chiding pat on the bottom, and said: 'Don't be sillier than you look now, Dolour love. You need your tea. Come and help me set the table.'

'I wish we was rich, so Roie wouldn't have to get married,' wailed Dolour. Mumma tck-tcked with exasperation, for Dolour's reasoning always had a most naive streak in it which made Mumma feel that she had neglected her daughter's worldly instruction.

They had hardly sat down to tea before Mumma gave them some news.

'Miss Sheily's getting married,' she said. Dolour choked unbelievingly. Hughie was peeved that he had been cheated of the glory of announcing the news himself, and hastened to cover it up.

'I told you as much the other night,' he expostulated.

'You didn't,' argued Mumma. 'It was only ten minutes ago that she told me herself.'

'You're batty,' said Hughie angrily. 'I told you just before we went to sleep. It was just an idea I had, coming from observation.'

'You never said a word about it,' protested Mumma. 'We was talking about me new maroon dress, and that was all.'

'Look,' he said. 'I was lying on me left side, and . . .' he went into a long description of detail. Mumma cast a despairing look at Dolour.

Dolour interrupted: 'Anyway, it doesn't matter, Dadda. She's getting married quietly next Friday, and she's wearing a grey dress and a grey hat with a veil, and she's going to leave the house.'

'So, don't you see? Charlie and Roie can have her room,' cried Mumma. Hughie's face darkened. He pictured himself coming home drunk as usual on Friday nights, and Charlie's presence damping all his performance.

'Young people ought to be by themselves,' he muttered.

'But they'll have their own cooking things up there and everything,' cried Dolour. 'And maybe Roie will ask me to tea.'

This seemed to her to be almost as exciting as being invited to the Governor-General's residence.

Mumma and Roie were equally excited about Miss Sheily's marriage, for that had seemed to be as unlikely as the remarriage of Queen Mary. They fossicked about, and dropped hints, and on the eve of the great event were invited to view Miss Sheily's going-away clothes.

Mumma wiped her hands on her apron and climbed the steps with difficulty, because her legs were troubling her; but Roie and Dolour sprang like young deer from one dark step to another, because they had done the same fifty times a day for most of their lives.

'Oh,' commented Mumma, as she looked at Miss Sheily's going-away dress laid out on the bed. It was dark brown, dark as mahogany, and with much the same effect on Miss Sheily's complexion as a polished table on a white tablecloth. A neat, sharp-toed pair of shoes with bronze buckles and a business-like air, also stood on the bed, and a brown handbag, severely plain. 'It's very tasteful,' said Mumma, disappointed, for she had imagined that Miss Sheily would have piles of lovely underclothing and perhaps a pretty nightdress or two, as brides always had in books. Roie nudged her, for her disappointment was plain to be seen.

'It's really fashionable, Miss Sheily, and you should look very nice,' she said gently, looking at the strange desiccated little woman with pity and interest. Did Miss Sheily love Mr Gunnarson, or did she marry him just to escape into another environment and another sort of life? Miss Sheily shrugged. She was making toast at the gas-ring, and took no interest in their visit. The prospect of marriage made little difference to her; she was as acid and unpredictable as ever.

Suddenly there was a firm tread on the stairs, and Miss Sheily ejaculated: 'Caesar's ghost! Can't the man stay away for five minutes?'

'Oh, it's Mr Gunnarson,' whispered Mumma, like a scared hen, trying to shepherd her daughters towards the door. But Miss Sheily waved the toaster.

'No, no, don't go. He won't stay long, I promise you.'

Roie and Dolour looked at each other with suppressed giggles.

A moment later Mr Gunnarson came clumping into the room, disappointment on his face plain to be seen.

'Oh, you've got visitors, Miss Sheily,' he said, flashing his bright light eyes at them.

'I can have my friends up, can't I?' snapped Miss Sheily, turning over the toast.

'Indeed you can, my darling,' agreed Mr Gunnarson, going over and kissing her tenderly on the cheek. Miss Sheily, her eyes glittering like black coals, immediately swiped him over the hat with the red-hot toaster. It left a black criss-cross pattern on the felt, and there was a smell of burnt wool.

'My living heart and soul!' whispered Mumma, swallowing hard, for never in all her life would she have thought anybody capable of swiping their prospective husband with the hot toaster.

'You stop that licking around me, or I'll brand you, you old octopus,' shrieked Miss Sheily. Roie and Dolour fled down the stairs. Mumma went more slowly, but before she left she caught a glimpse of Mr Gunnarson's face. It was almost proud, as though any moment he might say: 'Ain't she the one, now?'

'The wedding's off,' yelled Dolour, bursting into the kitchen and recounting the story with gusto to Hughie who sat washing his feet in a basin.

'Not that one,' said Hughie. 'He's one of them that loves his face trod on. You see.'

And they did. The next day a taxi called for Miss Sheily, and off she went without a word; she even had a shopping basket over her arm, and intended to pick up a few things after the ceremony. Mumma and Dolour, just bursting with curiosity, waited inside the kitchen door for her return.

'I wonder if he'll call her Mrs Gunnarson now, instead of Miss Sheily,' giggled Dolour. Mumma replied: 'I still think her name's Stella.'

'We don't even know his Christian name, either,' murmured Dolour. Her eyes sparkled. 'Sssssh, here they come.'

They heard the two pairs of feet ascend the stairs, and a few minutes later the door slammed and the feet descended. Mumma waddled across the kitchen and sat in a chair, pretending to be darning. Dolour drooped herself over the table and became engrossed in the pattern on the tablecloth.

Miss Sheily's sharp voice said: 'Don't pretend you weren't listening, because I saw your shadows on the wall. May I come in?'

'Oh, yes, Miss Sheily . . . Mrs Gunnarson, do,' said Mumma feebly, too taken aback even to become angry at the insult.

Miss Sheily came in. They saw Mr Gunnarson, laden with a suitcase, a hatbox so crammed with goods that its lid wouldn't shut, and with a palm-stand under the other arm, trot down the hall. Miss Sheily was all dressed up in her brown outfit, and they had never seen her look so plain.

'I came to wish you goodbye, Mrs Darcy,' said Miss Sheily. Her eyes flickered from one to the other. 'You were kind to poor Johnny.'

'I loved him, I did,' said Mumma simply, and the ready tears welled to her eyes. A brief flicker went over Miss Sheily's face.

'I don't suppose we'll ever see each other again, Mrs Darcy, so I want to wish you luck. Here's a month's rent . . . no, don't be foolish, woman, take it and be thankful. And here's a little present for Rowena.'

She put a white cardboard box on the table. Mumma blushed and stammered: 'It's good of you, Miss Sheily.'

She shook hands with them both, a cold, white, dead fish hand. Then she was gone. Dolour cast a desperate look at her mother. She felt she couldn't bear it if Miss Sheily went without . . . She raced after her.

'Miss Sheily! Miss Sheily!'

She faced her in the dark hall, and her courage failed.

'Well, what is it now?' asked the woman sharply.

Dolour stuttered: 'Please, before you go . . . would you tell me . . . we've often wondered . . . would you tell me what your Christian name is?'

Once she had it out it sounded preposterous. She cowered away from Miss Sheily, almost expecting to have her face slapped. But Miss Sheily, after a pause, said softly: 'Isabel.'

'Oh,' said Dolour. The relief was tremendous. She said: 'I just wanted to know.'

'I know,' said Miss Sheily, and it seemed to Dolour that never before had her voice been so kind. She watched the taxi till it disappeared down the street, and coming inside, stood for a while in the dark stair recess where Johnny had played, feeling as though she wanted to cry again.

Seventeen

'She was a mystery woman and no mistake,' marvelled Mumma, looking yearningly at the parcel which Miss Sheily had left. It was a great temptation to open it, but she conquered it, and it was there when Roie came in with Charlie that night. They had been out shopping, and Roie was both rapturous with and doubtful of the quality of everything she had bought. She had a breakfast-cloth in gaudy checks, and a set of blue-rimmed plates, and two knives and forks and spoons in cheap leaden ware from Woolworths. But Roie looked at them as though they were hallmarked silver.

'Gee, Charlie, our very own,' she had murmured over and over again. There was a curious change in him, as his marriage drew near. Many years ago, when he realized that the only way to face a bitterly cold and cruel world was to build refuge within himself, he had fought and laboured to become a content and tranquil person. This he had achieved, and the desolate, frightened little boy he had been vanished as though for ever. But now it was as though the little boy were back again, warm-hearted, excitable, needing to be comforted and reassured of love. Charlie was restless every moment he was away from his girl. Roie felt this, and loved him the more for it.

The present from Miss Sheily was a beautiful, white ruffled night-dress. None of them had ever seen anything like it before. It was like something Lana Turner, or some other delicious porcelain Hollywood princess might wear, not Roie Darcy from Plymouth Street. It smelt delectably, too, of freesias. Nobody knew the name of the perfume, save that it was the smell of the plain little creamy flowers that grew by the Sicilianos' fence.

When Charlie saw it he immediately imagined Roie in it, and

because that was disturbing, he put the thought out of his mind and turned to Miss Sheily. Queer little tragic harridan, what had she meant by such a gift? That she, too, might have worn such a nightgown on a bridal night if it had not been for some misadventure? What was her secret? Something had happened to her a long time ago, and a catalysis of the soul had taken place. She was a well of bitter water, and not even the adoring and masochistic Mr Gunnarson would change her, ever. Charlie looked at his own girl, her cheeks like poppies with happiness; her soft sooty hair in disarray, and her little sallow neck vanishing into her cheap cotton blouse, and loved her so much that he felt he would have to shout it aloud to them all. Funny, timid little Roie, whose words faltered so often, yet whose expression told him everything.

They went upstairs to Miss Sheily's room. Dolour whispered to her mother, 'I wonder if she's left anything behind,' for it was the delight of the Surry Hills children to rat empty houses after their tenants had shifted, and come laden home with all sorts of treasurable rubbish.

But there wasn't anything. The room was as clean as a scrubbing brush could make worn and hideous linoleum, and a manila broom the crude blue kalsomined walls. The bed sagged forlornly in the middle, and the blankets were stained with tea and coffee and a dozen other unanalysable things. But it was no worse than a thousand other lodgings in Surry Hills; it was a lot better than Charlie's present room. It had a door which locked, and it had a window which looked out on the alleyway which ran down beside the house, and, across that, into three crammed and hideous backyards full of garbage cans, tomcats, and lavatories with swinging broken doors and rusty buckled tin roofs.

But these were all things they were used to. They didn't mean anything to Roie and Charlie. A stranger in this attic room would have withered and died with the sheer ugliness and sordidness and despair of it; but to Roie and Charlie it was a room of their own.

Mumma pinched Dolour, and taking her by the edge of her sleeve, drew her towards the door. 'I've got to be getting the tea on.'

'I'll come down later,' protested Dolour. Mumma pinched her harder, and with a yelp they both disappeared down the stairs.

Dolour was furious. 'What's the big idea?' she demanded.

'Can't you leave them alone for five minutes?' hissed Mumma, red-faced at her daughter's obtuseness. Dolour asked: 'Whatever for?'

'What do you think for?' asked Mumma, busying herself at the sink. Dolour's face reddened with humiliation, and, more than that, with the strangest feeling she had ever had. She had always come first in Roie's heart; now she knew she had been taken from that niche and put elsewhere. Charlie was in her place, and she would never win it back.

From that moment Dolour hated Charlie. She pictured him upstairs, holding Roie, kissing her, touching her in a way that no one had ever touched her sister, except perhaps Tommy Mendel, for Dolour in her shrewd precocious way had her own ideas about Tommy Mendel. It made her feel sick with disgust and hatred.

The wedding was coming very close, and Mrs Drummy, who sewed, at last finished Mumma's maroon dress. It was in a shoddier material than the frock she had dreamed, and it did not fit very well over Mumma's upholstery, but there were stylish tucks, and a thing Mrs Drummy called a 'slimming panel' floating like a limp scarf from the right shoulder. Mumma did not fancy this much, but everyone told her it was elegant, so she didn't pull it off.

One day Charlie said to Roie: 'Is there anything your mother would like for the wedding . . . I mean, a little present from me?'

Roie said instantly: 'She's always wanted to have her hair permed.'

That was thirty-five shillings, and Charlie had to work many hours to earn as much as that, but he put his hand in his pocket and pulled out the money.

'Now, tell her it's from you,' he cautioned, 'not me, or she'll think things.'

'What things?' scoffed Roie, and ignoring his advice she went off to Mumma and jubilantly announced that Charlie had made her the present of a permanent wave. She was aghast when Mumma took it very badly, fulminating against upstarts who criticized their mother-in-law's hair, and telling Roie to tell him to go and get his own waved and not to be insulting her.

'But you've always wanted a permanent. It was me that suggested it,' wailed Roie. Mumma had known this from the start, but couldn't help seizing the chance to express a little of the jealousy and resentment a mother-in-law feels against even a man she likes. She said, grudgingly: 'Oh, well, then, I suppose I could get it done.'

'You needn't get it done at all if you don't want to,' flamed Roie. 'And you ought to be ashamed of yourself. It was a kind thought of Charlie's, that's all, and I give him credit for it.'

Mumma eyed Roie's hand with distrust, for it looked as if it were going to dart forth and take the thirty-five shillings back, but it didn't, and she said repentantly: 'Don't be listening to me, Roie love. I'm upset because the iceman didn't come, and the meat's gone funny. I'll get me hair done on Friday.'

Mumma's hair had never been done before. When she was young it was rich and wavy and chestnut, forever tumbling down from the knot in which her clumsy and inept hands twisted it. It was always a surprise to her to look into the glass and find that it was no longer that way, but grey and brindly and tousle-ended. She went to the hairdresser as one might go to the guillotine, frightened into stupidity; but she was happy and excited about it too. Mumma had visions of herself with glossy symmetrical waves like the ladies in the hair-oil advertisements.

But somehow her hair didn't turn out like that. The hairdresser did her best with it, but Mumma came out of the shop with a sort of electrified bolster on top of her head.

'It'll lie down in a couple of days,' said the hairdresser anxiously. She was a neat, harried little body with four children crammed into the dingy living-room behind her salon. Mumma surveyed it doubtfully. She couldn't quite believe that it was the same hair which had covered her head only a couple of hours ago. This had a virile frizziness like the hair on a strong man's chest; it almost crackled when she nodded, so dry and brittle it had become.

When she got home she was frightened to face the critical gaze of Hughie. Roie's sympathy and Dolour's mirth she felt she could withstand, but not Hughie's. As she walked down the passage and heard his loud Friday-night voice, her cheeks flushed in anticipation, but she forced herself to march in without any diminution of spirit in her footsteps.

'Goddlemighty,' gasped Hugh when he noticed her. 'Sweet jumping moses, whatjer done to yerself, woman?'

'I been permed,' began Mumma, with a piteous attempt at dignity. Hughie laughed until he nearly fell on the floor. Roie came out of the scullery and cried: 'Don't you mind him, Mum. All perms are funny for a while. Yours'll be good. You see.'

Mumma looked in the sideboard mirror and prodded the strange cushion of hair which still had an odd elusive perfume of ammonia about it. She felt hopelessly that it would never be any different. She would have to go to the wedding like this and have everyone laughing at her. Probably . . . Struck by a sudden awful thought, Mumma rushed into the bedroom, Roie following. There she was, trying to force her old navy hat down over the mass. It jammed tightly, and then, as though on invisible springs, slowly rose. Mumma looked aghast at Roie.

'I can't get it on,' she moaned. 'Now I won't be able to come to the church.'

Roie took the hat and pulled it down to Mumma's tortured eyebrows, but once again it slowly ascended. In the doorway Hughie rolled about in uproarious mirth. Mumma cried: 'You can well laugh, but what about me, not even able to go to me own daughter's marriage?'

'You'll come to my wedding, if we have to get Father Cooley to perform it in the backyard,' vowed Roie, and then the picture of the robed priest standing amidst the garbage tins and reciting the marriage ceremony overcame them all, and Mumma's first permanent wave ended in roars of laughter.

But that night, as she lay beside the snoring form of Hughie, she touched the tight kinky curls and spirited high-voltage frizz of her new pompadour, and murmured: 'It's that Charlie who's done this to me.'

Then came another thought, apologetic: 'Not that I'm blaming him. And it might turn out very well, for all that. I'll wash it tomorrow.'

So she washed it twice a day until the wedding day came, and by that time it had only a flyaway fluffy effect, which Mumma privately thought youthful, and indeed beguiling. It made her very happy.

Dolour dearly wanted a real wedding, with herself as bridesmaid. She said several rosaries for this end, but with a forlorn feeling in her soul all the time that her prayers were not to be answered. The idea of all the pomp and etiquette of a real wedding, with a best man, and confetti, and presents and breakfasts, and all the rest, terrified Mumma and Hughie and Roie and Charles into numbness. None of them had the slightest idea about the conduct of such a ceremony — who gave whom a present, or who walked on the right side of whom.

'I just want to be married,' confessed Roie to Charlie. 'And I'd like it best with nobody there at all.'

That morning Roie had gone to Communion and afterwards she knelt for a long time thinking of Tommy Mendel. Had it been a sin, or hadn't it? Roie knew that the Church thought so, and so she had confessed it, but she still could not work out the rights of it. She had committed a sin because she loved Tommy very much; there had been no thought of self in it. She felt that if it had truly been a sin then she was not worthy of Charlie. That brought a new idea; had she really paid enough for that sin, or would she, and Charlie perhaps, go on suffering for it ever after?

'I don't want him to be hurt ever,' she gasped, shuddering at the impact of that thought. 'Oh, I wish it hadn't ever happened. Please, please let me forget it.'

But she couldn't, and then she thought that perhaps Charlie was like Tommy Mendel, with the same instability and selfishness and inconstancy, and she felt that marriage with him would be intolerable bondage, and that she must run away from it now before it was too late.

The dread and fear were with her all day, but it was impossible to run away now. Mumma had her new frock, and Dolour a new hat, and Hughie had so steadfastly remained sober. Besides, Father

Cooley was expecting them at eleven. These things seemed to Roie to be insurmountable obstacles.

It was a lovely day, very soft, with an autumn pulse in the air. Roie got dressed with Dolour's hysterical help. Through the phoenix palm's radiating vanes she saw the blue sky like a flag, but it didn't comfort her.

'Ah, gosh,' groaned Roie. Dolour viewed her with dismay, for her cheeks were milk-pale and her eyes dark with fright.

'You're not going to be crook, are you?' she squeaked. 'You don't feel sick in the stomach?'

'No, I don't,' snapped Roie. She snatched up her blue halo hat, glared at her sister, and clattered noisily down the stairs. Mr Diamond, who had tactfully accepted an invitation to the 'breakfast' only, opened his door a trifle and peered at her. She looked slender as a wand in her blue dress, and pitifully young.

'Poor little devil,' muttered Mr Patrick Diamond, envisioning all the disillusionment and drab monotonies that lay ahead of Roie. He felt his indigestion coming on, and grabbed his stomach premonitorily as he clicked the door shut.

Mumma had been dressed for an hour, sitting stiffly on a chair so that she would not disarrange the pleats in her skirt. She had refolded the slimming panel a dozen times, for it worried her very much. Hughie's face was red with scraping, and his hair was slicked back unfamiliarly with brilliantine. Roie scarcely knew him. Also there was Charlie, dressed in his best suit, the one with the blue stripe. His tousled hair was already springing out of the sleek order into which he had combed it. He paced up and down the kitchen, smoking one cigarette after another.

'Charlie!' wailed Roie, jumping into his arms. They closed around her, big and warm, and such a good fit that all her fears immediately left her, and she thought: 'Gee! I'm lucky. I'm lucky!' as she listened to the steady beat of his heart through the too-stiff lapels of his five-guinea suit.

'Plenty of time for that afterwards,' said Hughie gruffly, for he was embarrassed and nervous. 'Come on, or we'll have his reverence suing us for overtime. Dolour!' he screamed up the stairs.

So they all went to the church, and Roie and Charlie were married in a very plain and ordinary way, kneeling there at the altar rails in the empty amber-lit church, with the stout red-faced priest standing before them in his black soutane with one button missing at the hem, and over it a surplice starched too much, so that the lace stuck out stiffly like a verandah roof and gave Dolour hysterical giggles.

In twenty minutes it was all over. One might have thought that anything so fast would be unimpressive, but Roie and her husband never forgot that golden morning when their paths met completely and continued as one.

Hughie was more nervous than any of them. It brought him out in a sort of rash of garrulity and exuberance; he couldn't get home quickly enough to toast the bride and drown his qualms in the comforting warmth of alcohol.

As soon as they reached home, Mumma set about laying the spread, and Hughie bellowed up the staircase: 'Come on down, Patrick man! The knot's tied. Come and have a swig,' and the door at the top of the stairs sprang open as though by clockwork, and Mr Diamond descended.

Roie saw with surprise and a queer feeling of tenderness that he had put on his best suit, and had shaved the back of his neck as far as he could reach, in a sort of makeshift haircut.

While all the preparations were going on, Charlie and Roie sat together on the old couch.

'Happy, Ro?' he asked, softly, so that Mumma wouldn't hear. Roie nodded, and the fugitive smile that flitted over her face filled him with joy and fierce determination that he would shield her from every grief the hard world might bring. For him, marriage was even more of a milestone than it was for Roie. She had known poverty of an inconceivably drab and sordid sort, but she had always had love and companionship, and the warm family circle that was broken only by her father's bouts of drunkenness. Charlie had had poverty, and the desperate panic-stricken loneliness of a small child. He had had homelessness, and the heat and cold and hunger of a bagman's gipsy life, the long silences of his strange eccentric companion, and the vast desolation of the outback. Marriage was for him the ending of all that chapter; it was the commencement of an entirely new life. There would not be much in it; children perhaps, and work and laughter, and sorrow, and eventually pain and separation. But it was a pain bestrewn with jewels for him, for Roie was to make it hers.

'Now you can tell us where you're going for your honeymoon,' cried Mumma, slapping down a dish of subsiding butter on the table. She had steadfastly refused to listen before, on the grounds that it brought bad luck.

'Narrabeen,' said Roie. 'You go in a bus. You can swim there . . . there's breakers.'

'I went there,' boasted Dolour. 'That's where we had Delie Stock's picnic.'

'You didn't, you went to Collaroy,' corrected Hughie. Dolour looked sulky.

'Well, it's near enough,' she said. Her nervous tension was high, not only because of Roie's wedding, but because of Roie's departure with Charlie, into a life in which she, Dolour, would never more have part.

They all sat around the patched and greyish tablecloth, that was set out in a prosaic assortment of hastily-assembled edibles; plates heaped with thick corned beef sandwiches, soup plates full of tomatoes and lettuce, and here and there a dish piled with sticky baker's cakes. Three sherry bottles and a port bottle shouldered each other with clinking familiarity in the middle of the table, and Mr Diamond eyed them thirstily.

There was not much conversation, but many smiles. Mumma was full of yearning for her daughter, so young, and, in spite of Tommy Mendel, so innocent, about to set forth on her new life like a small and inexperienced Christopher Columbus braving an unknown ocean.

'It's so hard, darling,' cried her heart. 'Not now, when there's love between you, but later on when you've got children, and them with the croup and you up all night with your back broken, and your mind crazy with no sleep, and your husband snoring on the bed with his boots on, as drunk as a lord. 'Oh, God, dear,' cried her heart. 'Make it easy for my little Roie.'

And Hughie, warming up with the drink, thought: 'I'm not an old man yet. There's many men grandfathers at forty, and who's to say I'm fifty-five? Not so long ago I was married . . . and Dad there with his face like a big red moon. God, he had a tongue on him, sweet as honey with the brogue . . . and Ma, too.' He tried in vain to remember his mother, but all he could recollect was a black dress with a sort of plaited gold brooch close up under her chin. 'She must have had hair,' argued Hughie to himself muzzily. 'And eyes . . . she must have had eyes. Funny how I can't remember them.' It seemed to him so ineffably sad that he couldn't remember the colour of his mother's eyes that he put his head down on his hands and wept a tear or two. Patrick Diamond, who was equally muzzy, clapped him on the shoulder.

'Ah, you should have remained a bachelor, mate; there's nothing like it for peace and contentment.'

'I wish I was dead,' sobbed Hughie.

'Then go off, for goodness sake, and cut yer throat and stop spoiling the party,' suggested Mumma hotly, for she had had a couple of glasses of spirit and was feeling full of courage. Charlie laughed. He knew it was all a surfeit of emotionalism, and took no notice of it. He sat quietly with Roie, holding her hand under the table, and looking now and then at Dolour, so as not to leave her out of the fun. But Dolour, stuffing cake into her mouth, thought: 'I hate him! Buck nigger! Buck nigger!'

Roie thought: 'I want to cry, or laugh, or something. Don't let me spoil it. I want to be what he wants me to be. I love him. I love him. I love the back of his neck and that little hollow in his cheek, and his eyebrows. I love you, Charlie, don't you hear me?'

She felt that the intensity of her thoughts was so great that he could not help but hear them. With shyness she looked away, from his lips that silently said 'Darling' above the merry uproar.

Hughie recovered suddenly from his sorrow about his mother, and said confidentially to Mr Diamond: 'I've gotta dance. I've gotta dance, mate.'

Mr Diamond cheered hoarsely, and winking at the company in general, pushed Hughie out into the middle of the floor. He looked all around with a beaming smile, promising all the entertainment of their lives. But because the alcohol had effected a strange sense of distance between his feet and his brain, he did not move, but stood on one leg and waved the other in and out and back and forth in a kind of stationary Highland fling.

Mr Diamond held his nose and let out a wild squeal, meanwhile pumping his left arm up and down against his side, in imitation of the bagpipes.

'Whoopsy-doopsy, oopsy-doopsy, up the leg of me drawers!' bellowed Hughie. Mumma banged the table with a fork.

'You stop that sort of stuff, Hugh Darcy,' she threatened, 'or I'll stick you in the gizzard with this.' Her mild eyes sparkled and her face was fearsome.

'Mumma gets funny when she's a bit woozy,' chuckled Roie.

'Yole spoilsport,' complained Hughie, collapsing, mainly because he was out of breath. 'Lookut ole spoilsport, Patrick. Lookut 'er,' he said, nudging Mr Diamond, who reluctantly gave up his pumping and looked.

'Don't you glare at me, you old tearer down of images,' cried Mumma, turning her wrath on Mr Diamond, who said placatingly: 'Now, now, missus, keep yer hair on. I didn't look at you.'

Dolour pushed the sandwiches over. 'Here, have one,' she invited, and Mumma took one and subsided, a little tearful, sniffing away her tears because she wanted very much to be happy at her daughter's wedding, and couldn't quite manage it.

There was a little precise knock on the door, and Dolour hissed: 'Bet that's the Drummy kids to see if there are any left-overs!'

But it wasn't. It was Lick Jimmy. Small and bowed, and yellow as soap with increasing age, he stood there, a narrow figure in his tight black trousers and coat. He bore a parcel, strangely wrapped in the exotic back-to-front newspapers he read.

'Come on in, Jimmy,' roared Hughie, waving his arm in an expansive gesture. 'Come on in, me old heathen, and join the bun-fight.'

Mumma's hospitable heart smote her that she had not invited Lick Jimmy to the party. 'Come and 'ave a cup of tea, or some sherry, Jim,' she invited.

Jimmy smiled. 'I bling plesent, then I go,' he announced. He gave the parcel to Roie. Roie was covered in confusion and delight. Lick Jimmy bowed.

'Many long years, missie Roie,' he said. 'Many sons. Many lands and houses, misser Charlie,' he said. There was a flicker in the doorway, and the quiet tiger padding of slippers up the passage.

'Gee,' gasped Dolour.

'He's a queer old coot,' said Patrick Diamond.

'Useful sometimes. You oughter know,' said Hughie meaningly, and laughed to kill himself when Patrick looked perplexed.

'Go on, open it, Ro,' urged Mumma eagerly. Roie undid the parcel. Inside was an entire flat bolt of finest silk, thinner than gossamer, a filmy glossy stuff that had unfortunately been dyed a violent salmon pink.

'What a pity. You couldn't wear that. You'd look like a nigger,' cried Mumma, and could have bitten her tongue out. But Charlie didn't seem to notice.

'You could make lots of pants out of it,' suggested Dolour. 'Shut up,' hissed Mumma fiercely. But Hughie unheeding, chipped in:

'Keep Charlie interested.'

'Yer don't need nice clothes after yer married,' said Patrick Diamond superiorly. 'You need good heavy working clothes that will stand up to a lot.'

'Fine life you think the girl's going to have,' flashed Mumma. They could all see that at any moment there was going to be a good old stand-up fight. Hughie said hastily: 'What's that fell out there?'

Roie picked it up; a little yellow card inscribed with a brush in sweeping black letters: 'Good luck from Lick James.'

'Lick James, eh?' Nobody saw the joke but Charlie. Mumma was a little offended.

'Well, you couldn't expect him to sign it with anything but his full name,' she expostulated. 'It wouldn't have been manners.'

And they all agreed.

Eighteen

As the time of going-away grew near, Roie became frightened. She felt the old trembling, prickling feeling rising at the base of her spine, and her head beginning to spin. Charlie noticed it even before Mumma did. He said quietly: 'It's going to be all over soon.'

And so it was. Soon she was jumping down the crooked stairs for the last time, still in her wedding dress. It was blue linen, with an exotic sort of beaded lily on the bodice, under which Roie's little breast bloomed with a pitiful slenderness. Hughie clasped her gingerly at first, and then gave her a good hug, muttering into her hair: 'Goodbye, kiddie. Hope you have a nice holiday.'

Mumma didn't cry. The wine had lent her a self-composure, and she looked long and gravely at Roie and said: 'Remember this is the beginning of your new new life. Start it well, and it'll end well.'

Roie nodded silently, for she was frightened she was going to cry. She looked around for Dolour, and there she was standing with her head ridiculously hidden in the curtain, like an ostrich. Roie went up and peeped around the curtain and there was Dolour's face, twisted up into dumb grief.

'Goodbye, Dolour, darling.'

'Ta-ta, Ro,' choked Dolour. Then she gave a long anguished snort, and everyone laughed, and Roie ran out quickly in case her tears should overbrim.

Soon they were in the tram, and Roie began to feel better. She looked at Charlie, and he looked at her, and they looked away again, each with a little shy smile. They liked the tram, but they liked the ferry better. It made them feel almost as if they were going on a sea-trip for their honeymoon, as lots of young people did. They looked about with awe at the hugeness of the ferry, and when the man with the mandolin came along Charlie gave him threepence with proud hauteur that was born of pleasure and embarrassment. He played 'Little Nelly Kelly' and 'Concerto For Two' with extreme hurry and eagerness, as though he were anxious to earn another threepence.

They managed to get a seat together in the crowded Narrabeen bus, and it was then that Roie really began to feel excited. The road unwound, white and curving, bordered with green paddocks, and little houses sitting comfortably under the lee of hills. Now and then there was a sapphire flash of sea, and after a while, as they rounded the bluff above Long Reef, a wondrous stretch of beach opened before them. Pale and oatmeal-coloured, curved in a half-circle, and rimmed with the uneven stripes of the great white breakers, it swung around into the far distant haze. Roie gasped. 'This is what Dolour told me about,' she said. Charlie squeezed her hand.

'Pleased I chose this place?' he asked.

'Is it here? Oh, it's like Paradise,' she cried.

The bus spun downwards into Collaroy, past a theatre like an exotic lime ice-cream. And soon it was impatiently chugging, waiting for them to get off at Narrabeen village. Charlie lifted out Roie in one hand and their suitcase in the other. He was excited with an exultant growing excitement. He wanted to laugh aloud.

'It's up this way.' He gestured with the suitcase to the little houses scattered amongst the dunes.

'I'm glad you didn't want to stay at a boarding-house or something,' panted Roie, skipping ahead of him, and looking around her like a delighted child.

'I'm glad *you* didn't,' he replied.

'I wanted our own little place for the fortnight,' she cried.

'I wanted to have you all to myself. Ah, gosh, Roie!' he cried in a sudden tumult of excitement and anticipation. Roie suddenly stopped. Her heart beat fast. She was all at once frightened. She was even more frightened than she had been when Tommy Mendel had wanted her. She wanted to run down to the bus stop again and go back to Mumma, and poor Dolour, who had so hated her going. Charlie put his arm around her, and felt her trembling. He said gently: 'Darling, don't be scared.'

'I'm not scared!' cried Roie angrily. She pulled away. 'Which is our cottage?'

Charlie pointed to a little house a hundred yards away.

'That's ours.'

Roie was delighted. She jumped up and down like a child and cried: 'It's pink! It's pink!'

And so it was, a tiny square pink cottage, with a sandy path, and geraniums and petunias struggling gallantly with the overgrown grass. Charlie fished the key out of his pocket. 'Here you are. You open it.'

Roie took it and ran forward. The key grated in the lock, and the door opened, a little protestingly. The tiny place smelt of the sea, and the white sand had sifted under the door, so that their feet crunched on the floor. There was a minute lounge gaily furnished with blue cane. Yellow and blue-striped curtains flew in the breeze as Roie threw open the casement windows. She cried aloud with joy: 'Oh, the sea! The sea!'

There it was, the whole Pacific, cobalt, glittering richly, tossing itself in foam-laced breakers against the castled Narrabeen bluff. It was magnificent and lonely, and the very essence of all blueness and sunshine, and it was the backyard that Roie and Charlie possessed.

They ran through into the tiny kitchenette, and laughed at the pygmy gas stove, with the row of bright saucepans hanging above it. Everything was clean, and smelt of the sea and the coarse blowing grass.

'Where's the bedroom?'

'Through here.'

There was a white-painted bed, with a blue spread on it, and pink ruffled curtains at the window. The floor was bare but for rag mats, and a big mirror hung on the wall. Roie bounced on the bed.

'Oh, it's hard! No dips!' she sang. Charlie bounced beside her.

'No bugs! and real white sheets.' Charlie pulled her back on the bed, buried his face in the hollow of her neck, and said softly: 'Darling Roie! I can't believe we're really married at last.'

'At last?' Roie wriggled away, because she was timid of the tone of his voice. 'It's only been a few months since we first met.'

'I wanted you right from the start,' he whispered. Roie lay in his arms looking up at his face, dark and beautiful in its odd way. She kissed him on the peak of an eyebrow, fleetingly, so that he laughed and dropped her: 'Let's go and have a swim.'

'I can't swim,' she protested.

'Neither can I. But we can fool around in the breakers.'

He flung open the suitcase, tossed her bathing suit to her, and picked up his own trunks. Unselfconsciously he pulled his shirt over his head. Roie watched, blushing a little because, although her instincts told her to turn her eyes away, she knew that she did not have to do so. It was like watching a stranger undress. Charlie noticed her discomfort, and said: 'I'll undress in the lounge. Hurry up, because the tide's on the turn.'

Roie didn't know whether to be pleased or sorry. She hurried into her own suit and joined him on the step.

They ran into the water. The sea spoke in vast sonorous vowel-sounds . . . 'aaaaaaaaaaaahhhhhhhh . . . ooooooooo-hhhhhhhhhhhh.' Roie screamed and pranced on the sand. She was frightened to go in, and yet longing to breast the cool and tingling water. When she was wet all over, she felt proud, as a child might, when it had conquered a fear. She became almost hysterical with excitement; it was such fun waiting for the great glossy bottle-green breakers, runnelled and channelled with a thousand gullies and hillocks, to lift her off her feet and carry her irresistibly to the shore. For the first time that year she felt the blood running strongly through her body, and her skin opening like a flower to the hot caress of the sun and the cold caress of the sea. She caught Charlie around the waist, and he stood like a rock before the approaching wall of the breaker. Then they were hurled together, breathless and laughing, upon the sand.

'Oh, oh,' gasped Roie, sitting up, with sand thick upon her swimsuit. 'I've never had so much fun in all my life.' Charlie pulled her to her feet. The water ran in little droplets off his smooth skin. He had a wide chest diminishing into his trunks, and long, well-muscled legs. Roie had never really seen a young man's body before. He grinned as he saw her surveying him.

'Well, do I come up to standard?'

'I think you look better with your clothes off,' she said seriously. She shuddered with a passing chill.

'Come on,' he said. 'You're cold. Let's go up to the house.'

'Oh, no,' she begged. 'Just one more dip.'

'We'll be here fourteen days,' he reminded her. They looked at each other and laughed aloud with delight. Fourteen paradisal days stretched between them and the drabness of their daily life. They ran up the dunes, playing like children.

Ten minutes later Roie saw the sun go down behind the bushclad cliff beyond the village. Her skin smooth and cold, her wet hair brushed into fluffiness, she stood at the tiny stove, grilling the steak and tomatoes which Mumma had packed in the suitcase. She had forgotten nothing. Bread was rolled up in Roie's nightdress, salt and talcum powder sat side by side; the pepper and sunburn lotion rubbed shoulders and the butter sat securely in a spare soap-holder.

'I can cook,' boasted Roie.

'You can do everything,' said Charlie. He ate as vigorously as he did everything else. Roie felt a stirring of vainglory as she watched him. It was good to think she could feed him. She felt scorn for all the brides who couldn't cook at all.

The evening came down, and the village sprang into a sprinkling of yellow lights. Roie was so tired after her surfing she wanted to go to bed at once, but she was frightened. On the threshold of a great experience, she stood tiptoe, timid and hesitant, and wondering, and longing to run away home. For a long time she put off going to bed. After a while, as she went past the couch where Charlie lay at ease, he put out an arm and pulled her close to him. He nuzzled his face into her hair and asked: 'Don't you want to go to bed with me?'

She put her head on his chest, and felt the deep slow pulsations of his heart.

'I love you, Charlie.'

'I know you do, sweetheart.'

'I'm just a little bit scared, Charlie.'

'Scared of me?'

'Oh, no . . . just, scared.'

Charlie was silent. Only his heart sounded in the stillness.

'Let's go to bed, Roie, and let me lie with my arms around you, and you won't be scared any more.'

'Yes. Charlie.'

She went into the bedroom. The light was soft and dim; through the wide windows came the mournful sound of the tide incoming.

She undressed slowly. 'I wish I was fatter. I wish I didn't have so many bones. I wish my hair was longer. I wish I was prettier. I wish I knew what to *do*;' and deep down was the wish: 'If only that hadn't happened, I mightn't be afraid.'

She got into bed and lay there, her little body making hardly a hummock in the blue field of the spread. Her heart was beating fast. She held her hands together to keep them from trembling. Charlie came in, his hair tousled from the shower, mopping the drops off his brown chest with a towel. He looked down at her.

'Are you scared of seeing me with my clothes off?'

'A little bit.'

He dropped the rest of his garments on the floor. He was slender and shapely and tawny-skinned. His neck rose out of his shoulders like a short pillar of bronze; his dark head was beautifully set on it. He looked at her without any selfconsciousness, without any shyness or embarrassment in his golden eyes.

'I'm just like other men.'

She nodded, without a word. He flicked off the light; and got into bed beside her. She did not move for a moment, and then, as his arms went around her, she turned to him, put her head on his shoulder and lay close to him. The warmth of his body lay all along her side; his velvety skin brushed her arm, her ankles, her cheek. Again she felt his heart. It was like some machine that had started twenty-four years ago and never faltered one hairbreadth in its steady throbbing. It was in some way like Charlie himself, deep, wise, undeviating.

'Oh, Charlie,' she trembled. 'I love you so much.'

'I love you and want you so much,' he returned. His hand stole down to her breast. 'You're so little, Roie,' he said inconsequentially. They lay there for a while. Roie's heart steadied. He said: 'I've never held a girl like this before, although I often thought about it. It's much nicer even than I thought it would be.'

Roie whispered: 'Haven't you ever had a girl?'

'No,' he answered.

'I thought all men did,' whispered Roie, shamefaced. She felt him shake his head.

'Lots of men don't. I've never touched a girl yet. No more than you've ever touched a man. I picked you right, didn't I?'

Roie was silent. In that moment the episode with Tommy Mendel, her illness, the baby she had lost, all went spinning away like dust down a corridor. They were a nightmare unreality, as though they had never been. How could it have been true, that silly, clumsy, ludicrous little experience? It wasn't anything like this. It was no more like this than a street lamp is like the sun. This was beautiful, exultant, the most overwhelming thing she had ever known.

She felt for Charlie's lips with her own. 'You're the first man I ever had,' she breathed. 'You're the last man.'

His lips met hers, young and warm and ardent. His arms held her more tightly, and she felt the glowing warmth of his flesh, his very bones. He was hers, and more than the whole world she wanted to be his.

Nineteen

It was strange when Roie woke up the next morning, and yet familiar, too. She woke quietly, opening her eyes suddenly on the bright, light room with the sea-dapple sliding over the ceiling. She turned her head, and right under her lips was Charlie's warm soft hair. His head was on her shoulder, his arm flung across her, one knee over hers. She marvelled that she did not feel his weight; it was not at all like sleeping with Dolour, who had been all awkward angles, and as heavy as lead.

She lay there for a long time, looking at his sleeping eyelids, and his face, relaxed and tranquil. His dark blood was plain now, but it gave to his face an exotic difference, a delicate difference in the line of his lips and the triangularity of his eyebrows.

He was hers and she his; the mystery had been consummated. She was different now, and it was not a physical difference; it was spiritual. Nothing she had ever dreamed had been even remotely like the reality, his passion and strength, his complete adoration of her and surrender to her. Roie had often read books that talked about a bride's surrender, but now she knew that the bridegroom's surrender was just as complete.

Suddenly he opened his eyes, looked at her and smiled. He slid his cheek along her bare shoulder and murmured: 'Roie.'

'What, darling?'

'Nothing. Just Roie.'

They lay in warm quietness for a long time, while the sea light glimmered all about them. Then, with mischief in his eyes, Charlie asked: 'Still frightened of me, Roie?'

She shook her head dumbly, frightened lest he should look into her eyes and discover that she loved him as the saints loved God, unquestioningly and exultantly. The knowledge was in her heart, but there were no words for it yet. Gently, tenderly, they would come to clothe it, until at last she would be able to tell him.

They stayed at Narrabeen for a fortnight. Every moment of it was a revelation to Roie, learning more about Charlie, and falling deeper and deeper in love with him all the time. She grew in mental stature; there were implanted in her the seeds of tolerance and sympathy that were to flower in her adulthood.

The two of them, barefooted, ran along the sand dunes, sliding and slipping, the little flat bright town on one side, and the steely glimmer of the lakes, and on the other side the wild and lonely shore. A fierce vigour seized Roie; she felt as though she had never been alive until now. She ran and played on the hard oatmeal sands, and taunted the great breakers to come and get her. She was fey, and Charlie felt almost an awe as he watched her. She, so delicately strung, so passionate in everything she did and felt, must surely have great pain and sorrow ahead of her. Where others found valleys, she would find abysses; where they climbed hills, she would climb mountains, and see from their peaks enchanted vistas beyond their comprehension.

Sometimes he felt frightened before this unknown quality in her future; he put his head on her breast and felt the palpitation of her heart.

'Happy, Roie?' She was silent a little, and then her breast shuddered and a sob rose out of her throat.

'What's the matter, my sweetheart?'

'If I died now, this minute, Charlie, it would have been worth it.'

The tears trickled under her closed eyelids, and he kissed them away. He did not say anything, for she knew what he meant. Her feeling was not his, for as much as he loved Roie, he, as a man, had a grip of years as she, as a woman, had a grip of moments; he knew that there was much more to come. But he understood in some wordless way how a passionate soul can achieve happiness so great that there seems no more to be experienced.

The blue sky was low about them on the dunes; they were islanded in air, in aloofness from the rest of the world. 'It mightn't always be like this, Roie. We'll never have much money. We'll have to live in cheap places, down in the dirt and drabness like everyone else. We'll grow old. Perhaps you'll be ill. Perhaps I will. Nobody can tell what life will bring to us.'

Urged by compassion he tried to shake her out of the rapture that might entrap her into so much pain. She shook her head. 'It won't matter. As long as we're together.'

'We mightn't always be together, either,' he said slowly; a premonitory shadow of the agony of their separation drew over him like a chill from the sea, so that he drew her closer and sought warmth from her body. He expected her to shudder, too, but she looked at him with eyes as innocent and unalarmed as a child's.

'You mean one of us will die?' She sat up; the wind flung out her hair. 'Of course one of us will . . . maybe it isn't so far off, either. But nothing can separate us. Souls don't die. Did you forget?'

Looking at her, he marvelled that she could accept so unquestioningly the fact that death would one day tear one from the other. A pang of pain went through his heart at the thought, and he forced it away from him and held her so fiercely that she cried out and protested, her body melting into his even as her words sought to thrust him away.

'Oh, Roie, if I lost you, I'd kill myself.'

She shook her head, smiling to herself, and thinking of her mother and Thady.

The fortnight might have been a thousand years. Every day Roie changed from what she had been to what she would thereafter be. Her pursuing, inward longing to make things what they were not had gone, because she had found that Charlie had changed the world to her desire. His presence made it all she had ever wanted. Her timidity now became a warm and self-contained silence into which she entered when she was with strangers. She was not self-conscious; it was just that she had a world of her own into which none but she and her husband might enter.

She said to Charlie: 'Would you give me a baby?' He was

surprised, for he and Roie had never discussed children. He had thought it was because she would, like most girls, like a year or two free before she entered upon motherhood.

'Why do you want a baby? Aren't I enough for you?' he asked, half-humorously, for a tiny jealousy had risen in his heart. She put her head on his shoulder confidingly.

'It's just that I want you to own me altogether,' she said. Words did not come easily to her when she was thinking her deepest thoughts. 'I want you to be part of me for ever and ever.'

He smiled. 'Perhaps it's already happened, Roie.'

Roie shook her head. She felt quite sure.

'Up till now you've only wanted me for myself, because we love each other. Can't you want me because you can give me a baby, and I can give you one?'

Fear rose in him, fear for her health and her life. He experienced in a fleeting instant that sense of loss which had been his when they spoke of death, upon the sands. It was almost as though the dark blood in him, nurtured on superstition for a thousand generations, trembled and was afraid before the doorway of life. Roie felt this. 'You're not afraid for me, are you?'

'You're not very strong, Roie, and it'll hurt you.'

'Oh, Charlie, you don't understand. Having a baby is different from all the ordinary ways of being hurt. It's worth it all. Other pain isn't worth anything, but that is.'

Roie was driven on by something she had to obey. She held herself guilty for the death of one baby; she felt that she had to conceive and bear another, and if God still deemed her guilty he would take that from her. She felt this as surely as if it had been written on a tablet of stone, feeling shadow-like the agony of a childless mother. Yet, at the same time, she wanted to laugh out aloud for delight that she could have a child, the seal of her union with her husband. She took him in her arms as though she were the lover and not he.

'My sweetheart, my own love,' she murmured.

The sea crashed again and again at the foot of the dunes, and the little house moved as though before the breath of the vast ocean. The pale water-glimmer on the walls quivered and wavered and fled before the sinking of the moon. In the bed Roie slept, untroubled even by dreams, her hair like filaments of jet over Charlie's shoulder, whilst within her the soul of her child trembled into existence.

Twenty

Dolour was so excited on the day Roie was coming home that she could hardly sit still in school. All her little memories of her sister merged into one enchanting whole; she felt that never had there been anyone as beautiful or romantic as Roie. Even her name seemed as distant and unusual as that of a film star. 'Rowena Darcy,' muttered Dolour into her geography book. 'Rowena Rothe.' That sounded even queerer. How could Roie have discarded her own name for that of her husband, so easily and unresentfully? Dolour felt suddenly very upset and angry. She was on the threshold of womanhood, borne this way and that by conflicting tides of feeling, often her muddled yearnings and dreamings dissolved into storms of furious tears. She felt angry with and disdainful of Roie, because she had been so weak. She, Dolour, would never fall in love; she felt fierce and pure and fortified against the soft call of the flesh.

'Ha!' snorted Dolour. Sister Theophilus looked up in amazement, and Dolour bent blushing over her book, while Harry Drummy kicked the back of her desk and sniggered inquiringly.

When she came out of school she paused for a while beside the brown stone house on the corner of Plymouth Street, and watched the rubbish men emptying all the tins which stood, like rusty sentinels, in a ragged line along the footpath. The men were great beefy-armed fellows in sacking aprons. They spread out a sheet of hessian in the middle of the footpath and emptied one tin after another upon it, until at last there was a huge stinking heap of week-old refuse. The dogs and toddlers darted in to pick up fascinating scraps, and the blowflies crawled, shimmering cobalt, upon the sticky masses of decomposing foodstuffs. There were cabbage stalks, a barrowload of rotten fruit from Lick Jimmy's, peaches that oozed yellow pulp from the rents in their brown-patched skins; there were old clothes, sad boots with calloused heels, and hats that were just misshapen basins of felt; old books and magazines, stained with tea leaves and the sodden heterogeneous mass of household garbage. Dolour poked away a bit of squashed pumpkin with her foot and picked up an old satin shoe with a diamante buckle. She jerked it off and walked away quickly, her heart beating fast for she had a magpie adoration of shiny things. It was so pretty, flashing diamond showers into the air, and reflecting little rainbows into her cupped palm. It made her feel happy all the way home.

She heard Roie laughing in the kitchen, and with her heart jumping with pleasure she galloped noisily down the passage and threw her arms around her sister.

'Gosh, you're brown, Ro! Isn't she brown, Mumma?'

She did not think for a while to see if Roie were different in any other way, but when her excitement had died down she looked covertly at her sister to see if her honeymoon had changed her. But Roie looked just the same; no consciousness of her new knowledge showed in her eyes, or in the way she moved. It was only now and then, when Roie turned her head and fell silent, that Dolour saw in the pure slender line of her cheek and mouth some elusive difference, some rich and peaceful expression that had never been there before.

She loved Roie more than she ever had, and out of her mind she thrust Charlie, who had taken her place and would for ever more come before her. In her pocket the diamante buckle lay cool and hard and square. Dolour danced up the stairs to her own room, so that she could gloat over it. It was funny with Roie not sleeping in her room any more. Dolour, though she was growing up, and her body enlarging, felt little and thin and forsaken in the bed which had always been too narrow for both of them. She missed Roie's grumblings and kickings, and the warmth of somebody to turn to when there was nightmare in the room. Sometimes she cried a little, for self-pity that her sister had left her, and other times she was ashamed to find herself listening to hear what Charlie and Roie talked about when they were alone. For Dolour's mind, less precocious than those of most Plymouth Street children, was awakening to curiosity, and all the formless hypotheses and muddlements of adolescence. It was not that she wanted to pry into Roie's private life; she just wanted to know. The physical manifestations of sex had always been before her, crude and blunt, but she longed to know if there was in her sister's love affair the sense of high glamour that there was in love affairs in books and on the screen.

It was only a few weeks before Roie knew that she was to have another baby. The little sick feelings, the faintness, and the fugitive pains brought back poignantly and nostalgically her longing for that other little baby that had never been anything at all. What had it been, a boy or a girl? A little creature with a face as soft as a petal, and tiny teeth like shells, with fumbling hands and uncertain fat feet ... like the ghost of a child its memory was always with her. She clutched her stomach, pain gripping her throat like a hand, and tears burning their way out of her eyes.

'Oh, dear Mary, say that I'm forgiven, and that God won't take this one. Let me be brave and not think about anything that might hurt my little one. Let me make up for the wrong I did to my other baby.'

She told Dolour before she told anyone else. Dolour, her heart sinking, and her stomach feeling slightly unstable, stood looking after her. Slowly but surely a wall seemed to be building between Roie and herself. Then all at once she felt glad. It would be nice to have a baby to look after and play with; it might even look like its auntie. Dolour rushed to the glass and examined her face minutely. Melancholy-featured and sallow with adolescence it looked back at her, but Dolour thought her mouth rather pretty, and her eyebrows not too bad at all. They would look well on a baby. She peered at a spot on her chin and rubbed it painstakingly with her finger, as though to erase it. Then she picked up the tube of tooth paste, said solemnly: 'This is a magic cream from the East,' and rubbed a little into the spot. She went downstairs, feeling spellbound, and entirely sure that when next she looked the pimple would be gone.

Mumma was very angry when she was told; she blamed Charlie, most unreasonably, and argued interminably about it with Roie as though the matter could be settled as easily as that. Finally she realized that Roie was very happy about it, and she began to think that perhaps it would be nice to be a grandmother.

'What are you going to call it?' she asked. Roie said eagerly:

'Moira if it's a girl, and Michael if it's a boy.' Mumma nodded approvingly: 'They're real good Irish names. Moira was the name of one of my sisters that died, and I had two Uncle Michaels, one on the Kilker side and one on the Mullins side.'

Charlie had never loved his wife so much. Now and then he came home and found Roie weeping on the bed. He was undisturbed, looking at her quietly, for he knew that she was easily upset, and would be laughing again within a few minutes. Tenderness filled his heart. He did not wish, as a woman might, that he could suffer her coming ordeal for her, but he hoped with all his heart that it would not be too agonizing for her little body and slight nervous strength.

'What's the matter, darling? Feeling bad?'

'No, I feel fine,' sobbed Roie. She fumbled for a handkerchief, and Charlie put his inky one into her hand. She rubbed streaks all over her face. Charlie shook his head: 'Lord, you're a goon. You look like a darkie going to a corroboree.'

Roie glared, throwing herself on the bed and sobbing heart-brokenly, kicking her heels in rage because she knew she was crying for nothing she could explain. Charlie laughed and tickled her, knowing that she would soon recover.

'It's just that I feel it's impossible for me to have a baby,' she choked ridiculously. 'I can't imagine me with a baby.'

'Well, I can't imagine myself as a father. It sounds as outlandish as riding a rhinoceros.'

'You sound like an old grandfather,' cried Roie petulantly. She jumped up, gave her face a cat-lick with a washcloth, and put on some lipstick. Feeling much better, she went beguilingly over and kissed Charlie under his chin. 'Gee, I love you Granddad.' She kissed him again, warmth and fragrance rising from her body, and he held her close and hid his eyes in her hair, so caught up in his happiness that he might have stumbled upon paradise unawares.

*

Everything in the lives of Roie and Charlie was bound up in sex. It was as though they moved in an atmosphere of their own, gentle, spellbound, warm as an island air, far from the rest of the world. It was so subtle that the physical expression of it, beautiful and ecstatic though it might be, was crude and vulgar compared with this spiritual knowledge that had come to both of them. The touch of a cheek, Charlie's arm across Roie's breast at night, her soft sleeping breath, his little murmur of drowsiness; all these things were expressive of wordless delight. During the day they did not always think of each other; it was just that each was in the other's thoughts like a shadow, or perhaps a light illuminating the swift-flowing river of mentation. And this was for all time; it was an actual transformation in their souls. Some love affairs come like extraneous things, and are worn by a personality as a woman wears a garment, to be flung away when worn out. But others are a sea-change, springing out of sex and bearing fruit in the spirit itself. Charlie's and Roie's marriage was like this.

Dolour still loved her diamante buckle. It was so treasured that she had not shown it to anybody. She flashed it back and forth, her eyes chasing the prickles of green amidst the blue and white glitters. It was the loveliest thing she had ever possessed. It took her a long time of anguished indecision, but eventually she bolted downstairs and gave it to Roie.

'It's a little present,' she stammered, her eyes beseeching Roie to take it and treasure it for its beauty as she had done. Roie answered warmly:

'It's lovely, Dolour. I've never seen such a pretty one. Thanks ever so.'

Dolour had for a few hours the exultant joy of the martyr, and when that died away she wished bitterly that she had not been such a fool. When Charlie came home she pressed her ear to the wall and out of the mumble of their talk she heard Roie say:

'Look what Dolour gave me. Funny kid.'

'What for? The baby?'

'I don't know. She just gave it to me,' said Roie with a tender, amused laugh. Dolour knew that it was, but all the same a sword went through her heart. She heard the tinkle of the buckle in a drawer, and leaning her head against the wall she cried silently, not only because she had humiliated herself with a needless sacrifice, but because she knew that nobody would ever fondle and adore the diamante bauble as she had done.

When the months went past without any trouble, Mumma grew easy in her mind, and boasted shyly to the shopkeepers that she was going to be a grandmother. Hughie looked at himself anxiously every time he shaved, to see if the white was coming out in his whiskers, and when they grew black and coarse and virile as ever, he, too, boasted to his friends that his daughter was to have a child. Only Mr Patrick Diamond resented the coming baby. He felt it a slur upon his barren life, and concentrated all his wounded vanity into one premature complaint about babies yowling all night.

'It won't yell at all, you see,' said Roie confidently. Already the baby was becoming a person. Roie's body was still slim, but her breasts were full and aching. She hugged the soreness to herself as though it were a blessing and a privilege. The rich autumn went past; Lick Jimmy changed the yellow chrysanthemums in his window for purple everlastings and the cold winds came from the interior of the continent as bitterly as from a fireless hearth. Roie was always warm; an inward fire made her body glow. She felt a rich and drowsy contentment, like a wheatfield, heavy and burdened with its own harvest. Often she placed a hand on her abdomen and felt her baby quivering. It was so alive; it jumped when a loud noise occurred, as though it heard. Charlie and she loved to lie in bed, feeling the baby between them, moving a tiny foot or hand, perhaps turning its head a little in its cramped and sheltered haven. There was a precious secret feeling about their love of the baby's little movements, so helpless, so pathetic.

'I'll work overtime till I drop,' vowed Charlie. He held her until she went to sleep, the deep protective instinct in him subduing his desire.

Just a few days before the baby was due, Mumma went shopping. Two winceyette nightdresses for Roie, a woollen singlet, for the weather was cold, and a pair of ugly mustard-coloured bedsocks. They had all the baby's little clothes ready, folded and immaculate.

Roie fingered them again and again, amazed that a baby could wear anything so small.

As she walked back from the shopping centre of Oxford Street, Mumma's feet were bothering her. She wearily meditated upon bunions, and the way they shot out radiating streaks of pain as a tree might send out roots. As long as Mumma could remember she had had bunions, mainly because from her childhood she had worn other people's shoes.

All at once her heart gave a painful thump, and she stood still, the string kit dragging from her hand, and all her faculties concentrated on the face of a young boy who stood talking to another at a tram stop.

He was fair, silvery-fair, with a wide freckled face, and teeth with little spaces between them. His blue eyes were crystal-pale, with dark blue rings around the iris. He was Thady . . . Thady grown up, and . . . and . . . Mumma began feverishly to count, as she had counted a million times. Ah, what was the use, when she knew it off by heart? Sixteen and six months and three days. Ten years all but eight days since he had vanished, at four in the afternoon. Mumma moved forward like a woman in a dream. She stared at him greedily; every silver hair on his cheek, the whorl of his ear, his slender neck, his big, hard, clumsy hands. She had no doubt. It was Thady. Her heart fell down in adoration. It was like a miracle.

'After all these years, these long, long years,' sobbed Mumma's heart.

The boy nodded to his friend, and they walked off in different directions. Mumma's bunions gave an awful stab of pain, and for a moment she thought that she might not be able to catch up with him. She hurried her unwieldy body forward, and, losing all sense of judgement, called out: 'Thady! Wait for me! Thady!'

The boy, unhearing, did not stop, and Mumma gave a great gulp of breathlessness and anguish, and he turned and looked at her curiously. 'You calling me?' he spoke roughly and abruptly, like many in that locality.

Mumma panted: 'You're my Thady.'

The boy screwed up his face, looked at her like a suspicious cockatoo.

'What's this? A gag?'

Mumma, seeing him closer, was overcome with love for him. Oh, he was a fine lad, with skin like milk save for the freckles; a real Irish buttermilk skin. She saw fleeting resemblances to Roie, and when he scowled, there was the young Hughie before her. She burst into tears. The boy stared. He wanted to swear, and walk away. But a feeling of curiosity intervened. What was the old hen cackling about, and her looking at him like a ghost just risen from the grave? He said: 'Here, can the waterworks, willya? What are you gabbing about?'

Mumma sobbed thickly: 'I'm your mother, Thady. Oh, me little boy, me little Thady!'

The boy became more and more convinced that the woman was mad. He looked with repugnance at her red, tear-blotched face, the hat pushed lopsidedly over her forehead, and the string kit, distended with odd-shaped parcels, dangling from her fat fingers. He ejaculated an obscene word, and walked off, very fast. Mumma, shocked into self-control, ran after him, crying: 'Don't go away. Don't. I want to talk to yer.'

'Go and cut yer throat,' answered the boy rudely, a little alarmed and annoyed at Mumma's persistence.

'You were taken off the street, ten years ago,' cried Mumma waddling along so fast that people in doorways laughed to see her. 'You were only six. Oh, Thady! Listen to me, Thady!'

'Go to hell, willya,' yelled the boy, his fair face so flushed with rage that his freckles stood out like a peppering of dark brown spots. 'Get back to yer bombo, yer old hag.'

He dived down a side-street. Mumma, her heart beating like a hammer, had to stop, holding to a fence and panting for breath. She had the sense to step back into the shadow, and she saw him jump a low gate and enter a house at the end of the street.

'God help me. God help me not to lose him now,' she prayed, aloud, so that people passing smiled pityingly, or amusedly.

She came to the house. It was neatly kept, and immediately a hatred for its keeper entered her heart. Here lived the woman who had stolen him, who had plunged his mother's heart into the intolerable anguish of the woman who loses her child. Ten long years of purgatory, of ceaseless worry and yearning had gone past Mumma, and she had never felt any hate for those who had stolen Thady, only wonder for their reason for so doing. But now she felt hate and fury as she never had before. Her eyes were blinded by a red-streaked mist; she had to bend low and fumble for the catch on the gate. Inside the house she heard words: 'God, there she is now. She follered me. Wouldn't it?'

A dark-browed man stamped out on to the verandah. 'Now, look here, missus, what are you chasing my boy for? State yer business and get hopping, will yer?'

'He's my boy,' cried Mumma, her lips trembling uncontrollably. 'He's my Thady, that you stole.'

'I told you she was bats,' put in the boy excitedly from the doorway. The man said with rough kindliness: 'Garn, get home, will yer? And sleep it off.'

Mumma said wildly: 'Thady, darling, don't you remember anything? You were six, Thady, remember? And yer had yer little navy pants on, with the patch, and yer red braces, new ones. You were so proud of them. And you had three marbles in a flour bag, a yeller connie, and a sort of stripy white one, and a big clay one you'd made yerself and baked in me oven.'

The man on the verandah eyed her with a fascinated stare. Her anguish, her earnestness, were beyond doubt.

'I ain't forgotten yer, Thady . . . not one inch of yer body, and you're still mine. I bore you down there in Plymouth Street, and I got every little bit of a garment you ever wore. Yer little shoes . . . Thady, darling, say yer remember.'

'I ain't remembering you nohow, yer old haybag,' said the boy sullenly.

A ruddy-faced middle-aged woman, who had been lurking down the hall, appeared with alacrity, her hands rolled up in her damp-spotted apron.

'Elsie,' said the man. 'This lady's in some sort of a mix-up about Brett, here. Get her a cuppa tea, willya?'

He pushed Mumma into a poky sitting-room, heavily overfurnished with sooty net curtains, an over-large chesterfield suite, and many oil pictures. She sat down gingerly on one of the rigidly upholstered chairs. The man rubbed a hand over the seat of his trousers, looked at the hand, and sat down himself.

'Now, missus, what *is* all this?'

Mumma, in a voice from which all the life had gone, explained. A heavy weight, so heavy that it seemed to compress her lungs, pressed on her heart. She was hardly able to breathe. She couldn't find a handkerchief and sniffed with increasing rapidity. The boy, standing awkwardly in the doorway, looked at his father.

'I don't know what she's gabbing about.' His eyes appealed to his father. He had a frightened, uneasy feeling that perhaps the old girl was right, and he would have to go away with her, a stranger, and live with her, and never see his own home any more.

The lady of the house entered, flushed and bursting with excitement. She put down a tray and said with gushing sympathy: 'Do have a cup, you poor thing.'

Mumma flared up, gave a last tremendous sniff and said:

'Don't you dare poor thing me. You'll be poor thinging on the other side of yer face when I get the police on to you for pinching my baby.'

'Now, look here,' began the woman, a brick red creeping into her cheeks.

The man said gruffly: 'Hold yer gab for a while, Else. She's talking the truth, as far as she knows it.'

'Of course I am,' said Mumma indignantly. 'You ask Father Cooley. You ask the nuns at the convent. Anyone. They'll tell you that what I've said is true.'

'You hold your tongue, too,' ordered the man authoritatively. Mumma subsided. 'Now, maybe you're telling the truth, as far as you're concerned, but all the same young Brett here is our son.'

'I had him in Paddington hospital,' interpolated the woman. 'Thirty-eight hours' labour, I oughta remember.'

Mumma scoffed. 'Easy to say that now. But can you prove it?'

'You can call in the neighbours,' cried the boy. 'Mrs Stead next door can tell you that we've been here for years . . . since I was seven,' he added lamely. Mumma's eyes flashed. 'There now,' she cried.

'There's his birth certificate,' said Else uncertainly. Mumma jeered: 'Do you take me for a fool? Do you think I'd be mistaken in me own son? Of course he's my Thady.'

She stared at the boy, who looked uneasily away. More and more she could see resemblances to Hughie and Roie, and even, now and then, to Grandma. The man laughed: 'You're batty, missus. It's just a resemblance, that's all.' Relief and triumph suddenly flashed into his eyes. 'Go on, Else, get out all them photos.'

'Oh, yes, I didn't think before.' Else rummaged in the sideboard, and brought out an untidy album bulging with photographs. She sat down by Mumma.

'Now, here you are, Mrs . . . er . . . here's Brett when he was six weeks.'

Mumma screwed up her eyes and looked at the bald-headed bundle of long clothes. It might have been almost any baby.

'And here he is with me and Dad, on his third birthday.'

Mumma looked eagerly at the fair-haired mite laughing between a smoother edition of the man opposite her, and a younger but unmistakable Else.

'It's me Thady. Glory be. It's me Thady.'

'Don't be a fool,' said the man brusquely. 'He's only three. How could he be?'

Mumma looked again. There was no doubt. The child in the picture was not six. Then how . . . her poor muddled brain snatched after the flyaway springs of her assurance, and failed.

'It's the resemblance, you see,' said Else with smug complacency.

She showed Mumma a studio photograph of a five-year-old child dressed in a black velvet suit which made him look like a gooseberry. It was undeniably Brett, but it was not altogether Thady. Mumma felt a slow hard pain at her heart, growing and growing.

She said faintly: 'I think . . .'

The man said firmly: 'You don't want to think. You want to *know*.' His wife showed her half a dozen other photos, all like Thady, but all with subtle differences. Was Brett's face wider, his hair fairer than

Thady's ... Mumma dropped the last photograph and her face collapsed into a thousand lines of misery, and she put her head down on the table and wept tempestuously.

Else dropped her mask of complacency, and became the warm-hearted decent woman she was. 'Here, you poor dear, have a cup, and try to forget it.'

After a while Mumma recovered enough to sit up and drink the tea, the cup rattling against her teeth. 'It's the disappointment,' she managed.

'I know. It must have been a dreadful experience. Losing a kiddy like that. Many's the time . . .' said Else, looking at her with grave, screwed-up face, as though to convey that she understood everything. Mumma picked up her hat, that had fallen off, and put it on with trembling hands.

'I gotta go. You been nice to me. I'm sorry I said some things I did,' she said. Else patted her shoulder.

'Don't you think of that, Mrs . . .'

'Darcy,' said Mumma drearily.

'You just try to forget all about it, Mrs Darcy, and I'm sure I hope that next time you find the right Thady.'

It was such a long way home and already the dark evening had come over the streets. The lamps winked out round and golden, and the cold wind blew the dust out of the gutters in miniature willy-willies. Mumma walked very slowly, her feet painful, and heavy as lead. She hardly noticed that the parcel of Roie's nightgowns had burst open, and the dust was streaking itself across the cheap furry winceyette.

'It makes you wonder what a body's born for,' said Mumma to the lucent cold blue sky, so far, so remote, so unhearing of pitiful human prayers.

At seven she reached home. Dolour was on the verandah. As soon as she saw her mother she called out the news. Roie had been taken bad, and had gone to the hospital.

Twenty-One

When Roie felt her pains that afternoon she was all alone in the house, and a little frightened. They were familiar pains, a shivering thrill of sensation through her abdomen. She felt the child lie quiet, as though resting for its ordeal which perhaps was just as great as hers. She knew that first babies are usually slow, and she sat down on the bed and packed her bag and brushed her hair quietly, as Charlie's ways had taught her. All the time she was saying: 'Please don't let me get frightened and lose control of myself. Make me brave. Make me brave.'

At half-past three Dolour came running in, up the stairs like a whirlwind, and banged at Roie's door.

'Where's Mumma? The fried fish man is open and maybe we can get some . . . what's up?' she asked, seeing Roie's white face. Roie smiled.

'I think you're going to be an auntie.' Dolour's face turned as white as milk, so that Roie forgot her own fear and said: 'Don't be silly, now. There's nothing to worry about. Can you walk up to the hospital with me?'

Dolour cried: 'Oh, you'd better not walk. I'll get a taxi. I'll get one right away.'

'No,' said Roie, 'it will do me good. The Sister at the hospital said it would.' She turned away, for the pain was sharper this time, and she did not want Dolour to see her face.

Dolour, sick at her stomach, faltered: 'Do you want to go now?'

Roie answered: 'If you'll just carry my bag, I'll be all right.' Now that the pain had gone, she felt wonderful. She rose and put on lipstick, saying: 'I'm glad I washed my hair yesterday.'

'Yes, it looks pretty,' stammered Dolour. She went ahead with the suitcase, and Roie climbed downstairs one by one, very carefully.

It was not far to the hospital, perhaps half a mile. They walked slowly down the broad street and into Murphy Street. Roie looked across the road at Number Seventeen; the tall brownstone house with all the jungle of pot plants looked as dark and furtive and secretive as ever. Roie had never seen it since that dreadful night when she ran away from the horror it contained. Now she looked at it only passingly. Charlie's love had almost destroyed her memory of that night. It was funny, she thought drowsily, how he could do that; he was something solid interposed between her and the nightmare. All at once her pain returned. It seized her in iron, merciless hands, and she had to turn and hold on to a fence, sweat coming cold on her forehead. Dolour chittered like a frightened bird.

'Are you all right? Oh, I wish Mumma was here! I wish Mumma was here!' there was hysteria in her voice. Roie took a deep breath. As mysteriously as it had come the pain was ebbing away. She relaxed and tried to smile.

'You don't want to take any notice of me, Dolour. Don't let this make you feel scared about having a baby. I'm pleased it's come at last . . . I was getting awfully tired of being big and clumsy and tired all the time. And the pain isn't really bad at all.' She had the age-old instinct of women to lie to younger women about labour pains, so that dread might not make things worse for them when their own time came. Dolour nodded dumbly, and they went slowly on.

The hospital was cold and white and incredibly busy. Roie felt forlorn and anonymous and unimportant when she entered the swing doors. She gave her name and they waited in a barren waiting-room until the nurse came along.

Roie cautioned: 'When Mumma comes home, tell her I'm fine. There's the potatoes on the back of the stove, and the pudding's in the oven. Turn the gas out when you get back. Tell Mumma not to come up to the hospital, for it might be a long time, and I don't want her waiting around with her rheumatics.'

'What about Charlie?' whispered Dolour. She had just heard,

from somewhere on the top floor, a frightful rending shriek, and her lips were pale and frozen.

Roie smiled faintly. 'He'll know what to do,' she said. 'Now, you'd better go now, Dol, and get the tea started for Mumma. She'll be tired.' Her cold lips touched her sister's cheek in a hurried caress, for she felt another pain starting. Dolour said nothing, not even goodbye. She tiptoed creakingly out, and ran all the way home, sobbing to herself, and hoping that Mumma would be there to take this awful burden of anxiety from her shoulders.

Now at last Roie was on her own, as she had not been since she lost her first baby. They came and led her away, unresisting, as though she were a puppet, for she was fast sinking into the abyss where one can concentrate on nothing except agony.

The night passed like an hallucination, splashed with violent yellow electric lights, the firm, often rough hands of nurses and interns, and the continual shrieking and moaning of other women all around her. Her baby was born early in the morning. It was the conclusion to nightmare. There was the coarse stinging smell of ether, much too late, and then she came to consciousness again, still muttering, as she had muttered all through her agony: 'Let me be brave. Let me be brave. I want to make up for the other time.'

Daylight was in the ward, blue and wan, and the lurid globes dimmed it into darkness. She saw the white forms of nurses at the bottom of the table, working over the little red body of her daughter.

One of them looked up. 'She's all right. Go to sleep,' she ordered brusquely, and Roie closed her eyes and drifted into the sleep of exhaustion.

Charlie came to see her that afternoon. They sat for a long time, rather shy of each other, looking at the baby at intervals, but most of the time staring at each other with delight and relief and happiness. They had little need to speak; her hand lay in his, and now and then he turned it over and looked at it. It was young and smooth, the nails short with housework, and already the stains of cooking and scrubbing upon it. How little and young she looked in the high white bed. It seemed impossible that she was a mother, that he had possessed her, and implanted his soul and personality upon her. He looked back at his hard and lonely childhood, and beyond that to other ancestors, black and strange, who had felt as he was feeling now, the piteous realization that time is fleeting and flesh is as grass.

Briefly and without words Charlie left his youth behind. He meant something now ... not only companionship and sustenance to a woman, but everything in the world to a child. He embraced the knowledge joyfully, for it seemed to him that although youth with its blitheness and beauty was to be loved, all of life was to be cherished.

Roie said suddenly: 'I didn't think she would be born all right.'

'Why, darling?'

'I don't know. I just didn't.' She smiled, and knew that instant that the old doubts and fears, born in her conscience, had gone for ever. The second child had wiped out the grief of the first. She passed her finger over its downy cheek, and it screwed up its pink face and whimpered.

'She's a little grub.'

'She's a little honey.'

They looked at her for a long time.

Until now their marriage had been ten months of careless happiness, now it became something else. Roie learned what broken rest was, hanging over her baby's cot until she was crazy with desire for sleep. She learned what it is to be bound hand and foot and heart to another human being, and to resent it a little, until at last mother love welled in her heart and made her slavery a happiness. Charlie, quiet and contemplative, watched her face; watched for the first fine tracery of the lines of irritation and disillusionment and monotony which mark like a seal the faces of slum women. But they did not appear. Roie had something which those other women had not, contentment and continued love. Charlie was the centre of her world. She ran to meet him at night, always with the same delight. In bed she lay behind the wall of his back, feeling little and protected and secure, as a woman of the caves might have felt long ago, as she lay with her man shielding her from the cave opening, and the great darkness and mystery beyond it. Charlie was a shield and a refuge to Roie, and she an endless delight to him.

'You're beautiful, Roie.'

'I'm not. I look like an old woman when I'm tired.'

'You won't always be tired. We'll get out of this, have a lovely house, and a garden . . . some day.'

They both knew that day would never come. Responsibilities anchored them, for Charlie's earning capacity was very limited, and day by day their bonds to the cheap and dirty portion of the city were made stronger. Perhaps they would struggle against it in their dreams, but no more than that. There were so many other things to consider too; their shyness and awkwardness with the people of the outside world, just as though they were inhabitants of an island lapped by the roaring traffic seas of the great city; their consciousness of poor, halting speech and inability to cope with any social standards; their tendency to shrink into and shelter within the warm, coarse, familiar things and places. They would grow old and die in Surry Hills, as people have been doing for five generations.

It was Mumma's birthday, and little Moira was four months old. Hughie had found in his nature strange depths of love for the little mite, for although he was Irish, and sentimental, he was also Australian, and thought the exhibition of it effeminate. He often talked to Moira, seeing in her birdlike blue eyes his father's Kerry eyes, and his mother's eyes, for they too had been blue.

'Wait till you're a big girl, little moke,' he said to Moira. 'You don't want a dirty old granddad staggering along in the gutter, being sick all over the footpath. You want a nice grandfather to take you for a walk and buy you an ice-cream. That's what you want.' And he pictured himself, with just a little drink inside to keep him warm, walking very upright, with a fine bushy head of white hair, and perhaps a decent little whisker down the side of his face, and beside him a prancing curly moppet of a Moira. And he pictured, too, all his old mates, purple in the face and bleary-eyed, sitting in doorways and being mighty envious of Hughie Darcy who had stopped when he oughter.

'I'll come right off it. I'm just weaning myself,' he explained to Mumma, as he had explained so many thousand times before. Mumma, since the time when she found Thady and lost him again, had been silent and often pale. For the first time in her life she began to think that perhaps it was not much use wishing and praying that Hughie would come off the drink.

'For what else in life is there for him?' argued Mumma with herself. 'He was a good husband when he was young.' And she convinced herself of this, in spite of all the appalling evidences to the contrary with which her memory presented her. 'I've put up with it for twenty-five years,' said Mumma defiantly, 'and there's no reason why I shouldn't put up with it till the end of me life.'

And because of this she did not argue any more with Hughie when he came home shouting drunk, nor did she demur when at her birthday he produced both Patrick Diamond and a bottle of ripe and turpentiny port. Mr Diamond looked thoughtful, as he usually did when he had a few in, and was considering casting down a few images. So Mumma said warningly: 'Now, not a word out of you, Patrick Diamond, about Pope-worshippers, for it's me birthday, and I'll worship who I like.'

'Not a word, Mrs Darcy,' promised Mr Diamond, and with a twinkling air of suppressed excitement he said: 'I've something important to tell yer later, Mrs Darcy. It'll make yer poor old heart warm, so it will.'

'Not so much of the old,' snapped Mumma, flushing as red as a turkey-cock, for she was only fifty-two. And Hughie burst in with: 'Yes, you keep yer long tongue between yer teeth, you old Orange beggar, or I'll tie a knot in it. Look at the fine figger of a woman all in and out like a pianner leg.'

Mumma said haughtily: 'That's enough of that filthy talk, then.' And so the evening began well.

Dolour came bursting in with pink cheeks and dazzled eyes from the darkness.

'What's the matter?' asked Roie. 'Where have you been?'

'Just to a choir practice in the school hall,' answered Dolour. 'It was good fun.' She looked at Charlie and grinned as though she could not help herself. This was so rare that he laughed aloud.

'What's on your mind, Dolour?'

Dolour blushed and ran outside. She stood outside the phoenix palm in the windy, gusty darkness, and looked up at the bright and piercing stars. Stray cats, empty-bellied and desolate, mewed feebly from behind the alley fence, but Dolour did not notice. Once again there was a spellbound, exciting world before her. She was not fierce and pure and fortified against the world after all, and she did not want to be.

'I know how Roie feels about Charlie,' she chanted under her breath, and giggled, and hugged herself.

'He's nice,' she whispered. 'He's got lovely brown eyes, and he wears a blue suit when he's all dressed up.'

It was a miraculous thing. She had gone to school with Harry Drummy, had yelled at him, kicked him in the shins, and been kicked in return. And now she had fallen in love. It was as sweet as a peppermint stick, and as pink and white. It made everything different. There was no sex in Dolour's feeling for him. It was as pure and fairylike and useless as the love of knights and ladies in antique ballads. But it was something to be gloated over at night time, hugged to her bosom, and cherished until, like a bubble, it floated unheeded away. For the first time Dolour was pleased that Roie wasn't sleeping with her any more. Now she was free to indulge as she wished in dream conversations.

St Anne of the Seven Dolours vanished with a swish of the skirts, and Dolour said softly: 'Mrs Dolour Drummy, Mrs Harry Drummy.'

'Ah, crumbs,' she said. The sweetness and wonder of it nearly overcame her, and she leaned her face against the spiky trunk of the unheeding tree and shivered for joy. Her Mumma cried crossly from the doorway: 'What are you trying to do? Imitate the ivy?' And Dolour, a little cross, and red-faced, marched in. Mumma! How should she know what her daughter was capable of feeling? Her life had only been housework, and babies, and trouble. Nothing like the glamorous, golden, and misty life which stretched out before Dolour Darcy. She drifted in and began handing around cups of tea, gobbling a tomato sandwich meantime, for love had not affected her appetite.

Mumma sat quietly, looking on, for she liked to see other people enjoying themselves. Her feet hurt, and she eased off her slippers under the table. It was nice to have a cup of tea and sit and watch

Hughie drinking port, and not care about it at all. She wondered why she had ever worried, forgetting that fierce hatreds and desires belong to youth and not to middle-age, which can at last learn to accept things as they are. Hughie noticed the absence of her cautioning voice, and this worried him so strangely that he stopped drinking, and even chided Patrick Diamond, who seemed to be putting away more than usual.

'It'll burn the guts outa you, Patrick man,' he cautioned. 'You with yer ulcers.'

'To hell with me ulcers,' retorted Mr Diamond blithely. 'I'm celebrating. Here, let me light yer little bit of a bumper, Hughie man.'

With an erratic hand he extended a lighted match to the cigarette butt which was protruding under Hughie's nose. There was an anguished yell, and a squirt of laughter from Roie and Charlie.

'Me nose, God damn it, you nearly burnt me nose off,' yelled Hughie, holding his hand over it. Mr Diamond shrugged foggily.

'It's yer own fault for having such a God-forgotten honker,' he answered reasonably. Hughie swelled visibly, for the nose was the Darcy nose, and had been handed down from one proud generation to another. Mumma interposed hastily:

'Now tell us, Patrick, what are yer celebrating?'

Mr Diamond's air of secrecy grew greater. Dolour said sarcastically: 'He's put a bomb in Father Cooley's bed, that's what.'

'Don't be speaking disrespectful of yer priest,' cried Mumma angrily, making a backhanded gesture at Dolour. Mr Patrick Diamond looked grieved.

'It's you who'll be taking them words back when yer hear me news, me fine young pullet,' he said to Dolour, who sniffed and stuffed half a tomato in her mouth. Then he announced:

'I'm entering.'

'What? A home for old men?' asked Hughie malevolently.

'I'm entering the Church,' said Mr Diamond pompously. There was a deathly silence, broken only by the juicy chewing of Dolour. Mumma gasped:

'You mean the Catholic Church?'

Mr Diamond nodded. Hughie began slowly to turn petunia purple.

'He's only being sarcastic,' ventured Roie.

Hughie suddenly exploded. 'You dirty stinking scoundrel of a scab, Patrick Diamond! To think that I've been nursing this viper in me bosom all these years, and now he does this to me.'

Mr Diamond was bewildered. 'I thought you'd be pleased. I've always had a strange discomfortable feeling in the back of me collar that you've been praying for me to turn.'

'But Orangemen never turn Catholic,' gasped Mumma. Mr Diamond said proudly: 'I do.'

Hughie exploded again. 'Drinking me wine and eating me tomato sammidges and then saying a thing like that. You're not fit for decent society, Patrick Diamond. You can't be trusted to stick to yer own principles.'

Mr Diamond, with the port mounting to his head, and his stomach beginnng to burn ominously, shouted: 'I'll do what I like when I like without the interference of any bone-headed tike.'

'There now,' cried Hughie triumphantly. 'He's blaspheming against the sacred name of the Church. And him talking about entering it. Why, the Church wouldn't have yer.'

'And why not, may I ask? Is it too high and mighty for such as me?'

Mumma flashed: 'It's not too high and mighty for any grey-bearded old sinner who wants to seek grace when he's on his last pins.'

Mr Diamond began to roar incoherently. He made a swing at Mumma, and Hughie clipped him under the ear. Charlie seized one by the shirt-front and the other by the coat-collar.

'Now look here, don't break up the party. Go outside and cool off.'

He shoved them both outside and shut the door. There was the anguished voice of a stood-on cat and the stamping of feet and mouthing of muffled oaths. Mumma cried to Charlie: 'Now they'll kill each other, and you'll be a murderer.'

There was silence outside; then they heard Mr Diamond slowly ascending the stairs. Hughie adjusted a triumphant expression on his face and entered the room.

'I gave him a swipe in the brisket,' he boasted. 'He's gone, and I never want to see his blaggard countenance again. The idea of him, wanting to turn at his age. The dirty old turncoat. Nobody would suspect an Irishman of doing such a thing, would they now?'

Mumma was repentant. 'Perhaps he meant well, Hughie love. There was no call to hit him in the stomach, anyway, and it so bad.'

'To hell with him and his belly,' cried Hughie. 'From now on he's wiped. I never want to see him again.'

'He's a poor old man,' said Roie softly. 'Perhaps he just wanted to bury all the differences, Dadda, and never fall out with you on St Pat's Day any more.'

Hughie reconsidered. He took a mouthful of port and let the strong stuff roll around his tongue before he permitted it to scorch his throat. 'Well, maybe I'll go up tomorrow and say I'm sorry,' he conceded magnanimously. 'Not that I am.'

Upstairs Mr Diamond lay on his bed and held his stomach and groaned. His pain was on him, and the agony was almost too much for him to bear. The little ugly room pressed on him as though it had a descending ceiling and contracting walls. He had a nightmare urge to shriek and scream and bellow and roar until someone came and knocked him on the head and put him out of this awful travail. He forgot all the scene he had just experienced; all he remembered was his complete loneliness. Somewhere he had missed his path, and now his only possessions were futile abstracts. Even they had deserted him. He did not care for either the green or the orange – nothing but the blackness and quiet of oblivion.

'One of these days,' said Mr Diamond between spasms, 'I'm going to turn on the gas.'

Downstairs Charlie said: 'Well, it's ten o'clock and I'm on an early shift. I'd better turn in.'

Roie rose, too. 'It's time the baby was fed.' She kissed her mother and father, and gave Dolour a slap on the tail as she passed. 'Happy birthday, Mumma, and I hope we're all here for the next one.'

They climbed the stairs. Near the top they stopped, and Roie leaned against her husband's shoulder and he kissed her soft, eager lips.

'Gee, I love you, Charlie.'

He whispered in her ear, and in the warm tingling darkness they clung together, exchanging kisses and whispered fugitive phrases, desire enveloping them both. Roie laughed, and ran into the dark room and flicked on the light. She picked up her baby and collapsed on the bed with it, holding it above her and laughing into its crumpled, drowsy face. Charlie sat beside her as she fed the child, and watched them both. His horizon grew smaller and smaller. It enclosed no vast field of dream or ambition, nothing but this small room and what it contained.

'I've got everything I want in the world,' he thought.

In the kitchen Mumma and Hughie fell into a silence, listening to the radio, which, now that the noise was gone, raised its voice and was heard. They listened for a long time, and it came to Mumma that almost all the songs she heard nowadays were sad songs. There were so many sad songs – not the virile, tragic ones of long ago, but little futile, piteous squeakings against the vast and bitter world. They were like the cryings of a bird overwhelmed by the ominous and sombre sandy winds from an encroaching wilderness. Some strange rot had settled in the hearts of the men who thought, the wise and educated and accomplished people of the world. They felt that there was no permanency anywhere; that all was vanity, and nothing under the sun was worth striving for any more.

In her peasant soul Mumma thought how strange it was. Her thoughts did not have words, and her pity did not even have thought. For the first time she felt equal and even superior to these people with the riches and the wisdoms of the world, who did not know even the simplicities she had been born knowing.

She told Hughie: 'I'm tired.'

She rose laboriously and put on her slippers, and went into the dark bedroom. Her hand was out to switch on the light when it happened. Thady was there. She felt the soft neck of a little boy, and his silver head, nuzzling into her lap. He was there, as light as a feather, as insubstantial as the wind, but real. She could smell the long-remembered smell of his body, and feel the gust of his breath. It was only for a moment, but it was as though her restless, tormented, mother's heart was stilled for ever into tranquillity. She knew now that Thady had died, long ago. What the manner of his death, where he lay now, she could not think, nor did she try. It was all over, long ago, and she possessed him again, little and defenceless and entirely hers. Perhaps some other time she would find him here in this room, this dirty dark room that had now been enhaloed and enchanted as was the tomb of Joseph of Arimathea after the Resurrection. She looked up at the ceiling; neither the stained plaster nor the clotted webs did she see, only the dark and fathomless and immortal sky, and beyond it to him who chose to walk in the ways of the poor and the forgotten as he walked in his garden.

Hughie came in and put his arms around her. He was tired and clumpy and middle-aged, and he smelt of port and sausages and cheap shaving-soap, but she loved him as she had never loved him before.

'Whatjer thinking of, old hen?' he asked, rubbing his whiskery cheek on hers.

'I was thinking of how lucky we are,' whispered Mumma.

READ MORE IN PENGUIN

In every corner of the world, on every subject under the sun, Penguin represents quality and variety – the very best in publishing today.

For complete information about books available from Penguin – including Puffins, Penguin Classics and Arkana – and how to order them, write to us at the appropriate address below. Please note that for copyright reasons the selection of books varies from country to country.

In the United Kingdom: Please write to *Dept. EP, Penguin Books Ltd, Bath Road, Harmondsworth, West Drayton, Middlesex UB7 0DA*

In the United States: Please write to *Consumer Services, Penguin Putnam Inc., 405 Murray Hill Parkway, East Rutherford, New Jersey 07073-2136.* VISA and MasterCard holders call 1-800-631-8571 to order Penguin titles

In Canada: Please write to *Penguin Books Canada Ltd, 10 Alcorn Avenue, Suite 300, Toronto, Ontario M4V 3B2*

In Australia: Please write to *Penguin Books Australia Ltd, 487 Maroondah Highway, Ringwood, Victoria 3134*

In New Zealand: Please write to *Penguin Books (NZ) Ltd, Private Bag 102902, North Shore Mail Centre, Auckland 10*

In India: Please write to *Penguin Books India Pvt Ltd, 11 Community Centre, Panchsheel Park, New Delhi 110017*

In the Netherlands: Please write to *Penguin Books Netherlands bv, Postbus 3507, NL-1001 AH Amsterdam*

In Germany: Please write to *Penguin Books Deutschland GmbH, Metzlerstrasse 26, 60594 Frankfurt am Main*

In Spain: Please write to *Penguin Books S. A., Bravo Murillo 19, 1°B, 28015 Madrid*

In Italy: Please write to *Penguin Italia s.r.l., Via Vittorio Emanuele 45/a, 20094 Corsico, Milano*

In France: Please write to *Penguin France, 12, Rue Prosper Ferradou, 31700 Blagnac*

In Japan: Please write to *Penguin Books Japan Ltd, Iidabashi KM-Bldg, 2-23-9 Koraku, Bunkyo-Ku, Tokyo 112-0004*

In South Africa: Please write to *Penguin Books South Africa (Pty) Ltd, P.O. Box 751093, Gardenview, 2047 Johannesburg*

READ MORE IN PENGUIN

The Shiralee   D'Arcy Niland

Everyone has their cross to bear – their swag, their shiralee – and for Macauley, walking across New South Wales in search of work, it is his young daughter who has to suffer his resentment at having her in tow. But then, as the real reasons for Macauley's journey become clear, he discovers that the ties that bind can be as much a comfort as a burden, and what he thought of as his Shiralee could be the one thing that will save him from himself.

Told with a gruff humour and a gentle pathos, D'Arcy Niland's classic Australian novel perfectly captures the spirit of the bush and the tough, resilient people of the outback.

'It has truth, strength and beauty, as well as humour and subtlety, deep feeling and brilliant craftsmanship' *The Sun*, Sydney

'Strangely moving, with its tough style and tender sentiment' *Observer*